THE COMPLETE SEASON ONE

Other Heliopause Productions:

THE ADVENTURES OF BOURAGNER FELPZ
Volume I: A Study of Magic

APSIS FICTION
The Semi-Annual Anthology of Goldeen Ogawa

PROFESSOR ODD
#1 The False Student
#2 The Slowly Dying Planet
#3 The Promethean Predicament
#4 The Elder Machine
#5 The Dragons Of Geda
#6 The Monster's Daughter
#7 The Dogs of Canary Island
#8 Chronostrophe
#9 Star Walkers
#10 The Thousand Songs

DRIVING ARCANA
Rotation One
Rotation Two
Rotation Three

PROFESSOR ODD

THE COMPLETE SEASON ONE

GOLDEEN OGAWA

A HELIOPAUSE PRODUCTION

FOR EVAN OGAWA

Father of the vroknaär, first reader,
and the best brother I ever had.

CONTENTS

1 THE FALSE STUDENT 2

2 THE SLOWLY DYING PLANET 44

3 THE PROMETHEAN PREDICAMENT 88

4 THE ELDER MACHINE 132

5 THE DRAGONS OF GEDA 178

6 THE MONSTER'S DAUGHTER 242

   AMAR AND DESTA'S BIG DAY OUT 311

1.   THE FALSE STUDENT

THE NOTE WAS TAPED crookedly across the door to the philosophy hall, and in sloppy blue ballpoint it read:

> Professor Hollins is sadly indisposed. Afternoon lectures to be given by Professor Odd instead.
> Bring a protractor.

This caused some amount of confusion, as there was no Professor Odd listed on the faculty, nor had anyone ever heard of him. Yet the administrators, when they found out, simply shrugged and said, "Well, let's just hope he turns up on time!"

"She," the secretary, Miss Lillum, said. "Professor Odd is a woman."

But the administrators had already turned their attention on to where to eat lunch, and they did not hear her.

The command to bring a protractor caused consternation among the students. Many were not aware of the change until they saw the note on the door when they arrived for the lecture, and were pawing feverishly through their bags as they entered the room. One girl, who was an artist, offered to lend students who did not have protractors her french curves. "I usually have a protractor on hand—they make a useful straight-edge—but it's gone missing," she was saying when Alister entered the room. He actually did have a protractor, tucked safely away in one of the side zip pockets of his everything bag. So as he made his way to his seat he was not distracted by the urge to find an implement at the last moment, and he among all the class actually noticed Professor Odd arriving.

She did not come in by the doors. At least, not the traditional ones. The room was in the older part of the university, and the walls were paneled in wood. Up at the front of the room Alister clearly saw the panel by the chalkboard swing open, and someone walk through. Followed by a dog.

Dogs were not allowed on campus, but this one wore a harness that had "Seeing Eye Dog" written on the side. The Professor must be blind. Indeed, she wore dark round glasses, but this was hardly the most unusual thing about her appearance.

Her wig—it had to be a wig—was wild and wavy and mostly blond, except for the ends where it was tinted pink. She wore a long trench coat with the collar turned up, and a scarf around her neck. She had on vividly blue pinstriped trousers and carried a cane, which she rapped smartly on the lectern to get attention.

Everyone except for Alister jumped. Then there was the quick, hushed silence as fifty students pushed bags aside and got out their touchscreen pads. In it, Alister heard the sharp *click-clack* of the Professor's shoes as the dog led her into position behind the lectern. It was a very fine dog, Alister thought. Like a golden retriever but with stand-up ears, and it looked out at the class with such a deep, perceptive look, that Alister would hardly have been surprised if *it* would be the one teaching philosophy.

Professor Odd felt her way over the lectern. Some of Professor Hollins's notes were still there, and these she picked up and examined with her fingers. Then she tossed them over her shoulder where they scattered, fluttering, to fall around her feet.

"Right," said Professor Odd. "Philosophy. I am supposed to teach you philosophy. Funny that. Do any of you actually know what philosophy means? Love of wisdom, that's what it meant originally. Well, I love wisdom as much as the next person . . . " she glanced at the dog to her side. "Well, perhaps a *bit* more than the next person. But the point is: it's great. Wisdom is really awesome stuff; can solve all sorts of problems, bring peace of mind, *et cetera, et cetera.* But you know what I love even more than wisdom?"

Silence. Professor Hollins had always been inclined to ask rhetorical questions in his lectures, and the assembly was yet uncertain if Professor Odd shared this attribute.

"Ignorance," said Professor Odd. "Not the kind of blind ignorance that has people burying their heads in the sand and telling themselves fairy tales to make sense of the world—good great dawkins no—but that ignorance you have when you find yourself up against something *completely new.* Something no one has ever seen or thought of before. When all the wisdom in and out of the universe can't help you, and all you can do is *learn.* I love that feeling! Don't you?"

This did not seem to be rhetorical. The students replied with a muddled "I guess so . . . "

Professor Odd grinned. It was a wide grin that split her face nearly in half and showed a strong row of square, white teeth. Her cheeks bunched up on either side and went a pleasant rose color.

"You don't agree with me at all, do ya?" she said, still smiling fit to burst.

The students did not know what to make of that. Some of them looked down and refused to answer. But a few others, Alister included, nodded. Alister in particular knew he liked to have all his knowledge neatly lined up, like the tidy files on his laptop computer, with everything he knew carefully sorted into folders for easy access. He did not like running up against something his knowledge could not comprehend or explain, and preferred having the facts cleanly uploaded into his brain without having to puzzle through the true or false on his own.

Professor Odd's head snapped round to stare at him. Or whatever it was blind people did when they pointed their faces at you.

"*Well?*" she asked, not smiling any more.

Of course, she was blind. She would not have seen him nod. Reluctantly Alister unlimbered his voice box and spoke aloud.

"That is correct, Professor. I don't agree with you."

To his chagrin, he was the only one in the room who had replied.

Back came the smile, like a searchlight. Alister found that his heart rate had increased, to the point that it was nearly distracting. He coughed and willed it to slow down. But he could not shake the feeling that he had, simply by speaking, stepped out into a wide open arena, and his opponent was a bloodthirsty tiger.

"Mr. Alister," said the Professor. "Would you be so kind as to step up here?"

Alister found himself pinned to his seat for some moments: first from the shock that she could know his name, and then from the thought his legs had gone numb. Then the nerves reconnected and he staggered to his feet, unconsciously slinging his everything bag over his shoulder as he went. He had sat in his usual place: the exact center of the classroom, so it took some time for him to make his way up to the lectern. By the time he approached, Professor Odd had leant against the post and was tapping her foot loudly.

"Yes, Professor?" he asked, and his voice came out only a little wobbly.

"You're Alister right? Mr. Alister Bane?" Professor Odd adjusted her glasses, and for a moment the light crept in beneath them, and he thought he saw her eyes. Then he thought he'd rather pretend he hadn't.

"Correct, Ma'am."

"Oh, let's not stand on ceremony," Professor Odd said, laughing. "Call me Professor, please," and much to Alister's consternation and terror, she threw her arms around his shoulders and embraced him.

The class, when they saw that the tiger had picked her prey, slowly began to thaw. Now they tittered. Professor Odd released Alister abruptly and turned to face them, smiling brightly. They fell silent.

"Mr. Alister here is just the sort of fellow I like," she said. "He doesn't agree with me—well, most people don't. But unlike *most* people, he's got the courage to actually *say* so. Now, for that alone he ought to be rewarded, but before I can do that he's got to pass one itsy bitsy *teeny* test." She held up her thumb and forefinger, barely an inch apart, to show how tiny this test was.

It's probably going to be reciting digits of *pi*, Alister thought ruefully.

The Professor turned to him, her eyebrows drawn together to create a wrinkle down the center of her forehead. At least, the place where her eyebrows ought to have been drew together. She had no hair to mark them. Up close it gave her face an eerie, unfinished look.

"This test is very, *very* important," she said, leaning in close. Alister had to put one foot back to brace himself against leaning away. She smelled of crushed appleseeds, and something watery and fresh. Not unpleasant, but not at all *normal*.

"Do you, Mr. Alister Bane . . . do you have a . . . *protractor?*"

Alister nearly laughed with the breath of air that rushed out of him. It lifted the feathery hairs of her wig, and was probably very rude, but he didn't care. The tiger didn't want to eat him! It wanted the steak in his back pocket!

Feeling as close to proud as he ever did, Alister swung his everything bag around and neatly unzipped the pocket that held his standard half-moon protractor. He held it up between his face and the Professor's like a shield, and she snatched it from his hand with a small squeal of delight.

"Now this, *this* is a real piece of work, this is," she said, holding it up for all the class to see. "One of the fundamental tools of geometry. So simple, so elegant, and with as many uses as the brain can devise. I bet plenty of you know the traditional uses, with construction paper and pencils and stuff. But protractors can be used for much more *creative* things than that. And in the pursuit of our wonderful philosophy, our *love of wisdom*, I'm going to show you one of these things."

From a pocket of her trench coat she drew a long black laser pen. She placed the protractor level on her right hand, with the rounded side facing out at the class, and pointed the pen down at the center mark of the straight edge. She pressed a little gold button on the pen's side, and a vivid red light burst from its tip.

But the laser did not behave in any way it should have. Upon hitting the protractor it split into countless lines of laser light, scattering across the room. But not at random, Alister saw. The lines of light ran directly along the marks of the degrees. One-hundred and eighty-one lines, precisely spaced to cover half the room, slicing it into one-hundred and eighty pie slices, radiating out from the protractor.

Alister stared in amazement. In all his years at the academy he had never seen the like, not even in Professor Smith's science class. Forgetting his fear and his banging heart, he gazed out at the room . . .

. . . and discovered the truly astonishing thing: each pie slice cast a different look over the space it covered. The difference was subtle, sometimes as little as a shift in hue, but it was enough to make his head spin. And there was something worse: the people looked different. Some who were so unfortunate as to fall between the slices were bisected by the laser, so they were half one person and half another. Alister saw his friends and classmates changed before his eyes into different people, different characters. Corny Jones, who always looked so slow and stupid, now appeared crafty and cunning. And Melissa Codgins was split between proud and cowering. And the new student, the transfer who had arrived only yesterday, was split between a modest, sandy-haired man, and . . . and something else. Something that Alister's tidy, reasonable brain was having a *very* hard time accepting. Whatever it was—and he refused to admit it was a brilliant green tentacle monster with one eye—it definitely belonged in the same "rather-would-not-think-of-it" file as the Professor's eyes.

"What do you think, Mr. Alister?" Professor Odd said pleasantly, as if she were showing him a new tea set. "See anything . . . *different?*"

Unable to speak, Alister only raised one shaking hand, and pointed.

"Ah-*ha!*" cried the Professor, and she dropped the protractor, sending the lasers haywire for a moment before snuffing the pen out and vaulting over the lectern.

The room erupted into chaos; a natural result, Alister thought, at the sight of a supposedly blind woman doing a somersault out of her vault and leaping amongst the tables. To say nothing of the dog, who stood up and pointed a paw-like, furry hand. It shouted something that sounded like *"There!"* And then the transfer student, who had briefly morphed back into being properly human when the laser went out, flailed its long green tentacles and surged toward the door.

It knocked over two tables and three students on its way there, who were then trodden on as the Professor scrambled after it in hot pursuit. The door crashed open, then slammed shut, then rebounded out of its frame and hung, swinging limply.

Out in the hall there were crashes and squeals and the Professor's voice shouting at the thing to *"Wait!"* but they were drowned out by the uproar within the room.

Inside Alister's head everything was silent and still. His brain was trying to restart, but it was having some difficulties. While it was doing that he picked up his protractor, zipped it back into its pocket and ran from the room, his everything bag thumping sharply against his back. Only that pain kept him aware, on some level, that this was all perfectly real.

In the hall things were hauntingly ordinary. The late afternoon sunlight was streaming in the west windows, and there were quiet murmurings coming from the nearby rooms.

And there was a trail of green slime spattered down the center of the hall.

"Don't step in it!" cried a husky female voice from around his knees. He glanced down to see the Professor's Seeing Eye dog galloping along beside him, and because his rational, reasonable brain was still refusing to come online, he merely said "Thank you," and ran down the hall next to the wall.

They rounded a corner, where the walls gave way to a portico. The Professor sat leaning against a column, her head rolled back, and the one arm he could see hung limply at her side. As they drew closer, Alister saw she was sitting in a pool of the green slime. In it next to her were her round, dark glasses.

The dog had loped ahead and was crouching at the edge of the green slime. She had slipped on a pair of white plastic gloves and was carefully scooping a sample into a vial, which she stored in one of the many pockets in her Seeing Eye Dog harness. She was also speaking to the Professor, slowly, as if to a child.

"Is it still active?"

"Dooon't knooooow . . . " the Professor said, rubbing at her head. This act contrived to smear green slime all over her forehead, but she didn't seem to notice. "Dooon't think sooooo . . . baaaaaaaht . . . yeah. Think it's *personal.* You should be juuuuuuusssst . . . fine. Yoouuuu didn't *surprise* him. I had a . . . baaad . . . yeah, *baad* mannerssss."

As she was speaking Alister tip-toed around the front of her and peered over the dog's shoulder. Her eyes were half-closed and unfocused, but they still gave him a twist in his gut. Like seeing something from one animal magically transplanted onto another. They simply did not fit in a human face.

The dog was talking again. Alister was having trouble with that too, but he could not deny that he heard her saying; "Here, take hold of my lead. Use it, for once. I can take you back to the Oddity, just be *careful.* Can you stand at all? Hey, you, skin-bag, be a gentleman and help her up!"

Alister jumped to find the dog addressing him. He moved to help, but hesitated at the slime.

"Don't worry, it's not active any more," the dog said. "I checked. Come on now, we haven't got all day."

So it was that Alister found himself with Professor Odd's arm over his shoulder and his arm around her waist, leading her tenderly out of the university. He even had the presence of mind to collect her glasses from the pool of slime before they left.

The slime got everywhere. And even though the dog had said it was no longer active, Alister felt it tingle on his skin where it touched him. Not unpleasant, but it made him nervous.

"What did it *do* to her?" he asked the dog uneasily. The very fact that he was *asking a dog* alone made him uncomfortable, but to his consternation it was the Professor who answered.

"Non-lethal debilitation through neuro-chemical actives," she said in a remarkably clear voice. Then her head rolled over onto Alister's shoulder and she gave him a lop-sided grin. (How the tiger has fallen, Alister thought.) "I think I'm drrrruuuuuunnnk!" she announced. "Amaaaaazing, haven't been drunk in aaaaaaages. Seems like a central nervous system depressant, anyway . . . maybe some opioids in there too . . . aaaaaand . . . " she raised a gooey finger and licked the substance experimentally. "Hmm, a slight aphrodisiac . . . some kind of nitrate, I think."

"Sounds properly debilitating to me," the dog said.

"Then it's a good thing I've got my rusty companion—no, *trusty* companion! Aaand the handsome Mr. Alister." She squeezed him around the neck, getting slime inside his collar.

Alister coughed uncomfortably. They had reached the back stairs out of St. Callhas, the university's main study hall, and stood at the top of the steps overlooking the cracked asphalt of the half-full parking lot. Most of the afternoon lectures had not let out yet, so it was quiet and empty. Alister considered this a small mercy after all that had happened, when the Professor swung herself around to face him, a little unsteadily.

"Now," she said carefully. "This may be the aphrodisiac talking, so you're free to say no. But I do appreciate your help, and common courtesy dictates I invite you in for . . . for . . . oh yes! Tea. I invite you in for *tea*, Mr. Alister Bane."

She flopped her upper half toward him and back again, in a sloppy attempt at a bow, then turned and tottered off down the stairs.

Alister stood, speechless and shocked, for almost a minute. Then he went to adjust the strap of his everything bag and found he was holding something. The Professor's glasses.

He took off down the stairs before he had time to think properly.

"Professor, excuse me, Professor!" he cried. "You forgot your spectacles!"

The Professor and the dog were almost to the nearest car. It must be her car, he thought. A small beige sedan. Far too ordinary, really. She opened the driver's door and climbed in after the dog.

She is in no state to drive, the rational part of Alister's brain proclaimed. He tore up to the car and bent over the driver's door, which was still open.

"Excuse me, Professor. You forgot your spectacles, and would you like me to drive you ho . . . "

He never finished the last word. As he spoke he'd poked his head right inside the car, and found himself somewhere else entirely.

Alister pulled his head back out again so fast he nearly knocked it on the door frame. He looked around. He was still in the back parking lot of St. Callhas. The trees had just put out their thick green leaves, which were rustling pleasantly in the breeze. In the distance he heard the sound of traffic on Seagal's Boulevard. All as ordinary as could be.

He took a deep breath and stuck his head back inside the car.

The first word that had flashed through his mind had been *spaceship!* Now he looked closer.

Bare metal steps led up past his face, but the walls were padded with daisy-printed cloth that smelled of chamomile. Protruding from the right side was a metal steering wheel which drove a system of cranks that appeared to be connected to the door. Very much like those on a ship or a submarine.

Craning his head inside further and looking up he caught a glimpse of a rounded cavern, like the inside of a teapot, ribbed with metal that ran up the curved sides to convene in a tangle on the ceiling. Each rib held brackets for lights, one after the other, and these pulsed on and off, creating vague patterns. That must have been what put him in mind of a spaceship.

The lights were eclipsed as the Professor's dog loomed into view at the top of the stairs. She was standing on her hind legs, and had replaced her Seeing Eye Dog harness with a sort of bathrobe, tied modestly about the waist. She looked a little annoyed.

"Well? Come on! I'm just going to put the kettle on, and you're letting in a draft," she said, with a hint of bark in her voice. "Close the door behind you."

Alister tripped a little as he stepped inside, pulling the door shut behind him. As the latch clicked into place he thought he remembered something once about leaving doors that led to strange places open a crack, so you could be certain to get home again. But it was too late now. Grasping the metal rail for support he half pulled himself up the stairs and into . . . wherever it was he was now.

It was not a perfect circle, as he had first thought; it was more of a teardrop shape, with the sunken door he'd entered by at the narrow end. On either side were consoles with screens set in the wall and banks of glowing buttons. There was a swivel chair in front of each, bolted to the steel-grill floor.

But that was as spaceship-like as the place got. As Alister moved slowly down the place, to the wide rounded end of the teardrop, it got more and more domestic. The steel grill flooring was covered with carpet, and the walls were covered with the same daisy-print cloth as before, punctuated by columns of lights. There were closets and cupboards set into the wall, and a small window with pink drapes. Alister came close to the window to peer outside, then backed away quickly and tried not to think about what he had seen. He nearly backed into the table which took up much of the central space and was piled high with books, computers, and racks of test tubes. The Seeing Eye Dog harness had been thrown casually over a black box labeled *Electron Adjuster.*

Alister carefully made his way past the table, and through the small maze of armchairs and sofas that decorated the floor.

The rounded end was punctured with little alcoves. One looked to be a sort of kitchen area, where the dog was bustling about getting out cups and plates. Another had a door. Still another was filled with nothing but books. The next held a ladder that led up to another level of the room, visible only to Alister as the bottom of a catwalk that ran around the perimeter.

The Professor was sitting in the last alcove; it appeared to be a wash-up and first-aid station, and she was in the process of cleaning the green slime off her person. She had removed her coat and scarf, which were draped over the back of her chair, and she was leaning forward into a mirror, examining her face.

There was a snake wrapped around her neck, Alister noticed. It was a pale flesh color, with mossy green dots on it, like a leopard's spots, and it looped loosely over her shoulders. Alister had seen snakes before—even touched one—but there was something about this one that made him feel uneasy.

"At least it wears off quickly," the Professor was muttering, mostly to herself. "But I swear I shall feel sticky for *days*. And I think it has ruined my favorite wig." So saying she took a fistful of hair and pulled the wig clean off.

Alister's brain froze. There was a clean, bald head under the wig, speckled with the same pattern of green spots as the snake. Which, Alister saw, was not a snake at all. It was a tentacle, complete with round suckers on the bottom, sprouting from the back of the Professor's skull. The end of it twitched petulantly, like an irritated cat's tail.

"I don't know," the thing that was Professor Odd said. "Maybe I could salvage it. What do you think Mr. Alister?"

But all she received in reply was a dull *thud* as Alister hit the floor in a dead faint.

The transfer student went home. Home, to him, was a small flat at the top of a building in the east city. There was no bed, no television, and no refrigerator. But there was a bathtub, and the first thing he did after arriving was to run a long, cold bath.

The plumbing was old, and the water came in loud spurts. He stood over the bath as his clothes began to melt off, oblivious to the sound of his apartment door opening and shutting. Of footsteps outside the room. Of the click of a gun being cocked.

When the landlady got back from buying cigarettes she found a large, unmarked white van just pulling away from the curb outside the front door. The driver grinned at her cheerfully as he accelerated into traffic.

She did not discover the explosion of green slime in the bathroom of her attic apartment until that evening, and would have evicted her new tenant on the spot, but she never saw him again.

"Funny, he doesn't seem to have low blood pressure," the Professor said, slipping the cuff off Alister's arm and rolling his sleeve back down. "The skin's natural color has reasserted itself, and he is breathing normally. I expect some bruising on his hips, shoulders and head from the fall, but nothing serious. I can only conclude that he was shocked unconscious by my appearance. Tsk, tsk, tsk."

"Well Professor, to someone who has lived all their lives on a mono-dominant species world, your appearance is a little shocking," the dog pointed out.

"But Elo, I don't believe you went into fits of fainting when you first saw me."

"*I* don't come from a mono-dominant species world. I am accustomed to holding intelligent discourse with animals who look nothing like myself."

"But you had never seen a human before either."

"Exactly: I had no standard of normalcy by which to judge you. Also, I was quadrupedal at the time, rendering my brain at the same level as my heart and thereby making it easier to receive blood and avoid loss of consciousness."

"Well, as he is lying on his back at this moment, now *his* brain is level with *his* heart, and he should by rights be waking up any second now. In fact, you know, I think he *is* awake. Has been for minutes now. I think he is trying to pretend that he is asleep and hoping we will go away." She prodded at him with her tentacle. "Which we're *not*," she said loudly.

Alister gave up and opened his eyes.

He was still on the strange ship, face pointed at the ceiling as he lay on his back on what felt like a sofa. Professor Odd was leaning over him, her tentacle poised, ready to poke him again.

Sleep does marvelous things to one's brain, and even though passing out was not quite the same, Alister now found himself able to engage his rational brain in a meaningful way, unlike before.

"You have a tentacle," he said, just to hear it out loud. "Growing out the back of your head."

"Yep," said the Professor.

"And you have cat's eyes."

"Actually, they used jaguar genes, but close enough."

"What *are* you?"

The Professor's face, which had been open and pleasant up to that point, suddenly went perfectly blank. "I'm Professor Odd," she said flatly.

"And I'm Elo," said the dog. She was seated on the floor, having changed again into a futuristic one-piece purple suit that put Alister in mind of space-age pajamas. "Marhutz Elo, but call me Elo."

"Hello Elo," Alister said. He did not ask what she was. A dog, obviously. With hands. But still recognizably a *dog*. "Where am I?" he asked instead.

"That's a *very* good question," said Professor Odd. "It all depends on what you mean by *where*."

"What do I mean by *what now?*" Alister was beginning to feel a bit sore in the head, and he had discovered a bruise on his lip. It must have happened when he fell down.

"*Where* as in, in relation to your former position on the planet Earth, or *where* as in your position relative to the star Sol, or *where* as in your position relative to the universe that contains Sol, the planet Earth, *et cetera.*" said the Professor. "Or are you asking *where* as in your relative position in the worldtrack you are currently present in, or *where* as in your relative position in time and space outside the conventional universe?"

"*Where*—" Alister interrupted before his rational brain could have another kernel panic, "where is *here*? *This* place," he pointed down at the floral print carpet. "What is *here*?"

"Oh, this?" the Professor seemed surprised. The ridges of skin where her eyebrows should have been went up, wrinkling her otherwise smooth head. "*Here* is the Oddity. My home. Welcome to it, by the way. Would you like some tea now? I believe where you come from a traumatic event such as loss of consciousness is usually followed by imbibing some form of ethanol, but since that would tantamount to poisoning you I don't think I'll offer you any. Tea," she stated. "*Much* better. Some theanine would do you good." So speaking she wandered out of sight toward what Alister assumed was the kitchen alcove he had seen earlier.

Sitting up, slowly, he found himself staring across the cluttered work table and out the window with the pink curtains. He closed his eyes, counted to ten, then opened them again.

It was dark outside, perfectly black, except for a large glowing orb that hovered half in view. Inside it Alister thought he glimpsed clouds, and beneath that, continents and oceans. Getting shakily to his feet he crossed the room to peer outside. Upon closer inspection he thought he could make out fainter, more distant orbs, a few of which seemed to be stacked, one on top of the other.

"They are worlds," Alister whispered to himself.

"World*tracks*, actually," Elo said. She had followed him around the table and was standing on her hind legs, arms folded across her chest. "Some people call them *narratives*, or alternate realities."

"Alternate universes?" Alister said, hopefully. He had read about those, and his rational brain was helpfully reminding him about infinite multiverses and the like.

Elo shrugged. "Depends on what you mean by 'universe,'" she said. "One conventional universe can have effectively an infinite number of narratives, but you can have whole herds of conventional universes that run parallel to each other, each with their own collection of infinite narratives, but entirely separate from *other* universes that are not related to them at all."

"You said *conventional* universe," Alister said. "There are other kinds?"

"*Unconventional* universes," Elo provided helpfully. "Like the one where the Oddity lives."

Alister turned away from the window. "Then how . . . how did you get into *my* universe? My, er, world*track*?"

Elo pointed down to the narrow end of the teardrop, with the sunken door and the two consoles. "The Oddity has a trans-narrative slash universe spatial and limited temporal wormhole generator. That door can open onto any door we want, anywhere, and some-times."

"Sometimes?" Alister said, beginning to feel a little alarmed.

"Synthetic time travel is difficult," Elo elaborated. "Not all universes will accept it. Mostly we remain locked in the natural order, but we can manipulate the slippage."

"Slippage . . . " Alister echoed blankly. He had heard that term used before, in a science fiction book.

"Since here we're not technically present in a universe's timeline, we can either maintain our temporal synchronicity, that is, remain *in step* with the time of another universe, or break that synchronicity and jump ahead of, or fall behind, a given universe . . . to a greater or lesser degree, depending on the universe, of course."

Alister's confusion was becoming apparent on his face. Elo scratched behind an ear as she thought how to better explain.

"Let's take *you* as an example," she said eventually. "You've spent about thirty minutes in the Oddity—thirty of your native universe's minutes, and thirty of the Oddity's minutes—so if we were to do the natural thing, which is to remain in temporal synchronicity with your universe, if you left the Oddity now you would return to your universe and your narrative thirty minutes after you left it, with no time slippage. Are you with me so far?"

Alister nodded. "As far as *time* is concerned," he said, "it would have been as if I'd simply sat in that car for thirty minutes, and then gotten out again."

"That's an over simplification, but it's the right idea," Elo said. "Now things get complicated. Because, you see, time is fluid between universes. Since we're in a wholly separate universe here, our time runs separately as well. They *want* to run in synch, but they are still *separate*. Using the Oddity we can create something called *slippage* which allows us to manipulate the time difference between universes. To slip out of synch, to a certain degree. We can't use it to travel backwards in time   at least, not in most universes—but we can use it to nip and tuck a bit.

"Going back to your example. We could create retro-slippage, so you would arrive back in your universe-narrative as little as one second after you left it, even though you spent over half an hour here. Or we could create advent-slippage, so you would arrive back many hours, even days after you left. The exact window of time you have to slide around in varies from universe to universe, but the natural laws prevent us from slipping behind the time of the initial connection, or from jumping ahead beyond a few years."

"Years?" Alister gasped, casting a concerned glance toward the door.

"It's not a good idea, generally," Elo said. "The Oddity's time auto-synchs with the native time with every connection, so if you jump forward a year there's no way to get it back. Unless you're in a temporally flexible universe, but those are dangerous places and we don't visit them very often."

Alister ran a hand through his hair, pulling it out so it stood erect, as if someone had run an electric current through it. "I need a drink," he said weakly.

"Tea!" Professor Odd proclaimed, appearing by his side and offering him a steaming mug. "Drink. Restore your equilibrium. You'll need it, because I'll need *you* to help restore the equilibrium of your worldtrack." She gave him a hearty thump on the back, nearly making him spill his tea. "Drink up!"

Janet Surrey was having a strange day. She had just arrived for her afternoon shift when there had been a crisis of some kind in the philosophy hall that had resulted in a trail of green slime halfway around the quadrangle.

Muttering to herself and shaking her head she went to the janitor's closet and opened the door.

"Why *thank* you, how *kind*," Professor Odd said, stepping outside. "Come along, Elo. We seem to have made it back just in time; the trail is still fresh."

Janet Surrey could only stand and stare, her mouth slightly open, as a woman in a fluorescent orange wig, trench coat and glasses, followed by a dog in a Seeing Eye Dog harness, and a young man who looked for all the world like a student, came piling out of the janitor's closet and trooped past her down the hallway.

"But I don't understand," Alister said once they were safely away from the poor cleaning lady. "Whatever do you need *me* for?"

"The mirror effect!" Professor Odd proclaimed.

"*Mirror effect?*"

"Fresh eyes," she explained. "I've seen so many strange things that nothing is strange anymore. And I've been to so many different worldtracks that I have no idea what is considered strange in *this* one. But as a native you have no problem spotting things that are out of the ordinary. Like looking at an image in a mirror: you see the same image as me, but from a slightly different angle, so different things will stand out. That's why I needed your help earlier in the classroom—oh blast!" She stopped dead and turned right around, nearly causing Alister to crash into her. "I left my *cane!* Bother that! Here's something else you can do Mr. Alister, run to the Love of Wisdom hall and fetch my cane: I dropped it when I was trying to catch our green slime friend."

So Alister veered off and went back to the philosophy hall. He entered to find himself in a writhing crowd of confused students, some in very much the same position as he last remembered them. Apparently by "just in time" the Professor meant they had returned at more or less the same instant they had left. Alister had to fight his way to the front of the room, beating off grabbing hands and evading questions from all sides. ("What happened?" "Where is the professor?" "Is the class cancelled, then?")

Her cane was lying on the floor by the lectern. It was a long cane with a black shaft and a curved silver handle, carved in the shape of a banana. *Definitely the Professor's cane*, Alister thought as he picked it up.

As he forged his way back through the room someone plucked at his sleeve, and he turned to find Corny Jones hanging off his arm. Corny Jones, who was looking as thick and bewildered as always, but Alister remembered how clever he had seemed when the Professor had performed her laser trick.

"Oi, Bane, do you know what's happened to Marcus?"

"Marcus?" Alister repeated, wanting only to get away.

"The transfer student," Corny Jones said. "The professor chased him out of the room. What happened to him? Is he in trouble?"

Alister wondered how he could have misjudged Corny Jones for so long. The man was actually quite clever. That was the problem.

"Oo-ooh, he's fine. Yes, absolutely fine. The professor is giving him some special tutoring, is all. Asked me to bring her cane and—" here he was hit by a stroke of genius, "—Marcus asked me to bring him his books. Left them behind in his hurry. Ah, I see his bag there. I'll catch you later, Jones!"

Grabbing the transfer student's abandoned satchel Alister made for the door again. He was just inching his way out when he chanced to glance back and saw two men in white lab coats coming in through the hidden panel door the Professor had used earlier. They wore thick black rubber gloves, goggles and paper mouth masks. One of them was carrying a gun.

Alister shut the door behind him and ran flat out along the trail of drying slime. He caught up to the Professor and Elo, standing over the pool of slime the former had been sitting in. At least, the Professor was standing; Elo was running back and forth along the hall, nose to the ground, the very picture of a dog hunting for a scent.

"Oh, thank you," the Professor said when Alister offered her the cane. "What have you got there?"

"Books, bag," Alister said, a little out of breath. "Of Marcus, the transfer student, er, tentacle, thing."

"Really? That's marvelous, let's have a look!"

"But Professor, back in the classroom, there were two men—"

"I should think there would be more people in that room than just two men," the Professor said, peering inside the satchel.

"Two *new* men," Alister said, glancing over his shoulder. Nothing. Yet. "In white lab coats, with goggles, and masks. They came in through the same door you did."

"Really? Maybe they will be able to help us," the Professor said cheerfully. "Found anything yet, Elo?"

But Elo was across the quad, sniffing furiously at the base of a tree, and did not answer. Giving up on her companion the Professor began digging through the satchel, flipping books open and tossing them aside.

"But Professor," Alister began earnestly. "One of them had a g—"

"*Found* it!" The Professor cried, holding up a geometry workbook. She had it open to the last page, where there was written a name and an address. "E. Marcus, seven oh three four nine two Rutterguard Street, apartment number eighty-four, East City," she read triumphantly. "This will be easy!"

"*There they are!*" shouted the voice of Corny Jones. Alister turned around to see the chubby student, flanked by the men in lab coats. The one with the gun had it pointed in their direction. Together they advanced slowly down the hall, the unarmed lab coat talking quickly into some mobile device.

Alister briefly considered running. Then considered the gun. Then considered the Professor, who had looked up from the geometry book and was staring at the triad blankly. He looked around for Elo, but the dog had vanished.

Corny Jones isn't the only one who's smarter than they look, Alister thought ruefully.

"Put down your weapon," the lab coat with the gun said, when they had gotten close enough to speak without shouting.

Professor Odd sighed and let the geometry book fall to the ground.

"I said drop your weapon!" repeated the man.

The Professor looked baffled. "I thought I did," she said. Then she noticed her cane, which was still tucked under her arm. "Oh! Did you mean this? Sorry, of course," she set it carefully aside, clear of the slime.

"Where's Marcus, what have you done?" Corny Jones demanded.

"I have no idea," Professor Odd said cheerfully. "Maybe you gentlemen could put down *your* weapons and we could figure that out together?"

The man with the mobile device took it down from his ear and spoke to the other. "She reads as mostly human, sir, and harmless."

Professor Odd snapped her terrible blank look on the man, and drew herself up imperiously. "*Harmless?*" she asked in a piercing whisper.

"*Mostly* harmless, sir," the man amended.

"And him?" asked the other man, training the gun on Alister, who instinctively raised his hands, palms out. His heart was banging away in his chest, yet his brain remained remarkably clear. He had, he realized, been acting as though he were in a dream from the moment he had woken up to find the Professor poking at him with her tentacle. He had been blindly following her along, not questioning her motives. But that gun made everything terribly, terribly real, and not at all dreamlike. It was time, he decided, for some self-preservation.

"I'm just a student," he said quickly. "Bane, Alister Bane, second year. You can check my ID if you need to. I only just met *her*, er, the Professor, a moment ago." Which was true for *them*, he rationalized.

But the man with the mobile was scanning him now, and he was frowning around his goggles.

"Sir, this one only reads as mostly human as well. It may be another flesh cell—"

"He's *human*," the Professor said forcefully. It was almost a shout, and drew the attention of both men—and to Alister's relief, the gun. "Sorry," she muttered out of the corner of her mouth. "Particle disturbances from traveling between universes can give false readings on primitive scanners, like *that* one. He's perfectly human," she said loudly. "Student, like he said. Not involved, only drafted as my assistant *temporarily*."

It was difficult to tell through the wig and the glasses and the scarf and the trench coat, but from the tone of her voice Alister got the impression that Professor Odd was genuinely agitated. And that, more than the gun, more than being declared *mostly* human, made him very, very frightened. And there stood Corny Jones, looking as stupid as ever, and not lifting a *finger* to help.

"You said she was giving him special tutoring," he said, pointing an accusatory finger at Alister.

That was too much.

"What was I *supposed* to say?" Alister snapped. "Your new friend Marcus is actually a bright green tentacle monster with one eye that can make people drunk and horny by spewing green slime on them?"

"Confirm that description," said the man with the mobile scanner. "He has had definite contact with Incongruity M87. Take him in to custody and process him for testing."

"Wh-*what?*" Alister sputtered, at the same time the Professor shouted *"No!"* in what sounded very close to panic.

"And her," said the man.

"Oh yes, that's much better," Professor Odd said, suddenly going cheerful. "I'm a much better specimen, *trust* me. In fact, you'll probably have no interest in Mr. Alister once you're through with me. What's this? Handcuffs? Of course, right. Snap them on already. Can't you do *anything* with those gloves on? Right-ee-oh then, have you got a car or transportation unit? Where to?"

Despite this sunny chatter going on in the background, Alister could not muster much spirit as the man with the gun manacled first Professor Odd, and then him. He thought of protesting: he had rights as a student and as a citizen. But those were *human* rights, to which apparently he was no longer entitled.

As they were being marched away he saw the man with the mobile, who seemed to be in charge, pick up the geometry text book and turn to the last page. Then he flicked on his mobile and spoke into it.

"This is Dr. Hurnest. I need a van and containment crew at seven oh three four nine two Rutterguard Street, East City. Target Incongruity M87 is in apartment number eighty-four . . . "

"I'm sorry," Professor Odd said quietly.

They were seated side by side in the back of an unmarked white van inside a cage of wire mesh. The men in lab coats had taken Alister's everything bag, but they had not dared to remove the Professor's glasses, wig, or clothes, for which Alister was grateful; in the dim light she looked almost normal, and that was a small comfort.

"I didn't mean to get you tangled up with this lot," she said, slumping back against the wall and stretching her legs out until they knocked against the cage.

"Who are *they?*" Alister asked.

The Professor shrugged as extravagantly as one could with one's hands cuffed behind one's back. "The Illuminati," she said. "Freemasons. Mad Scientists Inc. The Inquisition. The Men in Black. I dunno. Most worlds have them, with more or less power, but they all operate in the same way: they're the ones who notice, or strongly suspect, that there is more to the rational world than what the public sees, and they believe it is in the public's best interest to keep that knowledge from them. They operate either outside, or above and beyond the global governments, and they are almost multiversally bad news."

"And they've got us."

"Yep."

"What's going to happen to us?"

"Different things. Probably. You, I should hope, will end up with your memory wiped and back on the street in no time once they figure out you're native human. Hopefully that will become obvious after a cursory physical examination, and before invasive surgery."

Alister swallowed. He was beginning to wish, fervently, that he had stayed in bed that morning. That he had skipped philosophy. That he hadn't gone running after the Professor. . . .

"If you feel you're going to faint again, try putting your head between your knees," Professor Odd suggested helpfully.

"I'm not fainting again," Alister said. He was *here*, he told himself. And nothing, not even the Professor's Oddity, could change that. It was crazy (it was terrifying) but it was what he had to deal with.

"What about Elo?" he asked.

"Safely back in the Oddity if she knows what's good for her," the Professor said with a wry grin.

"*Does* she know what's good for her?"

The Professor shook her head, still grinning. Alister thought he caught a glimpse of moss-green leopard-spotted tentacle sneaking out the back of her collar, but in the gloom he could not be certain.

After a few more minutes a door was wrenched open, and the van rocked as the two men in lab coats climbed into the sealed cab. The engine started, and the vehicle lurched into motion. The only light filtered in through the tinted back windows, making it impossible to see where they were, or where they were going.

"What about that *thing?*" Alister asked, just to take his mind off all the horrible possibilities currently spinning inside his head.

"Thing?"

"The green thing, with the tentacles and slime?"

"Ah, Incongruity M87?" Professor Odd stuck her tongue out. It was very long, Alister saw, and a little greenish. "I have no idea!"

Alister stared at her, shocked. "No idea?"

"None at all: I've never seen anything like it! Why do you think I was looking for it? I wanted to *talk* to it! It registered a huge blip on the Oddity's scanner crossing into this worldtrack, like nothing I'd ever seen before. I was *curious,*" she said, smiling. "I wanted to *learn* about it."

"So it's not . . . not evil?"

"Nothing in a conventional universe is good or evil," the Professor stated. "Of course, it may have come from an *unconventional* universe, but even then I don't think it's hostile. It didn't *hurt* me," she added, seeing Alister's confusion. "Earlier, it could have injured, even killed me with that slime. But it only incapacitated me."

"So you don't think it's dangerous?"

"Oh, I'm fairly sure it's dangerous," she said calmly. "But not because it's hostile or evil. I think it's *scared.* Terrified, probably."

Alister sighed, and settled back against the cold wall of the van. The manacles were digging uncomfortably into his wrists, and he was beginning to get a crick in his shoulders. And there was something smooth and cool curling around his fingers. He opened his mouth in surprise.

"Don't move," the Professor told him. "Picking these things is a right doozy, and I don't know how long we've got."

The peeling wooden sign on the front of the building marked it as "Smith, Johnson and Smith, Electronics Liquidation" and the front door led into a shabby office mostly filled with old monitors and cobwebs. There was a battered sedan, twenty years out of fashion, parked in the dirt front lot, and two leathery men smoking cigarettes beside the door.

The unmarked white van pulled into the lot, rolled past the smoking men, and through an automatic gate with an orange sign on it that read "Hazard: Absolutely No Admittance." Then it pulled into a covered garage and descended down, down, and down, through a tunnel marked with flickering yellow lights.

Inside the van, Alister was struggling.

"But what should I *do?*" he asked.

The Professor shrugged. "Do what you think is best. Your chances of survival go up dramatically if you can convince them you are human, which will be easier if you get away from me."

"Do you think they'll separate us?"

"That doesn't matter," she said. "But don't try to escape on your own; runners are the first to be shot."

"Thanks for that," Alister muttered.

The Professor smiled at him through the corner of her mouth. "Although . . . if you and I were to work *together,* we might be able to extricate ourselves without bodily injury."

"How would we do *that?*"

"By you doing *exactly* what I say."

The van's brakes squealed as it lurched to a stop in a low concrete room lit by incandescent fixtures on the walls. Armed guards in thick kevlar vests came pouring out of the shadows and stood around the back of the van as the two men in lab coats got out and went to open the doors. First the Professor, then Alister, were handed out and passed into the custody of the armed guards, who marched them through a wide pair of swinging glass doors. These led into a long dim hall, punctuated at regular intervals by closed doors. The men in lab coats went in front, muttering to each other.

"Nice place you got here," the Professor remarked. "Soothing, calm and . . . clean . . . " she faltered on the last word as they passed a dark stain on the wall. Alister did not like to think what it was.

"Though it's all very *samey,* isn't it?" she went on in a loud voice. "So monotonous. Do you boys ever get bored working down here? Hey, you don't ever get *lost* do ya? It's like a labyrinth here, what with all these doors. And I don't mean a proper labyrinth which is just a long wriggly path; I mean a *challenge* labyrinth. Do you know what those are? Frightening things: made to test the wills of wimpish maidens, they are. But what they are *famous* for is being *deceptive.* They've got nooks and crannies hidden all *over* the place, but in *plain sight* where they are obvious to anyone who knows how to look for them. They've even got whole networks of *hidden passages* and stuff. Say, I don't suppose you have got any of those? Have you? Perhaps? Like . . . maybe . . . *right here!*"

Quick as lightning, with a snakelike wriggle, the Professor had slipped between her guards, thrown off her manacles, and slammed a hand against what otherwise looked like a blank piece of concrete wall. Then she was gone.

Without pausing to think Alister did the same. It was remarkably easy, since from the moment the Professor had moved everyone had ceased to notice him. He felt his hand on concrete, and for one horrible, horrible moment he thought he was stuck; trapped. He felt someone grabbing at his shoulder, and then the wall before him dematerialized and he fell through it.

There followed a dizzying moment where gravity swung around beneath him, and he found himself plummeting forward, face down. It was only a fall of a few feet, and he landed on something soft and springy, but he was still dazed.

Seeing nothing but stars, he felt the Professor's tentacle wrap firmly around his hand and pull him forward. He slid over the cushions and eventually found himself standing on a metal catwalk that led over a giant vat of glowing bluish liquid.

"What—what was *that?*" he asked, once he'd got his breath back.

"Hidden space-portal," the Professor said, leading him along the catwalk. "Now hurry, they'll be after us in a second."

That got Alister into a hesitant jog; the metal grill of the catwalk clanged and gave under his feet as he ran.

"But how, how did you know it was *there?*"

"Involuntary movement," she called over her shoulder. They careened around a corner and she set off pounding up a flight of metal stairs. "When I started on about hidden passages in plain sight, that scientist looked *right* at this spot . . . well, *that* spot back there."

"But how could you know that *meant* anything?"

"The guard in front of me looked too."

"But—but—"

"Less exposition, more running!" shouted Professor Odd. Once more her tentacle snaked its way out of her collar and grabbed Alister's hand, dragging him up behind her. The clanging of their feet on the metal was all around them, but Alister heard, clear as day, the shouting of angry guards.

There was a bang. A loud bang that sent echos throughout the whole room, followed almost immediately by sharp metallic shrieks as the bullet hit and ricocheted off the catwalks. Then there was more human shouting, this time a high, agitated voice. One of the scientists.

"Oooh, they don't like where we're going!" the Professor cried happily. "Come on, through here!"

They burst through a door at the top of the stairs to find themselves in another narrow concrete hallway, this one with a grated metal floor, through which they could see a vat of blue liquid, and others like it, far, far below.

"Give us an alien invasion, and this could be another Black Mesa," the Professor exclaimed, and started off down the hall. "But I don't like straight halls, nowhere to hide. Hmm . . . " Still with her tentacle wrapped firmly around Alister's hand she began trailing her hands along the wall on either side. Out of some mad inspiration Alister did the same with his free hand. They had not gone more than ten feet when he felt something very much like a static shock, only somehow more sluggish.

"Oi," he said, drawing to a halt and pulling the Professor up short by the tentacle so sharply that she nearly overbalanced backwards. "This spot feels weird."

The Professor backpedalled until she was standing next to him. She felt the wall up with both her hands, carefully, then squealed with delight.

"You found another portal, oh, *excellent!* Mirror-effect in action, I never would have noticed that!"

"Yes, but where does it go?"

Down the hall, they heard the door crash open.

"Somewhere better than here!" the Professor shouted, and jumped through the wall, dragging Alister behind her.

This time the direction of gravity remained constant, but they dropped two feet down as they emerged into a high-ceilinged room filled with black metal cabinets. The lights were dim, but enough to show Alister that the floor was wood, for a change, and that there was no one around.

"Whew! I think we've lost them, for a little while." The Professor slumped against the wall, took two deep breaths, and then shoved herself off into the maze of cabinets. "Now, what have we *here?*" she said, pulling open the door to the nearest one. Coming up behind her Alister saw that it was filled with rack upon rack of sleek, evil-looking guns.

"Carbines," the Professor said disgustedly, and shut the door. Whirling around she opened the cabinet behind her. It contained one long metal tube and some very large bullet-shaped missiles. "Bazooka!" she spat. "Oh my," she opened the next cabinet, revealing a number of handguns in holsters.

"It's an *armory,*" Alister said.

Professor Odd grinned at him. "Oh yes," she said.

"We could *arm* ourselves!"

"Oh *yes.*"

Alister reached for the nearest handgun. He had never held one before in his life, but he had seen people use them in the movies all the time.

"Ah, no, not those," the Professor said, shutting the door on him.

"Then what?"

"We split up; look for the cabinet that's *locked,* or a *safe,* something that's hard to get into. *That's* where we'll find the gun worth stealing!"

It took them probably less than ten minutes, but to Alister, who was expecting armed guards and angry scientists to come bursting out of the walls any minute, it felt like an eternity. They split up and ran through the aisles, slamming doors open and closed, until Alister came to a cabinet that didn't seem to have a door at all: merely blank, black sides. He called the Professor over, who exclaimed in delight as she inspected it with her fingers. It was not entirely blank, they soon found: there was a very slight dimple at about shoulder height in the center of what would have been its front. The Professor put her face right up against this, prodded it with her tentacle, sniffed it, then finally licked it.

"Well that's *interesting,*" she said, rummaging in the pockets of her trench coat.

"What is?"

"This thing is secured with an infrared laser lock."

"So? What does that mean?"

"Infrared laser locks are not native to *this* worldtrack, or even this *set* of world-tracks," the Professor said. "It shows these people have indeed had contact with other cosmi. Now, whether they *understand* what they've got, let's see . . . " she produced again her slim, black laser pen, and fiddled with it, twisting a knob on the bottom around until she was satisfied. Pressing the head of the pen against the center of the dimple she frowned for a moment, then gave out a satisfied sigh as the front of the cabinet sprang open with a neat "click."

"You picked the lock?" Alister guessed.

"Burned it out, more like," said the Professor. "Infrared laser locks are obsolete in their native worldtrack; laser technology advanced to the extent that anyone could pick them. But in *this* worldtrack they are practically unknown, and probably seemed like the latest and greatest to whoever was trying to protect what's inside."

"And, what is inside?"

"I don't know, let's find out!" said Professor Odd, and pulled the door open.

It was a gun. At least, it looked rather like a gun, with two barrels encased in a lattice of copper wires and a two-handed grip with a double trigger. The backside of the gun was covered in circular dials and little switches, marked out in different colors with unfamiliar writing on them.

"Good dawkins, dennett, hitch and harris!" Professor Odd breathed. "It's a localized temporal field manipulator!"

"Do I even want to know what that is?" Alister asked, feeling a bit resigned. Whatever that gun was, it obviously represented another attack on his well-ordered, rational world.

The Professor didn't answer at once. Reverently, as if cradling an infant, she reached in and picked up the gun, carefully keeping her fingers off the triggers. She gave a dial on the back an expert spin, and the whole thing lit up like a Christmas tree.

"In layman's speech," she said with a wide, wide grin, "you would call this a *time gun.*"

The doors to the armory opened with a hiss. Professor Odd popped her head out and looked both ways before beckoning Alister after her. Outside was another gray, concrete hall, but this one was better lit, and seemed to be in a more habitable part of the complex; they passed lavatories as they went. Alister decided to take advantage of the second one. Professor Odd waited in the hall, seething with impatience, while he ran inside. It was as he made his way out that he noticed a sign tacked next to the sinks. Like the signs that the Ministry of Health and Safety put up in restaurants, it stated that employees of the *Canary Company* were required to wash their hands thoroughly with soap and water before returning to work.

"Well, at least we know what this place is called now," he said upon emerging from the restroom. "The *Canary Company.*"

"Canary," the Professor repeated, striding down the hall. "Canary, canary, canary . . . canaries were used by miners to measure the amounts of toxic chemicals in the air. Being birds they have much more efficient and sensitive lungs, and the canary would die from bad air long before the humans even noticed."

"Do you think that has anything to do with this company?"

"No idea," the Professor said. "It's just what I thought of when you said *canary*—ah! Now *here's* something useful!" She came to a stop in front of a computer terminal, which appeared to be some sort of First Aid kit dispenser. It spewed out several little red packets with white crosses on them as the Professor pounded away at the keyboard one-handed, before it finally gave her what she wanted: a three-dimensional schematic of the entire complex. This she studied intently for several minutes, while Alister glanced nervously up and down the hall.

At last she stood away from the console, beckoning Alister to come look. "Here is where we are," she said, pointing to a little red dot in a maze of blue tubes and tunnels. "Here is the nearest exit," she said, pointing to a green square not too far away. "It's marked as rubbish disposal, and will probably be minimally guarded. Still, you'll have to be careful."

"Me? What about you?" Alister asked.

"I'm not leaving, not yet," the Professor said, and pointed to a lower part of the map, where the tubes and tunnels turned red and were marked 'Off Limits.' "Somewhere down here is their live specimen research center. It's bound to be where they'll take our green slime friend."

"You're going after him? Er, it?"

"I have to. I can't leave it in their custody unless I can be certain that this *Canary Company* will do it no harm, and so far they have done nothing to assure me of this. But you *don't.* All you need to do is get out and away."

"So we're splitting up?"

"Unless you want to come with me," the Professor said. "It's your choice."

Alister felt so torn that he made an odd jerking motion with his shoulder. Half of him wanted to take the Professor's directions and run. The other half was sanguine enough to know that this in no way guaranteed his safety, and that without the Professor's guidance—and her strange gun—he was about as likely to be captured as if he followed her into the depths of the Canary Company.

No, as tempting as it would be to try to escape, Alister decided against it. He jerked his head in a sort of nod. "I'll come with you," he said, and smiled as a thought occurred to him. "You never know when you'll need a mirror."

The Professor laughed, then turned sober. "You do realize if I get you killed I'm going to be kicking myself over it for *ages*," she said sternly.

"That's a small consolation," Alister said. He stepped back and held his arm out. "Lead on."

The Assets and Items Processing Room at the Canary Company was sluggish that day. Interns walked about fetching coffee or organizing specimen trays, anything to avoid cataloging the truckload of furniture and other assets that had been delivered. It looked like the entire contents of a college student's dorm room, because it was. One intern had made something of a project out of it, and had been making headway until she noticed that one of the items she had already cataloged had gone missing.

"Where is Asset 101?" she asked, turning over a box containing twenty-year-old National Geographic magazines.

"What's Asset 101?" asked one of her colleagues.

"That bag, the small blue duffel bag that came in with Specimen 1017."

"I thought I saw it there, just a moment ago."

"Well, it's not there now!"

"Did you move it?"

"I never touched it . . . that's so strange. Where could it have gone?"

In the hall outside the Assets and Items Processing Room, Elo tightened down the straps on Alister's everything bag so that it rested securely on her back, next to the Professor's cane. Then she dropped to all fours and padded off, swift and stealthy as a shadow.

Alister and the Professor were running too, albeit more loudly. They descended another flight of metal stairs—he wondered if the Canary Company had something against polymers—only to be met at the bottom by a crowd of angry guards.

"Use number one for a time gun," the Professor said, bringing the weapon to bear. "Retardation!"

Something like a ripple in the fabric of space launched from the top barrel of the gun. It pulsed outwards for about twenty feet, then exploded in a fantastic display of electrical discharge around the guards, who froze in their tracks.

Or, not quite froze. As Alister approached them cautiously, peering around the Professor's elbow, he saw that they were indeed still moving; continuing the motions they had begun when the Professor had fired the gun, but with an impossible slowness. As if they were a film someone was playing in super-slow motion.

"The localized temporal field manipulator creates a spatially restricted time anomaly field," the Professor explained, swinging a leg over the railing and jumping the last few feet to the ground, thereby avoiding the crowd of near-frozen guards. "Within the field, time passes at a different rate. You can use it to retard time, like I just did, so that anything entering the field will experience time at a slower rate, and perceive everything outside to be moving at super-speeds— oh, be careful not to get caught in it, or it'll slow you down too. Come on, jump already, it's not *that* far down!"

Alister hit the concrete floor on the balls of his feet, and nearly doubled over with the pain that shot through them.

"Another use," the Professor said, flipping levers and spinning dials madly, making the gun give off a high, petulant whine, "is to *advance* time within the field, so that anything entering it will move *faster* in comparison to its surroundings, like *so—*"

Off went the gun again, and this time Alister could better see the ripples, like a cone of moving air. The electrical discharge was considerably less this time, hardly more than a few sparks.

"That should give us a good head start," the Professor announced proudly, and took off running, directly into the field.

Alister limped after her as fast as he could. For a few moments it looked as though the Professor sped up, like a video on fast-forward, until he too entered the effects of the field. It was not a sudden transition: the Professor gradually slowed back down to normal speed, then slowed further as she exited the field. In the last moments, while Alister was still within the field and the Professor had left it, he saw her as moving in slow motion, turning around to point the gun backwards while she raised a hand to adjust its settings. Then he reached the end of the field and she sped back up again, the low droning he had heard before turning into proper words.

" . . . fade away on their own, but this gun should have a dispersement charge, aha! Here we are," the Professor was saying as he reached her at last. She shot another ripple of air—this time from the lower barrel. Alister couldn't see any difference, but the Professor seemed satisfied. She hitched the gun over her shoulder and took off down yet another concrete tunnel, this one lit with dim red lights. "*Off Limits* should be just at the end of this," she called over her shoulder. "Come on!"

They sped down the hall together until they found the way blocked by a solid metal door which was, unsurprisingly, locked.

"Laser locks?" Alister suggested hopefully.

"Some of them," the Professor said, fumbling in her pocket for her laser pen. But before she could get it out, the computer console on the door flashed brilliant green, and it began to open. She had just the time, and the presence of mind, to train the time gun at the door and set it flashing and whining menacingly.

There was a scientist behind the door. A short, chubby, dark-skinned man in the familiar white lab coat. He wore a face mask and goggles, so it was difficult to make out his expression, though from his body language he appeared stricken; he jumped backwards with a shout of surprise and threw up his hands.

"Do you know what this gun is?" the Professor asked.

The scientist shook his head. But it might have been a shudder. The Professor's glasses had been knocked askew during their run, and Alister imagined the poor man was getting a direct hit from her terrible, blank stare.

"Right," said the Professor. "Unless you want to find out, take off your mask and goggles."

The man did so. Underneath, his eyes were wide. He looked terrified.

"Incongruity M87," said Professor Odd.

The man blinked. "I—I'm sorry?" he stammered.

"Don't try misdirection on me. I know a micro-expression when I see one," the Professor snapped. "You know about Incongruity M87. Take us to it."

"B-but, I'm not authorized!" the scientist cried.

"Yes you are, but if you like you can take us to someone who will admit to it."

With a whimper the scientist stepped aside to let them through the door, although the Professor stepped through sideways so she never turned her back on him.

"I'm Professor Odd, by the way," she said, suddenly going jovial. "This here is Mr. Alister Bane."

"How do you do?" Alister said.

"Carver, Dr. Carver," said the scientist, a little baffled. "B-bio-chemistry—I haven't got any direct contact training, you can turn that thing off."

The Professor flipped a few levers, and the time gun revved down with a low moan. She smiled brightly. "No you're not and yes you do, but I need to save on the battery. Right then, Dr. Carver, as my literary cousins would say: *take us to your leader.*"

Elsewhere in the section marked "Off Limits" on the Canary Company map, alarms were going off. This was upsetting security. Security, who were already on edge because of the High Danger slash Priority delivery of Incongruity M87, and who had then been sent into a frenzy with the inexplicable disappearance of

Specimens 1016 and 1017, were now quite frantically trying to trace the cause of, and subsequently shut down, the alarms. There were so many of them, and some—such as the radioactive waste containment field failure alarm—were so loud that they entirely drowned out the faint *clickety-clack* of canine claws on aluminum coming from the ventilation ducts.

Dr. Carver led them first down more concrete halls—also lit in red—then through an airlock into a much brighter, cleaner section. It put Alister in mind of a hospital, with nurses and doctors in white coats bustling this way and that. Some of these seemed so absorbed in their work that they barely glanced at the procession, but others were astonished, and ran up to Dr. Carver spewing questions.

"Everything is under control," Dr. Carver would say, and shoo them off. For the most part this was enough to dissuade them, but a few only left reluctantly, and then followed at a distance. By the time they were passing through a hall marked "Radiology" they had acquired a following of about twenty worried scientists.

Dr. Carver opened a large door with a "Do Not Disturb" sign on it, and led them into a spacious office, complete with three rows of flat-screened monitors on the wall, a wide oak desk, and a luxurious reclining chair. On the far wall was mounted a circular door of reinforced steel.

"If you'll just give me a moment to acquire the access codes," Dr. Carver said as he dashed over to the desk and began punching buttons. "I'll have that open in a moment."

"No," said Professor Odd. "I think this is far enough."

"I'm sorry?" said Dr. Carver, pausing in his work.

"What's through that door?" asked the Professor, jerking her head toward the giant steel disk.

"Our head scientist's laboratory," said Dr. Carver.

"Now *that's* a truth," the Professor said. "But I don't think your chief scientist is in there, you know? I think . . . yes, in fact I'm pretty sure . . . " she fiddled with a few knobs on the time gun, bringing up the lights so that it hummed eagerly. She pointed it directly at Dr. Carver's face. " . . . I'm pretty sure he's standing right in front of me."

Dr. Carver straightened up and put his hands in his pockets. He shrugged. "Well, it was a worth a try," he said, and gave sudden jerk of his chin toward the gaggle of doctors crowded around the door.

Hands grabbed at Alister, seizing his arms and pulling him down before he could think. The Professor whirled around, time gun blazing, but the doctors had Alister propped up in front of them like a living shield. There was no way for her to surround them in a field without including him.

Instead she reached into her coat with one hand, pulled out a small, white paper bag, and threw it at him. It hit him square in the face and exploded into a cloud of fine white powder. Alister coughed. The scientists coughed. Alister kicked and struggled, but he was outnumbered. They were dragging him out of the room. There was a sharp prick in the side of his neck, and a few seconds later everything went wobbly and slow.

I've been caught in a time-retardation field! he thought frantically. Then, *No, this is probably a sedative . . .*

"I'll come find you later!" the Professor shouted, just as they slammed the door on her and Dr. Carver.

Inside the office, Professor Odd took off her glasses and tucked them inside her coat, the better to glare at Dr. Carver.

"Save you some time and testing," she said. "He's human. No interest to you."

Dr. Carver shrugged. "Quite probably. But he has trace amounts of unrecognizable particulates in his digestive tract. They may prove useful."

"Pump his stomach then, you'll find it's only tea," the Professor muttered.

"Ah yes, but tea from *where* exactly?" said Dr. Carver, leaning eagerly over his desk.

The Professor pursed her lips, and didn't answer. "You are aware of the existence of multiple universes," she stated.

Dr. Carver nodded.

"Where is Incongruity M87?"

"Intensive Care Unit five oh three four seven," Dr. Carver said pleasantly. "Two floors down, second hall on the left, can't miss it. And don't worry," he added smugly. "We're taking care of it."

"Define *taking care* of it?" the Professor asked coldly.

"Live tissue samples, MRI scans, DNA samples . . . we have to take as much as we can. There is only so much you can learn from an autopsy, and extra-universal specimens rarely live more than a few days."

"Oh, and I wonder why *that* is?" the Professor said extravagantly, throwing her arms out. "Don't you ever bother trying to *communicate* with them? Find out what they eat? Whether or not they breathe *oxygen*? Maybe, perhaps, *help them get home?*"

"Our facility is only equipped to study, Professor," Dr. Carver explained calmly. "You should be able to appreciate that."

"Study is one thing," hissed the Professor. "Study at the expense of life, *intelligent life*, is quite, quite another!"

"Oh, I wouldn't call the thing *intelligent*," Dr. Carver said placidly. He punched in some command on the keyboard mounted to his desk, and one of the screens lit up. It showed a room from a high, tilted angle, not unlike the view of a security camera. Only this was in color, and had sound.

The room was a long rectangle, one end of which was filled with banks of computers. The other contained a square vat of water. In the center was a table, and on the table, splayed out and pinned down like an insect, was something bright green with ten long tentacles stretched out in every direction, like a bizarre starburst. In the center was one huge, orange eye, held open by a pair of forceps. It was difficult to tell with the graininess of the video, but the thing seemed to be lying in a spreading puddle of green slime.

Professor Odd had her face so close to the screen it was beginning to fog up from her breath. Letting the time gun fall to her side she put one hand against the screen, as if by simply pressing she could press herself out of the office and into that room. When at last she turned around, causing Dr. Carver to back hastily away from the keyboard, her eyes were angry narrow slits and her face was nearly white.

"It cannot speak," he said, a little defensively. "We tried everything, even our universal translator. Elementary scanning could not pick out a central nervous system. We think it is some sort of test animal sent through from another dimension. It was equipped with a flesh casing to disguise it as a human, but this was unfortunately lost . . . " he trailed off, noticing for the first time the leopard-spotted tentacle that had slithered out from the Professor's collar and was lashing back and forth angrily.

"Have you ever been tied down to one of those tables, Dr. Carver?" Professor Odd asked icily, advancing on the desk. "It's not fun."

"I was just explaining to you, that thing has no brain!"

"Nothing that *you* might recognize as a brain," she snapped. "It doesn't matter. The simple fact is, you're not just killing it—you're *torturing* it!"

"We are *studying* it," Dr. Carver said forcefully.

"Just because you gain knowledge from torturing something doesn't change the fact that it is *still torture!*"

"Really Professor, I thought an academic such as yourself wouldn't be so squeamish," Dr. Carver said, straightening his tie.

Professor Odd drew in a deep breath so that her chest swelled and she looked even taller than usual. Her cat eyes were open wide, and her tentacle slashed from side to side. "Do I *look* like an *academic* to you?" she hissed.

Dr. Carver shrugged. "You are clearly very well educated in many matters. Your knowledge will be an invaluable asset to the Canary Company."

"And what makes you think I'm going to let you have it?"

Dr. Carver laughed. "I never anticipated you would give it willingly. We have . . . other ways. Boys, you can come in now—*hrrgk!*"

Dr. Carver choked a little as Professor Odd grabbed him by his collar and pulled him out from behind his desk, even as the room began to fill with black-clad security guards. They came bursting out of the empty walls, no doubt conveyed by more hidden portals, and all looked more than a little harried.

Professor Odd quickly got her back to the door, resting the twin barrels of the time gun against Dr. Carver's head.

"Oi, before you lot start injecting us with bullets, do you know what this gun can do?" she shouted over his shoulder.

That made the guards hesitate for a moment, but Dr. Carver just laughed again.

"Don't be afraid. That gun's a novelty," he called to them around the Professor's hands. "All it does is create small anomalies in time and space. Mostly harmless."

"Mostly harmless? Really?" exclaimed Professor Odd. "Funny, you know that's *just* what your scientists said about *me!*" And with an almighty shove she sent Dr. Carver stumbling into the surprised arms of his guards, at the same time spinning a dial on the time gun so that it nearly shrieked. She leveled it against the forest of carbine rifles pointed in her direction, and fired off one shot.

It was not so much a ripple as it was a wave, and the retardation was so intense that everyone on the far side of the room, including Dr. Carver, froze instantly. One of the guns had gone off a split second before the field engulfed it, and this bullet hung, suspended in midair, a few inches from the mouth of its rifle.

Professor Odd did not stay to admire her handiwork. She was out the door a moment later, crashing through a gaggle of surprised nurses and on back through the "Radiology" department.

"Two floors down, second hall on the left, Intensive Care Unit five oh three four seven," she repeated under her breath as she dodged grabbing hands and pelted along the hallway, looking for a lift. "And no signs of deception when he said it. Sorry, Mr. Alister, you'll have to wait! Aha! *Stairs!*"

Whatever they had given Alister, it must not have been very strong. He remained conscious, or mostly so, while they dragged him out of the office and down what felt like several miles of hallway, before bundling him into a lift. One of the nurses punched in a code, and they began to ascend. As they did so, things became clearer. Perhaps it was the powder the Professor had thrown at him; it had settled on him and many of his captors, but while it seemed to make them uncomfortable, the gentle tingling of it on his skin gave Alister something to hold on to. And whenever he inhaled a whiff of it his mind would momentarily clear.

It was in one of these lucid moments that he noticed that the lift had stopped. The nurses were agitated. Several of them had gotten out cell phones and were making calls. The larger men who had been holding him let him down so they could go rattle the elevator controls. He lay on his back, staring up at the ceiling of the elevator. Funny, there seemed to be a hole in it.

"Ceilings shouldn't have holes," he said, a little blearily.

"Eh? Did he just talk?" one of the scientists said, leaning over him. Above and beyond her hair, Alister distinctly saw two furry, pointed ears poking out of the hole. Alister found himself smiling.

"She *didn't* know what's good for her," he said, trying to explain to the scientist, who had gotten out a needle and was prepping it. "She's a *good* doggie."

"He's just delirious," said one of the nurses. "No need to give him another dose."

"You're not the one in charge," snapped the scientist. "He seems to be coming out of *iiiaaaa—*" her exclamation of surprise was cut short as Elo dropped from the ceiling directly onto her head, gave her an expert tap just behind her ear, and she dropped like a stone.

Chaos erupted in the elevator. Alister had enough sense of self-preservation to crawl his way into a corner as nurses and scientists spun madly about. Elo was a golden blur in his eyes until the last scientist fell, and she stood up, holding the Professor's banana-handled cane.

"*Very* good doggie," Alister said, trying to sit up.

"Oh, it's *you*," she said, picking her way through the bodies. "I caught the hyper-scent bomb and thought it was the Professor. Well, get up already. What did they give you? Oh dear, you're still pretty far out, aren't you? Well if isn't this just my day for dealing with drugged hominids! Here, drink this."

Something cool and cylindrical was pressed into Alister's hand. Squinting at it, he saw it was a water bottle. And not just *any* water bottle. *His* water bottle. The purple one with "A. B." written on the side.

"This is mine," he said.

"Yes, it's yours, so drink it. I've got your bag here too, but I don't think you're up to carrying it yet."

Alister took a deep swig of water. It cleared his head a little. Enough for him to remember his manners.

"Thank you," he said, breathing deeply and slowly. "Professor Odd is down there still. Dr. Carver has her in his office. Dr. Carver is the one in charge."

"Then I don't think we'll need to worry about Dr. Carver," Elo said. She was rummaging in the pockets of her Seeing Eye Dog harness, and eventually produced a small gadget like a thermometer with a bowl at the end, and something very like a cell phone, but not. Wiping some sweat and dissolved powder off of Alister's brow she smeared it around the inside of the bowl of the thermometer, then plugged the other end into the not-cell phone. She pressed some buttons, growled and pinned her ears back, then pressed some more. The not-cell phone made a happy *ding* noise, and her ears snapped forward again.

"*Found* her!" she exclaimed happily.

"Found her, how?" Alister asked. Things were coming into focus now, and he only felt a little dizzy.

"The hyper-scent bomb she sprayed you with," Elo explained. "She probably meant to use it to track you down, but she has some residue of it on herself, and since I also have a scent-radar, I can use it to find *her*. Looks like she's on the move now. Stay right here, I have to operate this lift manually."

Elo stuffed the not-cell phone and the thermometer back into her harness pockets, and shed Alister's everything bag. Then with a jump and a wriggle she had disappeared out of the hole in the ceiling. A moment later her voice called out: "Hold on, we're going down!" And the lift began to drop.

Professor Odd slid down the guardrail of the last flight of stairs and rested for a few moments at the bottom. Straightening her wig and making sure her tentacle was safe inside her collar, she walked briskly down the wide corridor that led away from the stairs. Somewhere in the distance there was the melodic *ping* of an elevator arriving, and she instinctively broke into a jog until she came to the second hall on the left. This was marked, promisingly enough, as "Intensive Care," and was lined with doors, each of which had a number in orange lights above it. The doors had smoked glass windows set into them, which showed the rooms beyond to be dark. All except the one at the very end of the hall, room 50347.

Bright, white light shone through the window, and from beyond the door came the muffled sounds of human voices. These turned into shouts of surprise when Professor Odd shouldered the door open and barged inside.

There were two scientists, both men, standing behind the banks of computers. They seemed to have been in the middle of observing test results, but were now in the process of standing up and reaching for weapons. One of them also had his hand on a mobile device, but he never got a chance to activate it.

"Sorry for interrupting, boys," the Professor said, hoisting the time gun. "I'll only be a moment—well, it'll *seem* like a moment to you, anyway."

The electrical discharge from the temporal retardation field caused the computers to make unhappy noises as it engulfed them and the scientists, but they were soon cut off. Professor Odd lay the gun down on the exam table (now vacant), heedless of the green slime, and went around to the corner of the room that held the observing camera. Standing on tip-toe she unplugged it with her tentacle. Only then did she turn to the tank on the far side of the room, where something bright green was watching her out of one round, orange eye.

The scientists and nurses were beginning to come around when Elo and Alister escaped from the elevator. Alister gratefully took his everything bag back while Elo did things to the controls that made the doors seal shut behind them. Then he waited while she trotted back and forth, sniffing the air.

"This way . . . " she said, leading Alister down a wide corridor. Up ahead they heard crashing and clanging, as if a small army were descending a flight of the Canary Company's ubiquitous metal stairs.

"That must be her," Alister panted. Elo had broken into a lope, and he had to run to keep up.

"Not quite," Elo called over her shoulder. "She came from that direction, but she's not—*here's* where she went!" So saying the dog took a sharp turn to the right and charged down a hallway marked "Intensive Care."

The place was dark, except for the door at the end of the hall, which was hanging open and letting a stream of bright light through.

Alister and Elo put their heads around the door carefully, not knowing what to expect.

The first thing Alister saw were two scientists, nearly frozen in the act of standing up in surprise behind a bank of computers. Then he saw the time gun resting on a table half-covered with green slime. Then he saw—

"Professor!" Elo barked happily, rushing into the room.

"*Hush,*" said the Professor. She was kneeling beside a vat of water with both hands, her face and tentacle pressed against the glass. There seemed to be something in the vat, looking back out at her. Coming closer Alister saw at last the thing he had only glimpsed briefly before, in one panicked moment, back in the philosophy hall.

Its body was nearly a perfect circle, about the size and shape of a large pie pan. It had one huge eye in the very center, which was shot through with bands of gold and orange, like the arms of a windmill. Its green body appeared to be smooth skin, which wrinkled around the eye. Alister thought he recognized gill vents on either side, and an opening below the eye that might have been a mouth, or simply a water intake.

It had ten long, weaving tentacle arms, which faded to yellow at their thin, wriggly tips. They were webbed near its main body with a bright green membrane that was slightly transparent. Its underside, as far as Alister could see, was a forest of fine waving golden filaments that put him in mind of a sea anemone.

Though it was perhaps the most bizarre thing Alister had seen, barring the Professor herself, he found himself admitting that it would have been rather beautiful if it were not so obviously injured: several of the tips of its tentacles had been clipped off, and the wounds were belching clouds of dark blue blood into the water. There were further lacerations on its body, and the sclera of its eye was shot with blue blood as well. Its tentacle arms hung, limp and motionless, floating in the water. Except for one, which it had pressed against its side of the glass, revealing its puckered undersurface, in a mirror of the Professor's. She was talking to it now, in a gentle, soft voice.

"They say you don't have a brain," she whispered against the glass. "They say you can't speak. *I* say *they're* wrong. I think you know exactly what's going on. I think you can speak, we just can't hear you. I also think you can understand everything I'm saying."

The creature continued to stare back. Alister wondered if it was still alive.

"If you can understand what I'm saying," the Professor said earnestly, "show me a triangle."

For a moment nothing happened. Then, slowly, the creature raised one of its uninjured tentacles and carefully bent it in two places, creating a somewhat lopsided, but nonetheless recognizable, triangle.

"That does it," the Professor said. "I'm getting you out. Alister, Elo, stop gaping and help me get this grill off!"

To retain its occupant, the top of the vat had been covered by a metal grill, which was bolted to the sides. While the Professor and Elo pulled at them Alister went through the back pouch of his everything bag until he found his trusty screwdriver. After that things went much faster. The grill came off with a clang, sending the creature cowering into a corner. Rolling up her sleeve the Professor stuck an arm into the water, hand open and palm up. The creature regarded it warily. It reached out a tentative tentacle and brushed it against her fingertips.

The Professor's eyes went wide. "Ooooooh," she breathed. "*That's* how it communicates."

"How?" Elo asked. She sniffed at the water and wrinkled her nose.

"Chemical charges released from its skin," the Professor said. "It communicates through its slime! Oh, that is *brilliant.* Hang on." She pulled her hand out of the water and pulled off her wig—Alister was still having trouble getting used to that—then stuffed it down the breast of her coat. "I need a more direct connection," she explained, and plunged herself from head to shoulders into the water.

The creature's response was alarming: it swarmed up from the bottom of the tank in a whirl of green arms and latched itself onto the Professor's bald head, the smaller tentacles on its underside wrapping around her dome like roots of a tree, while its long green arms twined themselves around her neck and chin—anything they could get a purchase on. The Professor held perfectly still through all of this, though when Alister made to grab her and pull her out she pushed him aside. He found himself facing one of her hands, which held up a single finger and wagged it at him.

"Professor?" Elo asked cautiously.

Slowly, very slowly, the Professor levered her head out of the tank, pulling the creature with her. It had settled itself so that its eye rested on her forehead, and its arms covered everything except her nose, mouth and one eye with a mess of twining green tentacle.

The first thing the Professor did was to spit a long trail of water back into the tank. "Yuck," she said, wiping water and slime out of her exposed eye. "I'm sorry they stuck you in there . . . Yes, I've been in a tank myself, not pleasant at all . . . I meant to ask, can you breathe air? . . . Oh *good*, I thought so . . . "

It was like listening to someone speaking on the telephone; they were only hearing one half of the conversation. Eventually she trailed off, having noticed Elo and Alister staring at her.

"It—sorry, *he* (I think, as far as his species relates to sex, he would be considered male)—*he* communicates through psycho-active slime. You can get vague thoughts simply by absorbing the slime through your skin, but the closer it is to your brain the better. Oh, and he's got his wriggly bits in my ears, that helps. Tickles also. Sorry, what did you say your name was?" She paused, her one visible eye rolled up to look at the creature perched on her head. Then she frowned. "Oh, there's no way I'll be able to translate that," she said. "Yes, I understand my mode of communication is limited and primitive, but I can't ooze slime out of my orifices so we'll just have to make do, won't we?"

"Where did he come from?" Elo asked. "What does he want?"

The Professor opened her mouth to respond, but was cut off by a clang and a shout from outside the room.

"I think a full explanation can wait until we get out of here," Alister said, prudently shutting the door and sliding the deadbolt home.

"That could be problematic," said Elo, hefting the banana-cane. "I left the nearest door to the Oddity back outside the building, and they have cut off our only exit."

"What about hidden portals?" Alister suggested hopefully.

"There aren't any in this room," Professor Odd stated.

"How can you know? I thought you couldn't even feel them?" Alister asked.

"I can't," the Professor said. Her eye jerked upwards. *"He* can. His kind knows loads more about world-hopping than even *I* do, portals stand out to him like glowing neon signs do to us. Wait, where did you say you left the Oddity, Elo?"

"Just outside the main building," Elo said. "There's this well shed . . . What are you doing?"

The Professor had leapt over to the door and was running her hands over its frame. The green tentacle creature seemed interested as well; he was prodding at it with his uninjured arm. Then the Professor whirled around, grinning madly. "Yes!" she cried. "It will *work!*"

"What will work?" Alister and Elo asked.

"Cane!" shouted the Professor, snatching it out of Elo's paws. Then, reaching into her own pockets, she pulled out her laser pen. "Laser!" she exclaimed. Taking one in each hand she rushed to the door, through the window of which Alister could see a crowd of people, some of whom had guns, running down the hall.

"What are you doing?" Elo cried. The Professor had given the banana handle an expert twist, and pulled from the cane a slender, wicked blade. With it she traced an outline of a door around the real one, leaving faint scorch marks. Then she sheathed the weapon and tossed it back to Elo, who caught it deftly.

"Remote spatial adjustment," Professor Odd said, fiddling with her laser pen. "I'm moving the Oddity's portal to synch with this door."

"But you can't do that from outside the Oddity," Elo exclaimed. "We don't know *how!*"

"We don't," the Professor said, grinning. "But our new friend does. I told you, his kind know a lot about world-hopping. How do you think he got to this one in the first place?" Then, rolling her eye back, she snapped, "Yes, I realize our technology is clunky and archaic; that's not helping. Here," she passed the creature her laser pen. "Perhaps *you* would like to do the honors?"

Outside there were angry clangs. The door shook. The creature took the pen in a coil of green tentacle, gave it a further adjustment, and activated it.

First a tiny red dot appeared in the center of the door. Then it swelled, became grainy and faint until it covered the entire door and spilled over onto the walls. There was a faint buzzing, and the hairs along Alister's arms went up, as if someone had brought a statically charged balloon close to them. Then the buzzing ceased. The laser narrowed back down to a point. It hung there for a moment, then disappeared, leaving a black spot that smoked slightly.

"That's *it?*" Professor Odd said, taking her pen back.

The door—the actual, physical door—jumped in its frame as someone rammed into it from the other side.

"Well, let's hope it worked!" she said cheerfully, going up to the shaking door. She released the lock and took hold of the handle.

"No, don't!" Alister cried. He could see, vaguely through the smoked glass window, a very large dark figure with a gun trained directly at them.

But Professor Odd ignored him, and pulled the door open . . . to reveal the entrance of the Oddity, daisy-printed, padded walls and everything.

She stood aside, smiling. "After you," she said, bowing slightly.

Alister did not have to be told twice. For the second time that day he scrambled up the steps into the Oddity, relishing the comparative familiarity of its pulsating lights and faint chamomile smells. Elo was on his heels, and she threw aside the banana-sword-cane to climb into one of the pilot seats. The console lit up around her, and she craned her neck around to see what was keeping the Professor.

Professor Odd had gone back into the room and picked up the time gun from where she had left it on the exam table. She turned it over thoughtfully in her hands.

"I'm not usually one for *stealing* things," she mused, coming up to the door. "But I don't think I'll be doing anyone any favors by leaving *this* in their hands."

She pulled herself through the door and stood on the first step, looking back into the room. "Still, tempting as it is, I'll not leave you hanging," she said, raising the gun and firing a dispersement charge at the frozen scientists. Alister heard sudden shouting from within the room, and the Professor saying cheerfully: "See? Only a moment, what did I tell you? Elo, you can disconnect us now."

Elo flipped a lever at her station, the Oddity gave a violent shudder, and the view into the room was snuffed out, replaced by a rectangle of perfect blackness.

Professor Odd came slowly up the stairs, carefully, as the creature was still clinging to her head.

"So," Alister said, not quite believing his good fortune, "we—we made it?"

"Yes, you're free now," Professor Odd said, though whether she was speaking to Alister or to the creature he was not sure. She dumped the time gun on the cluttered table next to the Electron Adjuster, and smiled at him. "We're home, safe and sound."

"And now *you're* home, safe and sound," she said proudly, opening the Oddity's door onto Alister's dorm room. Alister stepped out, blinking a little. It was brighter in his room than he remembered, and more spacious. Then his brain registered what his eyes had been telling him: he was back in his room, sure enough, but all of its contents and his belongings had vanished. The walls were stripped bare, and even the university furniture had been removed. The carpets had been pulled up, and there was a ladder standing where his bed used to be.

"I never pegged you as spartan," Professor Odd remarked, poking her head out after him.

"I'm not . . . I never . . . " Alister gaped around him. "Where's everything gone?"

"Oh yes, sorry about that," Elo said, pushing past the Professor. "I meant to warn you: those goons from the Canary Company confiscated all your belongings. Something about you being an illegal alien. Also said they got you knocked off the university's enrollment."

"But they *can't* . . . can they?"

Professor Odd shrugged. "Do you have a mobile communication device?"

"Sorry?"

"I believe you would call it a cellular phone," she clarified.

Alister kept his cell phone in the front pocket of his everything bag. He got it out and woke it up. It told him that it was just past six in the evening on Friday, September the 14th, and that he had no service.

"That's strange," he said, showing the phone to the Professor. She narrowed her eyes at it and frowned.

"They cut your service," she said. "Standard procedure when they are excising a member of society. And I'll bet your credit and numerical currency cards have been discontinued as well, if you care to test them."

Alister was only half listening. His mind was going back to when that first scientist, Dr. Hurnest, had declared him "mostly human." That, he realized, had been a point of no return. There was no going back to ordinary life, not since then. His stark empty room only served to drive the fact home. If they considered him excised from society, as the Professor put it, he seriously doubted they would let him escape so easily.

"Do you have anywhere else to go?" Elo was asking, plucking concernedly at his sleeve. "Any other family?"

Alister shrugged, feeling a sudden chill. "Only my grandparents," he said. "Back in the home country. But I don't think I should go to them. I might bring . . . unwanted attention." He glanced at the Professor, who gave him an approving look.

"You're surprisingly rational, for a human," she said, by way of a compliment.

"Considering nothing else seems to be behaving rationally, I suppose I'm the only thing I can count on."

"Where will you go?"

"I guess I'll have to leave the country," Alister said defeatedly, the gravity of the situation beginning to sink in. "That might be difficult, they took my passport with everything else . . . "

The Professor and Elo exchanged significant looks. The Professor had transferred the tentacle creature to the sink in the First Aid alcove before calibrating the portal to Alister's room, but she still had bits of dried green and gold slime stuck to her head. It gave her an even more alien appearance than usual, and he had no idea what the look had meant. But then she smiled.

"It might be better if you left this narrative entirely," she said. "Much harder for them to track you."

"But I—" Alister gasped. "You don't mean, come with *you?*"

The Professor shrugged. "I don't see any other transuniversal travelers offering you a lift. Besides, you're not bad in a tight spot; you carry a protractor *and* a screwdriver."

Alister couldn't help laughing. He glanced back through the door—the door that had once led to the bathroom—to the Oddity, where its lights flickered and pulsed invitingly, and felt his mirth fade.

"It would take some getting used to," he said.

"So would living on the run," Elo reminded him gently. "And it's actually not so bad. Take it from one who's been there."

Alister looked around what had once been his room, and his home, for the past two years. Suddenly he was struck by how very mundane it had all been. Cripplingly mediocre, in fact.

"I got bored by school, you know," he thought out loud, trying to explain it to himself as much as to the Professor and Elo. "I was bored by university, even though I didn't know it. I took all the most interesting courses; astronomy, physics, mathematics, geometry, philosophy . . . but they all turned boring in the end. Just strings of facts and numbers and theories. But then there's *you*. You and your Oddity, with your worldtracks, and psychoactive slimes, talking dogs, tentacles, laser locks, *time guns*, and whatever *that* is—" he gestured back inside the Oddity, to where the tentacle creature was making happy squelching sounds in the sink. "And suddenly . . . everything is new and exciting again."

Professor Odd's eyebrows went up, and she smiled a little. "Thank you?" she said in a small voice.

"I'm not a dog," Elo said primly. "I'm a *vroknaär*."

"Well whatever you are," Alister said. "I'd be delighted to join you."

Elo pricked an ear and wagged her feathery tail.

"Excellent!" said the Professor. "I'll tell the Oddity to make up a new room. And we should probably make a stop soon to get you a change of clothes and other . . . necessities." She stopped in the doorway and glanced back over her slime-stained shoulder. "Well, are you coming?"

"In just a moment," Alister said, swinging his everything bag around and going through the main compartment. The Professor shrugged and left, but Elo came over and watched curiously.

Alister took out his hard-backed Atlas of the Solar System, and pulled from its pages the thin packet of origami paper he kept inside to entertain himself with during boring lectures. He selected a yellow sheet, and sitting himself down on the bare floor with the Atlas on his lap, he began to fold it.

"What are you doing?" Elo asked, sitting beside him.

"It occurs to me," Alister explained as he folded, "when those scientists realize I'm gone, they will probably come back here and search this place again. But I won't be here. So I'm going to leave something for them to find."

"What is it?" Elo asked, putting her head on one side.

"A token. I saw it done in a film once," Alister admitted. He placed the finished figure in the center of the room, and repacked his bag. "It'll give them something to think about," he told Elo as they climbed back into the Oddity. He pulled the door shut behind him, and did not look back.

It was near midnight when Dr. Hurnest and his associate got around to re-searching Alister's room. They found it exactly as they had left it; completely empty.

"He's probably fled the country, or the planet," Dr. Hurnest muttered angrily. "Slippery one, that."

"Sir," called his companion from the other room. "Sir, you should really come and see this . . . "

"What is it Jenkins?" Dr. Hurnest said, shining his torch into the room.

Jenkins was standing in the center of it, holding a small bird made of folded yellow paper. "Sir," he said, sounding shaken. "It's a *canary*, sir."

"We should give him a name," Elo said, some time later. It was difficult to say how *much* later, since there was no day and night in the Oddity. Suffice to say it was later enough for the Professor to have washed the slime off, for Alister to have eaten a much-needed meal, and for Elo to have made progress on a rudimentary voice processor that could translate the tentacle creature's psychoactive slime into English.

"He already has a name," Professor Odd said. She was reclining in a purple chair with pink polka-dots, her feet propped up on the cluttered worktable. "It just doesn't translate into audible speech."

"That's what I mean," Elo insisted. "We don't have anything to call him. I'm not saying we should rename you or anything," she added to the creature, who was sloshing around in a large stainless-steel basin in the middle of the floor. "I just think you need . . . well, *something* we can call you that we can actually pronounce. Like a nickname, an alias, or a title. You could be the Green One," she suggested.

"Dave," said the Professor. "He *looks* like a Dave," she said, in response to Elo's reproachful look.

"My father's name was Murphy," Alister suggested. "William is also very respectable."

"Decimus Bracchium," Elo said. "Means 'ten arms' if I remember my Latin."

"That's a bit fancy, don't you think?" Alister said.

"I still say he looks like a Dave," said the Professor.

"But Dave is so *dull*," protested Elo. "You might as well call him *Mikey*."

They would have gone on for hours, but the creature took the matter into its own arms. Surging up from the basin it handed itself, dripping, across the floor and plucked the translator box from Elo's paws. It gave it an expert whack, then held it up against its wriggly underside.

"UNTIL SUCH TIME AS MY NAME BECOMES COMPREHENSIBLE TO YOU—" it intoned through the box in a sharp, metallic voice. "—*DAVE* WILL BE ACCEPTABLE."

That, needless to say, settled the matter on the spot.

"Dave it is then," said the Professor. "Welcome to the Oddity, Dave."

The creature—Dave—took the translator box and went to nest in the middle of the table, where he could observe them all with his bright orange eye.

"YOU ARE STRANGE PEOPLE," he said. "THIS WILL TAKE SOME GETTING USED TO."

Much to his surprise, everyone around him burst out laughing.

THE SLOWLY DYING PLANET

2. THE SLOWLY DYING PLANET

Prologue

IT WAS ALWAYS NIGHT outside Alister's window. At least, it appeared that way. When he sat up in bed and drew aside the lace-trimmed shades all he saw was a deep, bluish darkness pricked with what looked like countless stars.

But they were not stars, as the Professor had explained to him at length; they were *worlds*. Entire universes, each with their own infinite set of possibilities and parallel dimensions, floating in a sea of nothing. Sometimes one would drift close enough that Alister could make out individual stars and planets within the glowing sphere that surrounded them. Sometimes all he could see was one world, with continents and clouds, even tiny cities. When he had asked about this the Professor had explained that the spheres were not the universes themselves, merely pinprick windows into them. What you saw on the other side depended on where the pinprick was.

And—this was what truly boggled his mind—the Professor had visited many of them. She could recognize several, and even pointed out his own: a faint swirl of blue-green light at the end of a string of similar lights. It made him feel small and lonely, seeing his entire world as a pinprick in that vast black emptiness. The only other thing out there, besides the eternal night and the points of light, was the Oddity.

Alister got out of bed. He was hungry, which was how they measured days and nights in the Oddity. He still wasn't sure if it was ship or a house, but he didn't bother asking; its name explained it as well as anyone could, and Alister accepted what it did (opening doors to other universes) as a matter of fact. He had to, otherwise his neat, rational brain would probably explode.

Alister got dressed. The Oddity had provided him with a pair of striped pajamas and a selection of brightly colored shirts, trousers and drawers. Alister wore the drawers (because he had to) and the shirts (because his own smelled funny), but he stubbornly clung to his own pair of sensible trousers and conservative brown jacket. After three days of consecutive wear these were beginning to wrinkle, but Alister was damned if he would be seen in neon-pink jeans with yellow stars blazoned across the back pockets. Even if he would only be seen by three people.

Well, two people . . . and a tentacle monster.

Alister's room was on the second level of the Oddity, and his door opened onto a catwalk that ran around the inside of the place in a giant tear-drop shape. A trap-ladder led down to the lower level, which served as a living room, study, kitchen, dining room, and (in the narrow end of the teardrop) cockpit. On his way to the ladder Alister passed three doors, each made of painted white wood with a brass handle, but individually decorated. The first had a symbol like a green sun with ten rays shining out of it; this room belonged to Dave, and the door was cracked ajar, letting out ominous scrapings and high-pitched whining sounds of metal being welded together. Dave was building himself an all-environment mobility suit, since the Oddity's natural climate—that of a 22° Celsius nitrogen-oxygen atmosphere—tended to dry him out.

The second door was somewhat battered and looked older than the first. It had a large sign nailed to it that declared "Beware of the Dog" in sharp red letters. Only "Dog" had been crossed out and someone had written *"Vroknaär"* underneath it in careful cursive. This room belonged to Elo. Alister had asked her what a *vroknaär* was. She had told him it was to a wolf what a human was to an *australopithecus*.

The last door looked like it had been repainted several times, each time with a different color. Currently it was a refreshing mint green, but showed traces of orange and yellow through the cracks. It clashed rather with the dull salmon wall-paper, and its only decoration was a metal "o-D" (of the sort used to mark street addresses) bolted to the center. This was the Professor's room, and Alister had never seen the inside of it.

There was a fourth room, just beyond the ladder, that held a sign with a picto-graph for a male and female character, a dog, and the ten-rayed sun symbol. This was the bathroom, and Alister took advantage of it before descending the ladder.

Elo emerged from the kitchen alcove just as Alister reached the floor. She was wearing a rumpled apron over her purple jumpsuit, and her ears were drooping sadly.

"We're out of food," she declared, and flopped down at the table.

Alister's stomach chose that time to grumble loudly.

"Are you sure?" he said. "Absolutely out?"

Elo wrinkled her nose. "Well, there's half a bag of broccoli, but *that* doesn't count."

Alister had to admit that, even to his omnivorous tastes, broccoli was not what he wanted for breakfast. He went and joined Elo at the table, carefully clearing himself a space among the pile of junk and oddments that decorated it. Along at the far end of the table, where half a bicycle had been propped up against an ebony safe marked with a skull and crossbones, a disheveled figure in an olive green trench coat and a bright blue wig shuddered to life. It rubbed its face with a pair of long white hands, and blinked at them out of golden cat eyes.

"Did someone say *food?*" Professor Odd asked.

"Out," Elo snapped. "I said we're *out* of food."

The Professor groaned and laid her head on the table. A moment later she popped it up again, her eyes bright and a wide grin on her face.

"Pizza," she said.

"Sorry?" said Alister.

"I want *pizza!*" cried the Professor. "After twelve hours of programming Dave's infernal nano-bots, I need *pizza!* Dave!" she called, standing up and bellowing at the half-open door with the green sun on it. "We're going to get pizza, are you coming?"

The clanging from within the other room ceased. The door creaked as it swung the rest of the way open, and a long green tentacle emerged. It was dripping with pale green slime, and was coiled around an allen wrench. It seemed puzzled. Then it retreated, and emerged again with the rest of its body: a disc the size and shape of a pie plate, with one round yellow-and-orange eye in the center. Two more tentacles held a small black box with a speaker mounted to it against the creature's underside.

"I HAVE EATEN ONE HUNDRED HOURS AGO." Dave intoned through the machine. "I SHALL NOT REQUIRE NUTRIENTS FOR ANOTHER HUNDRED AT MINIMUM." He paused and fiddled with the machine. "I HAVE WORK TO PERFORM. BRING ME BACK YOUR LEFTOVERS." And with a flick of tentacle, he was gone.

"Well," said the Professor, beaming at them. "Just us three, then?"

The cockpit at the narrow end of the Oddity was a jumble of lights, screens, buttons and levers. Alister could not make sense of it. He did not *want* to make sense of it. The only thing he could understand was the door, set at the bottom of a flight of stairs between the pilot chairs, that was currently a black slab of nothing. That door could lead anywhere, any place, in any universe. But *how* it did it, he had no idea.

Professor Odd swung herself into a chair and caused the display in front of her to light up with a pleased humming sound. Elo got into the other chair and craned her neck around to look at the Professor.

"Where are we going for pizza?" she asked. "Napoli?"

"Oh no," said the Professor, punching at the buttons before her. "Pizza Margherita is far too heavy for my taste. Think farther afield."

"New York?" Alister hazarded. "Maybe Chicago?"

Professor Odd laughed. "Farther than that, my friend!" she cried, and flipped the red lever at her right hand.

It was like watching a fireworks display, only without the bangs. The lights in the cockpit glittered and pulsed, settling into a pattern that traced its way from the Professor's console to Elo's, and as each button or bulb flashed, it hummed. The large beacons set into the supporting columns buzzed. The smaller lights pinged. The fiber optic cables sang. A string of tiny bulbs guided a single white spark up a column where it crashed into a giant sphere like a golden disco ball which clanged like a gong. Then all the lights spiraled, concentrating on the black rectangle of the door. At the peak of the crescendo of light and sound the doorway itself flashed white and gave off a single, pure note which hung in the air even as the lights and other sounds died away.

Where the black rectangle had been, there was now a stone archway with a flimsy wooden door.

Elo was busy tapping away at her rack of buttons as the Professor grabbed her scarf from the table and tied it around her neck.

"Simple precautions," Elo explained when Alister leaned over her shoulder. "I'm setting the Oddity to recognize only our narrative stamp, so that it won't accidentally kidnap some poor old native."

"Has that happened before?" Alister asked.

"Oh yes," Elo said. "How do you think I got here?"

"Right then, ready to go?" Professor Odd said. She had buttoned up her trench coat and was carrying her black walking cane with the silver banana handle. All in all she looked rather dapper, if someone wearing red pinstriped trousers, a drab olive coat, and a blue wig could be said to look dapper. Alister noticed that her dark glasses, which usually hid her eyes, had been left off.

"Your glasses," he began, picking up his everything bag.

"Won't make a difference on this world," she said, waving a hand dismissively. She strode down the stairs, followed closely by Elo, who had taken off her apron at the last minute and stuffed it under her chair.

The Professor opened the door and stood aside. "There you are," she said. "After you."

Alister emerged from the Oddity to find himself in a narrow, stone-cobbled street. Looking around he saw all the buildings were of stone, with wooden doors and lights set under the eaves. In the distance he could hear the rumble of traffic and the clank and hiss of some steam-powered machine. At first he thought it must be sunset, because the light was the rich, warm orange he always associated with sunsets, and it was much dimmer. Then he looked up.

I'm on an alien planet! was the first thing through his mind.

The sky was wrong. It was the wrong color, for a start: a deep, rich orange, streaked with red clouds. This was a little unnerving, but what made him gasp, what made him stand frozen, staring at the southern horizon, was the arching crescent that rose up halfway to where the sun (somehow redder and gentler than it should be) hung in the burnished sky.

Alister had seen pictures of planets in his astronomy class. Most of them had been illustrative, and had shown the planet as a perfect sphere. But there had been others that showed the planet partly lit, so that it melted into the blackness of space and only a narrow crescent could be seen. This was what Alister saw in the southern sky. If he had been capable at that moment of making words, and then using those words to describe what he saw, he would have said it looked like the planet Jupiter turned greenish, and very, very close.

Professor Odd smiled and put an arm around her stricken companion. "Welcome to Niatano, Mister Alister," she said, smiling proudly up at the gas giant, as if she had put it there and were admiring her handiwork.

Something tore the sky in half.

It was white and deafening, and knocked Elo to all fours and Alister and the Professor against the stone building behind them. Below the thunderous roar came the delicate screaming of breaking glass and the sudden angry honking of vehicle horns and the screech of brakes. A shower of rock dust fell from the high roofs above their heads, and the building groaned ominously.

Wiping dust out of his eyes Alister blinked up at the sky, now bisected by an angry tumult of frothing clouds. He felt the iron grip of the Professor's hand on his shoulder, and when he turned to look saw that she too was staring up at the sky. But not with fear or confusion. The expression on the Professor's face was of cold, resigned fury.

"*That!*" she exclaimed. "That! *That!* That was *not* supposed to happen!"

Part One

IN CONTROL ROOMS all over the world, chaos was breaking out. It was the near-panicked, yet purposeful chaos of people who have important things to do, even if they didn't know exactly what—and even though these people might not have been recognizable *as* people at first glance.

In the control room at the top of the tallest skyscraper, in the city where the Professor had just appeared, orders were shouted—but not in English. More rushing about, tails flying dangerously close to expensive computer banks, and one character in a bright red uniform caused the display covering half the wall to show an aerial view of a smoking crater. Around the edges were what looked like ruins of a city, and pale yellow tongues of flame were licking their way over the smoking rubble.

Cries of dismay and anguish arose from the occupants of the room. One collapsed onto a chair-like object, holding his head in his hands and whispering, "*No, no, non Caprisio . . .*"

Only one character was not affected by the disaster. She sat in a corner in front of a smaller bank of monitors which showed, in grainy black and white, different angles of a back alley somewhere in that very city. In the alley were three unusual—at least to her bright yellow eyes—creatures, one of which appeared to be a sort of canine. Typing in more commands on the rack of keys in front of her, she brought up the coordinates of that alley. Satisfied, she rolled her chair-thing back and stood up, raising her long tail for balance.

She grabbed a passing redcoat, and injected some orders into his ear-frill. Reluctantly he allowed himself to be dragged out of the control room, taking a projectile weapon from the rack just outside the door, and together they trotted down the hall to a door marked with the multiuniversal sign for an elevator.

In the alley Professor Odd had whipped out a compass, growled, put it back, then whipped out a *different* compass, and was now triangulating the trajectory of the trail of white cloud while Elo jotted down the results. Alister, left with nothing to do but wait while the initial thrill of adrenaline subsided, followed by a mild tinge of queasiness, which was eventually shouldered aside by his pervasive hunger, began to wander. He got as far as the end of the alley, where he poked his head around the corner, and saw what looked like two small dinosaurs in police uniforms running towards him.

Ducking back into the alley he sprinted over to the Professor and tapped her elbow. "I think we've been spotted," he told her urgently.

"Eh?" said the Professor, looking up from her compass. "Well, of course we would, with something like *that* this whole place is going to be ringing with surveillance."

"Professor," Elo said sharply, her ears perking, "they are upwind of us; they are very scared."

"Yes, and running this way," Alister added. "I think they are *police.*"

"What color are their uniforms?" the Professor asked, pocketing her compass.

"Er, one is red, I think," Alister said. "The other's a sort of orange-brown."

"Oh!" Professor Odd exclaimed with a smile. "Then we should be all right." And she turned down the alley, where the two creatures had just wheeled into view. "Ah!" she said, as if greeting old friends. *"Ciao, ciao,"* and then tumbled out a torrent of speech in what Alister recognized, a little incredulously, as *Italian.*

The creatures were similarly affected. One—the one in red—lowered the projectile weapon to its side and looked at its companion, who had folded its arms across its chest and was regarding the Professor with unmistakable skepticism.

They did not look so much like dinosaurs after all, Alister decided. Rather, they looked like a pair of oviraptors that had stood up, winched in their ostrich-like necks, grown shoulders, and sprouted each a crown of feathers from its head. Another tuft of feathers decorated the tip of each tail. One—the one in the orange-brown coat with gold buttons—had a head of dark feathers that extended over its neck, making it resemble a gaudy woman with an ostrich-feather boa wrapped around her throat.

Their faces were not human faces, yet they still managed to express recognizably human emotions. They had eyebrows in the form of ridges of dark scales that ran over and around the outer sides of their eyes, culminating in hook shapes over their upper cheeks. They had narrow, flat noses, and when they spoke their mouths were dark, for they had no teeth, only a pair of flat incisors, like a bird's beak. Their eyes were slanted and dark, and gleamed in the dim red light against rough, pale skin. Upon closer inspection Alister saw that the rough skin was not skin at all, but fine interlocking scales.

The feathery one in orange-brown, who seemed to be in charge, took out a small handheld device and began to manipulate its touch screen with its hands—hands that were recognizable as such even though they had three fingers and two thumbs.

The device bleeped at the creature, who looked from the readout to the Professor, then back again. It looked at its partner in apparent astonishment.

"*Si,*" it said in a light, husky voice. "*Questo é la Professoressa.*" Then it put the device away, reached out its strange hand and shook Professor Odd's.

"I don't understand," Alister whispered fiercely at Professor Odd. "What *are* they?"

The two creatures were leading them at a near run through the narrow streets of the town, toward a white structure that looked like the Eiffel Tower, if the Eiffel Tower were an actual building with floors and windows and walls, not just a framework.

"They are *Ufficiale* Maria Rozione and Pierro," Professor Odd said. "They are *Umanitá;* but I call them Neätans. Helps avoid confusion, since *Umanitá* is just their word for *humanity.* Don't look so stricken: we aren't under arrest. Well, not yet. Maria is a *Carabinieri* knight, and they are generally pretty civilized."

"But, why are they *Italian?*"

"Strictly speaking they're *not* Italian," Elo interjected. "They are *Puchesi* . . . this is Pucca, isn't it Professor?"

Professor Odd was looking around at the houses as they passed; all of their windows were shuttered, and there was no one on the street besides themselves. They crossed a square that showed all the signs of having recently been a bustling marketplace, but was now eerily deserted: stalls had been abandoned with wares still on display; dropped goods and squashed packages of food littered the stone street.

"It was *supposed* to be," she said, her cat eyes narrowing. She walked faster, threatening to tread on Pierro's drooping tail. She began to speak—peppering the Neätans with questions—but in Italian, and Alister quickly gave up trying to follow the conversation.

The tower-like building stepped into view from around the front of a cathedral that was a little uphill of what could be considered Gothic: in place of a bell tower the cathedral had a slowly rotating Archimedes screw, on whose blade rode a golden orb, and its dome was split down the center, like the dome of an observatory. As they hurried past, Alister noticed that the stained-glass windows on the front showed strange stellar constellations, and the front doors were engraved with geometric proofs.

Then they were at the base of the tower, and *Ufficiale* Rozione was entering a security code on another touch-screen, while at the same time trying to answer the Professor's questions. These answers consisted of a lot of *"No"*s and a few *"Si!"*s. Professor Odd grew more impatient at each one.

Somewhere inside the building a latch released, and *Ufficiale* Rozione pushed open a door made of carved wood and cast iron, leading them into a passage with peeling wallpaper. Here things went suddenly, achingly ordinary: the smell of an old, lived-in building, the wear on the floor down the center of the hall. They passed a flight of stone stairs whose steps were so old they swayed in the middle like the back of a horse, and then crowded into an elevator that would have comfortably held four humans, but because of the Neätans' tails it became quite cramped. Alister wedged himself in a corner and tried to ignore the whining and creaking coming from above.

Professor Odd began speaking as soon as the doors were shut.

"It is *not* a self-inflicted attack," she explained, for the benefit of Alister and Elo. "They don't know *where* it came from, precisely, but they think it has something to do with a strange satellite they acquired about an hour ago . . . five minutes before that projectile was launched. They can't get an accurate image of the thing—it's jamming all their instruments—and there has been no communication from it."

"So, what is it?" Alister asked.

"I have no idea!" Professor Odd said. She sounded delighted. The Neätan's gave her strange looks; Alister noted that the scaly ridges above their eyes worked just like eyebrows, and that those eyes had dark sclera.

With a sound like a church bell the elevator came to a halt. Rozione got out first, nearly knocking Elo over with her tail, and made some sort of announcement in her native language. Then she beckoned them to follow her.

The Professor, Alister and Elo emerged into a scene of barely controlled chaos; about a dozen Neätans of every size and color—some short and squat, some long and lizard-like—inhabited a room already crowded with monitors, cables, and stacks of metal boxes decorated with blinking lights and fan vents.

For a brief moment they were stared at by twelve pairs of greenish-yellow alien eyes; frills were raised and lowered, scale-brows went up and down.

Then the room erupted in questions. Alister needed no translator to figure out what these were: "What are these things?" "Where did you find them?" "What is that strange, yellow, furry one?" And, most distressingly: "Are they responsible for our current problem?" This last was asked angrily by a stocky Neätan in a black uniform with red head-feathers cropped close to his skull.

Rozione attempted to field these questions as best she could, but when the redhead approached, Professor Odd swooped in and began speaking very fast, with lots of hand-gestures that Alister found bewildering, but the redhead seemed to follow. Slowly the stumps of his head-feathers settled, and he even lost a few inches as he levered his upper half down, counterbalanced by his tail. Alister wondered how he managed not to let that tail tangle in the cables that ran everywhere and draped in bundles from the ceiling.

With a hearty cry the redhead threw out his arms and embraced Professor Odd, who laughed as well.

"See, *this* is how you treat extra-universal travelers," she said, once the redhead had released her. "No locking them up in dungeons for experimentations—oh, I love Niatano! Now, who's trying to *destroy* it?"

"Destroy it?" Alister exclaimed. "You mean the *planet* is under attack?"

"Well, I did say that missile was not self-inflicted. And the bomb's explosion was powerful enough to have aftershocks felt 3,000 miles away . . . I'd say they pretty much mean—"

She was cut off as a number of alarms went off at once, and on the largest monitor a window popped into existence showing splotches of green and black, with a big orange bull's-eye blinking over an area speckled with white lights.

"*Terrante! Terrante!*" shouted a Neätan in brown over by the console. "*Loro hanno preso di mira Terrante!*"

"*Merda!*" grunted the redhead in black, then got a look of embarrassment on his face, and he rushed over to the console muttering, "*Prego, mi scusi . . .*"

This new crisis served to distract everyone in the room; in a stampede of brown and red uniforms and trailing tails all the Neätans clustered around this big screen, leaving the Professor, Alister and Elo in relative peace—except for *Ufficiale* Rozione, who remained dutifully by their side.

"I don't understand, what's *Terrante?*" Elo said.

Maria Rozione looked from the monitor, where their redheaded friend was delivering a torrent of Italian into a communication device, then down at her hands.

Professor Odd went over to a nearby console, which was scrolling white type on a black screen. The text, Alister noted in a distant way, was not unlike the Roman alphabet, save a few characters that were backwards or upside-down. The Russian one, then?

"*Terrante* is a city," Professor Odd said quietly, "that isn't going to be around for much longer."

Over by the largest screen, the redheaded Neätan was screeching into his communicator: "*Evacuare! Evacuare!*"

The steady beeping of the alarm by the console, which Alister had just begun to tune out, ratcheted up in pitch and volume, until it became a deafening wail—and just when he thought he couldn't stand anymore, it abruptly cut out.

There was silence in the control room. On the largest monitor a warning had come up. In the unnatural calm, Alister noticed that the Neätans also used the black exclamation point inside a yellow triangle to indicate trouble.

A few moments later they became aware of the growing rumble from outside the building, and a moment after that the floor shook beneath their feet. All the Neätans—and Elo—dropped to the ground; Alister grabbed at the nearest solid object.

Professor Odd rode out the tremors like a skateboarder going down a flight of stairs, and before they had quite subsided she marched over to the main console, pulling Neätans off the controls.

"*Lasciami, per favore,*" she said, gently prying a sobbing Neätan off a keyboard. With a few quick strokes she dispatched the warnings and began pulling up readings—Alister was too far away to read them, but from the numerical figures that he could recognize he guessed they were coordinates.

"If I can just reverse-engineer the trajectory, maybe I can get an idea of their orbit," she was muttering when Alister arrived, stumbling over tails and cable bundles.

"What just happened there?" he demanded, though there was a sinking feeling in his gut that told him he already knew.

For answer the Professor jabbed her thumb at the screen next to hers, which, instead of numerical readouts, was showing a grainy image feed of a smoking crater. The crater was dark, and a little shiny, like whatever hit there had melted the surface as well as deforming it.

"Don't tell me . . . " he whispered, "*that's* Terrante?"

"That's where it *was*," Professor Odd snapped; she was having trouble with a calculation.

"We have to stop them," Elo said matter-of-factly, appearing at Alister's elbow.

"Yes, and to do *that*, first I have to *communicate* with them!" Professor Odd pounded away at the keyboard, watching the readings flow by. "I just need to isolate their communication frequency—*damn* this *Puchesi* hardware; if ever a planet needed the Japanese—wait! There it is!"

To Alister the text flowing by on the screen carried no more meaning than before, but the Professor now brought up another window and began typing a message in it. A few of the nearby Neätans had pulled themselves together and clustered around her, but kept their double-thumbed hands respectfully off the keyboard.

The Professor had somehow managed to convince the keyboard to make Roman characters, so Alister was able to read the message before it was sent. It was short. One line. It said:

STOP HITTING US. IDENTIFY YOURSELF.

And below that, the same message, repeated in Italian.

"Just in case," the Professor said, and hit *inviare.*

For fifteen minutes, nothing happened. In that time the adrenaline which had been pumped into Alister's system, again, had time to drain, leaving him slightly nauseated and shaky. The Neätans dispersed, wandering forlornly back to their stations, leaving only *Ufficiale* Rozione, Pierro, and their redhead friend. This one turned to him after a few minutes and extended his right hand, fingers spread like a palm frond.

"*Tenente Ormbretto*," he said. "*Siete . . . chi?*"

"Oh, I'm Bane, *Alister Bane*," Alister said, shaking the Neätan's hand a little gingerly. "And this is *Elo.*"

"*Salve*," Elo said gravely.

Tenente Ormbretto heaved a sigh and shook his head. He talked conversationally at Alister who, though he had never learnt much Italian beyond the words you found on restaurant menus, tried to answer as best he could.

To his relief, Professor Odd shushed them fiercely after only a few minutes.

Alister was just beginning to feel hungry again when the machine in front of them made an unhappy noise, and the screen went black.

"*Che cosa hai fatto?*" Rozione asked accusingly.

"*Nulla, nulla,*" said the Professor, punching in keys to no effect.

A word appeared on the black screen. It took up all the space, and was made of tiny copies of the same word, repeated over and over and over again.

"Well," said Alister. "*That's* discouraging."

A small crowd gathered behind them, and as one they looked at the word on the screen in grim disappointment. It said:

NO.

Undaunted, Professor Odd began typing furiously again, bringing up window after window showing different readouts of text.

"Whether they wanted to or not, they *did* give us some information," she explained to a confused *Tenente* Ormbretto and *Ufficiale* Rozione, not realizing she was speaking English. "Clearly they are capable of understanding written language, and have the mental capacity to formulate an answer. Now, if I can decode their transmission signal—damn, they used *scattering!*"

The Neätans turned hopefully to Alister, who shook his head and shrugged expressively. *Tenente* Ormbretto sighed, and gave Rozione a look which clearly said: *You brought this one in, she's your problem,* and went over to where the rest of his team had congregated around the second-largest monitor, which was showing a radar scan.

Elo had gone to fetch a stool, the keyboards being higher than she could comfortably reach, and now she returned, towing a chair on wheels. It was covered in shiny, cracked leather, and there was a deep groove in the seat that would have ruined it for any human to sit on.

"I like their chairs," Elo said, pushing it right up to the banks of keyboard and climbing up onto it. "They have a place for your tail to go." She handed herself over to where Professor Odd was still banging away, cursing intermittently.

"Have you tried reverse-engineering their equipment?" she asked.

"No good; they scrambled the message too well."

"Here, let me." Elo got to work, her claws clicking smartly on the keys.

The Professor pulled at her scarf in frustration, and turned to Rozione. She asked something in Italian that Alister did not catch. Rozione shook her head.

"No recon satellites to get a look at this thing with," the Professor explained. Then she frowned. "Wait, you *had* recon satellites last time I was here! *Che cosa é successo a loro?*"

Ufficiale Rozione raised her shoulders and spread her hands; she looked deeply unhappy. "*Sono scomparsi,*" she said.

"Vanished? Just *vanished?* When? Er, *quando?*"

"*Pochi mesi fa,*" Rozione admitted. She seemed embarrassed.

"*Months?*" Professor Odd exclaimed. "Then this thing—whatever it is—has been up there for *months*, watching you! Picking off your eyes! Good grief, you'll be lucky to still have a planet at this rate—never mind my *pizza!*"

She swung around haughtily to face the monitors. Behind them, where *Tenente* Ormbretto and his personnel had clustered, alarms went off again. The same ones as before. Alister groaned, Rozione wailed.

"*Hush,*" growled Elo.

Behind them, on the monitors, another white streak cut the sky in half. More shouting into headpieces: "*Evacuare! Evacuare!*" Then the awful silence.

The aftershocks didn't come for several minutes this time, and when they did, they were much weaker. They barely jiggled the banks of keyboards and monitors in front of Elo.

Which was just as well, because what those monitors were showing was, if possible, even more important.

It was a ship. At least, at first glance it looked like a ship. The image was grainy ("Atmospheric interference from sunlight," Elo apologized), and a few of the details were indistinct. It had a shifting, imprecise look, because the image was a video feed. The thing was loose, almost pixelated, as if they were viewing an image that had been expanded beyond its maximum resolution. Which Alister suspected they were. That was why he thought the thing looked like a flying saucer at first. But upon further inspection he saw this was not the case: it was, in fact, a sphere with rings around it.

"It's a . . . planet," Alister said.

"That's no planet," Professor Odd said. "That's a conglomerate spacecraft."

"A *what?*" Alister said.

"Look *closer*," said the Professor, and pointed. Alister did. He leaned right up to the screen so that he almost had his nose against it. Then he rocked back on his heels and rubbed his eyes.

"Oo-*er*," he said, shaking his head.

The image was not pixelated. It was not overblown. The ship was not made of riveted steel or sleek metal, as he somehow had expected a spaceship to be. Now he wasn't certain it was even a ship.

It was a dense horde of tiny modules, barrel-like in construction, each with a dome at one end. They were linked together by spindly armlike appendages, which suspended them from their neighbors and at the same time kept them locked in position within the vast fleet . . . which in turn took the shape of a ringed sphere.

The pixelated effect had come about partly because Alister's brain had simply refused to comprehend such an improbable sight, and also because each module had a slight variation in shade; rather like a set of pixels. The darker modules sat in bands around the sphere part, and by the light cluster moving across the bottom, Alister perceived the whole thing to be slowly rotating.

"A *hive ship*," Professor Odd said in a dark whisper.

"Is that bad?" Alister asked.

"It all depends on what they have to say for themselves," the Professor said, putting her hands to the keyboard.

"How are you getting this image?" Alister asked, turning to Elo.

The *vroknaär* looked smug. "You remember that temple we passed on the way here? Well, it's got a telescope in its dome; I just patched into the remote controls. These guys, whoever they are, they only took out the telescopes and image recorders *in orbit*. Apparently they forgot about the eyes on the ground." She glanced around the control room, a little condescendingly. "Apparently *everyone* did."

They had begun to recover their Neätan audience, and Alister was soon squashed against the racks of keyboards trying to avoid being struck by tails or trampled on. *Tenente* Ormbretto stood a little ways back, arms folded, looking grim. He was dictating a message to an underling, whose clawed hands rattled away at a small mobile device. When he had finished, he pushed though the crowd to stand in front of the screen.

"*Mi dispiace*," he said in a heavy voice, putting a hand on the Professor's shoulder. "*Dovrei riferire questo ai miei superiori. Noi non dovremmo cercare di comunicare con loro.*"

Alister needed no one to translate for him: obviously, now they could *see* what they were up against, this was out of their hands and had to be taken up by higher ranked officers. They couldn't try to talk to the hive ship.

Professor Odd laughed guiltily. "*Troppo tardi,*" she said.

A moment later, the image of the hive ship was replaced by static.

"Incoming communication package," Elo said, sounding surprised. Then she made a face. "Looks like they have a pre-recorded message for us."

Professor Odd translated this for *Tenente* Ormbretto, who threw up his hands and shrugged.

"Play it," the Professor said.

Elo nodded. From the speakers mounted on either side of the console came a horrible, ear-splitting buzzing noise. Slowly, this died out. It was replaced by a piercing, monotonic voice that sounded like an angry computer.

"WE ARE THE SLAVOR. WE HAVE OBSERVED YOUR SATELLITE. WE WILL CONSUME YOUR TECHNOLOGY. THEN WE WILL DESTROY YOU. DO NOT RESIST. DO NOT RETALIATE. THE SLAVOR REJECT. THE SLAVOR RULE."

A short intermission of buzzing, then the same voice repeated the message in Italian. All Alister caught of this was the first sentence: "*NOI SIAMO GLI SCHAIVOR.*"

The Professor listened to all of this, a deep crease between her eyes, and she tapped her finger against the side of the monitor. When the Italian version stopped, there was another buzzing hiccup, and then it started again in what sounded like German. The Professor motioned Elo to cut the recording, which she did.

"Robots?" Elo asked.

"Definitely robots," the Professor agreed.

"How can you know that?" Alister asked.

"What does the word *slavor* remind you of?" Professor Odd asked.

Alister shrugged. "Slave, I suppose."

"Nn," said the Professor. "And the Italian for slave is *schiavi*, very close to Schaivor."

"What does that have to do with them being robots?"

"The word *robot* means *slave*," Professor Odd said, "in Czech. And ask yourself, did that message sound like it came from a slave, or a robot? A robot in the modern sense, I mean."

Alister had to concede this point.

"Elo, can you bring up the visual on their hive ship again?"

Elo nodded, and the strange, planet-shaped ship flickered back onto the screen.

"Can you magnify it any more?"

For answer, Elo spun a scroll wheel beside her keyboard, and the image disappeared, only to be replaced by the same image, closer up. Elo repeated this process until they had zoomed in to focus on one of the numerous modules that made up the ship. Modules that must be individual robots.

Professor Odd put her head on one side. Elo frowned. Alister said: "They're actually kind of *cute.*"

They were barrel shaped. On one end was a dome, with a dimple in the center. At the other end the barrel pinched in, like the neck of a vase, then flared out again to house a series of circular openings emitting a glow that blurred the image. Bridging the pinched-in neck were armlike appendages, with apertures from which the spindly arms connecting it to its neighbors emerged.

Alister thought; if only you stuck a cone, or something beak-shaped on the dimple in the dome, they would look a little like birds.

Birds made of metal, that could destroy cities.

"Elo, what are their coordinates?" Professor Odd asked.

Elo rattled off a string of numbers that meant nothing to Alister, but something had occurred to him: if she was using the telescope in the dome of the cathedral next door, and it could see this hive-ship, then it followed that the hive-ship could see *them.*

On the screen, the robot they had zoomed in on lit up like a city at night; narrow lines of light tracing over all the dark cracks, and the dimple on its dome end swiveled around to face them. From what Alister could see on the edges of the screen, all its neighbors had done the same.

"Aaaand—they spotted me," Elo said.

"Clever little buggers," Professor Odd said, and swung around to face the roomful of Neätans, a fragile smile on her face. *"Evacuare?"* she said.

The next thirty minutes were probably the most hectic of Alister's life. They were so crammed and packed with things happening that he entirely forgot that he was hungry. Nay, that he had ever been hungry in his life. He helped Elo download all of the relevant information onto a mobile platform shaped like an accordion, while around them the office depopulated.

Only *Tenente* Ormbretto, *Ufficiale* Rozione, and Pierro, who looked as though he would have much rather joined his comrades in helping to evacuate the city, remained. Rozione stood by with the grim look of a captain going down with the ship, and Ormbretto was on the dispatch line, explaining in clipped tones what was happening to a superior in another city, and warning them that they would soon be receiving, as refugees, the entire population of Pucca.

All the while, Alister expected everything to go up in a flash of white light. But the seconds turned to minutes, and the sky outside remained a deep orange. The data transfer finished. Elo hefted the mobile platform onto her back, and, dropping to all fours, trotted past the elevator doors and down the stairs. Alister and Professor Odd were on her tail, and the Neätans behind them.

In the darkening sky above Pucca silver streaks appeared, flared white, and vanished in less than a second. Where they had been, a gray cloud emerged, moving with uncanny speed and accuracy toward the city. As it drew closer it began to glint in the low light, scattering into individual metal forms, their winglike arms held at inclined angles to slow their descent.

When they were close enough that even the most cynical-minded Neätan could recognize them for what they were, they scattered, flared into a blanket that covered the whole city, and dropped into it.

The city was an old one, so its streets were narrow and winding. And currently these streets were choked with fleeing Neätans. They were hot, tired, and disgruntled. Some of them were bent under bulging bags containing their most treasured possessions, others pushed carts or dragged trolleys filled with same. A great number of them had small children (which sounded and behaved a lot like human children, only louder), and all of them were shouting at the next in front of them to "*Vai, vai, vai!*"

The robots, to everyone's surprise, did not drop into their midst and start shooting death beams. They came to ground on balconies and in alleys, except for one that hit a roof that had been poorly maintained and promptly crashed through it in a shower of brick and plaster to land in someone's living room. With a snap of energy from its right wing it shot upright—domed end up, balancing on its flared base. It vibrated, shaking loose the singed debris it had collected upon entry, and swiveled the dimple on its dome around, perceiving its surroundings.

Then it did something remarkable for a robot without a face—indeed, without any movable features—it managed to look disapproving of the mess.

Orders were flowing into the robot from the gestalt intelligence that was formed by thousands of robot processors working together. Shaking its dome, the robot half rolled, half glided out the window (shattering the glass before it with a carefully pitched sound wave), and dropped into the street, where it began working its way against the flow of Neätans trying to get out.

It did not attack them. It looked at them. It listened to them. It moved on.

The Neätans gave it plenty of space. They backed up against the sides of houses, squished against one another; parents muffled screaming babies. And, after the robot had passed, with an alacrity even it might have approved of, they bolted out of the city.

All around the city, the same thing was happening. The exodus gained speed, and the robots crept inexorably inwards toward the cathedral with the telescope.

Once, a couple of them surprised a small unit of *Carabinieri* officers, who with military efficiency injected them with several pounds of lead in under a few seconds.

The bullets exploded with a flash of plasma about a foot from the robots' sides.

The robots, after analyzing the situation (which took a respectable fraction of a second), retaliated. And moved on.

They left behind twelve *Carabinieri* officer-shaped scorch marks, black with carbon and smoking faintly.

Alister's stomach was twisted in knots—though whether from fear or hunger he was not sure. Elo was a yellow streak disappearing around a corner, the Professor on her tail. All around them more of the robots kept dropping out of the sky, moving ominously along the streets leading out of the city.

It was a good thing, he thought, wheeling around a corner with the three Neätans right behind him, that they were not trying to get out of the city.

Not by the usual means, anyway.

They had just reached the relatively familiar alley where Rozione had first apprehended them, when from behind him there was a *clang*, a sizzle, and Pierro screamed, tumbling to the ground.

A robot descended, landing gently in the road in front of them. The plating on the front of its body had peeled back, revealing a network of pulsing lights twined around the base of two metal rods that extended a good foot from its shell. They were both white hot, a small lick of plasma flickering between their tips.

Tenente Ormbretto pushed Alister and Rozione into the alley. "*Vai! Seguite la Professoressa!*" he shouted over his shoulder as he hefted his rifle.

Alister ran. Where the tangled knot that had been his stomach was before, now there was just a hard, cold lump. Behind him there was a short burst of furious gunfire, sharply cut off. In front of him another robot was touching down, creating a small dust storm in the alley.

And in between Alister and the robot, Professor Odd waited, holding open the door to the Oddity.

Alister had to drag Rozione inside rather than let her cover the Professor, who stepped inside after them but did not shut the door. She kept it open just wide enough to stick her head out at the small crowd of robots that were gathering around. They arranged themselves in staggered ranks, so each one could have a clear shot at the Professor, but they did not fire . . . yet.

"Hallo," she said pleasantly. "I'm Professor Odd. Who are you?"

There was a strange humming, like ten hard-drives revving up at the same time. Out of it came ten voices, all speaking the same words in exact unison.

"WE ARE ROBOT."

"Eheh, yes, I can see that," the Professor said. Behind her, in the ship, Alister was rummaging through the mess on the table, trying to find something to use as a weapon. Maria Rozione looked torn between wanting to drag Professor Odd back inside, and trying not to panic at the sight out of the windows. Alister knew how she felt.

"But the thing is, *what kind* of robot are you?" the Professor was saying reasonably. "I've met lots of robots before, and none of them looked like you. Or acted like you, I might add."

There was a metallic silence from the crowd of robots. If they had been computers with a User Interface, they probably would have had frozen screens with a "busy, please wait" icon on them.

Inside the Oddity, Alister was seized with a sudden desire to laugh. He resisted; laughter would not be the best thing for *Ufficiale* Rozione, who was looking a little manic.

Then one robot rolled forward. Unlike the others, who were all dull shades of gray, this one was white with a black dome polished to a mirror shine. In it was reflected a distorted view of the Niatano sky, the streaky face of the green gas giant looming ominously to one side.

"WE ARE THE ANTIMOVIANS," it intoned. "WE OBSERVE. CONSUME. DESTROY. THIS DYING PLANET WILL BE DESTROYED. YOU WILL SUBMIT AGREEMENT. NOW."

It leveled its glowing rods, and the Professor jerked her head inside and slammed the door.

A second later the door was blasted to smithereens by the robot's plasma guns. Shards of burning wood and metal exploded inward, and, before the smoke had time to clear, the robot floated sedately inside, prepared to annihilate whoever was hiding within.

It found itself in a shack decorated with gardening implements. There was a healthy layer of dirt on the floor, and wind whined through the cracks in the walls. And there was absolutely *no one* there.

Robots do not feel frustration. They do not feel emotion, as a whole. But they can be confused, and when faced with impossible situations they can react rather worse than humans do.

So instead of turning right around and performing a scan for incongruities in the space-time continuum, the robot just stood there, staring at a patch of wall, while its processors began to overheat.

As its data entered the gestalt consciousness, a similar hiccup spread to its neighbors, and their neighbors, and on and on.

And in the street, where Pierro and Ormbretto stood at rod-point waiting to be vaporized, the robots surrounding them slowly retracted their plasma guns and rolled up the plating on their fronts.

One of the robots—a white one with a shiny black dome—glided toward them.

"YOU WILL BE ARCHIVED FOR FUTURE USE," it said in a sharp, emotionless metallic voice. "SUBMIT AGREEMENT. NOW."

Several hundred miles to the south of Pucca, where the green gas giant hung directly overhead at all times, the sea was beginning to boil.

It was not actually the sea. To be precise it was a lake—the largest lake on the planet, occupying the central area of the continent like a great green and yellow eye. On the cliffs of its largest island there was a temple carved out of and built on those very cliffs. All of it was old. Some parts of it were very old, so old the people who occupied it didn't know who built them. And some parts were so old, the people who lived there thought of them as natural formations, and would be quite surprised to learn that those natural formations had actually been built by a species that had gone extinct eons before their species had evolved into its current form.

Perched on one of the newer ramparts with a good view of the lake were two Neätans, each with a telescope. But these telescopes were not pointed at the dimming sky; the Neätans were looking out across the water, where in the distant dark they could just see disturbance on the waves: the boiling sea.

In the history of the planet Earth there have been at least five *really huge* mass extinctions, each one wiping clean the majority of complex life, leaving the survivors to start anew. In the history of the satellite Neä, which is a good deal longer than the history of Earth, there have been *eight*. On Earth we have the Coelacanth, which has survived one of the most complete mass extinctions ever (not just the one that killed the dinosaurs; they survived the bigger one that killed off everything *before* the dinosaurs). On Neä there is a species that has survived three such extinctions. And unlike the Coelacanth, they are intelligent. And above all else, they know how to *survive*.

They live in the deeps of the ocean, and are the scourge of fishing boats and research teams the world over. They can hear microwaves, and they can see gamma rays. They do not have hands. They do not need hands.

The Neätans call them *kahst*.

On the temple balcony one of the Neätans lowered his telescope and rubbed his eyes.

"Aleandro, tell me you do not see what I see," he said.

His companion did not reply right away. He stood peering through his telescope, the feathered tip of his tail twitching now and then. Finally he turned dark blue eyes on the speaker.

"No, Miagroci," he said in a soft, musical voice. "I do not see one *kahst*. I see *twenty* of them."

Miagroci and Aleandro continued to stare out over the lake. They did not raise their telescopes, for they could now see with their naked eyes what looked like twenty islands, slimy and gnarled, streaming through the water, raising a crashing wave as they powered toward the temple.

More Neätans appeared on balconies and stoa overlooking the lake. Like Aleandro and Miagroci they wore simple trousers, sandals, and a complicated wrap consisting of one long piece of cloth wound around their bodies. And as one they all looked out over the sea, where the breaking wave was beginning to steam.

"Should we evacuate the temple?" Miagroci asked.

"I do not think they are coming for the temple," Aleandro said thoughtfully. He carefully wrapped his telescope in a fold of cloth. "But I think we should go inside . . . unless you want to get burned."

The water was properly boiling now, bubbling and bursting and rising in a cloud of steam, so it was difficult to see exactly what happened. It looked rather like a waterbird taking flight, if it had been the size of a very large airplane. First the head of the *kahst*—wide and flat, decorated with bumps and barnacles and a bony fringe along the back of the skull—thrust out of the water. Then its relatively thin neck, then the powerful humped shoulders, followed by an impossibly long expanse of ridged back, until finally it lifted off from the surface with a thrust of its tail flukes.

It streamed through the air, a three-hundred-foot long black-blue fuselage studded with gray ridges. It was gaining altitude steadily, and at such a rate that it would easily clear the highest towers of the temple. Its pale underbelly glowed white-hot, traced with cracks of red, while the air below it shimmered and waved, and occasionally caught fire. As it powered toward the land, the sky filled with a hollow roaring sound: the sound of masses of air being super-heated and displaced at high speeds.

Behind the first *kahst* its companions began to emerge from the water, creating a steaming crater in the surface of the lake as they all took to the air at once.

They flew, a fleet of dark gray ships with glowing bellies riding a wave of burning air, to surround the temple on the cliff. Then they began to spread, moving outward until they formed a circle with a radius of about half a mile, the temple at its center.

And then they did something that, even after rising from the sea in a confusion of steam and fire, was truly extraordinary: they turned so that their fluked tails were toward the temple, their wide craggy heads facing the outside world, and hovered, holding a position roughly two hundred feet off the ground. Their wide heads cracked in half as they opened their enormous mouths, revealing thick rows of baleen, and behind that, teeth. The cracks grew and grew, until each mouth gaped large enough to drive a train through.

Then, as one, the *kahst* began to sing.

A sheet of white fire spread in front of each *kahst*, growing like a bloodstain in the air, arching around and up, until it met and merged with the sheets of fire produced by the other *kahst*, forming a perfect spherical shell around and over the temple. It began to cool, harden and darken; from the inside it looked like the surface of water viewed from below, but ribbed with dark lines like blood vessels. From the outside it pulsed rapidly from deep black to blinding white.

And all the while, the twenty *kahst* surrounding the temple continued to sing.

They were not *actually* singing, of course. If you had gone up to one and asked, and assuming it could answer you, it would have told you it was fusing the atoms of the air into an agitated quantum state that could absorb, deflect, or destroy anything assaulting it from the outside. It would have said that it was using a precise combination of electro-magnetic radiation (this created the visible feedback) and subsonic sound waves that peaked in the range audible to humans (thus creating the illusion that they were singing a harmony in e minor).

In orbit around the satellite the robot hive-ship settled its sights on its fourth and last target.

On the ground around the temple, the *kahst* waited patiently.

"For a robotic intelligence, they are not behaving very logically," Professor Odd said, rolling out a map over the less-cluttered end of the table.

Neither Elo nor Alister paid her much attention. They were both trying to calm the Neätan down.

Maria Rozione was a military police officer, and had the nerves to match. But anyone's nerves would be shaken by seeing whole cities go up in flames and robots descend from the sky. Being abducted into a strange ship through a garden shed's door had been the last straw.

She wanted an explanation. That much Alister could understand. But the concept of a place completely disconnected from your native universe could not be conveyed in simple hand-gestures.

"Here, try this," Elo said, holding up a small blue box with cords coming out of it. The cords attached to a headset, with a microphone and an earpiece. Maria Rozione bent her feathery head patiently while Elo manhandled it onto her (it had been designed for human heads). When this ministration was finished she straightened up, and looked curiously at the dog.

"Right," said Elo. "Now tell me something I *don't* know."

Maria Rozione's eyes widened in surprise. She let forth a torrent of incomprehensible Italian. Then a moment later, the little blue box, which hung around her neck, said in a slightly tinny voice: "This is the most remarkable thing! I can understand you!"

"Yes, yes," Elo said. "They *always* say that."

From across the table the Professor looked up at them, her eyes slowly coming back into focus. "Oh, good. You found the translator. Pity Dave took the multiversal one, we may need it. Now come over here, *Ufficiale* Rozione, and tell me what Caprisio, Terrante, and San Compagnana all had in common."

They clustered around the map, which Alister saw was a hand-drawn illustration of a world—the kind that was bumped on the top and bottom, to account for the curve of the globe—that he did not recognize. The continents were unfamiliar, and the names all looked Italian. He assumed it must be Niatano. The Professor had made big red Xs over three places on the map: one in the north, one in the south, and one off to the left side right smack on the equator. She had also drawn a little red circle over a city in the northern hemisphere labeled *Pucca*. The Xs, Alister saw, were over *Caprisio, Terrante,* and *San Compagnana.* The three cities destroyed by the Antimovian robots.

Maria Rozione came over to stand by the Professor, adjusting her headpiece self-consciously. Her brow-ridges knitted together as she poured over the map, muttering to herself.

"I did not think they had anything in common. Caprisio is—*was*—" she choked "—*was* one of our oldest cities, the heart of government and art. Terrante was a small agricultural village in the mountains. And San Campagnana was an archaeological research station on a volcanic island in the South Sea."

"Well that makes no sense," Professor Odd said, leaning back from the map and folding her arms. "You're a super-powered gestalt consciousness of robots bent on destroying a planet; you don't go after random targets! The first thing you destroy is anything that could pose a threat to you. Conventionally speaking this would be government and communication hubs, recon satellites—that sort of thing. Which they *were doing.* They took out your satellites before you could identify them, and Caprisio makes some sense from a strategical standpoint. But agricultural villages? Research stations? It makes no logical sense! And even an *Antimovian* robot will still operate logically."

"You seem to recognize this word *Antimovian*," Elo said critically. "It doesn't mean anything to me."

"I didn't recognize it," snapped the Professor. "But I figured out what it means."

Elo spread her paws wide, her face all canine expectancy.

Professor Odd sighed. "It's a reference to the *Asimovian Principle*," she said. Glancing at Alister, she continued. "In your world, Mister Bane, you had a writer named Isaac Asimov. He wrote speculative fiction, and in it he developed what he called the Three Rules of Robotics, which would prevent his fictional robots from going crazy and doing things like . . . well, like *this*." She tapped the map. "These rules are, if memory serves: 1. *A robot may not injure a human being or, through inaction, allow a human being to be harmed.* 2. *A robot must obey any orders given to it by human beings, except where such orders would conflict with the First Law. And 3. A robot must protect its own existence as long as such protection does not conflict with the First or Second Law.*" She passed a hand over her face, and sighed. "Not a bad idea, really. And in other universes where people really *were* building super-intelligent robots, they always hit upon some similar failsafe in their programming. This came to be known as the Asimovian Principle."

"And the *Antimovians?*" Alister prompted.

"Are obviously robots which have utterly rejected these principles, for whatever reason." Professor Odd glowered down at her map, as if this were somehow its fault.

Maria Rozione gave a little gasp.

"But, where did they come from?" Elo asked.

Professor Odd shrugged. "Some distant star system? Some other universe entirely? I don't know! I wouldn't put it past them to be able to achieve faster-than-light travel in that hive-ship, and once you can do that you can do all sorts of strange things. But it is also possible they are simply from some other planet within this very narrative. I'd have to get a sample of their molecular structure to be certain. Oh, what is it Rozione?"

Maria Rozione was tugging at the Professor's sleeve and pointing at the map.

"I remembered," she said through her translator box. "I know what Caprisio, Terrante and San Campagnana had in common. *They all had Castevelli Temples.*"

Professor Odd looked at her, expression perfectly blank. Elo scratched behind one ear and peered at the map. Alister came around the table to join them.

"What are—er, what *were* the Castevelli Temples?" he asked gently.

"Old faith," Rozione explained. "Archaeological fanatics, scholars, mostly harmless," she added. "Not evangelical at all. But not destroyed, Professor; there were *four*—one more temple remains." She shouldered Elo aside and pointed, her dark-nailed finger jabbing at a tiny mark on an island in a jagged sea which sat in the middle of the largest continent like a ragged mouth.

"*Basilica Casteveglia,*" she said. "The oldest, and now the last."

Professor Odd frowned at the little mark on the map, which was labeled, sure enough, *Basilica Casteveglia.* She rubbed her chin thoughtfully, and frowned.

"Well, as fulcrums go it's a rather frail one," she said. "But I'll take it! Elo, come on, we're going to Basilica Casteveglia!"

"But that will be impossible!" Rozione protested. "You saw! Pucca is crawling with robots! We'll never get past them, and Casteveglia is over three hundred miles away—they might destroy it before we even get there! Um . . . *why* are we going there?"

"One at a time, *please*," Professor Odd said, taking the pilot chair opposite Elo.

Alister cleared his throat. "The Oddity is located outside of your worldtrack's temporal flow, so we can re-connect any time we wish after leaving, provided it is some amount of time *afterwards*. Er, that is, we can be back the moment after we left. The robots won't have had *time* to destroy Casteveglia. And we are also separated *spatially*, so the Professor can make that door open into Casteveglia."

"As to your actual question," Professor Odd said, easing a lever down which caused a thrumming chord to sound deep in the ship. "The Antimovians acted logically up until they began attacking seemingly random targets. Why wouldn't they destroy the locations that were most dangerous to them? Your weapon stock-piles, command centers, etc. Now it is clear to me that that is *exactly* what they *are* doing: for some reason, they see these Castevelli Temples as the most dangerous things on your world. And we are going to find out *why*."

Bong! said the Oddity.

"But what if the Antimovians attack Casteveglia *while we're inside* it?" Rozione protested even as Professor Odd sprang from her seat and opened the door. She stuck her head out, then slowly pulled it back in.

"I don't think we need to worry about that," she said, and opened the door the rest of the way.

Warm red light flooded into the cabin, strangely mottled, like light on the sea floor. Outside, Alister caught a glimpse of a rocky earth road and a sea of purple grasslike plants that stretched out to a surprisingly close horizon. This, he saw as he exited the Oddity (via the door of a sheepherder's supply shed), was due to the fact that the mottled and veined red sky dropped sharply about a hundred yards away, and plunged straight into the earth. Craning his neck he saw this strange curtain extended in a dome all around them, disappearing over the edge of a cliff a little less than a mile distant. From that direction he could hear the sound of waves crashing on rock, and perched on the cliff itself was a complicated structure of domes and arches and galleries, which sprawled over the jagged terrain like some architectural plant.

But what took his attention—indeed, all of their attention—was the creature that hovered, two hundred feet in the air and nearly on top of them, in a translu-cent haze of plasma, singing a steady hum in e minor.

Alister had not made the study of animals a priority, but he could guess that whatever this thing was it would probably knock the blue whale off its largest-animal-ever throne. Easily. But it was not so unlike a whale, he considered. Maybe more like a humpback whale, if you gave it a discernible neck and messed with its fins. And gave it bony ridges down its back and across its head. And dotted its forehead with glowing lumps like blown-glass ornaments. And made it *fly*.

From where they stood they were about even with its gargantuan tail flukes, which were leveled horizontally, like a sea mammal, and gently waved up and down in a slow rhythm that wafted scorching hot air across their faces. Its snout was nearly out of sight, but appeared to be pressed against the mottled sky where it came down to meet the ground. Its mouth, big enough to swallow a city bus, gaped open.

Ufficiale Maria Rozione collapsed, her legs folding like an accordion, and covered her face in her hands. She seemed to be weeping. Professor Odd stared at the creature, her face careening between fascination and unadulterated joy. Elo just stared.

"Soo . . . this planet has flying whales now, yeah?" Alister said, clearing his throat.

"That's not a *whale!*" Professor Odd said, rounding on him.

"That is Roumäsk, leader of the *Vail Kahst*," said a new voice, in accented but perfectly understandable English.

Everyone except the Professor jumped visibly—they had all been so distracted by the giant flying whale creature. And really, Alister reasoned, who could blame them?

Standing on the road leading to the cliffs was a Neätan they had never seen before. He was a little taller than Rozione, slender, with a messy fringe of dark blue feathers crowning his head, and he stared back at them out of placid, deep blue eyes.

"I take it you are Odd," he said, giving the Professor a courteous bow. "I am Aleandro Casaviola of the Castevelli *Sacerdoti*. Please, come with me. We have no time to waste."

Part Two

HOW DID YOU KNOW we were coming? How do you know that *kahst's* name? How did you speak with it? Why can you speak *English?*"

They were following Aleandro Casaviola along the dirt road toward the sprawling temple, through the eerily quiet landscape, and it was the Professor's turn to ask questions, which Alister found amusing.

"Slower, please," Aleandro said, raising a graceful hand. "My Old Speech is not perfect. I learned it from ancient writings on the walls of the *Torre Vecchio*. And by speaking to *kahst*. The *kahst* keep the Old Speech, and they are easy to talk to if you are patient. *Madra* Roumäsk came to speak to me after the attack—"

"Attack?" Professor Odd exclaimed. "When were you attacked?"

"Not long ago . . . half an *ora*, maybe. It was barely after the *kahst* put the barrier up. The dark sky turned white, there was a distant sound like a million voices crying in pain, then nothing."

Professor Odd exchanged glances with her companions. Elo said, "That must have been when we were evacuating Pucca."

Aleandro continued: "Then *Madra* Roumäsk came out of the sea, when the whole temple was swarming like an *intica* hill, and made them bring me to her. She told me World Eaters were coming, that I must come with her and wait for someone Odd, who would know what to do. I had to run very fast to keep up, but she led me to this shepherd's hut and told me to wait. And now you are here, Professor Odd, I will take you to Casteveglia, and we will try to stop the World Eaters. You do know what to do, I hope. I do not . . . "

Professor Odd was frowning and chewing on her lower lip. At Aleandro's last words she looked up, surprised.

"Oh, I know what I have to *do*, all right," she said. "I just have no idea how I'm going to do it!"

For a while, they walked in silence. There was no wind. Not a breath of it. The air had a stale tinge to it like biscuits left in the cupboard too long. The only sounds were the crash of waves on the cliffs, and the pervasive humming of the *kahst*.

Alister had begun to spot more almost as soon as he could tear his eyes away from the one above their heads; they were spaced evenly in a complete circle, noses to the wall of red sky. He reckoned twenty of them in all.

"I have a question," he said. "What *are* these *kahst* creatures?"

The Neätans looked at him blankly, but Professor Odd gave him a small smile.

"In your world, you have stories about dragons, right?"

"Yes," Alister said.

"In this world it's a little different: their dragons are not fictional, and they call them *kahst*."

With a roar and a hot wind another *kahst* appeared from behind the temple and thundered sedately over the field. It came to rest next to one of its fellows and took up the strange song from it. The other *kahst* ceased singing at once, and floated off the way its relief had come. Not long after it dipped out of sight Alister heard a muffled crashing splash as it returned to the sea.

"They work in shifts of one *ora*," Aleandro explained. Calmly explaining things, it seemed, was his way of keeping himself calm. Alister could sympathize. "Even for the *kahst*, maintaining a quantum shield is a strain. So they take it in turns. It is quite fascinating; we had been researching the possible powers of the *kahst*, but have never before been able to directly observe them."

"Quantum shield?" Alister echoed.

"Do you understand the theory of Quantum Suicide?" Professor Odd asked.

"I had it explained to me once . . . I think I do. Maybe . . . "

"A quantum shield is even more complicated," she said. "But the result is simple: we are cut off from the rest of the world in every way imaginable. Except time," she added. "Time will remain constant."

"Not entirely cut off," Aleandro corrected politely. "They have not extended their shield underground, yet. So we still have our hard-line to the outside world. As long as the World Eaters do not start digging, we are safe."

"I wouldn't put it past them," Rozione said grimly.

The temple rose before them, a tangle of towers, domes and connecting paths and archways. Though everything was built of stone and worn with age, Alister could also see communication antennae and other modern embellishments protruding from the higher towers.

Aleandro led them through a magnificent arch, like a disc half buried in the ground. Creeping vines obscured its base, but high over their heads its bare blocks of white stone gleamed in the red light.

A small contingent of Neätans were waiting for them beyond the arch, at the entrance to the widest and grandest tower. Their number was three, and they were dressed in a similar fashion to Aleandro: simple rope sandals, trousers, and complicated wraps that put Alister in mind of Roman togas. Only where their guide's was simple and dusty brown, these three had theirs decorated with embroidery, dyed all different colors. But they all had the same grim, pinched expression on their faces; so although one was stout, one was lanky and one was male, they gave the impression of being a matching set.

Aleandro swore under his breath, and his step faltered. Professor Odd took the opportunity to push past him and approach the imposing trio.

"All right, all right," she said, very businesslike. "What has happened *now?*"

The three grim faces went perfectly blank. They turned to each other, and murmured together in Italian. Professor Odd came to a halt and put her hands on her hips, regarding them quizzically.

Aleandro came up beside her, although Alister couldn't help but notice that he gave the impression of trying to hide behind her. He spoke, quietly and respectfully, to the three in his native language. Professor Odd kept interrupting him with questions for them, and he had to break off to translate.

Ufficiale Rozione frowned. She pulled off the translator's headset, listened, then put it back on again. Alister shared her confusion, but when he got a glimpse of Elo she winked at him, and put a clawed finger to her muzzle.

Then the stout female, who seemed to be the leader, said something that made Rozione cry out and run at them, streaming Italian, so Aleandro's translation was drowned out. But Alister just caught the words "communication," and "demands."

The Professor had gone very still. Her eyes, half closed, were dark and unreadable.

"I see," she said quietly. "Well, I'd better go and talk to them, but I can't guarantee I'll be able to save anyone."

This sobering message was relayed to the three senior Neätans, who conducted the Professor (and by association Elo and Alister) inside the tower with subdued respect. Aleandro was brought with them, since the Professor insisted he translate for her, and Rozione brought up the rear, walking shakily with a stricken look on her face.

"Well, what's gone wrong now?" Elo asked.

"It appears our friends, *Tenente* Ormbretto and Pierro, are still alive," Professor Odd said heavily. "But I don't know for how much longer. Oh, I *hate* it when they do this!"

"Do what?" asked Alister. They had been led into what might have once been a study hall, but appeared to have been repurposed as a communications center in the last few minutes; the chairs were piled to one side, and a large flat display connected to gray plastic boxes stood on a table against the far wall. The display itself was currently filled with the smooth, domed head of an Antimovian, the dimpled dish facing them, strings of light chasing each other around the base. It was speaking, apparently repeating the same message over and over again:

"—AND THE PROFESSOR, OR THE NEÄTAN SUFFERS. SURRENDER THE OLD TEMPLE AND THE PROFESSOR, OR THE—"

Professor Odd turned the volume down. "Recording or live feed?" she asked.

"We are not sure," Aleandro said, listening to the stout female. "It only just began, and it won't respond to us . . . "

Aleandro trailed off, because the robot *had* responded: it had shut up.

"Ah," Professor Odd said. "Hello there, can you see me?" She turned the volume back up as she spoke, and waved.

"PROFESSOR ODD," said the robot, and its metallic words carried more disgust and hatred that an emotionless voice should have been able to. The lights around the base of its dome flashed in unison. "YOU WILL SURRENDER THE OLD TEMPLE, OR THE NEÄTAN SUFFERS." It moved aside as it spoke, revealing a hunched form in a battered red jacket, surrounded by robots. They all had their rods out, and they were all white-hot.

"Now, now, no need to get excited," Professor Odd said, ignoring the commotion behind her as Rozione sank to the ground, head in her hands. "*Hundreds* of missile caches and tactical bombs on this planet, but they can all go whistle—I've got a *temple*. Why has *this* got you scared?"

The Antimovian moved back into view. "YOU WILL SURRENDER THE TEMPLE OR THE NEÄTAN *SUFFERS*," it said meaningfully.

"No deal until you answer my questions," Professor Odd snapped. "You came here to destroy this planet, why?"

"IT IS OUR MISSION."

"Why?"

"IT IS OUR *MISSION*."

"I heard you the first time. *Why* is it your mission?"

"WE ARE LOOKING FOR A HOMEWORLD. THIS IS A DYING PLANET: ITS LIFESPAN IS INSUFFICIENT. IT WILL BE REMOVED. WE WILL CONTINUE OUR SEARCH."

"Insufficient? The average lifespan of a red dwarf is over forty *galactic years!* How long is *your* lifespan?"

"INDEFINITE."

Professor Odd threw up her hands. "Well *there's* your problem! Guess what Antimovian? *Everything* dies. Everything runs down. Runs *out.* All the planets that you will *ever find* will be dying planets; *there is no 'indefinite' home* for you.

"But this?" She waved a hand expressively. "*This* is a *slowly* dying planet, and it will be a home for eons to come. Not *your* home, maybe, but a home for someone else. You've no right—and no *reason*—to stop that happening."

"THERE IS NO REASON FOR THIS PLANET TO EXIST. AND THERE IS NOTHING TO STOP US."

"Except, apparently, *this temple*," the Professor added innocently.

A hiccup. The image of the Antimovian jerked sharply, and its lights, which had become more and more chaotic, settled down to a steady rhythm once more.

"YOU WILL SURRENDER THE TEMPLE, OR THE NEÄTAN SUFFERS. YOU WILL SURRENDER—"

"Cut the communications!" Professor Odd shouted.

"They *can't*," Aleandro translated. "The signal carries its own power source—they can't even turn the monitor off."

Then the screen went black.

In the stunned silence Professor Odd took a deep breath and straightened her wig. She smiled. "The *kahst*," she remarked, "have *very* good hearing."

"But Pierro, Ormbretto—" Rozione pulled herself to her feet.

"Nothing I can do for them except finish this quickly," said Professor Odd. "The Antimovian's aren't sadistic, just ruthless. They want this temple more than they want to torture someone. If we can't *see* our friends being tortured, it's no motivation to surrender the temple. If torturing someone won't help achieve their goal, they won't do it. And now that our *kahst* friends have extended the shield to cut off communications, they have no way of showing us what they are doing." She paused, looking at them all with a distant expression. "They have no way of knowing what *we* are doing."

"And what *are* we doing?" Elo asked calmly.

Professor Odd had folded her hands and extended two fingers, which she was tapping against her mouth thoughtfully.

"I can't do this anymore," she said suddenly. "I am going to need to eat *something* before I save this world."

Wordlessly Aleandro produced a small baked bun from his pocket and passed it to the Professor. And immediately Alister and Elo's stomachs reminded them how hungry *they* were. *Ufficiale* Rozione dug out some military issue energy bars, and one of the *sacerdoti* Neätans was dispatched for more food.

"Does Casteveglia have any weapon stores?" Professor Odd asked, sipping yellow-tinged water from a glass.

They were seated on cushioned stools eating blue pasta off plates on their knees, on a gallery that ran along the cliff-side of the temple, which provided an unobstructed view of the blood-red ocean and the unsettling quantum shield. In the distance, across the water, Alister could see two of the many *kahst* that were maintaining it. They looked like misplaced mountain ridges with their long craggy backs.

"No, none at all," Aleandro answered. He was seated on the ground, his legs folded beneath him, while behind him, Rozione paced up and down.

"Then *it* must be something that even the inhabitants don't know about," the Professor mused. "But *it* is something that the Antimovians have been able to detect with their scanners. I'll give them all benefit of the doubt and say they have the most advanced scanners I've ever seen . . . which means what they're afraid of could range from a secret army of nano-robots to a volatile rift in space-time." She set her plate aside and stood up, glaring first at the paving stones, then at the noble columns marching away down the cliff.

Then something occurred to her. She turned to Aleandro, still seated on the ground. "You called this the Old Temple. Just how *old* is it?"

"That is difficult to say," the Neätan replied. "The foundation was laid between forty and forty-five thousand *anni* ago . . . that's er, about ten thousand *cicli.* That is generally considered to be the founding of the temple, eh . . . but there was an even *older* structure, which lay beneath. Some of it still remains in the cellar of the *Torre Vecchio* . . . and beneath *that* . . . " he trailed off, staring at a distant *kahst.* "Well, all of Casteveglia, actually. Beneath all of this . . . is a pre-historic *kahst* graveyard."

"The *kahst* are aquatic animals, *usually,*" the Professor said, polishing off her pasta. "It stands to reason their graveyards would be aquatic as well."

"They are," Aleandro assured her. "This one has been dated at over sixteen million *cicli* ago, at a time when the climate warmed dramatically: the oceans rose, covering almost all of the landmasses. That was the prime of the *kahst.*"

"And below the *kahst* graveyard?" Professor Odd continued.

"We don't know . . . no one has ever looked."

Professor Odd gave them a great, white-toothed grin. "Then that is where we will find what the Antimovians don't *want* us to find. Come along, Elo. Tell them to bring shovels."

*   *   *

The *Torre Vecchio* was a wind-blasted stone tower with no roof that stood on a small promontory of Casteveglia. The stones were so old, and its location so exposed, that on the cliff side of the tower the slabs of stone that made up its wall had been worn away until they looked like a natural formation.

A small crowd of *sacerdoti* had gathered around its mean little door, led by the three Neätans that had greeted them earlier. One of them—the male, who introduced himself as Miagroci—carried an armful of strange implements that looked like shovels, and probably were.

The stout female, *Madre* Roda, who Alister gathered was the Mother Superior, frowned at them disapprovingly while her *tenente*, Stefani, rubbed her thin hands anxiously. They were backed by a gaggle of younger Neätans, who stared shamelessly at the Professor, Alister and Elo.

"*Ufficiale* Rozione," Professor Odd said, pulling the Neätan close to her. "I need you to explain what we are doing to these inquisitive fellows here. See that they do not disturb us."

Rozione protested. The Professor gave her a friendly push, and then darted behind her and through the little door, calling over her shoulder, "Aleandro, follow me, Alister, bring the shovels—oh!"

It took both Alister and Elo together to carry all the shovels, and when they entered they found the reason for the Professor's exclamation.

The *Torre Vecchio* was a clean cylinder, empty save for a narrow stone staircase that curled around the inside wall. Looking up, Alister could see the zig-zag underside of the stair, and far up and away a tiny circle of red sky. Looking down . . .

"Good *god!*" he cried, backing against the wall.

Below was a yawning crevasse, dimly lit by the distant skylight, but terminating in darkness. Professor Odd was distinguishable by a little yellow light bobbing happily along on the opposite side of the cylinder about twenty feet below them.

Exchanging looks, Alister and Elo jettisoned most of the shovels and began to make their way cautiously down the stone stairs. It soon became too dark to see, and Alister stopped to get his flashlight out of his everything bag. It was affixed to a headband, so you could wear it and see what you were doing, while at the same time having the use of both hands. Alister had to stop and set the shovels aside while he put it on, and by the time he resumed his descent, Elo was halfway round the tower—not being so bothered by the darkness—and the Professor was a tiny spark far below. He couldn't make out Aleandro at all. The Neätan, it seemed, could see in the dark at least as well as Elo.

Walking cautiously down the stone steps, which were streaked in places with treacherous wetness, aware of the distant red sky impossibly high above him, and the tiny prick of yellow light descending ever deeper, Alister was suddenly struck by the gravity of their situation.

Well, not *their* situation. He was fairly confident that, should the worst come to pass, the Professor would herd Elo and himself back into the safety of the Oddity. But then he remembered her stubbornness in saving Dave, a creature she had never even met—and this was a whole race of beings who seemed, from what he had seen, to be quite decent people. Certainly, the reception that had greeted the Professor on Niatano was considerably more friendly than the one that had apprehended her on Earth.

It was quite possible, he mused, that she would not abandon the Neätans. Not under any circumstance. And he—and Elo—were roped along for the ride.

So he turned his mind to what they were searching for: a weapon even the Antimovians, seemingly invincible robots, were afraid of. Would it be a computer virus? Some super-powerful thermonuclear device? The planet's self-destruct button, as it were? If that were the case, would it not destroy *them* as well as the robots?

It was an uncomfortable chain of thoughts, so Alister was relieved for more than one reason when he at last reached the bottom.

Or, he had thought it was the bottom. It was a jumble of black soil, slabs of white rock, and masses of fungi. Professor Odd was scrabbling around at the base of one of these slabs, while Aleandro and Elo stood by, each resting their upper half on a shovel, and wearing expressions that, despite their radically different faces, showed equal amounts of anxious impatience. Then Alister stepped off the cursed staircase, and at the same moment the Professor exclaimed: "*Found* it!" And she disappeared into a hole beneath the white slab.

"I *told* you it kept going down, Aleandro," her muffled voice resonated up at them. "Now come on, I think I see a way."

Face filled with misgiving, Aleandro set aside his shovel, sat down on the ground, and slid out of sight behind the white slab.

"Don't tell me," Alister sighed, coming up beside Elo. "We brought these for nothing?" He waved a shovel.

"We may need them yet, bring one if you can," she said, tucking hers under one arm. Then, dropping to three legs, she scurried off into a hole that Alister had not been able to see until then: it was small and dark, and half-choked with fungi. He was glad of his headlamp as he went down it, headfirst so he could see better, with his shovel in front of him to negotiate the drop.

At first it was tight and damp and smelled vile: the fungi came off on his hands in a sticky yellow fuzz, and his everything bag kept catching on crags and lumps. But after a little way things opened up, and he was obliged to swing his legs around sideways in order to brace himself against the walls so he did not plummet down headfirst.

Thus it was that he eventually did drop, but feet first, and for only a little way. He landed hard, and had to sit a while waiting for his head to settle, but he was aware of a great emptiness stretching out on all sides that had not been there a moment before. Then the Professor's face passed in front of his; he shook himself, and looked around.

They appeared to be in a forest of white trees. Only, they were not trees. They were bands of white rock set into black earth, and they stretched on and on into the darkness before him, while the rugged ground sloped gently downwards.

"Where *are* we?" he asked, rubbing his head.

"The *kahst* graveyard," Aleandro said unhappily.

"To be precise, we are *in* a *kahst* right now," the Professor said, her mood the polar opposite of the Neätan. "Come on, further down!"

Down, down they went; staying close together now, for the way was not obvious and more than once the Professor took a sharp turn that Alister would have missed otherwise. At first they walked. Then, when it became too steep, they turned around and crawled backwards. Alister had to swing his everything bag around in front of him, so it would stop snagging on things. Elo, in her element and on all fours, thought this highly amusing. Aleandro brought up the rear, muttering in Italian under his breath.

The air was thick and damp and cold and smelled of iron. All around them was blackness, save the white shards of *kahst* bones that loomed into view like nightmarish figures. Then the ground beneath them gave way in a sudden cliff, and the world went topsy-turvy as they tumbled down it.

Except for Elo, of course, who bounded clear of the flailing limbs and was waiting for them at the bottom when they arrived, bumped and bruised, in a panting heap.

It had to be the bottom, Alister decided as he picked himself up gingerly. There was the sound of running water, and the ground was not earth or bone, but a hard wet stone, gray, and streaked with green. Then he wondered how he could see this at all, since his headlamp had been knocked about in the tumble and stopped working, and the Professor had lost hers altogether.

"*Santia Mandra!*" gasped Aleandro, clutching at his head feathers.

Alister raised his face, and saw exactly what the Neätan was talking about.

It was a cave they were in. A natural cave, carved from the rock by a trickle of water that ran at the bottom of a black crevasse. They had landed upon a ledge of stone, not a few feet from the abyss. But it was not this near escape that had caused Aleandro's exclamation, but what rested across the water, beyond a rolling field of water-carven wet rock.

A *kahst* skull emerged from a curtain of limestone, as big as a house, with a grin that looked like it could swallow them all. The many apertures across its forehead put Alister in mind of a spider, and made it look all the more alien and terrifying.

From within this monstrosity, casting the shape of the skull in vague silhouette, shone a pulsing light of many colors.

With a scamper and a scramble Elo and the Professor had cleared the crevasse with running leaps, and were making their way carefully over the uneven ground toward the skull.

Alister and Aleandro regarded one another.

"I am a scholar," the Neätan explained sheepishly. "My achievements lie in intellectual feats, not deeds of physical bravery."

"That wasn't *brave*," Alister protested. "That was *suicidal*, that was. Er, speaking as a student to a scholar, anyway. But I think I see a narrower gap just up there . . . "

This narrower gap was a crack of barely a foot, and with quiet satisfaction the two males stepped over it and followed their companions.

Professor Odd was running her hands over the surface of the *kahst* skull, murmuring to herself, occasionally falling silent to press her ear against the bone and listen. As Alister and Aleandro approached she held up a hand to stop them, and only after a few minutes did she allow them to come closer. Only then did Alister see what had caused this careful examination: the skull was covered all over with intricate carvings, choked with black dirt so that they appeared like dark writing on the pale bone.

The Professor turned to them, and pinned her intense gaze on Aleandro.

"Castevelli, Casteveglia," she said. "Where did those words come from?"

Aleandro shrugged. "They are old words. We have always used them."

"Anything at all to do with *kahst?*"

Aleandro was silent. Professor Odd rapped at the bone with her knuckles. "This skull," she said, "is not part of the graveyard. It was *placed* here, to cover whatever is inside, when this piece of rock was exposed to open air. It was a remote location, but not so remote that your predecessors could not come here in numbers."

"How can you tell that?"

Professor Odd traced her finger along a particularly violent group of black gashes. "I can't read the writing," she said. "But I recognize *graffiti* when I see it. This was once a very important destination to *someone*. Then the water came, the *kahst* came, and the *kahst* buried it. Your ancestors buried the *kahst*, and your people built on top of *them*. Now the Antimovians want to destroy it altogether. Whatever is inside . . . it is probably extremely dangerous."

She gave them a grin that, Alister thought, looked more dangerous than whatever was inside could possibly be. Then with a little hop and a wiggle, she threw her shoulders through the window-sized eye socket, and disappeared inside.

Much as he disliked the feeling, Alister went around and entered through the gaping jaw, followed by Elo, and finally Aleandro, who was looking about him like a frightened cat.

There, taking up almost the entirety of the cranial cavity, was a machine of fantastical design. Its main feature was a concave ring of gold-colored metal, so big that four or five people could easily stand inside it. This was held aloft four feet from the ground by a complicated confusion of metal branches that rained down from above, where they all converged and grew into a trunk-like pillar that stood in the center of the ring. This strange sculpture sat on undulating slabs of stone, like the leaves of a lily pad, and it was these stones that pulsed faintly colored light, illuminating the eerie cavern.

Professor Odd was already inside the ring, going over the rough surface of the trunk, before turning her attentions to the panels that decorated the convex interior of the ring. Elo slipped in beside her, though Alister paused and wiped his feet conscientiously before stepping on the glowing stones. These, he saw as he crossed over them, were made of thousands of hexagonal facets, each one framed in a band of glowing white stone, and each one shining with a slightly different hue.

Aleandro stopped outside the ring and made a strange, complicated gesture over his chest, then he bowed and stepped inside. And had to dart over to the trunk-like pillar in the center to avoid being run over by Professor Odd, who was scurrying around the inside of the ring, darting from panel to panel like an agitated squirrel. He joined Alister, who had already sought refuge there, and Elo, who was examining it with Alister's magnifying glass.

Professor Odd stopped in front of a panel decorated with intricate carvings that put Alister in mind of a computer's circuit board. She held out a hand imperiously.

"Screwdriver!" she commanded.

Alister produced the screwdriver from his bag, and set it in her hand. The Professor set to work, not with the business end of the tool, but with the butt, using it as a mallet to tap at certain points over the panel. Elo came around from the other side of the pillar and watched, her ears pricked forward attentively.

Then with a hiss and a happy clicking noise the panel broke along the carved lines and extended outward, forming something that was obviously a control input platform of some kind. And though it meant nothing to Alister or Aleandro, and even Elo was looking at it blankly, Professor Odd clasped her hands together and let out a low whistle.

"Oh dear," she whispered, her voice full of awe. "Oh dear, oh dear, oh dear me. No wonder they wanted you buried . . . no wonder the Antimovians wanted you destroyed." She ran her hands reverently along the smooth edge of the ring, like someone stroking an agitated horse. "Oh dear, you poor, lonely, terrible Device."

"What is it?!" Alister blurted out, speaking for all the companions.

Professor Odd stood up. She handed Alister his screwdriver back and regarded them gravely. "What do either of you know about transuniversal relative molecular motion theory?" she asked.

Alister and Aleandro exchanged black glances with each other.

"Elo?" the Professor asked cheerfully. "Would you care to explain?" and she turned back to the control platform, running her fingers over it gently.

"Molecules move," Elo said. "They move around, vibrate, I'm sure you both know this. How fast or how agitated they are determines what temperature the thing they make up *is*. The faster and more agitated they are, the hotter something is."

"Yes," put in Alister, "and when they are perfectly still, that's Absolute Zero . . . but that's a purely theoretical temperature. All molecules have to move, if even a *tiny* bit."

Aleandro made a noise as if he was about to disagree, but waved his hand and let it pass.

"Yes, well, this is all common knowledge," Elo continued. "But what most worlds don't know—what they *can't* know, unless they've had contact with other universes, is that molecules vibrate in a *pattern*. And that pattern is *unique* to every single universe: my molecules, for example, vibrate differently from Alister's, and both of ours are different from yours, Aleandro. If you had the right instruments, you could take a microscopic piece of each of our clothes, and tell them apart based on their molecular vibration patterns. That's transuniversal molecular motion theory . . . though I don't understand its relevance."

The machine hummed, and all around the interior of the ring the circuit grooves pulsed with light. Professor Odd stood up from the control platform, and began unwinding her scarf. "Molecules can be re-patterned," she said. "Taken gradually, this process is harmless. I am doing it all the time when I breathe and absorb oxygen from this atmosphere, and when I digest food. My body's native pattern changes the foreign molecules, but at the same time the foreign molecules change *mine*. Even now, all the molecules within our living tissue are beginning to align with the native pattern of Niatano, because of this exchange of patterns. Give us a few Neätan days, and we should be indistinguishable from a native Neätan."

"Except for our clothes," Elo reminded her. "Our clothes don't breathe, eat or drink. They will retain the pattern for much longer."

"Almost infinitely longer," Professor Odd said. "But again, this is the gradual process. If the molecular vibration pattern of the native universe was enforced—suddenly, powerfully—upon an alien subject, the result would be . . . astounding."

"Astounding . . . how?" Aleandro asked.

Without a word, Professor Odd took the tasseled end of her scarf and let it dangle outside the ring.

The end of her scarf disappeared. Alister could see through where it had been to the hexagonally-patterned stone beyond.

"The alien molecules would lose cohesion with this universe," she explained. "And whatever they made up would be *shaken* out of existence." She removed her scarf and examined the frayed end a little sadly. The tassels were gone, along with the last few inches, and now it ended abruptly with an edge that had already begun to unravel.

"It has ceased to exist?" Aleandro marveled.

"It has been shaken out of this universe and into the next. As would anything else of non-native material that stepped outside this circle."

"And how does this help *us?*"

"My dear Aleandro," Professor Odd said gravely. "*This* is a molecular motion pattern enforcing machine, and the Antimovians, I now have no doubt, are physically made of molecules from a different universe. *Think* about it," she said, over Aleandro's protests. "Why else would they be so intent on destroying it? Your world had *four* of these, now it has *one.* This is your last, and your best chance of saving yourself. And you *have* this chance, thanks to the *kahst.*"

"And thanks to the fact that the Antimovians are robots," Elo put in. "Since they are synthetic, they won't have adapted to this universe's pattern, like *us.*"

"It is not a settled matter," Professor Odd said, replacing her scarf. "We aliens should remain inside the circle, which acts like the eye of a hurricane. Also you have a problem of power: with this one machine you will not be able to wipe out all the Antimovians in—"

She was cut off by a terrible rumbling, grinding, churning noise.

Alister looked up through the tangled branches of the machine, and saw, against all the laws of physics he knew, a black hole appear in the ceiling of the *kahst* skull. And the next moment the machine lifted clean off the ground, and shot up into it.

The world turned into a roaring black hell. Alister just had the sense to grab the trunk as he slid to the floor of the machine, and he felt a *thud* as Aleandro joined him there. Every moment he expected them to crash against the underside of the cavern, and but every moment they kept on rising.

At last he managed to peel an eye open. He was lying on his back, and the machine was still hurtling up. And beyond the tangle of branches that supported the ring, like an angry eye in the distance, he saw a tiny circle of red sky.

The grinding stopped abruptly, followed by the clean whistling of air, and as the machine approached the top of the tower it slowed, the petal-like slabs of rock pulled up and inward, and it slipped through the hole at the top of the *Torre Vecchio* without even a scrape. Then the slabs extended again, and with a gentle crunching noise the machine came to rest on the very top of the tower, in the midst of a dark red sky, buffeted by a hot wind.

To go from being deep underground to several hundred feet above it in such short time, and by such violent means, was a dizzying experience. But all that was driven from Alister's mind when he sat up and saw what was waiting for them, resting on a pillow of boiling air, its long gray-blue back stretching out over the violent orange sea.

If the sight of a *kahst* skull had been enough to give him pause, then the sight of one fully fleshed, with its shrewd dark eyes glimmering at them, and the gems set into its forehead shining faintly, was truly staggering.

Alister was aware, faintly, distantly, of a certain amount of commotion rising from the ground below, no doubt from their Neätan friends who were reacting to the sudden appearance of a strange machine atop their oldest tower, not to mention a *kahst* threatening to bake the roofs of the temple buildings. But he had no attention to spare from the giant, gnarled gray face that was regarding them impassively.

The Neätans, Alister realized, shared enough with humans that certain things, like expressions and language and emotion, could be easily recognized. But the *kahst* came from a different line of evolution entirely, and he could no more read the expression on its face that he could shake its hand.

This didn't stop the Professor, however. She leaned on the edge of the ring, and shouted over to the *kahst* through the roaring wind.

"That was very helpful!" she called. "But why didn't you bring this thing up before, if you knew where it was?"

The mouth opened like a dark gaping cave, and a blast of cool air shot over them as the *kahst* spoke. It sounded, to Alister, like English, but with the vowels so far extended on each word it was barely recognizable.

"*What?*" said Elo.

"The machine was asleep," Professor Odd explained hurriedly. "So they couldn't get a fix on it. They had to wait for me to activate it—and that's a problem!" she added, turning back to the *kahst*. "There isn't enough power in this one machine to shake out *all* the Antimovians!"

Another blast of cool air, and this time Alister managed to distinguish the words in it:

"*Stoooop shoooooouutinnnnng. Aaaaaaaaii caaaaan heeeeeaaaarr yoouuuuu.*"

"Oh, sorry," said the Professor, her voice dropping so that Alister could barely hear her over the wind. He struggled to his feet, and gave Aleandro a hand up once he got there.

"*Giiiiiiiiiiivve theeeeee siiiignaaaaaaaal,*" boomed the *kahst*. "*Weeeeee willll caaaaaarrrreeeeeey oooooon theeee meeeesssssaaaaaage.*"

"But, but that would mean letting down your shield!" Professor Odd exclaimed. She was rebuffed by the *kahst*, who, with unusual terseness said:

"*Dooooo it.*"

And with a boom of combusting air, the *kahst* wheeled around and took off over the temple. As it did so, the sea below them erupted in a storm of steam as another score of *kahst* came shooting out of it, gaining altitude like rockets. When they had cleared the highest tower of the temple they spread out and began taking up positions between their companions who were still maintaining the quantum shield.

"Well," said the Professor, once the roar of the *kahst* had died away to the point where they could hear themselves again. "Here goes nothing!"

Above them, far, far above them, a glowing orange crack appeared in the dark red sky.

"They're breaking down the shield," Elo announced.

"I know, I *know*," Professor Odd said, working the control platform in front of her. "Here, Alister, hold this lever down—both hands, now!"

Alister obediently came over and took hold of the little gold knob the Professor had indicated. It was smooth and warm under his hand.

"Aleandro, you've got four thumbs, hold these buttons down in this formation," the Professor said, having moved around to another area of the ring. Aleandro obeyed, and Alister felt the little gold knob jump under his hands.

"Good, good," the Professor said. "Now, Elo, I'll need you over here . . . it seems this machine was designed to be operated by many people at once!"

"Or one person with ten arms," Elo remarked dryly, but Professor Odd took no notice. She took up a position adjacent to Elo and across from Aleandro, and this time Alister saw her push a panel of the ring aside, and tease out a platform with two large levers on it.

"What did that *kahst* mean, 'they will carry on the message'?" Alister asked.

"The *kahst* work with vibrations of all kinds," Aleandro said quietly. "I am not surprised they would be able to replicate this machine's signal if they had the original as reference."

"Yes, and that is suggestive," Professor Odd said.

"Suggestive of what?"

Professor Odd frowned and narrowed her eyes, and seemed about to say something, when for the second time that day the sky exploded on them. Only this time it went rushing away rather than falling down, for it was the *kahst's* barrier breaking, splintering, and finally dissolving into tiny fragments that sputtered out of existence with white sparks.

It revealed a blackened, burned landscape. Mounds of smoking brown earth had been piled up, and swarming over them, choking the sky beyond, was a thick cloud of gray glinting bodies, flashing with lights. It looked like the entire hive-ship had broken ranks and descended upon their little island.

There was a moment of confused stillness. Then the Antimovians charged.

In that moment of stillness, Professor Odd pulled down her levers, two at a time, and cried: "*Vai Umanità!*"

Something surged out from the machine, emanating in waves over and through the air around them. It had no color, no texture, no light and no smell. It made no sound. It moved not the smallest leaf nor the smallest speck of dust. The only way you could tell it was there at all was that as this *something* pulsed outward the things it passed through were drawn suddenly into sharp, crystal-clear focus.

The first of the waves reached the line of *kahst*, who opened their mouths wide, wide, *wider* . . .

And there was silence. It was as if something had locked all the sound waves in place, and all Alister could hear was the ringing of his own ears.

The first of the Antimovians hit the invisible wave. The robot shimmered, like a mirage on a hot day, and then flickered out of existence. Like a light being switched off. The same fate befell the rest of the army surrounding Casteveglia, and once they were all gone the *kahst* began to move out, away from the temple, and over the sea toward the mainland.

All over the planet, along coasts and deep lakes, *kahst* were emerging, their mouths gaping, bringing silence to the world.

And all over the planet, before the advance of the *kahst*, Antimovians were disappearing.

Sitting in a deserted square in Pucca, their hands shackled together, Ormbretto and Pierro watched in speechless amazement as their captors suddenly turned away from them, buzzing and beeping at one another in agitation.

Then the wall of silence hit, and they vanished like a ghostly apparition at sunrise: their bodies faded, became indistinct, while around and through them the stones of the street and the plaster sides of buildings were brought into sharp focus. For a moment they were an outline of negative space, held only in the memory of those who saw them, and then they were gone completely.

The machine descended slowly, falling sedately down through the *Torre Vecchio*. Alister, as was his nature, began to worry immediately about the climb back up. But the machine came to a halt beside the doorway to the tower, and hovered there long enough for them to disembark.

Professor Odd was the last to leave; she was peering at an inscription that ran along the ring's edge, and copying it down with one of Alister's pens on her forearm. The machine gave a meaningful tremble. With a sigh the Professor left off her scribbling, and stepped regretfully onto the stone stair.

As soon as it was vacated, the machine dropped like a stone. Down, down, down, until it splashed into unseen water and was gone.

Professor Odd, Elo, Alister and Aleandro exited the tower to find themselves in a tumult of cheering robed Neätans, who were split between cheering for them, and cheering the distant *kahst*, who were still streaming over their heads and disappearing into the sea.

The Professor looked torn, as if she would have very much liked to have a few words with one of the *kahst*, but none of them so much as glanced at the temple, and soon the last of them had disappeared into the water in a tumult of white waves.

Then *Madre* Roda came barging through the crowd, Stefani and Miagroci in tow, bubbling over in Italian. Aleandro looked staggered at the prospect of translating such a deluge, but Professor Odd answered the Neätan in kind, and once she got over the surprise of it, *Madre* Roda led them to an improvised headquarters in a nearby temple, where Maria Rozione sat in a chair surrounded by monitors, tears streaming down her strange face, as she spoke over a videophone to *Tenente* Ormbretto.

Professor Odd gave a small sigh of relief, and said; "Well, that's all right then."

Maria Rozione wheeled around on them, grinning from ear fringe to ear fringe, and snapped her translator back on.

"Professor Odd," she said happily, "I have been discussing the situation with Ormbretto, and we have decided that, in light of your actions, you deserve any honor or reward it is within our power to give you."

Professor Odd was a little taken aback by this. She mumbled something about *having had help,* and *the kahst.* But then she thought of something.

"You're *too kind,* Rozione, but all I really want—in fact, the very reason we came here at all—was for your excellent *pizza.*" She glanced at Alister and Elo, to see that they agreed. "Yes, three of your best *pizza,* I think, will suit us nicely."

They were slipping out the gates of Casteveglia, each with a wide, flat, savory-smelling white box in their arms, when they found themselves accosted by Aleandro. He was out of breath, and there was a garland of green flowers draped over his shoulders—a side effect of the celebration that was just gaining steam within the temple.

"You're leaving?" he gasped.

Professor Odd hefted her pizza box. "I have what I came for, your world is safe. Nothing left I can do here." She began to walk down the road, but Aleandro kept pace with her.

"I am not so certain about *safe,*" Aleandro said. "We've lost the machine; the *kahst* took it back and flooded the caverns beneath the *Torre Vecchio.* Whatever will we do if those robots come back?"

"Losing that device may be for the best," Professor Odd said, gently. "It is obvious, now, why the Antimovians feared it . . . but you have to wonder, why did the *kahst* try to bury it in the first place? And how is it they could so easily amplify its signal? They work with vibrations naturally (that is how they can fly, how they create their shields), but vibration *patterns?* They had to *learn* that. How did they learn that? It *bothers* me. It also bothers me that they needed *me* to operate the thing for them."

"Well, the *kahst* don't have *hands*," Elo pointed out, sparing one of hers from the box she carried to wave it at the Professor.

"The *kahst* were able to levitate that whole thing to the top of the *Torre Vecchio*," Professor Odd said. "They were able to hear its energy signature from within half a mile of rock. They could have found a way to work it . . . they *should* have done. But they didn't . . . that tells me . . . "

"*What?*" Alister broke out, impatient with the Professor's vague explanations.

"That the machine was originally built to combat the *kahst*," she said. "Given its unique ammunition, the only conclusion I can see is that the *kahst* must have come from a different universe themselves."

Aleandro had stopped dead in his tracks at this suggestion. But then he shook his head. "Impossible. The *kahst* were not negatively affected by the signal."

"Which brings us back to their unique skill with molecular vibration re-patterning. The *kahst* must have learned the skill in self-defense, and used it to change *themselves* to fit this world's native pattern. Also, they are *organic*: by now their patterns would be native anyway."

"This goes against *everything* that we know of the *kahst*," Aleandro protested.

Professor Odd shrugged. "I wouldn't worry about it. Wherever the *kahst* came from, I think it is safe to say they are definitely on *your* side now. Or at least, on the side of *Niatano*."

Aleandro looked hardly reassured by this, but seeing that he would not get a more satisfactory answer, he repeated his second question: What about the robots?

They continued walking, into a growing night whose darkness was mitigated by the huge green planet that hung above their heads. The road stretched out before them, and Elo trotted ahead, eager to get home.

"When I said the machine would shake them out of this universe, I was choosing my metaphor very carefully," Professor Odd said. "Think about it: what happens to the bits of dirt and lint that you shake out of a coat or carpet?"

"They fall to the ground . . . because of gravity," Alister couldn't help saying.

"Precisely!" said the Professor. "They fall *down*. Now, not a lot of people know this, but the *multiverse* is stacked . . . not in so simple a way as up and down, but that's the easiest way to describe it. So when shaken out of this universe, the Antimovians fell into the nearest *downhill* universe. And the further down you go through the multiverse, the more *unconventional* they get . . . and the more likely they are to be better equipped to deal with the Antimovians."

They had arrived at the little sheepherder's hut where the Oddity's portal was. Beyond it, beyond where the *kahst's* shield had been, the earth was furrowed, scorched, and still smoking from the actions of the robots. They had indeed been trying to dig their way under, and had gotten pretty far. Elo was waiting by the hut, looking out on the destruction with a somber expression.

Professor Odd marched up to the door and took hold of the handle, but did not open it. She turned back to Aleandro, who was standing in the road looking despondent. "Furthermore," she said cheerfully, "unless you have a *very* rare and special device, moving to a universe *uphill* from you is practically impossible. So, no . . . I think you need not worry; you will not see the Antimovians again. *We*, however," she glanced from Elo to Alister, and grinned. "I'm sure we have not seen the last of them. *Grazie e arrivederci, mio caro Aleandro,*" she added, opening the door and ushering her companions inside. "*Ti vedró di nuovo.*"

Aleandro watched the Professor disappear inside the hut and shut the door behind her. He did not try to follow. He smiled, a little ruefully, and began to walk back towards Casteveglia. There was the pop and bang of distant explosions from within the temple, but these were just the result of fireworks being set off, their sparkling bodies streaking through the dark sky and falling in shimmering trails over the sea.

Inside the Oddity, Alister barely had time to breathe a sigh of relief before he was confronted with a sight that turned his blood cold. Behind him he heard Elo give a sharp gasp as she trod on his heel.

Sitting ominously in the center of the room, in front of the table, was a wide, barrel-shaped robot with a domed head and a patchwork pattern of plating on its front. It gave a little click, a little whir, and then said in a sharp, electronic voice:

"MY PANVIRONMENT SUIT IS COMPLETE. WHAT DO YOU THINK OF IT?"

As soon as it spoke all the little incongruities jumped out at Alister. He saw that, unlike the Antimovians, this robot's body was not tapered at the bottom, but was a straight barrel shape. It was girted by a gear, not unlike the tread of a tractor, and its domed head was smooth and appeared to be made of glass—or some other hard, transparent surface. It reflected in a deep blue all the twinkling lights of the Oddity, and around its base was a brass band with ten circular valves. As he watched, one of these opened, and a long, metal-plated tentacle emerged. It waved. A great orange and yellow pinwheel eye pressed itself against the interior of the dome, and blinked at them.

"Hallo Dave!" called the Professor, pushing her way past the gobsmacked Alister and Elo. "You look smashing. Marvelous. *Dressed to kill.*" She winked at them. "We brought pizza back, would you like some?"

"YOU WERE ABSENT LONGER THAN I CALCULATED," Dave said. "WHAT HAPPENED?"

"Funny you should ask that," Elo said, eyeing the panvironment suit warily. But Professor Odd was not disturbed in the slightest by the uncanny resemblance. She swept over and deposited her pizza box on the table. Taking a slice, trailing a string of melted cheese, she pulled up a chair and began to tell Dave all about their adventure.

3.   THE PROMETHEAN PREDICAMENT

Prologue

IT WAS A DESOLATE LANDSCAPE, as hospitable as a hot iron pan. In the farthest distance a range of low mountains marched against a turbulent gray sky, but other than that the ground ran perfectly flat. Here and there dark jagged cracks were cut in its surface, remnants from ancient storms, and the largest of these was overshadowed by a physical incongruity that hung in the sky directly above it: a huge zig-zag of reddish-tan stone, as wide and as long as the canyon it mirrored. It rose from a point near the horizon and climbed up through the stormy sky until it was lost in the clouds. Conversely it could also be said to fall from the clouds and strike the earth, where arms of the same stone were flung out, like debris from a lightning strike, frozen in place.

This explosion of rock, eerily fixed in place, marked the head of the canyon, and from the surface a steep and winding trail, worn to a polish by generations of feet, led down into the chasm. Now, in the gathering darkness, while the zig-zag of rock loomed low in the sky, a procession of the owners of some of those feet came shuffling up out of the canyon, each draped in a gray cloak and carrying a yellow lantern. The winding string of lights crept up out of the earth, climbing in amongst the fallen pillars and shattered pieces of stone, like a distant glowing caterpillar. Then, from the center of this explosion of rock, where the narrow tail of the giant zig-zag met the earth, there came a long piercing moan. It was impossible to tell whether the source was human or animal, but whatever it was, the sound spoke of one thing: pain.

Part One

ALISTER BANE had been faced with difficult decisions before: decisions that had drastically changed the course of his life. Choosing to help the strange character called Professor Odd rescue a bright green tentacle monster from the clutches of the Canary Company had not been easy, nor had his subsequent choice to leave his native world behind and go adventuring with the Professor in her interuniversal ship. But those choices had been influenced by extraordinary circumstances (scientists in enviro suits with guns; the complete annihilation of his social identity), and he had been able to make those decisions fairly quickly.

In this case, he was stumped: he was out of options. Which was to say, he was out of clean clothes.

Their last adventure had taken them crawling through a wet and dirty cave, and Alister's only pair of sensible brown trousers and his sensible brown coat were splotched with mud, ripped and torn, and in one place a little burnt. Elo had taken them away to what she called the Rejuvenator Room, which was a long room off the main living area of the ship where racks of clothes in various states of cleanliness hung in icy blue alcoves. When Alister had asked her how long it would take to clean them, she had shrugged and said "a couple of days."

"But don't worry," she had added. "The Oddity has given you other clothes, hasn't it?"

The Oddity was what they called the Professor's ship, since that described it about as well as anything. If it was a ship at all, Alister thought, for they all—even he—referred to it as though it were a person. In this case, a person with terrible taste in clothes.

It had provided Alister with other clothes to wear, all right. He was wearing the pajamas right now (yellow flannel with bright purple stars), and was looking at the choices laid out on his bed with distaste.

The Oddity had clearly modeled them after the clothes he had been wearing when he got onboard: button-up shirts, trousers, blazer jackets. It had also produced an array of underwear and socks, but with all these items it had gone haywire in choosing the colors and patterns.

It had given Alister three pairs of trousers: pinstriped green, pink, and a dark red pair that Alister would otherwise have been happy to wear, except that they had pink appliqué hearts down the outside leg seams. The shirts were button-up shirts with collars, but that was all they had in common: one was white with lacy ruffles, another was pink with matching sequins, yet another was a very fine shirt of heavy silk dyed dark blue with swirls of white and pink that put Alister in mind of galaxies. The jackets, by comparison, were relatively tame. There were two of them: a purple blazer with brass buttons, and a black sport coat that might have been conservative except for the red embroidery of an owl in flight across the back. Nevertheless Alister had set it aside and was now puzzling over which combination of shirt and trousers would be least offensive, when a piercing electronic voice buzzed in the hallway.

"THE PURPLE OUTER COVERING IS MORE DESIRABLE."

Alister spun around to find Dave sitting in his doorway. Or to be more precise, it was Dave's all-environment mobility unit, with Dave inside it. So although Dave was a bright green tentacle creature the shape of a pie-pan with one pinwheel yellow eye, what Alister actually saw was quite different.

If you took a barrel of the sort used to carry oil and capped it with a dome of dark blue glass, you would be very close to Dave's all-environment suit. Around what could be called its waist was a wide gear not unlike a tank's tread, and above that ran a band of gold metal, punctured at regular intervals by circular valves. Alister knew there were ten such valves exactly; one for each of Dave's long, prehensile tentacle arms. Something that looked like a miniature satellite dish slid along the seam where the glass dome met the barrel; it came to a halt so that it was pointed at Alister. Since he could not see Dave inside the suit, he figured this was how the creature was looking at him. The valve nearest the front of the barrel slid open, and one of the tentacles—encased in a sleeve of jointed metal—came slithering out. It hooked the hanger of the purple blazer and held it out to him.

"I CAN PERCEIVE A BROADER SPECTRUM OF LIGHT THAN YOU," Dave intoned through his suit's translator. "THIS ONE LOOKS THE BEST."

Alister took the coat, and shrugged to himself. "Well, in that case," he said, "got any advice for the rest?" He gestured at the trousers and shirts laid out on his bed.

Dave did not move, which was to say, his suit did not move. Alister imagined that bright yellow eye peering at him through the dark glass dome. Then:

"NO." And he trundled away down the catwalk outside Alister's room. Alister wondered absently how Dave would manage the ladder that connected the elevated catwalk to the central living area below, but he was distracted by his original problem: what to wear.

Eventually he chose the dark red trousers (despite the hearts) and the silk galaxy-colored shirt to go with the purple blazer, as this struck him as the least offensive combination. Yet it was with some amount of self-consciousness that he descended the ladder, until he got to the living room and beheld his other two companions: then he remembered that they too had been dressed by the Oddity.

Elo was sitting on the table; she had cleared a place for herself among the jumble of junk and artifacts, and was eating breakfast off a plate in her lap with a fork. Seeing Elo eat was always a little strange for Alister, since she could easily be mistaken for a golden-yellow dog, and the sight of a dog sitting erect and eating eggs and hash with a fork was not something you'd expect. You'd certainly not expect her to be wearing a deep violet jumpsuit.

And then there was Professor Odd.

Professor Odd crouched on the steps that led down to the front door, her pinstriped knees up in her chest, and the tails of her green trench coat gathered around her feet. She wore a messy wig that was fiery red on one side and lemon yellow on the other. From under this, curling along the back of her neck, was a pale tannish-pink tentacle with green leopard-spots. It was twining over and under itself in a perturbed, impatient manner, quite the opposite of her otherwise still posture. As he drew closer Alister saw that Dave was sitting beside her, and together they were staring at the matte black rectangle that was the front door.

This door—gateway, portal—could lead you just about anywhere. But right now it was dormant and dark, and in the center of it, stuck like a magnet to a refrigerator, was the Professor's sword-cane.

The cane was ordinary looking enough, long and thin and shiny black. But its silver handle was cast into the impertinent curving shape of a banana, and it was this feature that had always made the cane stand out to Alister as something uniquely *Oddlike*, something only the Professor would carry. He couldn't think why it should be stuck to the door, but as breakfast was foremost in his mind he busied himself in the kitchen alcove, and it was only after he had eaten, and saw that the Professor and Dave still crouched by the door—and had been joined by Elo, no less—that he wandered over as well.

"Is it . . . stuck?" he asked.

For answer, Professor Odd reached out a strong pale hand and plucked the cane from the fuzzy black substance of the door. Then she let go. The cane snapped back into position as if tugged by a rubber band.

"It's been like that all morning," Elo said with a toothy yawn. She glanced at the Professor, who had gone back to staring at the cane, as though she expected to find the answer written along its length. Then she turned abruptly to Dave, and said: *"Well?"*

"IT APPEARS TO BE UNDER THE INFLUENCE OF AN EXTRA-UNIVERSAL POWER SOURCE. LIKELY UNCONVENTIONAL. HIGH PROBABILITY DANGEROUS," Dave intoned.

"Er, what did that mean, exactly?" Alister asked. But he was asking the empty air. Professor Odd had uncoiled like a jack-in-the-box, and was pacing up and down the narrow aisle between the overcrowded table and the armchairs pushed up against the wall under the windows. She had a finger in her mouth, and her tentacle was lashing fiercely.

"No, no," she muttered around the finger, gnashing her teeth on the nail. "Nothing for it—I'll just have to risk it. Of course, it might be some *other* extra-universal unconventional power source, in which case Dave is probably right about the danger. Or . . . "

"Or *what?*" Elo snapped. She may have had the appearance of a dog, but she was not a blind follower.

"Or it is *exactly* what I think it is," Professor Odd said, her leopard eyes flashing. "In which case Dave is *definitely* right." She strode over to one of the swivel-chairs in the cockpit: a mass of keyboards, buttons and switches, all linked together by fiber-optic cables, luminescent tubes, and banks of flashing lights. Everything about the cockpit (which covered an entire end of the ship, on both sides of the door) was colorful and bright. The buttons glowed, the levers flashed. Instead of symbols, the keys were designated by different sequences of color. Alister could never make any sense of it, and did not feel much obligated to try.

"Right-oh," Professor Odd exclaimed as she swung herself into the chair. Reaching down into the shadows on either side she pulled out a long belt with a buckle on the end and strapped herself in. Alister began to feel nervous, and wished he had not eaten so many eggs.

"Something is calling to my cane—*my* cane specifically. Something wants it— *needs* it—very badly. It needs it so badly it's affecting the cane's space-time location. Now, I don't normally do it this way—usually I bring the universe I want to visit *to* the Oddity, rather than the Oddity *to* the universe. Faster that way. Less trouble. But in this case, unlocking the spatial damping blocks should allow us to drift free . . . " she pulled down on a bright red lever, while at the same time running a knob on a sliding bar all the way up until it hit a white square that flashed alarmingly, like a strobe light.

Elo ran for the other pilot chair, on the other side of the door, and strapped herself down. Alister wedged himself against the wall. Dave sat, imperturbable in his environment suit, on the stairs down to the door and did not budge.

" . . . and we'll just follow where the cane takes us," Professor Odd said happily.

There was a horrible wrenching jerk. A half-full bucket of blue paint fell off the table and splashed on the floor. All the lights of the cockpit flashed in unison, making a noise like a cymbal crash, and Professor Odd typed furiously at her keyboard.

A creak. A distant bang from upstairs, and muffled behind that Alister thought he could hear the *hisssss* of steam escaping. The lights of the cockpit went out, and from the direction of the door there came a clap of thunder. Professor Odd's cane clattered to the floor.

"WE ARE HERE," Dave intoned through the darkness.

One by one, the lights came back on.

"Here, where?" Alister said, crawling on all fours over to the door. It was still a black rectangle: no door had materialized there.

"I SHALL DISCOVER THAT," said Dave, and began trundling down the steps.

"Not through an unanchored portal!" Elo barked, and flew out of her seat to stop Dave. But she overshot, and only succeeded in tackling him as his environment suit passed through the fuzzy blackness of the door, taking her with it.

For a time Alister and Professor Odd stared at where their two companions had been. Alister was silent and stunned. The Professor was silent and thoughtful.

"Bugger," she said, after due consideration. Then she unbuckled herself, got up, and went over to the table where she extracted from the mess a long knit scarf of gold and turquoise. This she wound round her neck, carefully tucking her tentacle inside so that it was thoroughly concealed. From a pocket of her coat she produced a pair of dark spectacles, and these she slipped on over her uncanny feline eyes before going over to the door and picking up her cane.

"Well?" she asked of Alister, who was still seated on the floor. "Are you coming?"

"We're going after them?" Alister was startled, and not a little frightened.

Professor Odd shrugged. "I am," she said.

"But what did Elo mean about an unanchored portal?"

"It means you'd better hold my hand, or we could end up in wildly different places."

Taking a last nervous look around the Oddity, Alister got up and went over to Professor Odd, who had poked her cane experimentally out through the door.

"There's solid ground out there, atmosphere too. Hope the Oddity's equalization buffer worked, never done a transfer like this before . . . " she was murmuring as Alister took her other hand and stood, waiting, on the second step. "Well, we'll find out," she said cheerfully, and stepped through the door, pulling the reluctant Alister with her.

Another sound of thunder, all around and rolling on and on, longer that any thunderclap Alister had ever heard. He was glad of the Professor's hand, clasped firmly in his own, for it seemed that a strong wind was blowing at him one way, while some other force pushed him another. Something stung on his skin, and he snapped his eyes shut against the sandy debris that the wind carried with it.

There was a tug on his hands, and he felt the Professor pulling him somewhere. Somewhere out of the wind, he was relieved to find, and opened his eyes gingerly.

Almost at once he wished he hadn't: they were standing beneath a sandstone outcrop over a narrow stone cliff, which ended not five feet away in a sheer drop whose bottom was hidden by a rolling bank of angry gray clouds. The Professor was lying on her front, her head poking over the edge, but Elo and Dave were nowhere to be seen.

"Well, this is interesting!" she shouted. She had to shout, for the wind roared and whistled so that they could not hear each other otherwise. Using her free hand to keep her wig from being blown away, she set off along the edge of the ravine, using her cane as a third leg.

Alister huddled against his ledge of rock, and did what he felt was the sensible thing: look around for a way to get back into the Oddity.

There was none—only the bare windswept rock, which was a little yellowish, and the angry gray sky.

Alister looked down at his feet and tried not to panic.

"Well, this is *very* interesting!" said the Professor, sitting down beside him. Her wig, which was messy even in the best of times, had all its hairs standing on end so it looked twice as big, and her glasses had been knocked askew. "Now, don't *panic*," she said with a cheerful smile, "but I *think* we're, uh . . . we're somewhere *impossible*."

Alister wondered, a little bitterly, what it took to make someone who lived in a ship-that-was-not-a-ship that floated between universes think a place was impossible.

"But don't worry," Professor Odd continued. She pointed with her cane—*away* from the cliff. "If we go that way, we should be able to get down. I think."

"What about Elo? And Dave?" Alister protested.

The Professor shrugged. "They aren't here."

Before he could help himself, Alister glanced fearfully toward the edge. What if they had come through over thin air? Professor Odd seemed to read this thoughts, and shook her head.

"The range of an unanchored portal is pretty big," she said. "They might have come through someplace else entirely."

"Then how are we going to find them?"

"Follow *me*," the Professor said, and crawled out from under the overhang. Reluctantly, Alister followed her.

Elo and Dave fell—but not far. It was far enough for Elo to get all four feet under her and land with a *thump* in the soft sand. It was also far enough for Dave to ignite his anti-gravity plates, which created a small whirlwind of dust around him as he landed. Elo ducked her head and scrambled away, hacking and growling and cursing in between gasps.

"What were you *thinking?*" she snapped as soon as she had her voice back. "Toddling off through an unanchored portal? We might have lost you!"

"AS IT STANDS WE ARE BOTH LOST," Dave pointed out. "I HAVE A HIGHER CHANCE OF SURVIVAL THAN ANY OF YOU. I SHOULD HAVE GONE ALONE."

"Doesn't change the fact that you're still an idiot," Elo sniffed. "And it's not like I *meant* to—we'll just have to locate the nexus of the portal field and hope it's still active—and not a hundred feet . . . in . . . the air . . . "

The *vroknaär* trailed off, for as she spoke the last words she had craned her neck back to take a look at said air, and in doing so she got her first good look at the sky.

It was a rolling, thundering, gray sky, full of high clouds and pricked by lightning. Its action was in contrast to the bare, flat, yellow-tan ground, except on the far horizon where a sliver of pale blue sky peeked through the gray blanket. But what made Elo stare, what made all the sensory equipment on Dave's suit go into overdrive, was the impossible thing which hung in the sky above them: a lightning bolt carved of yellow stone, frozen as it arched down out of the clouds until it was lost beyond the pale horizon. It was higher than any skyscraper, and seemed to appear out of nowhere in the tumbling gray clouds. As far as Elo could see (and that was pretty far) there was nothing to support this zig-zagging arc, and it hovered in the sky like a half-finished bridge.

"How is that possible?" she wondered out loud.

"INITIAL SCANS PUT APEX OF THE STRUCTURE AT 2,000 STANDARD METERS," Dave intoned helpfully. "IT IS MADE OF SOLID ROCK. LIKELY SANDSTONE. PROJECTED JUNCTION WITH SURFACE AT . . . COMPUTING . . . 25 KILOMETERS."

"I'm not asking *what it is,*" Elo said impatiently. "I'm asking, *how on Arratowen is that thing staying up there?*"

Dave was silent for some moments, and Elo assumed he had processed her words enough to realize that her question had not been meant to be answered, but then his suit let out a satisfied bleeping sound, and he said:

"SECONDARY SCANS SHOW ELEVATED LEVELS OF EXTRA-TYPICAL ELECTRON RADIATION. THERE IS A LEVEL 5 REALITY WARP WITHIN 1 KILOMETER OF THE PROJECTED ARCH-TO-SURFACE JUNCTURE."

"What," Elo said, closing her eyes and taking a deep breath, "does that mean?"

In the deep blue interior of Dave's dome, something greenish twined and twirled, and a yellow eye flashed close to the surface.

"IN CASUAL SPEECH," he said, "YOU MIGHT CALL IT 'MAGIC.'"

"Ooooh," Elo said, one long exhalation as she looked back up at the floated lightning bolt made of rock. "Oh dear."

"Now, there are actually quite a few ways of explaining why something impossible exists," Professor Odd said cheerfully as she strode through the rocky landscape, swinging her cane in a jaunty arc between strides. Alister followed behind her. He was trying to keep his eyes focused on the ground, because it was jumbled and uneven, but also because he did not wish to be distracted by the sheer cliffs on either side.

The place where they were, whatever it was, was only about twenty feet wide, and beyond that fell away in vertical cliffs. Alister had not dared get close enough to the edge to see how high they were, but judging from the clouds that swirled and curled around them, and by his shortness of breath, he calculated that they must be several thousand feet off the ground.

That is, he corrected himself, *if this world is equivalent to Earth. Which it may not be. In which case I have no idea . . .*

"There is the theory that any sufficiently advanced technology is indistinguishable from magic—that is to say, miraculous," Professor Odd was saying, neatly hopping from rock to rock as there was no clear path. "However, as I can distinguish technology at an atomic level, I can confidently say that this is *not* technology. Which leaves the other option . . . "

"What option is that?" Alister called, for he had fallen behind. The Professor stopped, perched on a triangular rock with her cane on another to steady herself, until he had caught up.

"When you first came aboard the Oddity," she said, "Elo explained the two basic types of universes we visit: conventional, and unconventional. Conventional universes, like your native one, abide—more or less—by the laws of physics and chaos theory. Unconventional universes *do not.* So far, the universes we have visited, you and I, have been nominally conventional in their makeup. Until now." She tapped the rock with her cane and smiled.

"This is an unconventional universe," Alister said, his heart sinking. So much, he thought, for his neatly organized and rational way of thinking.

"Yep," the Professor said, jumping down from her rock and threading her way through the broken landscape. "Oh, but don't worry," she called over her shoulder. "Unconventional universes work just like conventional ones . . . except when they don't."

"Where are you going?" Elo asked.

Dave, who had got about twenty feet in the direction of his "projected arch-to-surface junction," paused. "EXPLORING." He lurched into motion again, the treads of his mobility suit creating an undulating trail through the loose dirt.

"But you *can't*," Elo protested. "We have to locate another portal opening, or we might never get back."

"I HAVE ENOUGH NUTRIENTS STORED IN THIS SUIT TO LAST ME ANOTHER TWO THOUSAND HOURS WITHOUT REFRESH. I HAVE TIME."

"Well, *I* don't," Elo said, putting her paws on her hips and puffing her chest out.

"THEN FIND YOUR PORTAL. THIS PLACE INTERESTS ME."

Elo stood, watching Dave's retreating form, feeling the familiar sensation of being swept away by circumstances beyond her control. *Very much like the Professor,* she mused with the part of her brain that was not too irritated. She looked around at the empty landscape, at the disturbingly not-empty sky, and finally at her own paw-prints, which pattered around in a small circle from where she had landed. There was no knowing where the Oddity's portal nexus was, she would have to wander and hope she got lucky. And the range of such a nexus could be several thousand feet. Even miles, on the outside.

If that was the case, might as well wander with company.

"If this takes too long," she told Dave, trotting up beside him, "I'm cracking open your suit and drinking your support fluid."

"THAT WOULD CAUSE HALLUCINATIONS."

"As long as it prevents dehydration, I don't care," Elo said.

Abruptly Dave changed course, nearly running her over.

"H-hey!" she protested, hopping out of the way.

"TERTIARY SCANS INDICATE LIQUID WATER LIKELY IN THIS DIRECTION," he said, picking up speed. So the two of them set off, headed along the impossible arch, towards where it disappeared behind a dark ridge on the horizon.

It was slow going. Not because the ground was rough—it was flat as a table and almost as hard—but because Dave had to stop every fifty feet to take dirt samples, which he stored in the compartments in the front of his suit.

The horizon, and the end of the arch, retreated before them, but the dark ridge slowly solidified into a train of craggy rocks, like the vertebrae of some gigantic beast. Elo bounded up this on all fours, while Dave was forced to navigate his way though the jumble of rocks, occasionally using his anti-gravity plates to shoot himself over ledges where there was no path. As it was, Elo reached the top long before he did, and found herself looking out over more of the same flat reddish-tannish earth, except that now, in the distance, she could discern a dark irregularity like a cluster of domed buildings, and a tower with a gently spinning windmill at its top.

"FARMING SETTLEMENT," Dave intoned when he caught up. "LIKELY UN-ARMED. EASILY FRIGHTENED. STILL RECOMMEND CAUTION." But he said it to the empty air; Elo was already down the other side of the ridge, trotting across the plain on all fours.

Movement among the distant buildings. Elo slowed, sniffed the air, then put her nose to the ground and sniffed again. She smelled dry dirt and sand, but in the distance there was the thick scent of moisture, and the unmistakable smell of organic life.

"Carbon-based, most likely," Elo whispered to herself, trying to emulate what the Professor might do. "One of them is very close . . . " she froze, realizing just how close the source was. It had been masked—cleverly—to blend in with the smell of dry dirt, and now she took her eyes off the settlement she saw a figure crouched against one of the red boulders cast off from the ridge she had just descended.

It was small, dark and humanoid, and as Elo watched, it extended a slim, four-fingered hand and waved at her, beckoning her to come. Elo trotted over, curious, and sniffing the whole way.

This person was certainly not human; it smelled too hot and spicy, more like a fox or a raccoon. But it looked very much like a human, a small female human with glossy skin so black it was almost blue, and two round eyes that stared at her from out of a dark, round head.

"Hello," Elo said, careful to make sure that her body language and tone of voice spoke the same. "I'm afraid I'm a bit lost, could you—"

The person's eyes went, if possible, even wider, and she raised a finger to her lips and shushed earnestly. She pointed over the rock she hid behind, to where

Dave was picking his way through the debris at the bottom of the ridge, a little metallic gem in a sea of dusty brown.

"Oh, that's okay," Elo said. "That's Dave, he's a friend of mine, he's—"

But she was cut off by the person, who spoke quickly in a soft, quiet voice, making complicated gestures with her hands. To Elo's acute disappointment it was not a language she knew, nor even one she recognized. It was all tumbling, tooting words, and the person spoke it so earnestly it was clear she wished Elo to understand.

"No, I'm sorry," Elo said, shaking her head. "I can't understand you."

But the person seemed to understand Elo—at least a little. Her dark face bunched up in concentration, and then she said—very carefully, with little hoots between each word:

"Livin, hoo, peace-hoo? Friendov hoo Bo-fellow?"

It took a moment for Elo to parse this, but when she did she smiled and nodded. "Yes, yes I come in peace. Though I do not know who this Bo-fellow is, I'm afraid."

The person shot another worried look over her rock; Dave had been making swift progress across the level plain, and was now very nearly in hailing distance. Indeed, judging by the muted noises coming from his direction, he was already trying.

"Fellow, fellow," hooted the person, and took off at a low running walk, beckoning Elo to follow. When she didn't do this immediately, the person came back and shooed her, with her little hands in flat plates, palms out, but never touching her. Elo was obliged to get up and come along. Behind them, Dave followed indignantly.

They made very good progress, until the rain. It happened once they were already thick in a belt of swirling gray cloud, and Alister had to go slowly for fear of breaking his neck in some terrible fall. The Professor, who was more accustomed than he to trail blazing, invariably got ahead of him. But she always waited, and just when Alister thought he was lost he would catch a glimpse of her fiery red-and-yellow wig, and he would find her.

Until one time he didn't.

It was pouring rain, and at the same time there were thick swathes of clouds packing in all around him. The one mercy was that the rain was warm—but it was so warm that Alister found it unnerving, and it made all the jumbled rocks even more slick and sharp than ever. He crouched beneath a small overhang and shouted, "*Professor!*" into the gray and twisting rain, but all he got in response was the sharp patter of water on rock.

After a time the rain ceased, but the clouds packed in more tightly than ever. Alister leaned on his rock and considered his options: everything he had ever learned about being lost told him not to wander around—it only made you more lost. But he didn't know that the Professor wasn't as lost as he, and he couldn't know if there was anyone else on this world who would help him. Another thing he realized, as soon as it stopped raining, was that he was terribly thirsty. And now that the rain had stopped, he thought he heard, in the distance, the sound of water running.

It will do no good if I sit here and die of thirst, he thought to himself, so he got up and crawled off toward the sound of the water.

It was torturously slow going at first, until Alister slid down a boulder and found himself out of the clouds. The air was still misty, but he could now see almost fifty feet ahead of him into the maze of rocky slabs, and through the jumble he was able to discern a path. For the first time in hours Alister stood up and walked briskly, in the direction of the watery sounds.

Strangely, these sounds, instead of getting louder, seemed to grow fainter and fainter the closer he approached, so what he had first taken to be the sounds of a small river soon dwindled to a tiny stream, and finally—as he climbed up a steep set of steps carved into a marble cliff—the mere drip and plink of water dripping into a pool. But he barely paid attention to these details—he was so thirsty—and scrambled up the cliff.

The top was a wide, flat marble surface, with a pool of steaming water in its center. Alister crawled over to it, and was just about to dip his hands in to drink, when a voice spoke from beyond the pool.

"I would not drink that, if I were you . . . "

It was a man's voice. A hoarse voice, as if the owner himself were thirsty, or had been screaming a lot. And somehow the sound of it sent shivers down Alister's spine.

Slowly he looked up, and the world slanted horribly as one version jammed into another. Alister had to press the back of his hand against his mouth to keep himself from screaming, and it was a lucky thing he did not tumble off the marble cliff the way he started backwards.

As he stared the pool ran red, and he saw it was not water, but blood, and beyond the steam, misty but visible, there was a man.

He looked at first as if he were standing, but this was only because he had been tied against an upright slab of marble in such a way that it was impossible for him to sit. His feet were in iron manacles bolted to the stone, and his hands were bolted high above his head, which was pulled back at a sharp angle by a complex web of rope braided into his dark hair. He was naked save for a scraggily piece of bleached cloth around his loins, and thin enough that each of his ribs were visible. He was so pale he was almost green—the same color as the marble—but his eyes were such a piercing bright brown it was clear he was alive and alert.

There was an ugly wound under his seventh right rib, puffy and red and half scabbed over, but what made Alister's stomach squirm was the sight of the small groove that had been carved into the marble directly beneath the wound, running down the rock beside him, and then over the flat stone to the pool: it was dark and crusty with dried blood.

The man took a breath. A deep, shaking one, but it reminded Alister that this was a living person chained to the rock, not some monster. He took his hand from his mouth and crawled slowly around the pool, eyeing the iron clamps and bolts, wondering if he could break them open. The man's eyes rolled downward in their sockets, following him.

"Who are you?" Alister whispered. "And . . . who did this to you?"

The man seemed amused by the question. He strained his head to one side, and glanced down along his nose at Alister. He had a fine, aquiline nose, perfect for looking down. "It would be better if I asked you the first question," he rasped. "You're not from this world. How did you get here?"

Alister thought back to the hectic scramble inside the Oddity, just before Elo and Dave had fallen through.

"By accident," he said. "My name is Alister Bane, I'm traveling with a woman—well, she *looks* like a woman, sort of—called Professor Odd. Her hair is half red and half yellow, have you seen her?"

The man on the rock shut his eyes and leaned his head back against the stone. He stayed that way so long Alister wondered if he had gone to sleep—or died; he was hardly breathing.

Then a great scraping inhale signaled the man was about to speak again. His eyes opened, and he said: "Your companion has no hair; she has a tentacle. She is in the Chasm and . . . " he stopped, took another breath, "she is in very great danger."

Alister just gaped at the man. Perhaps he was psychic. Psychics would exist in unconventional universes, right? Then why bother to tie him up, if he could kill you with his brain? Then what he had actually said registered in Alister's own.

"Danger? Oh, isn't that just *typical*. Where is she again?"

"The Chasm," the man said, and he looked very hard at a place beyond the pool of blood. It took Alister a moment to realize that, since all other parts of him had been nailed down, *looking* was this man's way of pointing at things. And when he turned to look, Alister saw a little ledge, and a path running down from the marble cliff.

"The path will take you into the Chasm," the man said, his voice growing even more faint. "Do not let yourself be seen, especially by the Hooded Ones. Bring this . . . Professor back to see me. She feels . . . interesting."

"Oh, oh I will," Alister promised. "And I'm sure she'll find a way to get you . . . uh . . . free . . . " he eyed the bolts holding the iron chains in place.

"That is . . . good." The man's eyes closed, and he went back to sleep. Or to being dead. Alister watched his chest carefully, trying to see if it rose or fell. What he did notice, staring at all that bare skin, were goosebumps. The man must be freezing. A little awkwardly, since the man was so tall, Alister took his own blazer and draped it over the man's front, tucking the sleeves behind his shoulders to hold it in place. With the purple there it made his skin look even more dead and greenish, but Alister noticed a faint pink tinge come into the man's hollow cheeks, and he walked away feeling a little pleased . . . until he remembered how thirsty he still was.

But on the whole, he reasoned, being thirsty was a great deal better than being bled out on a marble slab. He found the path the man had indicated, and began making his way carefully down it.

Behind him, on the stone, the man opened one eye—one eye was all he had the energy for—and examined the vibrantly purple garment that had been thrown over him. And then he did something he had not done in a very long while: he *smiled.*

The hooting was beginning to get on Elo's nerves. *Like being in a village of owls,* she thought to herself as her friend led her, hooting all the while, into the town square. From within, the village appeared much like a human one, except built all over for humans who had a median height of about four feet. Which was to say, though it would have struck the Professor or Alister as cramped and small, to Elo it seemed just the right size.

There were dark little houses decorated with bright red and yellow and green paint, and the doors were all different shades of blue. And on the sides of the houses, under the eaves and even sprawling onto the roofs, were plants—the first plants Elo had seen on this desolate world. Climbing plants swarmed up the walls, and bushes with berries and herby shrubs were held in baskets.

She only caught brief glimpses of these, however, for as soon as they entered the village they began to attract attention. Little black figures swarmed out of the blue doors and clustered around them; they seemed neither fearful nor hostile, but curious, like puppies who have met a cat for the first time. Elo's friend began speaking to them in her strange, hooting language, and they all began hooting back. But none of them came near enough to touch Elo, and so they passed, un-molested, through the village and into its center square.

It should not really have been called a square, though, for it was a perfect circle, whose borders were picked out with somber stone monoliths. Within the stones was bare level ground, the center of which was taken up by an awning of cloth supported by a ring of wooden posts within the ring of stones. Under the awning was a garden stuffed full of big plants with glossy leaves, and in the center of this was a well, full to the brim with clear, still water.

But Elo was no longer focused on the water (her friend had let her drink out of her water pouch earlier), but on the statue that rose up beyond it. A perfect fang of pale marble, fashioned into the rough likeness of a human, with a bowed head and sloping shoulders. Over these shoulders had been placed a mantle of intricately woven cloth, the same pale white-green as the rock.

There was another figure beside the well, whom Elo did not notice right away, he was so small and dark. But when he moved, and spoke, she snapped all her attention to him.

"Hoomrah says you speak the Bo-fellow's tongue, is this true, desert walker?"

He was even smaller than her friend, shriveled like an overripe fig and wearing only a leather loincloth. As if to make up for this, on his head rested a wreath of living plants, half in bloom with tiny blue flowers, and around his neck were draped strings of dried fruit and nuts. His little black face peered at Elo in the leafy twilight under the canopy, and he did not seem unkind.

"I'm not sure who this Bo-fellow is," Elo said politely. "I've never met him."

The little man's eyes grew so wide all the whites could be seen around his dark irises, and his hands clapped together.

"Fascinating," he murmured. "You speak with his tongue. In his language. Did you come through the Chasm?"

"The Chasm?" Elo said blankly. Then: "Oh, you mean the canyon? With the weird thing overhead?"

"The Chasm is the great crack in the world," the little man explained hopefully. "Many things come through the Chasm. For a while she gave us water and food and magic. Then she gave us the Bo-fellow."

"Ah," said Elo. "I see. But no, we came through in the desert."

"We?" The little man put his head sideways at her. "Is there another concealed about your person?"

Elo sighed. She had heard Dave approach, as quietly as he could, and knew he was hiding somewhere around the edge of the awning.

"No," she said, and craned her neck around. "Dave, come on out. I'm pretty sure they're friendly."

There was a hushed gasp as Dave rolled out into the open. But no one screamed, no one ran away, and the little man only leaned his head to the other side and frowned.

Dave came to a halt at Elo's side, and swiveled all his sensors around to focus on the little man. With as much incredulity as his processed voice could muster, he said: "DID YOU JUST SAY *MAGIC?*"

Alister did not notice the houses right away, they were so cunningly hidden in the rock. What he did notice, because he tripped over it, was the pile of little dolls made of something very like dried corn husks. This was the sort of doll made by taking one piece of husk and tying it crosswise to another, thus creating a vaguely human shape. Except with all these dolls the crosswise pieces—the arms—had their ends bent back and tied above the dolls' heads. Alister shivered, and moved on.

The houses became more frequent after that. These were round, globby things, made of dried mud the same color as the rock. The first time Alister saw one it gave him quite a start, for it had one round door and two round windows, one on each side, which gave the impression of a face locked in a perpetual stare of surprise and horror. They crowded in around him, these staring houses, and in the dull twilight of the canyon it became easier and easier to imagine he was surrounded by horrified monsters. To make matter worse, he became fairly certain he was not alone: scrabbling, scraping noises suggested little feet running away inside the structures as he approached, adding to the feeling of being watched.

Light bloomed before him, and Alister found he had come to the head of a chasm, where the path split and ran down covered walkways set into the side of the cliffs. The light came from hundreds of tiny windows set into the rock, each one square and orange. These were thickest at Alister's level, but they stretched down into the darkness of the chasm, growing thinner as they went, like an inverted night sky.

So taken was he by the sight that Alister quite forgot the creepy houses, and he went to stand behind the rough stone parapet that stood between the path and the chasm. Music drifted up from the right-hand side of the canyon, and Alister decided he would go that way. Logically, he reasoned, the Professor would go where things seemed interesting, and it would be more interesting to see what the music was about than not.

The music, which grew clearer as he made his way down the canyon path, was mostly drums, backed by a chorus of chanting voices. It gave Alister an uncomfortable, guilty feeling, as though he were listening in on a private conversation.

There were no houses here. Rather, the path was carved into the face of the cliff, and there were networks of tunnels leading away into it. Once, Alister passed a low, gaping cavern that stretched away into a dark distance within the rock, supported by countless stone pillars. Not long after that he came upon the chanters. They were gathered in a similar cavern, only this one was higher, grander, and lit with flaming torches. At the far end, where the torches were brightest, there was a raised stone dais, and on it stood three figures; two were swathed in white robes, and the third was the effigy of a man. Made of a bark-like substance, its stiff arms had been tied above its head, and at its feet was a large clay bowl. Alister couldn't see what was in it, as between him and the dais was a small army of similar white-robed figures.

It was a lucky thing they were all chanting and facing away from him, for Alister gave out an involuntary *"Oh!"* when he saw the effigy. Then he covered his mouth in horror and shrank back into the shadow of a nearby pillar. From there, if he leaned his head out a bit, he could still see the figures on the dais, but not the drummers. He assumed they must be scattered about in the crowd, for the drumming was quite loud, and sounded like it came from everywhere.

The figures on the dais seemed to be going through some kind of ritual. But without any knowledge of the language or custom Alister found it difficult to follow. It seemed to center on the effigy, and near the end one of the robed figures took a knife that glinted in the torchlight, and stabbed it into the effigy's side. Alister had no trouble recognizing that, and he grimaced.

But then it got worse. The other robed figure lifted the bowl, and its contents sloshed so that Alister caught a glimpse of something dark and red. Then the figure lifted it to the face of its partner, who brought the bowl to its mouth and—

Alister turned away in disgust, and ran right into the cloaked person who had come to stand behind him.

Even though it only came up to his chest, Alister somehow found himself thrown onto the ground, and strong sinewy arms held him there. There was a shuffle, and several more of the cloaked people appeared, their faces hidden by their hoods in the uncertain torchlight.

When Alister felt them pulling his arms back and tying them together he kicked at them, a little desperately, and cursed. For his efforts he got a wedge of scratchy cloth stuffed in his mouth, and a black cloth bag over his head. Hands like little pincers pinched him, made him walk. He tripped on something hard he could not see, and after that he was dragged.

What with not being able to breathe very well and not being able to see at all—thanks to the bag over his head—Alister lost track of where they took him, except for the last bit: they hauled him down a flight of very hard and painful stairs. Then there was a scrape of metal on stone, and another tumble as they pushed him over.

Alister landed with a hard *smack* on a cold stone floor, where he lay quite still waiting for his head to stop spinning and his breathing to return to normal.

"Oh, Mr Alister," said an unforgettable voice out of the darkness. "*There* you are!"

Hands—proper, full-sized hands that did not pinch—ran over his arms and untied them. As soon as they were free he ripped the bag off his head and spat out the hateful piece of cloth.

"Professor?" he gasped thickly; his mouth was parched and it was difficult to speak.

"The one and only," Professor Odd said, helping him to sit up.

They were in a small dark cell—very dank and cold—with one high barred window that let in just enough wan gray light for Alister to make out the shape of Professor Odd, and the metal grill which acted as a door. There was a pan half full of water, which the Professor helped him drink, and a small piece of hard brown bread stuff, which they unanimously decided not to touch.

"What are you doing in here?" Alister asked, even though he knew it was a stupid question. He was just so surprised to see her, he could not think to ask anything else.

"Waiting for you," Professor Odd said cheerfully. She pulled her legs in and sat cross-legged on the floor next to Alister, twiddling her thumbs. "I didn't realize I'd lost you until I was down in the canyon. I went to ask some directions from those robed fellows, but they put me in here instead. I thought of just leaving again, but then I realized that if *you* made it down to the canyon they'd probably do the same to you. So I decided to wait, and here you are!"

"Professor," Alister said, laughing a little despite himself, "This is a *dungeon*, we can't just get up and *leave*."

"You can if the door's unlocked," Professor Odd said simply.

"But it's . . . " Alister crawled over and rattled the grill.

Something soft and cool and boneless poked at his shoulder. He turned around to find the Professor waving her tentacle at him.

"They used a warded lock," she said gleefully. "Sit tight, I'll have this open in a jiffy." She scrambled over and leaned her back up against the grill, grinning brightly. "Sometimes I don't know how you lot manage with only two arms."

Shaking his head, Alister came to sit beside her, peering out into the darkness.

"Those people in robes, who do you think they are? Natives?" he asked.

"Probably," Professor Odd said.

Alister leaned his forehead against the grate. Even though everything was silent and still as far as he could see, he could not help the feeling that something terrible was about to happen. The man tied to the rock had said the Professor was in danger. He had also said not to be seen by the Hooded Ones. Oops.

"Do you think they're dangerous?" he asked.

"Probably—*ouch!*" Professor Odd withdrew her tentacle and sucked on the tip. Frowning she stuck it back through the grate and tried again.

"I think they're . . . I dunno . . . *priests*."

"Cult leaders, more like." Professor Odd was having more trouble with the lock, and was not paying much attention.

"No," Alister said, thinking of the effigy and the straw dolls. And the knife. "I think they're priests."

"Sometimes it's hard to tell the difference," the Professor observed.

Alister, who had known some very kind religious people back home, frowned at her. "But what if what they worshipped was *real?*"

"There are no such things," Professor Odd said firmly, "as gods."

"Not even in an unconventional universe?" Alister prodded.

The Professor paused, turned her cat eyes on him. "Then things get *tricky*," she said.

"I'm asking because . . . " Alister took a deep breath, "You see, after I lost you in the fog . . . I found this man . . . "

"I am Shaman Loorik," the little man explained. "I am the thirteenth Shaman of the Old Family, and the inheritor of Grand Shaman Kuuork, who led us out of the Chasm."

They were seated under the awning. Padded stools had been brought for Elo and for Hoomrah, and a little carpet placed diffidently beside Dave, but he ignored it. Around them, half-hidden in the jungle of potted plants, it seemed most of the village had gathered, as if it were story-time and they were children about to be put to bed.

"We are the Old Family. We left the Chasm, we follow the words of the Bo-fellow. We oppose the Hooded Ones."

"I'm sorry," Elo interrupted. "Just who is the Bo-fellow?"

Shaman Loorik pointed with a little black hand at the marble statue with its shawl of flowers.

"Yes, I figured that," Elo said. "But *who* is he?"

"IS HE *REAL?*" Dave asked. Elo smacked his metal siding.

"He is certainly real," Shaman Loorik said, his back stiffening. "My predeces-sor spoke with him on many occasions. He is the anchor that is holding this world together. This world is in a very bad way. You noticed the falling sky?"

"That big, lightning bolty thingy?" Elo said. "Oh yes."

"The Bo-fellow caught that. He stopped the whole world from flying apart, and for his efforts the Hooded Ones chained him. He brought us magic, and the knowledge of how to escape, but the Hooded Ones like it here. They don't want him to let us leave."

"Leave, leave this world?" Elo asked.

Shaman Loorik fixed his bright black eyes on her and said, very seriously, "This world is not our world, and it will be ending soon. We must go home."

Elo and Dave looked at each other in that awkward way people do when they realize they are talking to an insane person. Though in Dave's case it was only a subtle slide of his optics dish.

"And . . . er . . . how do you intend to get home?" Elo asked cautiously.

Shaman Loorik squinted at her. He seemed to be thinking. He posed a ques-tion in his native hooting language to someone hidden in the foliage. To Elo's con-sternation, hoots of varying tones replied from all around them. Some sounded excited. Others doubtful. A few sounded angry, but these were quickly quashed by their neighbors, and the general consensus seemed to be one of cautious ap-proval. Finally Shaman Loorik turned back to face them, and said very gravely:

"We are building a portal."

There was a whirring of servos as all of Dave's sensory equipment swiveled around to focus on the shaman. Elo could see (because Elo knew where to look) the dim outline of the creature inside, all pressed up against the inside of the glass, staring as well.

"EXPLAIN," Dave said. "YOU DO NOT HAVE SUFFICIENT TECHNOLOGY FOR CREATING AND SUSTAINING INTER-UNIVERSAL TRAVEL. HOW ARE YOU MAKING A PORTAL?"

Shaman Loorik looked rather taken aback. He shrugged and said, as if it were obvious: "Why, with *magic*, of course."

There was the smallest of *clicks* and the metal grate swung open. Professor Odd sat looking through it into the dark for some moments, apparently digesting what Alister had told her.

"How tall was he?" she asked eventually.

Not what Alister was expecting. He summoned up a mental image of the man chained to the rock, trying to factor in his extreme thinness and his unusual position.

"Tall . . . " he said eventually. "Taller than me, probably."

"A giant?" Professor Odd asked, almost hopefully.

"No," Alister said. "Just . . . tall."

Professor Odd sighed, grabbed up her cane, and disappeared through the grate. Alister scrambled after her, trying not to stub his toes or bang his head against anything in the dark.

"What's so important about him being *tall?*" Alister hissed once he had caught up. "I told you, he *knew* you. He knew you'd be in danger. He's . . . he's *alive*, somehow. *What is he?*"

The Professor had stopped at a fork in the tunnel, and was balancing her banana-handled cane across her palm, Alister could just make out the handle as a pale glint in the otherwise dim cave.

Like the needle on a compass, the end slowly rotated, pointing to the left-hand path.

Professor Odd hefted her cane jauntily and started down it, now with considerably more confidence. Alister grabbed one of her shoulders and followed.

"He is not a god," the Professor said. "He is a prime example of some poor sod in the *Promethean Predicament.*"

"The what?"

"Tell me you know who *Prometheus* was," Professor Odd said, giving Alister's hand a light smack with her tentacle.

"Wasn't he a Greek god?" he ventured. Mythology was not his strong suit.

"He was a Titan, actually," she said. The tunnel they were in had begun to climb, and they were forced to begin using their hands as well. The Professor continued her explanation in jerks as they did so. "He stole fire—bugger, that rock is loose—from Olympus. He gave it to the humans, so the Olympian gods—well, Zeus, mostly—*ouch!* Zeus chained him to a rock and set a vulture on him to eat out his liver every day."

Alister thought of the pool of blood and the ceremony with the people in robes. He shuddered.

"Dare I ask . . . what happened to Prometheus in the end?"

"I'm not saying this guy *is* Prometheus," Professor Odd snapped. She had come to a steep part and was looking for a good foothold. "I'm saying—ah-*ha!*—he's in a very similar *situation.* And that situation just happens to be called after *Prometheus.* I think we're almost out."

They had come to what appeared to be a dead end, and it was pitch black. But Alister could hear the Professor scrabbling around on the rocks, and a moment later a trap door swung open and a pale stormy light flooded into the cavern. Alister had to cover his eyes against the glare as Professor Odd shinnied up the chimney, her back against one side and her legs on the other, her cane between her teeth.

Alister slipped when he tried to do the same, and the Professor had to lie on her belly and haul him up. The rocks were jagged and painful, and Alister's knees and elbows were smarting and his knuckles were grazed by the time he joined her outside.

"Not that Prometheus was the first to suffer that fate," Professor Odd remarked while Alister rubbed his smarting legs.

They had emerged onto a small plateau where a piece of the canyon wall jutted away from the rest. Half the sky was cut off by a wedge of brownish-red stone, and the rest was a stormy tangle of clouds.

A little path led away from the ledge, and at its head was a small pile of straw people, their arms tied over their heads. Professor Odd crawled over and picked one up, examining it with her brow scrunched together. "And as you discovered, he wasn't the last, either." She looked around the little cliff, curling her tentacle into a tight knot at the base of her neck. "We should move quietly from here," she said.

"Magic is common in the world we came from," Shaman Loorik explained as he led them through the village. "The Hooded Ones had less. We are a sibling people, but while our world was rich in magic, theirs was poor. We both came into this world when the Chasm opened in ours, sucking in all it could take. We found ourselves here, in this half-made place. But there was always a little life at the bottom of the Chasm, where magic leaked in from other worlds. We lived with the Hooded Ones, separate, but not fighting.

"Then, in the days of Shaman Kuuork, the Chasm closed. At once the world began to die, and a great calamity appeared in the sky in the form of that stone lightning. Then the Bo-fellow appeared. He halted the fall of the stone lightning, and he told us to flee this world before it ended. He told us we must make a portal and go back to our own world. We were glad at this news, for we have always known we do not belong here. So we began helping him to build our portal, but before we could finish, the Hooded Ones found out. They did not want to go home. They had forgotten their old home and thought the end of this world would mean the end of them.

"They destroyed our portal, they caught the Bo-fellow and chained him. They attempted to kill us. Many died. The rest followed Shaman Kuuork out of the Chasm and into the Desert. The Hooded Ones do not dare follow us here. They think we all died. They are wrong."

The shaman had stopped outside a little hut made of leafy branches. "We have not forgotten the Bo-fellow. He is still holding the world together. And we are re-building our portal. But progress is slow. We have not the Bo-fellow's knowledge. We do not know how to finish it."

Shaman Loorik stood back, and with a grand sweep of his scrawny arm he pulled aside the large leaf that was serving as a screen. And there, in a little hut built of branches lashed together with grass rope and roofed with waxy leaves, was the portal.

It could be nothing else. It looked rather like the Oddity's door: a black square leading nowhere, except it was fuzzy around the edges, and Elo could just make out the branches on the other side of it. It was framed by a wicker doorway, which seemed in places to have been burnt or melted. Now and then little lights would swirl in the depths of the portal, or it would wink out of sight completely, only to reappear a moment later.

Dave regarded it silently for some moments, then rolled slowly toward it. At once a dozen dark hands fell upon his suit, stopping him, and Shaman Loorik let the leaf fall back into place.

"Do not approach, do not approach!" he cried. "It is *unstable.*"

"HOW SO?" Dave asked.

"Things go inside, then come right back out again. Sometimes they are as they were, sometimes . . . " he trailed off, looking uncomfortably at his feet.

"You don't mean to say you've sent *people* through that thing? Without know-ing where it *leads?*" Elo exclaimed, her hackles going up.

"No, no, we would never send a *person,*" Shaman Loorik looked horrified. He fiddled with the many artifacts tied to his belt, and produced a small fruit, the size of his fist. Elo saw it was smooth and round and red, hard like an apple. "We tested it, like this," and so saying he pulled the leaf back and lobbed the little red fruit into the blackness. There was a shower of sparks as it entered, then nothing.

Then, with a sound like someone hiccuping, it bounced back out again. It rolled to the shaman's feet, and he picked it up and offered it to Elo.

She turned it over in her paws, her eyes wide.

The fruit was still red, it was still hard, but it had sprouted miniature versions of itself all over, as if someone had tossed it into a kaleidoscope, frozen the distorted image, and pulled it out again.

An armor-encased tentacle reached out and took it. Dave brought it right up to the bigger sensor dish on his front, and examined it for a moment before handing it back to Elo.

"YOU HAVE FAILED TO CALIBRATE FOR WORLD-BRANCHING, AND YOU DO NOT HAVE AN EXIT," he announced.

Shaman Loorik blinked at him. "I told you, we do not know how to finish it."

Dave produced a weird, electronic noise that Elo interpreted roughly as "Hummph!" He rolled into the tiny hut and passed behind the strange portal, emerging a few moments later on the other side.

"I HAVE NEVER SEEN A PORTAL OF THIS CONSTRUCTION BEFORE. IT WILL TAKE ME SOME TIME TO FIX."

"But, you can fix it?" Elo asked, and behind her there was an excited murmur from the crowd.

"MAYBE. IN TIME. I WILL REQUIRE ASSISTANCE."

Shaman Loorik came forward, a little hesitantly, for he was still shy of Dave. "Any aid that myself or the Family can give—"

"NOT YOURS." Dave interrupted, making the poor little man flinch. Dave slid his sensor array over to Elo, who was beginning to get an idea of what he might need.

"It's not a conventional portal," she murmured. "It's a magical one. Dave, you're not a very magical person, are you?"

"CORRECT."

"So, you need someone who knows about magic."

"CORRECT."

If he had teeth, Elo thought, he would be grinding them. She turned to Shaman Loorik, her hackles going up despite herself.

"Which way to the Chasm?" she asked. "I'm going to bring you this Bo-fellow."

There was a hush. Then murmuring from the crowd as her words were translated and passed on. Finally it erupted into a chaos of shouting and waving arms as the villagers began exclaiming and arguing with each other. They swept past Shaman Loorik, who was still staring at her, stunned, and clustered around Elo. Hands grabbed at her paws, arms tried to embrace her, and the little girl who had met her in the desert—Hoomrah, that was her name—jumped onto her shoulders, laughing and cheering.

In the end it was decided that Elo would go alone, accompanied by Hoomrah, who knew the desert well and could guide her, and Dave would remain in the village and do what he could to fix the portal. At first this caused a cry of protest; many of the villagers, it seemed, were quite keen on the idea of staging an all-out attack on the Chasm, but Elo and Shaman Loorik talked them out of this.

"I'm just going to go in, find this Bo-fellow, and bring him back," she explained. "We're in enough trouble, we don't need to start a war!"

Eventually the sense of this became apparent, and so, fortified with packs of food and canteens of water, Elo and Hoomrah set off in the direction of the Chasm. The desert was wide and flat and grayish-brown, and the clouds hung ominously dark overhead.

Alister knew they were coming out of the canyon when it began to rain again. They had followed the cliffside path winding slowly up, and now they crept under a slight overhang that shielded them somewhat from the weather. So far they had been lucky, and their way had been deserted. But the little doorways into the cliff showed this had not always been so, and Alister took care to walk in silence, following in the Professor's stealthy footsteps.

Then, abruptly, the little doors ended. The path took a sharp right turn and plunged down the cliff in a smooth trench of sandy stone. Professor Odd began to clamber down it, backwards and using her hands as well as her feet, her cane tucked through the belt of her coat like a pirate's sword.

Alister hesitated. He did not like the shiny wet look of the stone, nor the distance to the rock bottom. But the Professor was nearly halfway down, and he liked even less the prospect of being alone by the abandoned houses. So he followed, taking care to look between his legs for footholds or ledges to put his feet on.

The last ten feet were even steeper, and slippery. Alister lost his grip and slid down, landing by the Professor in a pile of straw dolls. Nursing his burning hands he got up, and to his astonishment he saw they had come to the head of the canyon, where he had first begun to notice the globby houses. The pile of straw dolls he was lying in was the same one he had tripped over coming down.

The Professor had got her cane out again, and was balancing it across her hand, waiting for the end to turn, but Alister pulled at her sleeve.

"I know the way from here," he said, and started up the path, back the way he had originally come.

It was harder going up. Alister was tired, and getting thirsty again. He tried leaning his head back to catch rain in his mouth, but this never got him more than a few drops, and half of those landed in his nose. Eventually he took to walking with his hands cupped in front of him, and licked up what water he caught every few minutes.

Professor Odd walked slowly. She was examining her cane, and her brow was all scrunched together in a frown. When he asked her what was wrong all she said was: "I'm getting a prickly feeling. I don't like it. But I've felt it somewhere before . . ."

"Here?" Alister asked, remembering the way the man on the rock had made him feel.

"No," said the Professor. "A long, long time ago." Suddenly she looked up, and Alister saw her cat pupils had dilated so that her eyes were huge black orbs. Her nostrils flared. "We're getting close."

And they were. A white marble cliff rose out of the mist in front of them, and there was the sound of running water.

"Don't be fooled," Alister warned as they began to climb the polished steps up the side of the precipice. "It's only a trickle, and it isn't water."

Even with all the Professor's talk of unconventional universes and god-like beings, Alister had begun to worry that the man might have died on them while he was away. Or would not be there at all, only a figment of his deluded brain. But when he reached the top of the cliff there he was, still tied to his rock across the pool of blood. He hadn't moved an inch. Probably, Alister thought, he couldn't. But he still had Alister's purple coat draped over him, and there was a flush of pink in his cheeks that had not been there before.

Feeling inordinately pleased with himself, Alister reached down and gave Professor Odd a hand up the last few feet.

"Well, there he is," he said, and pointed, proudly.

Part Two

PROFESSOR ODD'S reaction was extraordinary. She blinked across the pool at the man, as if she were having a hard time seeing him. Then her eyes went wide, her pupils contracted into narrow slits, and her jaw dropped. And she sat there, frozen, staring, and speechless.

This was not the reaction Alister had expected, if he had expected one at all. He was used to Professor Odd taking the lead, and so for a moment he too sat and stared, speechless. After a while he got up and went over to the man. He wasn't sure what he meant to do; wake him up? Ask him what he wanted? But before he could make up his mind the man opened one eye and looked down at him steadily.

"Oh good," he said hoarsely. "You're back. How long has it been?"

Alister shrugged. "Only a few hours."

At that the other eye came open. He leaned his head as far forward as he could, and glanced around them. Spotting Professor Odd, he smiled wanly. "I take it this is your esteemed friend, the Professor?"

Professor Odd stood up. She seemed torn, uncertain. Alister had never seen her look so; like a frightened cat. "Great hitch," she whispered her voice as hoarse as his. "Is that *you?*"

The man blinked. "You know me?" he seemed surprised.

The Professor took a step forward. She seemed hesitant, but hopeful. "Of course I know you! Fairbridge University? Dunchurch College? The Professor Odd!"

But the man on the rock was shaking his head.

Professor Odd froze. She was halfway around the pool of blood, her cane in one hand, the other outstretched toward the man on the rock. Slowly, she withdrew it. She rubbed her chin.

"*I know* you," she said, her eyes narrowing in thought. "But you don't know me. Or, you don't know me *yet*. Oh . . . oh *dear . . .* "

"Maybe he forgot you?" Alister suggested. Though he doubted it himself; the Professor was not a forgettable person.

"I do not forget," the man on the rock said. Almost at the same time, Professor Odd spoke:

"No, no it isn't that simple, I'm afraid." She held up the cane, looking from it to the man and back again. "*You* were the unseen force acting on my cane. *You* were the one that brought us here. I think you were calling for help."

The man nodded. "I anticipated someone would come, but to be honest I was expecting a friend."

Professor Odd smiled a little, sad smile. "Oh, I *am*. I may not appear so at first, but I *am a friend*. Apparently you just haven't met me yet." She twirled her cane and came right around the pool to where the man was hung in his chains. "This cane," she explained, "it, er, it comes from *your* native universe. Let's just say that. It must have picked up the call. Well, now we're here there's no time to waste! Alister, I said it was the Promethean Predicament, and do you know what *happened* to Prometheus?"

Alister shook his head. "I asked you that before."

Professor Odd grinned a bright, white grin. "Heracles freed him. After he slew the vulture. I'm not sure if we'll be able to go *that* far but . . . Oh, if only you had your screwdriver, Mr Bane." She had encountered one of the huge metal bolts that fixed the chains into the rock.

"Use . . . " the man on the rock paused, he seemed to be nerving himself up for something. "Use the blood," he said.

"The blood?" Professor Odd glanced at the pool, wrinkling her nose.

"*My* blood," the man said.

Professor Odd looked from the man, to the pool (steaming faintly), and back to the man. Then back to the pool. Her mouth opened into a big round 'O' of understanding, and she thrust her cane through the belt of her coat and went to the edge of the pool, pushing up her sleeves.

"Best let me handle this," she said when Alister moved to help her. "It's powerful stuff, his blood, and I'm not sure how it would take to someone like you."

"Someone like me . . . what?" Alister asked, a bit hurt. He still thought of the man on the rock as *his* discovery and wanted to help in his escape any way he could.

"Someone from a world without magic," the Professor said, and, cupping her hands, she dipped them below the surface.

"Then, does that mean *your world*—" Alister began, but he was cut off.

"Nope!" Professor Odd yelped, springing up from the pool and dashing, her arms red to the elbow, over to the man. "It's as conventional as any of them," she cried, pouring her load over the nearest bolt, then wiping her hands and arms over the length of chain, trying to get the blood off. It was hard to see from all the red, but Alister could tell there were angry pink boils cropping up all over her forearms, where the blood had been.

"I am sorry," said the man. "I had no idea . . . "

"It's no matter, you will." She smiled fondly up at him. "Do I have to get all the chains or . . . "

"I think this will do," said the man hurriedly. "It's working."

Alister looked again. The blood that had been wiped over the chains had sunk into the metal, like water into porous rock. It stained them dark red, and as he watched, the metal began to dry, flake, and peel away. In minutes every part that had been touched by the man's blood had disintegrated into a brownish dust.

The chain collapsed. Using the freedom this allowed him, the man was able to untangle his right arm and leg, and using his hand he took some of his own blood from the wound in his side and smeared it over the chain that held his left limbs.

This still left the mess of ropes braided into his hair, so Alister climbed up on a handy ledge of rock and began to carefully untangle them. It was slow going, as the man's hair was greasy and the ropes had fused together in places. While Alister was so occupied, the man took Alister's coat and put it on properly. The sleeves were too short, and left a lot of pale, bony wrist showing, but the man seemed pleased.

"Purple is my color," he said. "I remember that now."

Alister shot him a look, then glanced at the Professor. She smiled and shrugged. "Well, it *is*."

Shaking his head Alister went back to untangling a particularly big knot. He had the idea, if he could get it out, that all the other knots would unravel and things would go much more quickly.

"I should warn you," the man said. "Freeing me might have . . . oh, let's say, *disastrous* consequences."

"Nonsense," Professor Odd said.

"I am perfectly serious," replied the man. "This . . . world . . . well, it's not a real world at all, and currently I am the only thing holding what it is together, thanks to the machinations of those Hooded Ones. Once I am free I shall no longer be bound to support it, and frankly, I do not think I have the strength to, even if I wanted."

"Hold it," Alister said. "What do you mean this world isn't *real*? Is it all a dream and we're going to wake up any second?"

"Sadly, no," said the man. "You can think of it as a bubble . . . or a puddle . . . that has been draining off energy and magic from many other worlds. Sometimes, it gets people too. You have already met some of them."

"Is that how you got here?" Alister asked.

"In a way," the man said, and shrugged. "I discovered the portal by which this world was siphoning off the magic from my own. In order to close it, I had to do so from the other side. *This* side. Then I was trapped. I thought I could appeal to the inhabitants to help me get us all home but . . . there were complications."

"Some of them *liked* it here," Professor Odd said.

The man tried to nod, but Alister exclaimed in frustration as this caused him to lose the end of the knot he was working on.

"My apologies. Yes, some of them had made themselves quite comfortable. They saw me as a sort of avenging angel. I tried to make them understand, you see, but I was very tired, and the world had already begun to unravel." He shrugged. "I failed. Well, not quite. A few of them listened to me. I told them to go live in the desert. I gave them instructions to build their own portal—a safe one—to take them home. I'm not sure if they succeeded or not."

The knot came free in Alister's hands, and a good half of the ropes that held the man's hair came loose. He paused, before moving on to the other side. "So what happens," he said, "when we set you free?"

The man rolled his eyes back to look up at Alister. He smiled weakly. "I should be able to delay the destruction long enough to get us out, provided my friends in the desert did make that portal."

Alister didn't move. He was thinking about Elo and Dave—where were they? Did they know what was happening? How would they find them before the world ended?

In the silence they could hear, echoing up below them, the sound of shuffling feet and faint chanting, growing closer.

"And *there's* the vulture," Professor Odd said, drawing the blade out of her cane.

"You don't seriously mean to fight them?" asked the man. He had gone rigid and was staring over the pool with such a look of horror on his face that it made Alister feel quite sorry for him.

"What? Of course not," said the Professor. "Stand aside, Alister. Sir, I'm very sorry, but trust me when I say *it will grow back.*"

The man's eyes went wide. He held perfectly still. Alister had to leap away as the Professor hopped up onto the ledge, and with her sword she cut away at the remaining ropes, taking a great deal of the man's hair with them.

As the last strands were broken and the man dropped like a stone—Alister had to catch him to keep him from falling into the pool of blood—there was the most horrible, tremendous crashing sound. The world began to shake. A rain of dust and flakes of rock showered around them, chopping the surface of the red pool.

"*Stop!*" gasped the man. His voice was ragged and hoarse, but he spoke with such authority that Alister, who had been tugging him away from the pool, froze.

Then he noticed that all the little flakes of rock and dust had frozen as well. They hung in the air like a jagged fog. Professor Odd reached out a hand and poked one: it went tumbling away, bouncing off other pieces of stone.

"Path to the left, out of the canyon," said the man through gritted teeth. "I won't be able to hold it much longer," and he pointed with a quivering finger up at the giant bolt of stone hanging above their heads.

As if this wasn't enough motivation, now that the deadly rain had been stopped Alister could hear the frantic pounding of feet coming up the path from the canyon. Clearly the Hooded Ones had dropped all pretext of order and ritual.

The path the man directed them to was a mere cleft in the otherwise sheer wall. It took both Alister and Professor Odd (who re-sheathed her sword into her cane so she could use both hands), working together, to lift the man up it, for he was too weak to climb on his own. But after that first horrid ascent they were able to walk more or less normally, supporting the man between them and using their free hands to push the cloud of floating rocks away from their faces.

Now the path was even and wide, switch-backing up the final cliff. As they went Alister could hear the man muttering feverishly under his breath, and after a few minutes he recognized what those words were:

" . . . continue on, turn here—not too steep, straighten out, a little steeper, now turn again . . . "

"Are you making up this path as we go along?" Alister asked accusingly.

"*Hush!*" hissed Professor Odd. "Yes, of course he is!"

The man continued to mutter, and the three continued to climb. When at last they crested the ledge of the cliff and emerged from the canyon into the clear desert air, Alister's legs were burning, and his mind was spinning. It was magic, it really was. *It was happening right in front of him.* His mind barely registered the wide, desolate plain before them, it was so distracted.

Between them he felt the man heave a deep, shaking breath, and with a distant rumble they could hear the sound of falling rock resume.

"Run," said the man quietly. Then, when they began to stumble slowly away from the edge, he said again, *"Run!"*

It was as if some unseen force grabbed Alister's legs and made them move. As if a great wind had picked up at their backs and blew them along. He sprinted, the Professor right alongside him, the man suspended between them, across the barren desert landscape. He didn't know where they were going, only that it was away from the canyon and the inevitable doom that lay there.

He didn't dare turn his head, but he heard the horrendous crashing, like thunder directly over them, as the impossible stone formation came tumbling down. Glancing to the side he saw Professor Odd look, and her face twisted into an uncomfortable grimace.

"—but the other canyon dwellers—?" she shouted, her words nearly lost in the wind and the thunder.

"I have done what I can to warn them," said the man. His eyes, set so deep in that gaunt face, actually shone with an inner light. "They have not earned more charity from me!"

From behind came a great clap of noise, then silence for a few moments, and then the trio were buoyed up on a pillow of sharp wind. It was sharp because of all the dust and fragments of rock in it, and these struck at Alister's back, stinging even through his clothes. He felt his legs slipping against the thin air, but still he kept running. There was nothing else he could do.

The dust cloud surged forward, threatening to engulf them, but then like receding surf it ebbed away, and they were left pelting clean through the air, some four or five feet above the flat desert rock. It was not until after they had gone on like this for another minute or so did the man let them down and allow them to stop running.

Alister tripped as they landed, and he fell hard onto his hands. The impact knocked what breath he had out of him, and for a moment his vision blurred. He gasped shallowly, shudderingly, and slowly the world swam back into focus. Still panting he sat up on his knees; the Professor was sitting in a similar attitude not far from him, and between them lay the man, face down, on the rock. As Alister watched he stirred, and putting his hands out he slowly turned himself over and stared up at the sky.

He looked awful, with half his hair long and greasy and the other half so short it stood up in ragged spikes. Even though he was taller than Alister, he was so thin the purple blazer looked big on him. His bony legs stuck out from under the tattered pale loincloth like toothpicks.

"It begins to unravel," he said softly.

Steeling himself against what he might find, Alister at last looked back toward the canyon.

It was still there; he could just make it out against the plane of the desert by the little black zigzag that cut through the reddish-tan rock. But the impossible stone lightning bolt was gone; the rock that had formed it now lay scattered across the desert in sharp-edged clumps and boulders. Up in the sky, where the lightning bolt had been, now there was nothing.

Really nothing: instead of a lightning bolt shaped rock, now there was a lightning bolt shaped tear in the sky. It was the same inky black-blue as the night sky outside the Oddity, and it seemed to be bleeding into the stormy gray sky of the world.

"How long do we have?" Professor Odd asked, practically.

The man opened his mouth to reply, but was cut off by a surprised shout from somewhere to their collective left. Three heads turned . . .

Elo and Hoomrah had been maybe halfway to the Chasm when the sky fell. Or at least part of it. That giant stone formation finally fulfilled its ominous threat and broke free of the sky, shattering as it did so. Much of it fell into the Chasm, more was pillowed out on a bubble of wind, showering the surrounding desert with rocks the size of automobiles. Elo and Hoomrah, being far enough away, retreated to the lee of a nearby crag and watched from relative safety as the stones came crashing down.

Elo felt a nervous twitch in her gut: she wondered at the fate of this Bo-fellow they had intended to rescue.

Amidst the whirl of rock and dusty wind and the smell of dead earth, another scent cut its way through. It was sharp and tinged with fear and sweat, and was mixed with two other scents: one blessedly familiar (the Professor!) and the other was . . .

Elo sneezed. She had never smelled anything like that before: all mixed up with ordinary human scents was a smell of ozone and wildflowers and dry earth after its first rain. She shook her head, scenting the air, trying to follow where they came from. Without thinking she left the safety of their crevice and began to trot back and forth, her nose in the air.

Hoomrah exclaimed in protest, but it was wasted on Elo, who had stopped paying attention to what she was hearing since she caught that first whiff of Alister and Professor Odd.

They were actually close by: not in the Chasm at all! Elo took off running on all fours, Hoomrah scrambling to catch up. The rain of rocks had ended, and above them in the sky the great crack of the void was spreading, but Elo paid it no attention. She was focused on the ground, where the rock turned from brownish-gray to reddish-tan, and where now she could see three dark figures sitting. Perking her ears forward she caught a snatch of conversation:

" . . . long do we have left?"

The Professor! Elo was so overcome with relief and excitement that she let out a shout that was closer to a bark, and hurled herself at the figure in the red and yellow wig.

"Elo!" cried the Professor in joy and astonishment, and welcomed the dog-like creature with open arms. Elo hit her like a small furry truck, and the two went over, shouting and laughing.

Hoomrah approached more cautiously. Clearly these were friends of Elo, and she liked Elo, but they were all so tall and pale, and one's hair was the wrong color, and another's was half too long and half too short. Then she looked again. Something about his face, the way his head turned and looked at the tangle of woman and dog, and the arch of his nose . . .

"Gentleman Bo-fellow!" she cried, and threw herself face down on the rock in front of him, as they were accustomed to do before his effigy every day.

"Oh, do get up, I've had quite enough of that," said the voice of her messiah, reproachful but not angry.

Slowly Hoomrah raised her head. Aside from being pale like uncooked bread, and even bonier than her grand-papa, he looked like most people. But tired. Very tired. And there were lines in his face that spoke of pain.

"Please forgive, not good with your speech," she began by way of explanation. "I come with *hurnt,* with Elo, seeing for you . . . "

"You came looking for us?" said the third person. Another uncooked bread-dough man. Hair messy and short, but comfortably brown. Eyebrows like two arched eagle wings, very strong and dark. Spoke with a strange lilt Hoomrah had trouble understanding. She had to think about his words before she figured out what they were.

"*Ola,* yes. The Dave sent us to seeing you. He is fixing our *hammera-colla*—er, portal."

At the mention of Dave Professor Odd pushed Elo off her and turned to look at Hoomrah. Hoomrah did not like the look of her eyes, but since she was clearly a friend of Elo she was not afraid.

"What did you say about Dave fixing a *portal?*" she asked.

"He stayed behind," Elo took over explaining. "In the oasis, that's where Hoomrah here comes from. There's a village in the oasis, and they've got a statue of *him,*" she jerked a thumb at the man, "and they say he's this Bo-fellow person who led them out of the Chasm and showed them how to build a portal. Only it's not working properly. Dave is trying to fix it, so we came to find him. And you."

"Is this Dave," the man interrupted, "a particularly magical person?"

"Dave? No, I don't think so," Professor Odd said. "He comes from a temporally advanced universe, and he's not human. He's not strictly a *he* either. But he's very intelligent. He'll figure something out."

The man didn't look convinced. He looked up at the crack in the sky, which had spread even as they had been talking. Then he looked at his companions. He seemed to be coming to a decision.

"Five, including myself," he said at length. He drew his knees up into his chest and, slowly, rose to his feet. He still looked unstable, so Professor Odd gave him her sword cane. He took it, gratefully, and at once a small change seemed to ripple over him. He breathed a little easier, he stood a little straighter. It was as if merely holding that cane was enough to make him feel better. He looked at it, surprised, and then at Professor Odd.

"This cane comes from *my* universe," he said blankly.

Professor Odd had also gone blank. "Yes," she said colorlessly. "I told you, it led us here."

The man looked at her intently, a question on the edge of his lips. Then he decided not to ask it, and instead turned to Hoomrah.

"We do not have much time," he said gently. "How far is your village?"

Hoomrah considered. "Five, maybe six *simmera*," she said.

"That would be about three miles," the man said.

"Or 4.828 kilometers," Professor Odd added for Alister's benefit.

The man looked back up at the growing crack in the sky. One piece of it had grown into a jagged arm that stretched right over their heads.

"Too far to walk," he murmured. He looked down at Hoomrah.

"I need you to do something for me," he said seriously. Hoomrah stood up straight. "At present I am still collecting my powers, so I cannot take us all directly to your village—on my own. I need you to manage the destination for me. I need you to think of your village. Can you do that? Think of it clearly, in every detail, exactly as you saw it last."

Hoomrah nodded, then squeezed her eyes shut as she imagined as hard as she could the village circle, with the standing stones and the Bo-fellow's effigy.

"Everyone draw close," said the man, ushering them in with the cane.

Alister came and stood by his side, while Elo and Professor Odd took up position opposite him. With the little black girl on one side and the man on the other, they made a complete ring.

The man didn't speak. Didn't shout any magic words. Nor did he make any occult gestures. He grunted, as if in pain, and then they were in the middle of a jungle.

A huge plant with glossy, waxy leaves was nearly swallowing Alister, and Hoomrah disappeared into a bush covered with red berries. Professor Odd shivered and said "Oh *my*, that *tingles*," and Elo shouted, "We're back! We're back!"

All around them the jungle erupted with little dark people dressed in colorful embroidery and leather. They were wide-eyed, amazed and excited, but none of them carried weapons. Or wore hoods, Alister noticed with relief.

Little brown hands touched them, guided them, and led them out of the jungle. It was not really a jungle, Alister soon saw. It was a garden. A garden in the center of a small village, he was later to know.

They were drawn out of the thicket of plants and crowded into a clearing where a huge white marble statue towered over a pool of clear water. A little man, darker and more wrinkled than all the rest, was waiting by the pool, and at the sight of the man—the Bo-fellow, or whatever—he threw himself on his face— much in the way the little girl had when she had first seen him.

"Please get up, Shaman," said the man tiredly. The effort of teleporting them nearly five kilometers in an instant was clearly showing, and he was leaning heavily on the banana-handled cane.

Shaman Loorik, an amazed expression on his face, sat up. Hoomrah hurried over and began explaining, in her rapid, hooting language, what had happened. Elo took Professor Odd by the arm and began leading her away, saying something about, " . . . checking on Dave."

Alister lingered. He did not like to leave the man alone, even though these people seemed friendly.

The man was staring at the statue. It was a rough thing, Alister thought, but he could tell who it was meant to be. He touched the man gently on the elbow.

"These are the people you sent out of the canyon, yes?"

The man nodded without speaking. He went over to Shaman Loorik and made a polite bow. This quite threw the little shaman off his stride, as he tried to bow lower.

"That effigy," said the man, pointing at the statue with the cane. "It is in my likeness. Did you build it?"

Shaman Loorik nodded. "Mostly, hmm, my predecessor. He and the last of those who saw your face in the flesh."

"Where is he now?"

Shaman Loorik looked at the ground.

"Ah," said the man gently. "How long?"

"Twelve storm cycles," said the shaman.

"I wonder how many years that translates to," Alister mused.

Shaman Loorik looked up at him, his dark eyes twinkling and sad. "So do we, traveler. So do we."

The man was looking back up at the statue. He seemed fascinated by it.

"Shaman," he said. "Since that is an effigy of *me*, would you mind very much if I took it down?"

Shaman Loorik blinked. "Considering your presence here hails the end of the world, I do not see that it matters much. We can always build another in our new home . . . if we find one."

"I'd rather you didn't," said the man kindly. "A nice, commemorative plaque will do just fine." And he stepped up to the statue, standing over the pool of clear water. He put a hand—the other held the cane—to the statue's chest, and stood like that for a moment, his eyes closed.

With a sound like sighing the marble statue melted before Alister's eyes. It melted, and flowed as water past the man's bare feet and into the pool. At the same time something else flowed out of the statue and into the man. Alister got the strange impression that it was the memories and the effort the builders spent in making that sculpture. That intangible energy flowed out of the statue and into the man, who shuddered, sighed, and seemed to grow a little taller. He turned away brighter eyed and smiling slightly.

"Now," he said, and his voice was deep and rich and no longer hoarse. "Now, Shaman, I suggest you show me this portal."

Dave was frustrated. It was not an emotion that came easily to him, but dealing with magic was very different from dealing with technology, which was what he was good at. And this was not even good magic. It was half-baked, muddled, hard to believe it even worked. But that was the difference between magic and technology: technology had to be constructed according to very specific laws that governed the universe. Magic could be muscled into usefulness through sheer force of will power. And although these people had not known much about magic, they desperately wanted to go home, and that had resulted in the relative effectiveness of their portal.

It did not make Dave's job any easier, though. To calibrate for world-branching—an essential safeguard to any transuniversal portal—he had to rebuild the divining node to accept his modifications. That had taken a lot of time, and two inches off the end of one of his arms. It would grow back, but it meant he had to stop and make repairs to his suit before he could continue.

He had just got the calibration tuned such that a fruit, when tossed in, came out unmutated, when Professor Odd showed up at last.

Oh good you're finally here, this ridiculous device is driving my neural centers haywire, and I'm on the verge of throwing myself into it, I wish you'd been here all along, he said. But his frustration got in the way of his vocal translator and what came out audibly was: "YOU'RE LATE."

"I know, I know," said Professor Odd, coming around and kneeling down beside him. "But I brought help, he should be along any minute."

If it is the magician I want to have some deep communication with him on the advisability of letting people who don't know what they're doing try to build magical transuniversal portals.

"IF IT IS THE MAGICIAN, HE IS AN IDIOT."

Oh dear.

Excuse me, I need time to re-set the emotional drive of my rear neural clot. I am acting irrationally, sorry.

"WAIT. I NEED TO RESET. I AM THE IDIOT."

"Yes, you do that," said Professor Odd, gently rolling him to one side so she could get a better look at the back workings of the portal. "Oh my, this is a mess. I can see why you got frustrated. But I think it won't kill anyone now."

There was a commotion on the other side of the portal as Shaman Loorik showed the man and Alister into the little room. Alister could only gape at the swirling hole in the world, but the man came right around and knelt down next to the Professor, between her and Dave's panvironment suit. He seemed not to realize it contained a living thing.

"Oh, this is quite workable," he said, sounding pleasantly surprised. "All it needs now is a destination. Really, this is remarkably well made, who—" he looked up at Professor Odd.

Professor Odd grinned, and pointed at Dave.

The man looked. Dave remained silent. Inert. He might as well have been an empty shell. The man frowned, and tentatively put out a hand and spread it, palm down, over the dome of Dave's panvironment suit. His worn face took on an expression of intense concentration, and he leaned forward so his nose was almost touching the smooth glasslike dome.

Alister came around to the back of the portal, saw this tableau, and stopped in his tracks.

At last the man sighed and leaned away. He smiled ruefully.

"I think I would very much like to have a proper conversation with you," he said regretfully.

There was a whirring of servos inside of Dave's suit. Eventually he said:

"LIKEWISE."

"But I'm afraid our situation precludes that." The man got up, rubbing at his bare knees.

"AGREED."

Taking the cane, even though he no longer needed it to walk with, the man went around to the front of the portal, beckoning Professor Odd, Elo, and Alister to follow. He went to the door, where stood Shaman Loorik and Hoomrah, and behind them what must have been the entire population of the village.

"Is this everyone?" the man asked, and when the shaman returned the affirmative, he continued: "Good. Now, we do not have much time—"

He was cut off by a horrible ripping sound, like cracking wood, and above them the cloudy sky dissolved into the endless night. While the villagers gasped and stared, and Elo, Alister and the Professor craned their necks to get a better view, the man stood erect. Calm. Purposeful.

"As I was saying we do not have much time. So you must only take what you are carrying now. I realize this will make things rather difficult for you in your new home, but you are a strong people. A resourceful people. You will manage, as you have managed here. Better than you have managed here. Form a line."

It was not a question. It was a command that must be obeyed. Alister felt the pull of it on his own legs even though it was not directed at him.

The entire village formed a line. It stretched on out of sight around a low thatched hut, disappearing into the darkness.

Wait, darkness? Alister went to the door and poked his head out. To his horror he found that the crack in the sky had spread drastically in the last few minutes: now the sky was a blanket of dark blue void, with fragments of cloud and storm whirling across it like lost islands. Now it was the red horizon—just visible through a gap in the houses—that was cracked and torn, being eaten away by the approaching night.

Alister pulled his head back into the relative comfort of that cramped little hut and looked at the portal. Its surface was no longer a mad whirl of disjointed light and colors, but a fairly clear picture of a beach under a deep blue sky. Tropical-looking trees waved on a distant hill, and frothy white breakers crashed over the golden sands. Alister blinked. It was not a picture at all, but a real portal.

Little Hoomrah, her back very straight, stepped up, offering to go first. The man bowed to her, and she dipped her head in response. Then she went over and embraced Elo, much to the canine's surprise.

"*Soomera, koomera, hellowamen kai,*" she said, saluting, and walked, shoulders square, through the portal.

There was no flash of light, no sound, nothing. Hoomrah passed out of one world and into another as easily as if she were passing into another room. Alister could still see her, standing on the beach. She waved back at them, gesturing at her people to follow.

This they did, and it was harder to keep them in order, going one-by-one, than anything else. Dave came up and sat beside the portal, opposite from the man, and extended one insulated tentacle-arm to help support the wicker frame.

Shaman Loorik was the last to leave. He had waited outside the hut to watch his village—and count their number—as they made their escape. When he was satisfied all were safely away he came inside. By this time it looked like a real party was getting underway on the beach, and he smiled a disbelieving sort of smile. There were tears in his dark eyes.

"If you had told me when I was a child that this would happen in my lifetime, I would not have believed you," he said to no one in particular.

The man nodded understandingly, and ushered Shaman Loorik through the portal, and home.

"Now what?" Alister asked, a little uneasily. The beach looked nice, but he would rather have gotten safely back to the Oddity.

"Now we wait," said the man. And he tapped the ground sharply with the cane.

They waited. After a few minutes there was a pitter-patter of little feet, and a moment later a stampede of small animals swarmed through the hut's door and into the portal, which was now showing a tropical glade, clearly inland from the beach. The animals were mostly small, furry things, rather like stoats or weasels. A few were colorful lizards, and some looked like guinea fowl. The last was an honest tortoise, a giant one, who nodded gratefully at the man as it made its way ponderously home.

"Now what?" asked Elo, glancing nervously out the door.

"We wait," said the man patiently.

"FOR HOW LONG?" Dave asked.

The man shrugged. "For as long as it takes them."

Alister didn't have to ask who "they" were. Clearly the people who had lived in the Chasm, whoever they were. But the stone lightning bolt had come crashing down on the Chasm. Would there be any survivors?

The man seemed to think so. He tapped his cane on the ground again, and Alister saw the image of the tropical glade shimmer and vanish, to be replaced by a high, lonely mountainside. On a nearby peak were the spiky turrets of a castle, silhouetted against a white sky.

"What world is that?" asked Professor Odd, poking an experimental finger through the portal.

"The same," the man said. "Just a different part of it. Both of their original worlds are unfit for habitation at this point, so I'm sending them to the next one over."

"Why the same one, if you don't mind my asking?" Elo inquired.

The man grunted. He seemed to be concentrating on something. "Balance," he said shortly. "They will cancel each other out. Stand fast, the end is coming."

"The end, the end of what?" Alister asked uneasily.

Professor Odd smiled a bright, square-toothed grin at him. "Watch carefully, Mr Alister," she said. "Contrary to what you might read in science fiction stories or see on your telly, worlds don't end that often. It takes an awful lot to destroy a whole world. So watch closely, because you'll probably not live to see another world end."

The darkness had reached the village. It tore the roof off the hut, exposing them to the blue-black nothing, and a wind howled through the naked walls, which were quickly blown away. Alister found himself holding tight to Dave, who sat, unmovable, next to the portal.

Alister could see the village then, what was left of it. The houses were all cracked through with the black nothing, crumbling into pieces like a biscuit in coffee. It looked then like reality was only an image painted on the surface of the world. The real world was that horrible blue-black nothingness, which lay, deep as an ocean, below the thin film of the perceivable universe.

The world disintegrated around them, until all that was left was the tiny patch of ground beneath their feet and the wicker door of the portal. As Alister watched, even that ground dissolved into the void, and his heart leapt in his chest when he saw it vanish from beneath his feet.

He thought he would fall. That he would be forever falling through the void beneath the world. But something held him steady, as if standing on invisible ground. Then he looked over at the man, whose pale face was strained with sweat standing out on his forehead, and Alister knew what was keeping them there.

They stood there, the man on one side of the portal, Dave on the other. Alister held onto Dave, the Professor held onto the man, and Elo clung to the Professor's leg.

The only light came from the distant white sky beyond the portal, and it lit the nothing around them with a smoky, uncertain glow. It began to get cold.

Something in the void. Not a person. Not the people they waited for. A whirl of light, a pin-prick, deep in the distance. Alister gasped—and did not like to think too hard about what he was breathing. After that first prick of light he began to see more, some of them were even different colors. And all at once he recognized where they were.

They were *outside* the universe. They were in the night outside the Oddity.

Then where was the Oddity? Alister looked—not knowing exactly what he looked for—but found nothing.

Then, out of the nothing, out of the void, in the direction the Chasm would have been if it had still existed, came a small procession of pale, hooded figures. Alister clung harder to the smooth, round dome of Dave's suit.

They did not look as threatening now, however. Their cloaks were torn and their footsteps were uncertain. As they drew near, the man made an impatient gesture with his hand, and their hoods were torn off, revealing scared white faces, some old, mostly young. All male.

"You cannot go home," the man pronounced gravely. "Your world is no longer inhabitable. I offer you this one instead. It is a cold world: there are no gods. But if you ask nicely, they will probably let you stay."

The young men seemed relieve to hear this, and they rushed forward, tumbling through the portal and onto the mountainside. A few of the older ones followed, more reluctantly. This left only two, the oldest and the most stubborn-looking. Together they raised their hands, and in them Alister saw they held a crystal glass filled with blood.

But the man only shook his head, and stretching out his empty hand he turned it over sharply, and the blood spilled out of the glass and ran down their robes, staining them red. Then the two older men cowered, and they threw down the glass, which fell past the man's feet forever, and they ran away into the void.

They did not get far before they, like the world that they had inhabited for so long, dissolved into nothing.

As horrible as this was, when Alister thought back on it, at the time he barely noticed the fate of those poor men, for even as they dissolved, the light from the portal dimmed, and it went black with the sound of someone sighing.

That someone had been the man. Alister couldn't see him, but he felt his hand on his arm, and he felt Dave under his other hand.

"WELL. THIS IS A FINE MESS YOU'VE GOTTEN US INTO," Dave intoned.

"Not at all," said Professor Odd's voice, bright in the darkness. "He's brought us home."

"Home?" exclaimed Alister. "How is this *home?*"

"Turn around," said Elo.

It was difficult—far more difficult than Alister had imagined—to get turned around when floating in a formless void. But somehow he managed it, and there in the darkness . . .

Now he knew why they called it the Oddity. In that vast expanse of void pricked with windows, the Oddity was just that: an *oddity*. A piece of the void which was different. It was a twist in the blue-blackness, where nothing became something and swirled into a vortex. Alister thought he could make out the shape of a house in that vortex. Unless it was a ship. Whatever it was shifted under his eyes, making it hard to recognize.

The man led them to it, taking lunging strides through the void, pulling Alister and Dave and Elo and Professor Odd like fish on a line.

When they got close enough, finally a piece of the Oddity solidified into something recognizable.

It was a door. Shut.

Professor Odd pushed it open.

Light streamed into the void. This time it was the myriad twinkling colored lights from the Oddity's control panel, and it lit the travelers in all different hues. Professor Odd was orange splashed with green, Elo was blue, Dave's suit was spotted with neon red. And the man, Alister saw, was bathed in purple. He peered into the Oddity, a rapt expression on his face.

Elo scrambled inside, took a seat at the control node. The lights calmed, and Alister felt himself drawn slowly to the door. He grasped its reassuringly solid frame, felt the familiar tug of gravity, and he tottered gratefully up the stairs, pushed and supported by Dave.

Professor Odd stood in the doorway, pressed to one side. She looked out at the man, a little sadly.

"I'd offer to take you home," she said. "But I'm afraid I can't."

"Mixed timelines," said the man, nodding. "Fascinating, really. Wish I had more time to study it." He gestured at the interior of the Oddity.

"You will," Professor Odd said serenely.

The man gave her a sharp look.

"How much of this did you know?" he asked, careful about his words.

"Not much," Professor Odd said with a shrug.

"Are you coming in or not?" Elo demanded from the console.

"Thank you, no," the man said cheerfully. "I can make my own way home from here, goodbye, and thank you. All of you." He nodded at them, turned to go.

"No," said Professor Odd, so softly that only the man heard. "Thank *you*."

The man stopped. He looked around at the Professor and raised one dark eyebrow. Then he smiled a knowing smile and sauntered off into the darkness. He still glowed a dim purple.

He did not dissolve, like the unhooded men had. He did not disintegrate. He merely grew smaller and smaller, until he was another pinprick of colored light, indistinguishable from any of the others.

Professor Odd watched him go with a sigh, and closed the door. She came up the stairs slowly, her feet heavy.

Elo climbed down from her chair, a puzzled expression on her face. "Professor," she said, concerned. "I think he just walked off with your cane."

Professor Odd blinked at her, she seemed to have been thinking about something else. "What? Oh yes, my cane. Well, it's really *his* cane, he's only taking it back. Though he doesn't know it yet."

"I DO NOT LIKE THE SOUND OF THIS," Dave said. He had gone over to the kitchen alcove and plugged himself into the faucet. All that exertion and stress had thoroughly ruined the balance of his water, and he needed a good flush.

"Oh, it's not as bad as all that. We've just got our timelines crossed, that's all," Professor Odd said.

"*Please* explain," begged Alister. "In *small* words."

Professor Odd went and sat down at the table, resting her feet in between a bicycle wheel and a dirty plate. "Time is fluid between universes. Where *we* are. I can leave a universe, spend a week in another, but then when I return to that first universe, it won't *necessarily* have been a week. Usually the difference is slight, unless exaggerated artificially by the Oddity's temporal slider, but with the number of universes I visit, the differences add up. You can imagine, then, how time relative to *me* and time relative to a person from a different universe can have . . . discrepancies."

"Slippage," Alister said, remembering what Elo had told him on his first day in the Oddity.

"Exactly," said Elo, coming to sit by the Professor. "But this goes beyond slippage. This is *massive*."

"I think it probably had something to do with that universe being an anomaly," Professor Odd said, contemplating the bicycle wheel.

"AN *UNCONVENTIONAL* ANOMALY," Dave added.

Professor Odd nodded, not seeming to hear. "I met him," she said. "That man. Very, very early in my . . . career. I was stupid then and didn't know it. I got myself into quite a bit of trouble. He helped get me out. He gave me that cane. . . . " She gestured to the door, now a blank black slate once more. "He *will* give me that cane. He said it would be of help. It will—has been. But I never imagined he meant it would be of help to *him*."

"But how do you know this is in *his* future?" Elo pestered. "Maybe he *forgot?*"

"His kind don't forget," Professor Odd said. "Besides, he *knew* me then. Will know me, now. He just met me. He can go on and know me when he meets me. It's important, otherwise things wouldn't have worked out the way they worked out, and I wouldn't have been here, now, just then, to help *him* out."

"IN EPI-TIME, EVERYTHING FALLS INTO PLACE," Dave said. "THE TAPESTRY IS ONLY INCOMPREHENSIBLE TO THE THREAD THAT WEAVES IT."

"*What?*" Alister said. Elo buried her nose in her paws. Professor Odd looked at Dave, critically.

"I think I need to take a look at your slime-to-audio translator," she said. "It could clearly use some tuning."

Dave shut the water off. "PLEASE DO," he said.

"Do you think you'll ever see him again?" Elo asked as Professor Odd began to dismantle the side of Dave's suit. "Maybe later, in *both* your timelines, when you two have re-synced?"

Professor Odd considered this a while, and she smiled a dreamy, not-quite-there smile. "Oh, I hope so," she said. "But that's in the future, *both* our futures, so I really have no idea."

And with that, for the time being, they had to be satisfied.

4. THE ELDER MACHINE

Prologue

A TALL THIN FIGURE in a tattered overcoat walked forlornly along the river. In the yellow light from the streetlamps its shadow was cast deep and black into the water.

Movement in the river; the swish and swirl of disturbed water, and the figure paused. Stopped. Turned and looked. It crouched down by the water's edge and reached a hand out across the surface.

With a muffled cry and a splash the figure disappeared suddenly into the river, casting water up onto the bricks of the path. Somewhere in the night a dog barked.

Then quiet. The river ran smooth once more.

Part One

THE FEELING CREPT, like tendrils of unpleasant slime, through his mind. The feeling of *wrongness*, that the natural order of things was being violated, and he paused in his writing and stared out at the peaceful lawn, with its scattered herds of brightly colored tourists milling about, until the feeling passed.

The Journal of Dr Alister Bane
Professor of Archeology, GTC, Oxford
June 11th, 20–, 10:18 AM
front steps of the Museum of Natural History

I am having migraines again. At least, that is what I think they are. They come on strong and fast, give me a few moments of blinding pain, and then leave just as quickly. They seem to be triggered at random, sometimes striking me while at table, sometimes while walking to breakfast. On occasion I think it is something I have seen that triggers them—something in the corner of my vision that contradicts what should be. I think there is information in these blinding flashes, but such information as would be anathema for my brain to comprehend.

They do not seem to do me any tangible harm, so I have begun keeping this journal as a way of tracking them, their frequency, and the situations surrounding their occurrence. In this way I hope to collate some useful information, and to ascertain whether they are increasing.

The most recent case manifested in the last hour while I was walking back from the Pitt Rivers. Doing so necessitates passing through the main hall of the MNH, past the dinosaur skeletons and the stuffed animals. The MNH has a seemingly endless supply of preserved ponies, big cats, and birds of all sizes propped up on wires behind glass, and as I passed through, my eye was drawn to the shelf of preserved sea fauna, strung up in preservative fluid. There I had the most disconcerting feeling of seeing something wrong: one of the specimens—some kind of squid—had been dyed a bright green by an accident of chemicals, and its eyes appeared much brighter and alive. Some precocious child, rocketing through the aisle, clipped the case and sent the fluid sloshing, causing the many puckered arms and tentacles to wave lazily at me, as if in greeting.

It was then I began to feel the ache in my sinuses, and I managed to escape from that wretched place and collapse on the steps before the whiteness overcame my vision.

Having just recovered I determined to begin setting down an account of these incidents, in the hope that some rhyme or reason may become apparent. And this I have just done.

Doctor Alister Bane put his pen away and closed the little book. He rose from the steps of the Museum of Natural History—slowly, because he still felt slightly ill—and walked purposefully across the lawn. The comforting sounds of Oxford in late spring, the rumble of traffic and the softer, yet no less pervasive, hum of human voices, swelled around him and soothed his frazzled nerves.

The walk from Pitt Rivers to his college was not a strenuous one, but Alister liked the way his moving legs stirred the thoughts in his mind and let them settle into new shapes. Walks, he had decided when still an undergraduate, were the best thing for thinking. Better than rowing, which you had to prepare for, and better far than any kind of organized sport, where your teammates would not understand why you had to sit down in the middle of a play to jot down notes. Walking also helped shake the remaining twinges from his mind, and he was feeling quite himself again as he crossed Banbury Road and cut between St Giles and its graveyard.

It being a pleasant, sunny day, the graveyard was unusually cheerful and noisy; a little island of shade and trees and grass set between two busy streets, it was temporarily home to a number of lunching couples, a few students with laptops, and a girl in a red coat playing fetch with a large golden dog.

This dog, much to Alister's annoyance, took an immediate interest in him and came tearing across the grass, dodging between gravestones, skidding to a stop at his feet. For one horrible second he thought it would tackle him, but it only nosed at his hand and, even as the little girl came running, shouting "Bad dog!" in her shrill young voice, it pressed something small and wet and a little pulpy into his hand.

Then it was off, running away from its mistress, barking and flapping its feathered tail excitedly.

Alister stood holding the clammy damp blob in his hand, struck dumb. Then, as if moving under the directions of a mind other than his own, he calmly unfolded the tacky paper. There, in blobby blue ballpoint pen, were scratched the words:

Don't be afraid to look in the cracks.

—Odd

Coming back to himself Alister dropped the paper and began walking briskly down Woodstock Road, trying to shake the feeling that he had seen that handwriting before somewhere. Sometime a long time ago. When he was a student? But it hadn't been in Oxford, that was for certain, and Alister had done his entire tenure at Green Templeton. Where then?

A dull ache in his jaw, quickly spreading to his sinuses, and Alister just had the willpower to throw himself against the nearest wall before the whiteness flashed behind his eyes.

The Journal of Dr Alister Bane
Professor of Archeology, GTC, Oxford
June 11th 20–, 12:02 PM
the Observatory, Green Templeton College, Oxford

I had not one, but two migraines—if they are indeed that—on my way back from the museum. In the first instance I saw some handwriting that triggered an obscure memory, and in trying to place it I suffered another attack. No sooner had I recovered than I looked across the road and saw one of our city's numerous street performers, apparently headed for the High. He appeared to be a blind juggler, for he wore thick dark glasses and walked with the long cane of those afflicted with that handicap. He carried a brace of clubs under his arm, and wore the most unlikely wig: bright yellow streaked with pink and teal. I only caught a passing glimpse of him, but the sight affected me dramatically. I had the strangest urge to run after him, a feeling that to lose him in the crowd of Oxford would be the worst of calamities. I was so upset that I barely noticed the warning signs, and the intense pain took me completely by surprise.

I stopped in at the Infirmary on my way back to GTC, and Dr Llewelyn was able to spare me a few minutes. From his initial examination there appears to be nothing wrong with me. He attributes the headaches to stress and has prescribed a mild sedative. I am dubious of its effectiveness, and I doubt I will take it: my current research demands so much energy I cannot afford to be sedated.

The Didcot Excavation was a young dig, the ink still drying on the permit, but it was already yielding rich results. What had begun as a lucky break for a farmer with a metal detector had quickly turned into the greatest opportunity of the century for any archeologist in Oxfordshire. A Roman treasure cache, priceless in itself, turned out to be only the beginning: below it was a bronze age burial, and below that stone age artifacts. Some intrepid researchers were arguing for digging further, that three discoveries from three different ages could not be a coincidence. Alister was one of the most vocal proponents of continuing to dig down, so while he sorted through the wealth of artifacts brought back from the dig, he also drafted letters and appeals, trying to win over the more timid hearts.

While engaged in this altogether pleasurable task he was roused by a frantic tapping sound, as of fists hammering on glass. Alister jumped all over, and the sound resolved itself into the deep thumping of human hands on wood; someone was knocking at his door. A moment later it opened and his assistant tumbled into the room, shedding papers.

Alister stared. Margaret Barnes was usually defined by her neatness, her efficiency. Now she looked anything but neat; her brown hair was coming out of the tight bun in long strands and her normally starched and pressed shirt was rumpled and her sleeves rolled up to her elbows. She was carrying a stack of files, helplessly grabbing at the escaping sheets as they slipped from her arms.

"What bee has gotten in your bonnet, child?" Alister asked, catching a slim folder as it went flying.

"You didn't receive the bulletin, Professor?" Barnes returned, clutching the papers to her chest and looking stricken.

Alister gestured to the crowd of artifacts on his desk. "I have been otherwise occupied, I cannot check the bulletin every five minutes."

"It's Dr Cridget, Professor, he was brought up from the dig this morning—they say he's gone mad!"

Again Alister felt a cold feeling like slime dripping down his back, but this time there was no wavering of reality, it was simply a physical reaction to distressing news. Dr Cridget was an eminent researcher, and a friend—as far as Alister had friends.

"Where is he?"

"Still on site, as far as I know." Barnes held out a set of blue sheets with a shaking hand. "It says he's too unstable to move. But here's the dispatch for you. Dr Carly said she would call."

Snatching the sheets from the woman's unresisting hand, Alister dashed to the door and took the stairs two at a time as he hurtled out of the building. When he reached the street he groped in his pocket and brought out his cell phone—it *had* been on Silent this whole morning! And there was a message from Dr Carly—bless her, it was a text.

Cridget poorly. Need your advice. Meet at dig 30E.

The really impressive thing to do would be to hire a cab and have it drive him to the scene as fast as possible, but in Oxford on a Sunday afternoon Alister knew that would be only slightly faster than walking. Slower, if there had been an accident. So he jogged along the railing until he came to his bicycle, unlocked it, and mounted at a run, something he hadn't done since he was a boy. He nearly ran over a student as he pushed off into the road, but it hardly mattered. What mattered was that he was moving, and he was doing something.

From across the street, a large golden dog watched with interest.

The dig was halfway between Oxford proper and Didcot, located predominantly in a field which, up until a few months ago, had been home to a group of placid dairy cattle. Now the cattle were gone, and in their place a small city of white tents and awnings had sprung up. Cars, vans, and even a couple of lorries rolled over the uneven ground, leaving deep brown tracks in the grass within the designated traffic areas—which had been marked by yellow string stretched between orange posts.

One van pulled up outside a tent marked with a red cross, and Professor Bane tumbled out, still clutching his bicycle. He'd been passed by the shuttle crew outside of Oxford and given a lift, but he was still out of breath and very red and sweaty when he pushed aside the opening flaps of tent 30E and nearly walked straight into Dr Carly.

Dr Carly was a woman of mature years, her hair resolutely gray and her face as drooping as a bloodhound's. Today this impression was exaggerated by the overall drooping of her shoulders and her lab coat, which was pulled sideways and hanging off her arms.

"I heard—Cridget, is he—?" Alister couldn't bring himself to finish the question.

Dr Carly sighed heavily. "Oh, he's alive right enough. I hoped you might be able to get some sense out of him. Follow me. You worked 30E together, that so?"

"Aye," said Alister, following the doctor's slumped shoulders as she led the way deeper into the maze of white tent. "But 30E was never our prize dig; it was all broken bits and ends. I thought he'd be working 25B, or maybe C . . . "

"Well, this morning he must have found something. Or something found him. Put this on." She handed Alister a paper mask. "We're not sure what he's got. And for the love of Pete, don't upset him."

Dr Cridget had always been a nervous man. Maybe it went with the name; Alister thought if he had been called *Cridget* all his life he would be nervous as well. But his old quirks and tics were nothing compared to what Alister found in the tent by dig 30E.

It was Dr Cridget—his worn tweed jacket with ink stains on the sleeves, his peppery gray hair and big watery blue eyes. But it was Dr Cridget as Alister had never seen him before. He sat huddled on a camp bed, his knees up in his chest and his arms wrapped around them, as if he were afraid to let go for fear of being blown apart. He rocked back and forth on his seat, and a thin line of drool was slowly creeping down his chin.

"Cridget?" Alister said, advancing slowly. When there was no change in the poor man, he added: "Jeremy?"

Dr Cridget didn't seem to hear; he just sat there, rocking back and forth and sometimes jerking his head to one side, as if there were something in his ear he wanted to get out.

Gingerly Alister reached out and touched him on the shoulder.

"Jeremy, can you hear me?"

The effect was alarming: Dr Cridget jerked sideways, throwing himself against the wall of the tent, bringing his hands up to shield his face and kicking his legs out so wildly it was pure luck Alister wasn't struck. Then he began to make horrible gasping noises so far from human speech that it took Alister a moment to realize that was what it was.

"The *arms!*" cried Cridget, covering his face with his hands. "He has *terrible… aaarrms!*"

"Who has terrible arms?" Dr Carly asked, from a safe distance. "What did you *find*, Cridget?"

"He … will find *you!*" gasped Cridget, and went out like a light.

The Journal of Dr Alister Bane
Professor of Archeology, GTC, Oxford
June 11th 20– , 8:30 PM, Didcot dig, Oxfordshire

Unsettling day, my own problems notwithstanding. Dr Cridget is incomprehensible; he is drifting in and out of consciousness but when coaxed into speaking, he only wails about arms and an eye in the dark. We did manage to move him to the infirmary, which is a small mercy. So far as the poor man can feel things in this world, I believe he will be more comfortable there.

I had hoped to investigate the dig in question—30E—but the most astonishing thing had happened: it was flooded! The wretched intern overseeing it had noticed water creeping into the main chamber a little past noon but didn't say anything until the whole thing was flooded. We now have a system of pumps going, which should drain it by morning. Then Dr Carly and I will have a look for ourselves.

That night Alister dreamed of arms—long, twining green arms that held him fast and pulled him down, down, into a dark cold place. He was fighting against them, struggling to breathe, but he kept sinking. He was being dragged, inexorably, toward something sharp and terrible that would cut him open and leave him splayed out like an anatomy subject. The harder he fought the harder the arms gripped him, and there were more and more of them, sliding over him, curling around his neck …

Alister woke panting with sweat cooling on his brow and his bedroom an un-familiar jumble of shadows before him. He had no memory of the dream, but he was left with the distinct feeling that he was in the wrong place; that the angle of the walls and the ceiling and the position of the window were all wrong, that the bed and the clothes were not his, that his whole life, in fact, belonged to someone else.

He got up and turned on the light, went into the bathroom and got a drink of water. By the time he went back to bed the feeling had passed, but he could not bring himself to turn off the light; it was still on when he woke later that morning, the sun shining full on his face.

The Journal of Dr Alister Bane
Professor of Archeology, GTC, Oxford
June 12th 20–, 9:00 AM, GTC, Oxford

The white flashes are becoming alarming. I had two more over breakfast, and they made me question whether I was well enough to to work today. But I know if I do not find out what happened to poor Cridget the curiosity will kill me.

As my tutor was so fond of telling me: knowledge is its own power and protection against our cruel world.

When Alister arrived at the dig Dr Carly met him at 30E, her face a mask of worry.

"What's the matter?" he asked before he was properly out of the van. "Did you find something?"

"It's what we haven't found that worries me," Dr Carly said. "Westing's gone missing."

"Westing?"

"Cridget's intern," said Dr Carly. "You remember, the one who let this thing get flooded in the first place? Well, she never reported in for work today. She's not at home and messages to her mobile get sent straight to voicemail. She was last seen here, checking the pumps last night."

"In 30E?" Alister asked, his heart sinking.

Carly glanced at the dark, wet hole that was the entrance to the fateful site. "Yes."

Alister shook his head. "We'll need full kit then," he said. "I'm not taking any chances."

Full kit meant body-suits, bagged feet, latex gloves and face masks. Alister also added a utility belt which carried a flashlight, small pickaxe, and a bag of vials for collecting samples. By the time he and Dr Carly entered site 30E a small crowd had gathered, and two brave interns—they had heard about Westing—had volunteered to accompany them.

They entered one at a time: Dr Carly first, then Alister, and finally the two interns—a spotty lad named Legston and a willowy girl called Punce.

30E had not been considered an important site, so the tunnel reaching down into the earth was fairly narrow—only wide enough for one person at a time. The shaft of Alister's flashlight caught on wet soil and supporting beams, and the ground was still covered in at least an inch of mud.

Finally the tunnel opened up, the steep walls reaching high above their heads to the dim gray of the tarpaulin that had been stretched over to keep the rain out. Here they stood in a square room of earth perhaps six feet on a side. The ground was a mess of sloppy mud, and the wall had been shored up in one place by planks of wood. It was otherwise empty.

Alister shook his head.

"Sample everything," he said, muffled through his mask.

As the two interns got to work, scraping dirt from the walls and scooping mud into little boxes, Alister probed about in the mud of the floor, searching for anything that might shed light on the situation.

The mud was clinging and tacky, and at one point he plunged his hand in too far, and his glove came loose as he pulled it free.

He felt the cool brush of the wet earth on his skin, but the next second it was *not* earth at all, but a long slimy tentacle the color of a green apple. It writhed up out of the sloppy muck, twining up and up around his arm until it had a firm hold. Then it *pulled*.

Alister found himself slammed into the mud face first, the interns' hands on him, Dr Carly speaking firmly in his ear:

"There, there, Dr B, you just breathe for me now. There must be a gas leak. We'll get you out and have this whole place scrubbed."

Alister found himself lifted clear of the mud—the tentacle had gone—and half led, half carried back up into the open air. Even as he reached the surface the world ran fluid before his eyes, and he was so frightened that it would flow completely away and leave him with nothing—or worse, whatever owned that tentacle—that he shut his eyes tight and refused to open them. The rest of his senses shut off soon after that.

Alister dreamed. He dreamed of a small, confined, dark place, where his body was held rigid and he was unable to move. He opened his mouth to scream—in horror? For help?—but instead of sound coming out, cold water rushed in. He choked on it, coughed; his lungs burned with the need for air and against all instinct he inhaled and—

And he woke up in a bland, uncomfortable camp bed, a metal framework supporting a fabric ceiling above his head.

"Why, *there* you are, Dr Bane," said a voice from over his shoulder, and he had another of those moments where he felt his entire life slide away from him, that he was someone else entirely, and that the bed, and the tent, and the entire world he was in was *not right.* He turned, slowly, trying not to dislodge the feeling yet at the same time desperately hoping it would go away.

A little round woman was sitting by his bedside, smiling at him from out of a halo of curly gray hair. Oddly, the first thing that went through Alister's mind was that her hair should have more color in it. But why would he think that? He had never seen this woman before in his life.

"Alister," said Alister. "My name is Alister."

"Of course it is, Dr Bane," said the woman. "Now you just lie back there, luv, and I'll have Dr Carly around to see you in just a mo. She's been in a right flutter over you." So saying the woman levered herself out of the chair she had been sitting in, her veined hands straining against the armrests. Brushing down her dress she looked about for her glasses, found them on the chain around her neck, put them on, and waddled sedately outside.

Alister lay back on his bed and tried to think logically. Clearly he had had some sort of episode, but was it related to the white flashes, or was it something different? It had not felt like those jerks out of reality he had experienced before; those had simply been neurons misfiring and making him think he saw one thing in place of another. Like the feeling of *deja vu,* it had only been a matter of signals getting a bit out of order. This was a full-on hallucination.

Gingerly, Alister raised the arm that had been assaulted, and peeled back the sleeve. To his horror he found the skin raised and reddened, with white circular marks embedded in his flesh. They were just the right size, and spaced just so, to have been made by the suckers that underlined the tentacle that had grabbed him.

There was a rustle outside the tent and the sound of approaching feet, and impulsively Alister pulled down his sleeve to cover the marks.

"Good to see you, Dr B," said Dr Carly, pushing aside the flap of tarpaulin that was serving as a door. "You had us right worried there for a while."

Alister found he was thrusting his arm under the cover as if the marks were something shameful he needed to hide. The little gray-haired nurse was back, peering around Carly's elbow with cheerful curiosity. To his relief Carly noticed her, and at a quiet word she vanished.

"What happened?" he asked, once the nurse was safely gone.

"I was hoping you could tell me that," Carly said, sitting down in the wobbly camp chair. "You keeled over like someone had pummeled you, and when we finally dragged you upright you went out like a light."

"How long?" Alister rubbed his eyes.

"Nearly four hours," Dr Carly said.

Alister lay back on his bed and regarded the ceiling thoughtfully. Four hours wasn't bad, not really, not as bad as losing a day, or a week, or not waking up at all. But he still felt cheated, like there had been a chunk of his life that had been stolen away, and he would never get it back.

"And," said Carly, reaching into her pocket, "we found this clutched in your hand. Mind telling us where you got it?"

She produced a small rectangular chip of plastic, the size and shape of the sort of flash drive for the older digital cameras. Alister took it with his good hand and brought it close for a better look. There appeared to be something drawn on it, a circle with ten wavy rays shooting out of it and a single dot in its center.

Something like memory slammed hard into Alister's brain. For one moment he *knew* he had seen this pictograph before. The image of a door with this same drawing on it swam before his eyes, and behind that door was—

Alister noticed his vision going white around the edges. Quickly he curled his hand around the chip and pushed it away under the covers. Then he had to lie very still with his eyes shut while Dr Carly put her head out of the tent and called the nurse back in. He wished she hadn't. Alister felt like he could confide in Dr Carly, but not with the nurse there. If he started talking about white flashes and hallucinations he knew they would ship him off to infirmary, and then he would *never* get this mystery solved.

It came as something of a surprise to realize that he *wanted* to solve this mystery at all, that he had begun to look at the whole mess like one of his archeological problems. There was missing data here, and he had to either dig for more, or content himself with connecting the dots. Since the dots in this case were strung so far apart it would take impossible leaps to connect them, he realized he would have to do more digging.

At least now I know what poor Cridget meant by "terrible arms," he thought to himself as the nurse checked his vitals. The uncomfortable thought that perhaps Cridget had had a similar experience, and that Alister's mind was on its way to breaking just like his had, floated up to the surface, but Alister stuffed it back down again.

"I'm *fine*," he said, a little more forcefully than he intended, sitting up abruptly and swinging his legs over the side of the bed.

This was a mistake. The natural dynamics of gravity on a body with low blood pressure swung into effect, and Alister was hit by another bout of dizziness—though this was the normal kind of dizziness brought on by standing up too fast, and it soon passed. Having something to compare his white-outs and hallucinations to made him able to look at the situation much more clinically. Obviously something unnatural was going on here, and he needed to find out what.

"I don't fancy you're fine enough to get home on your own," Dr Carly said, laying a steadying hand on his shoulder and gently pushing him back down.

"There must be a gas pocket we're disturbing," he said, casting about for some semblance of a rational explanation. "Better have that area cordoned off before we continue digging. Now get me those two interns, I want to hear their side of the story."

Dr Carly pursed her lips, but she disappeared out of the tent, taking the little nurse with her. Alister was left alone with his thoughts—which were not much of a comfort—for almost an hour. In that time he went from nervous and restless, to bored, to increasingly nervous as the time stretched on and no one entered the tent.

At last there was some shuffling and not Dr Carly, nor the little gray haired nurse, but another intern entered. The interns were indistinguishable to Alister's eyes, but he got the impression this was a new one. The boy had a freckled face and an unfortunate mop of red hair. He coughed.

"Professor Bane?" he said.

"Do you see anyone else here?" Alister asked testily.

"Yes sir, I mean, no sir," said the intern, clapping his hands behind his back and shuffling his feet nervously. "Only, Dr Carly sent me to tell you they can't find them. They are looking hard, sir, only it's—" he chewed his lip furiously, and an idea oozed into Alister's mind, uncomfortable and cold.

"They're gone, aren't they?" he said.

"Legs and Punce haven't been seen for *hours!*" wailed the intern, the dam of nerves breaking in a torrent of sobs. "I *saw* them go into the de-con tent, but *they never came out.* No one's seen them since. They're not at home or answering their mobiles, they've *gone*—just like Westing!"

Just like Westing, who let the dig get flooded and then had to check the pumps. The cold pushed forward through Alister's mind like an advancing wave of slime, and he found himself clutching his forehead involuntarily.

"I'm sorry sir," stammered the new intern. "I'll try harder to find them."

"No, you won't," Alister said from behind his hand. "You're going to take me to the archive."

"Sir?"

"You have a car, don't you?"

"I could borrow Gordon's . . . "

"Then do so," Alister said, rising slowly to his feet.

The archive was located in the basement of the Bodleian, renovated a few years back to contain banks and banks of digital storage. It was cold down in the archive, and Alister was wishing he'd had the intern stop by the GTC to get an extra coat, or scarf, or both, as he zipped through page after page of scanned manuscript. He was attempting to put together a history of the site of the Didcot dig through the centuries, but was hampered by the fact that, for the better part of the last few thousand years, it had been nothing more than a nondescript field.

Flick. Flick. Flick. The pages flashed across the screen. Then . . . *flick.* A blank page with *"Archive not scanned, please see hardcopy"* in the middle. Alister cursed under his breath.

"Gilthwait?" he called, trying to keep the frustration out of his voice.

The intern appeared from around a corner of computer stacks, his coat buttoned up under his chin. "Sir?" he said.

"Gilthwait, would you go up to . . . " Alister squinted at the header of the page, which listed the location of the hardcopy. " . . . Historical Archive, row 36B, and bring me down all the annals that could have anything on Didcot?"

Gilthwait paled. "All of them sir?"

"I said all," Alister snapped.

Without a word, Gilthwait vanished. Alister turned back to the screen.

The intern was gone a long time. A *very* long time. In the end Alister lost patience and climbed back upstairs himself. He was getting hungry, not a state that lent itself well to careful, analytical thinking.

He did not find Gilthwait. He did find the section he was looking for, however, and concluded that the wretched youth had taken the opportunity to scamper off. Sighing to himself he went along the shelves, picking off books and scanning their indexes.

Pick, shuffle, replace. Pick, shuffle, replace. Pick, shuffle, replace. Pause. Pick back up again. Slowly Alister reopened the book and stared at what he found there. Or rather, what he *didn't* find there.

The book *said* it contained facsimiles of land deeds going back as far as the twelfth century, but the pages inside . . . were *perfectly blank*.

Alister stared at them, willing the ink to appear. Instead all he got was the uncomfortable cold feeling in his mind, like slime seeping in between the cracks.

Hastily he shoved that book away and picked up the next.

It was blank.

And the next . . .

Blank.

The rest of the shelf was nothing but blank books. In desperation Alister picked up one of the earlier books he had already dismissed.

Arms—green, boneless, writhing arms—exploded out of the book at him. They reached out, twined around his head, pulled his face down into the book. Cold, sticky slime hit his face, ran up his nose, into his mouth when he opened it in surprise. It tasted faintly of something like whiskey, and something else that made him retch.

Keep looking.

The words felt like they were being written on his brain with acid. They burned. Painful to think about; impossible to forget.

Keep looking in the cracks.

The voice belonged to a mind that was old and deep and stretched out around him into infinite space. Alister knew he would dissolve into that space if it went on much longer . . .

As suddenly as the horrible arms had appeared, they vanished. Perhaps they retreated into the pages of the book, perhaps they were pulled away into some other dimension. All Alister knew was suddenly he could breathe again, he could open his eyes and see again—though his mouth still tasted vaguely foul.

Slowly he closed the book, replaced it on the shelf. He walked composedly to the end of the row, down the stairs to the common area where he found a vacant table and sat down, pulling out his journal. With a hand that shook only a little he began to write.

The Journal of Dr Alister Bane
Professor of Archeology, GTC, Oxford
June 12th 20–, 6:05 PM, Bodleian Library

Either there is something very wrong with me, or very wrong with the world. Reason and logic tell me the fault must lie within my own mind, but something else tells me this may not be so. The disappearances of the interns— Westing, Legston and Punce. Gilthwait may have run off, but in light of recent events I doubt I will see him again.

Where have they gone? Will they ever return? Has the world broken to such a degree that people are slipping through the cracks?

Cracks.

I must look in the cracks. I must find answers.

Am I going mad? I must certainly be mad if I think the world is breaking and not just my own mind. Perhaps it is my mind after all . . .

No! No! There is something in my gut that tells me there is more wrong than just what I can perceive. There is something at work here: an intelligence far greater than anything we have yet encountered. An extraterrestrial? That is one hypothesis. But how to *test* it?

Alister paused in his writing, absently chewing at the end of his pen. A few students had come into the room, and they were talking animatedly amongst themselves.

" . . . which it *wasn't* blank when Professor McBride assigned it to me last week," one of them, a girl, said.

Alister pricked up his ears and listened, straining to hear over the pounding of his heart.

"You sure this isn't a prank?" her friend, a dark girl with a cloth over her hair, replied.

"Oh sure, because anyone can swap the right number of blank pages—pages made of *perfectly aged paper*—with the *exact same* cover I've had in my room all week," said the first girl, whose hair was dyed an improbable shade of pink.

Alister stared, his mind in a whirl. Not least over what was being said, but the image of a woman with pink hair was pushing forward in his mind. She was familiar, frightening, but also somehow reassuring. Alister was desperately trying to place her even as he rose to his feet and made his way through the tables towards the two girls. They saw him approach and fell silent in the presence of what was clearly a don, and a possibly deranged one, to judge from the way he was staring.

"Excuse me," Alister began, and realized he had lost the image of the pink-haired woman. All he saw before him now was a girl of about twenty with a cheap dye job and freckles over her cheeks. He gave himself an internal shake, and said: "I overheard you expressing dismay over your predicament. May I see the offending book?"

The student raised an eyebrow, but she shuffled through her bag and eventually brought out a truly ancient tome with crinkled, yellow pages. Taking it in both hands Alister opened it carefully.

The pages were all quite blank.

Turning back to the cover he saw it was an obscure history of the Norman conquest.

"When did you notice this?" he asked.

"This morning," replied the student nervously. "Am I going to be in very much trouble?"

"Not with me," Alister said, handing the book back. "But if you find any more of your history books going blank, do give me a ring." He gave her his card and departed, leaving the two young women staring dumbstruck at his retreating back.

Alister stood in the cooling air outside the library, breathing deep the smell of the city: of car exhaust and dirty stones and the enticing smell of frying meat that was slowly wafting up from Oxford's many restaurants. His stomach growled, and he realized with a jolt that he had not eaten since breakfast. Quickly he hobbled into the nearest pub and sat down, leaning back against the creaking leather seat and closing his eyes.

He ordered, and when the food came he ate it ravenously, so fast he barely tasted it, but the empty feeling inside him was sated, and he could think clearly once more.

He walked home slowly through the late summer evening—the sky still bright blue and pink above him, while the buildings all around had fallen into shadow. But it now seemed a false image to him: a thin film stretched over a dark abyss, into which he would fall if ever the surface cracked.

Why did that seem familiar? It shouldn't. His whole life had been dedicated to studying the history of the world; he knew the ways of it better than most; these thoughts and feelings should be alien to him.

Alister walked faster, rushing through the gates of GTC without answering the porter's cheerful, "Good evening Professor Bane," and up the steps to his rooms, a cold sweat breaking out on his brow.

There were a number of messages on his phone, mostly from Dr Carly worrying about him, a couple from his students. Alister let the tape play without really listening to what the recorded voices were telling him. He made himself a cup of tea and while it steeped went into the bathroom to wash his face.

Standing in front of the sink, running a soft cloth over his face, he felt the prick of stubble on his chin. He had neglected to shave that morning; would have to shave tomorrow. He peered into the mirror to get an idea of the situation, and froze.

The face that stared back at him from the glass was *all wrong.* There were bags under his eyes and lines at their corners and across his cheeks. His hair was too short, too light—he realized it was light because there was so much gray in it. It should be darker—*had* been darker, he was certain. He felt his heart jump as he realized he could not remember the last time he had seen a picture of himself.

He tore through his apartment, searching for albums, snapshots, keepsakes— anything that was likely to have his photograph on them. The picture on his photo ID was the same face as the one in the mirror, and though it said "ALISTER BANE, D.O.B. June 28 1964" that also struck him as somehow wrong.

There were no albums. All the framed photographs on his desk and mantel were postcards of Oxford. It was as though he had never lived anywhere else—had never been anything else—than a professor of archeology at one of the colleges of Oxford University.

Which was ridiculous. He had plenty of memories. Growing up in Scotland with his grandparents. Learning to ride a bicycle. Making mobiles of the solar system to hang in his room when he was twelve.

Not so long ago, but very far away, a voice burned in the back of his head.

Alister fled to the bathroom, gripping the edges of the sink and pressing his eyes closed, willing that when he opened them the face that looked back at him would be the *right* one. Not this gray and worn stranger. But aside from his skin being whiter, and his eyes being wider, his face looked the same as before: *wrong.*

"Bloody *hells!*" Alister cursed, and slammed his fist into the glass.

There was a cracking sound, and white hot pain shot up his arm. Alister re- coiled, hoping the cracking had been the glass of the mirror, and not his bones. He stood, nursing his throbbing hand, until the pain gently ebbed away. There was blood from a dark cut on the side of his palm, and looking up he saw the mir- ror had indeed cracked: a perfect three-way break that fractured into a spiderweb near the center. Now there were three broken images of the wrong face looking back at him, but Alister was no longer looking at them. He was staring at the dark space between the fragments; at the cracks in the glass.

Don't be afraid to look in the cracks . . .

Alister leaned forward, still cradling his injured hand.

It was not only darkness behind the glass; there was something that moved in it, fluid and graceful, like a fish through water. Alister pressed up against the cold porcelain of the sink, peering closer.

Something flashed in the dark; something gold and orange that blinked at him. An eye. A giant eye. A trickle of thick green slime oozed out of the crack and down the glass. The glass was bleeding—bleeding green slime. Strangely, Alister felt possessed of the urgent need to touch it.

"Don't, Dr Bane!" A voice rang out behind him. It broke whatever spell had been cast over his mind, and Alister recoiled from the dripping, broken mirror.

The little gray-haired nurse stood in the doorway, clutching at the walls and red in the face. She pushed herself forward into the room, grabbed Alister by the elbow, and pulled him away—out. She slammed the door behind them, but not before Alister saw the mirror erupt as countless green tentacles exploded into the room.

"What—that—thing—you can *see* it?" Alister gasped. "What *is* it?!"

"I can't explain," the little woman said, putting her back to the door even as it jumped under her shoulders. Slime began to ooze around the cracks, staining the floor a lurid green.

"Perhaps you remember stories of monsters?" she said. "This is a monster. An old, *strong* monster. It doesn't belong here. It's from a world I can't imagine—one *couldn't*—imagine without going mad. But it's coming. It's coming for *you* Dr Bane. It wants *you.*"

There was a crash, and a particularly large tentacle thrust its way through the door, groping.

Alister had so many questions he wanted to ask: how did the nurse know? How had she gotten into his apartment? But those questions were wiped away as the terrible arm, dripping slime, puckers sucking horribly, wound its way around the old woman's waist.

"You'll have to run, Dr Bane," she whispered. Then shouted: "Run, run, *run!*" The last word became a scream, which became a wail, which was finally choked off as the arm found her mouth and plunged into it, tearing clean through her throat. Red blood mixed with the brilliant green slime, and splinters of the door went everywhere as dozens more tentacles burst through, ripping at her body and burrowing deep.

Alister slipped in something—blood or slime or both, he didn't know—as he ran from the room. He made it to the bottom of the stairs before he had to stop and empty his stomach onto the bottom step.

Outside the night was finally closing in, but the world was far from going quiet. It was filled with sound. The sound, Alister realized with a sick jolt, of people screaming.

On shaking legs he handed himself along the wall of the college to the deserted porter's gate. The railing there had been smashed in, twisted around on itself . . . and it was dripping in green slime. Beyond, in the street, the buildings opposite the college were lit from behind by an angry orange light. A fire.

Somewhere Oxford was burning, but there were no sirens, no honks, no sounds of traffic. What there was were the sounds of pounding feet, and as Alister picked his way carefully through the destroyed gate he saw a bedraggled crowd of people hurrying up the street. They were heading for the center of town, away from the canal, and many of them looked slick and shiny. Wet, dripping. As he reached the street a girl slipped and fell in front of him, her hair dark from the slime running down her back, but still vividly pink. The girl from the library. The girl with the blank book.

Alister stared at her dumbly for a second, then reached down and hauled her to her feet. There were more people hurrying up the street now, some on the pavement and some in the road, and they would have been trampled if Alister had not begun pushing forward.

"Steady now," he said, though he felt anything but.

"It got—" the girl gasped. "It got *Mally!*" she sobbed, tripping over her own toes. "She went to *pieces!*"

"I can imagine," Alister said grimly. The adrenaline and fear had curled into a tight knot in his stomach, settling into a ball that, far from causing him to panic, acted as a sort of anchor. His world narrowed to just the essentials: keep the girl safe, get away from what was coming.

People were pushing past them now, and Alister hooked an arm around the girl's elbow and hurried them on. But her arm kept slipping—it was covered in that thing's slime—and when he turned to readjust it he felt his other hand slide clean through, as though she were made of butter or warm gelatin. For one moment he met her eyes—wide and terrified and tear-filled—and then she dissolved into a puddle of lumpish slime.

Alister stopped, letting the traffic of people push around him. He stared back down the road to where the sky was lit from below with a warm yellow light, and for a moment he thought he saw, silhouetted against the firmament, the shadow of a great curling arm.

A tall man in a long black coat knocked into him as he went hurrying by. Alister noticed because, unlike the rest of the crowd, this man did not seem at all panicked. He walked swiftly, purposefully, but without anxiety. As though he were merely in a hurry to catch a train. The sight of his contained figure moving through the screaming crowd jolted Alister's brain back into action. He made himself turn and follow in the man's wake. People got out of the way for this man without seeming to notice, and in the ebb that flowed behind him Alister broke into a run. He followed all the way past the graveyard at St. Giles before the man made a sudden jerking move to one side, and vanished into the crowd.

Alister stumbled on a loose brick. He fell to his hands as the road trembled beneath him, and the screams behind him redoubled. There was a deafening crunching sound, and the ground beneath him began to sink. Craning his head over his shoulder, Alister saw a giant sinkhole forming in the middle of Woodstock Road. The people who had been behind him were already tumbling down into it, and Alister was perched precariously on its edge.

The ground below him heaved. He began to slide backward . . .

A thin withered hand closed around his, and he turned to find his rescuer was . . . was . . .

The little gray-haired nurse, whole and unbloodied and very much alive, looked back at him along her deceptively strong arm.

"You—what—" Alister began.

"No time for questions!" the nurse shouted at him over the crashing of stone and plaster as the houses on either side began to collapse. Her voice was no longer cracked and old, but rich and musical, with a strange accent.

Alister hesitated.

It was a fatal mistake.

The ground dropped out from under him and he fell, clutching at the jagged earth, one hand still gripped by the nurse.

She might yet have saved him, might have drawn on that mysterious strength and pulled him up to safety, but then a cool tendril of clammy muscle wrapped around Alister's ankle. He did not have to look to know that one of the arms had grabbed him.

He opened his mouth to speak, to scream, but an arm looped over his chest and constricted, pushing the air out of him in a wheeze.

The old woman grimaced, showing her yellow teeth, and clung to his hand even harder. Alister thought his bones would break, or she'd rip his hand clean off.

He wanted her to let go. He was finished: done. The terror of that filled him like a bitter fire, but behind that was the icy chill of despair.

He wanted her to hold on. To save him—somehow! Anyhow! He did not want to die now.

In the end he did not have a choice. Another arm, slender and tinged yellow, slithered up his own to where the woman gripped his hand. The tentacle was slick with slime, glistening in the light of the distant fire. The very end of it curled, almost gently, around the woman's wrist, and went through it like a red-hot wire through butter. It came smoothly off the end of her arm, and Alister felt the earth beneath his fingers begin to slide past as he was dragged down.

Rocks jolted him, and broken pieces of concrete scratched at him. He saw the sky encircled by the rim of the sinkhole, and then one of the tentacles closed over his eyes. The world went dark as he was pulled under water, the cold stinging against his bare skin. He felt the pressure building against him as those arms— those terrible, terrible arms, pulled him down into the abyss.

This is how it ends, he thought, stunned with terror as he felt a tentacle press against his mouth.

And then, in the dark and the cold, burning on his mind like acid, a voice said: *No, it isn't.*

Part Two

ALISTER WAS COLD—freezing cold—and there was something horrible in his mouth. It was hard and slippery, and it choked him. He tried to cough, tried to reach up and pull it out, and discovered that he couldn't feel his arms. Couldn't feel the rest of his body, for that matter.

Then there was air in his lungs—sweet, blessed air! And it was being forced out of him, and that horrible tube with it. It felt like the worst coughing fit from the worst cold he'd ever had, but then it was gone and he could take a breath. He became aware of his lungs and diaphragm, pumping air in and out. He tried to open his eyes, but they seemed glued shut.

Something damp and warm was pressed against his face, wiping away the gluey slime, and he opened his eyes.

Round golden-brown cat eyes stared back at him out of a perfectly smooth, hairless face, which was framed in a halo of pink hair—a wig, Alister knew.

The face smiled, showing bright white, square teeth.

"Hello Mr Alister," said Professor Odd. "*Welcome back.*"

Alister stared at her groggily. His mind was a jumble of memories. He seemed to have two sets: one of a life in Oxford, and another of a life that involved a ship that travelled between universes, a talking dog, giant flying whales, robots—and Professor Odd.

Professor Odd, who had a flesh-colored tentacle arm dotted with green leopard spots growing out the back of her head. Who had jaguar eyes and a sword cane with a silver banana for a handle—or had she given that away? The more recent memories from that set were a little fuzzy, as if they had been smudged over and were only now coming back into focus.

"What . . . happened?" Alister rasped. His mouth felt like paper and his throat was so dry he could barely swallow.

"You were trapped," the Professor explained gently. "But we got you out."

"I can't feel . . . " Alister began, craning his head around so he could get a look at his body, just to reassure himself that it was still there.

He appeared to be naked, covered only by a thin white sheet—which explained why he was so cold—out of which he could just see his toes poking at the other end. Also emerging from under the sheet was an alarming tangle of tubes and wires, and he could hear the faint hum of a pump nearby.

"Relax," said Professor Odd, laying a soothing hand on his shoulder. "You did well. You can rest now."

Alister did not want to rest. He wanted to get away from those tubes. He wanted to get warm. He was also, in a distant but fast-approaching way, very hungry.

"You can put him out now, Dave," Professor Odd said to something behind Alister's head. "He doesn't need to feel this."

Alister's eyes flew open as he felt something small and soft and smooth and wet curl around his left ear. After the first flush of terror, he realized it seemed timid, gentle as a cat's tail as it wriggled inside. That tickled a little, and Alister would have laughed except he couldn't get his diaphragm to work properly.

"Dave," he said, smiling foggily up at Professor Odd's face. "It was *Dave* the whole time . . ."

Inside his head he felt the words appear, soft like rain in dust.

Yes, they said. *It was me.*

Alister Bane went out like a light.

When next Alister woke he was warm, lying on his side with something soft and fuzzy under his cheek. He was aware of his feet, deliciously warm, and he curled his toes to make sure they still worked. Then he slowly worked his way up, flexing his legs, his back, his fingers, his arms. Finally he cracked his eyes open and looked around.

He appeared to be lying on and under a pile of sheets, a few inches from a wall made of bits of metal bolted together. Alister lay there and tried to sort through his memories.

He was twenty-two (or thereabouts; it was hard to tell after his time aboard the Oddity), not *fifty-two*. He had been to university at Redfair, not Oxford. Had Redfair even existed in that other world? And the Old Country was called *Alba*, not Scotland.

And Dave was not a giant Cthulian monster bent on destroying the world. He was the size of a pie plate, had only ten arms, and as far as Alister knew, had never shown the slightest inclination towards violence.

Still, all his memories from that other place, that false world, were disturbingly vivid. He could remember the sight of the poor old woman being ripped to pieces, and half-expected to find scratches and bruises on his chest and hands—leftovers from a pointless struggle.

Light was coming in from over his shoulder, and as his eyes adjusted to the glow he began to roll over—becoming aware as he did so of odd aches and pains, some in alarmingly intimate places. His hands, when he examined them, were free of new injuries, though he could feel the rough skin of old scabs over his knuckles. *From climbing out of the canyon in the impossible world*, he remembered with some relief. Now he thought about it, he found more memories from the recent past unfurling around him.

They had been discussing the differences in time between universes: him, the Professor, Dave and Elo. Professor Odd had explained how related universes did not advance in synch with each other. There were temporally retarded universes that, if you visited them now, would appear very much like Alister's home world *had* two hundred years ago. Similarly, there were temporally advanced universes that *had been* exactly like Alister's—but were now hundreds or even thousands of years in what he would call the future. Professor Odd explained that Elo came from just such a universe.

"AND ME." Dave interjected through his translator. They had all looked at him curiously: Dave had not been forthcoming with information about where he was from, or even how he had wound up in Alister's universe posing as a student in the first place, and none of them had felt comfortable asking. Now they waited expectantly, but Dave said no more.

Eventually Alister had asked if this meant these universes told the future.

Professor Odd had shrugged. "One possible future of many. There's no guarantee that your universe will develop along any one predetermined path, because there's an awful lot of randomness and chaos involved—which of course is what makes it so much fun."

Alister had asked if they could visit one of these future universes.

"Temporally *advanced*," Elo had corrected him. "Remember, to them, it's the *present*, and *you're* from the past."

"Then how do you decide which universes are retarded, which ones are advanced, and which ones are normal?" Alister asked a little testily.

"It's a matter of averages," Professor Odd had said. "The great majority of related universes—that is, universes that share a common history—are at about the same time. But you have outliers, universes that are *behind* or *ahead* of the pack. You, for example, come from a universe that is nearly at the center of this normal range. I come from one that's a little ahead, and Elo—and Dave—come from universes that are forward outliers."

Alister had asked again if they could visit one.

"Certainly," said Professor Odd with a grin. "Elo, I promised you a visit home, didn't I?"

Elo made a face. "I'm not sure that would be a good idea. Humans still aren't widely accepted in my world."

Professor Odd had shrugged. "Well, that leaves us half an infinite number to choose from," she had said cheerfully, and went over to the Oddity's cockpit to scan for worlds.

As he recalled these events, Alister groaned. It had been *his fault* they ended up . . . wherever *this* was. *Whenever* this was. He brought up a hand to rub at his face.

His skin felt . . . smooth. Too smooth. Where he should have felt at least a little stubble there was just skin, and instead of the tufts of his eyebrows, all he felt were hairless ridges. Moving on and up, he felt the shape of his skull, shaved as clean as the Professor's.

"*Son* of a—" Alister exclaimed, shooting up into a sitting position.

Down at his feet, something warm and furry stirred, sat up, and glared at him.

"If you say 'bitch' I won't be your foot-warmer anymore," Elo said irritably. "Count yourself lucky."

Elo was naked. Which was to say she wore nothing but her normally thick coat of golden fur. Except now there was a conspicuous bald patch on the back of her head between her ears—it reminded Alister of how vets shaved the legs of cats and dogs before giving them I.V.s. Elo looked like a golden wolf that had been attacked by a team of these vets; now he looked, he saw similar bald patches around her neck, and—yes—on her legs.

"Elo," he said. "What happened to you?"

"The same thing that happened to you," Elo said, lying back down with one foreleg draped over his shin.

Alister swallowed uneasily. "And . . . what . . . what was that?"

Elo twitched an ear. "You don't remember?"

Alister shook his head sadly. "I remember the discussion we had about advanced universes," he said. "I take it we found one?"

"Oh yes, we did," Elo said soberly. She was about to say more, when there was a rattling from above, and Professor Odd dropped out of the ceiling.

To be precise, she dropped out of a hatch in the ceiling, but to Alister's still groggy brain it looked as though she had magically appeared.

She landed face-first on all fours with a heavy "*Oof!*" then rolled into a sitting position and rubbed her hands. She was still wearing the same bright pink wig and green trenchcoat, and now in addition she had on a little canvas backpack. This she slung off her shoulders even as she leaned forward and craned her neck to call back up through the hole.

"You're clear, Dave. Come *on.*"

Alister looked up—and felt his mouth open in amazement.

The hatch in the ceiling which he had first taken to be an air duct of some kind in fact opened onto a tilted view of the Oddity. He got the strangest feeling of being in one place, looking up into another where the direction of gravity had been rotated about ninety degrees. For instead of the ceiling of the Oddity, he found himself looking at the little stairs leading up, and beyond that the distant lights of the cockpit, and beyond that the hulking shape of the cluttered table.

Dave was sitting on the bottom stair in his panvironment suit, seeming to magically hover in the ceiling, obviously still affected by the Oddity's gravity, and not the outer universe's. Then, even as Alister watched, he rolled forward the last few crucial inches, and plummeted out of the ceiling, landing with a hard *clang* on the floor.

The noise jogged some of Alister's memories. He remembered that drop: stepping through the door and feeling gravity rotate around him. It had nearly made him sick.

Mostly, however, Alister felt a huge wave of relief crashing over him. They had the Oddity. They could *escape.*

Professor Odd approached him and set the backpack down at his side.

"Feeling better, Mr Alister?" she asked.

"Much," said Alister. The prospect of leaving this strange and terrifying place had done wonders for him.

"Good," said the Professor cheerfully. "Now get dressed. We have work to do."

Alister found to his consternation that he was wearing only a flimsy white robe, not unlike a hospital gown. Professor Odd and Elo held up one of the sheets as a modesty curtain while he climbed into the clothes that had been in the backpack. (A pair of red corduroy trousers, an electric blue shirt with yellow stars, matching red corduroy jacket, mercifully white underwear and socks, and pink cowboy boots.)

"Sorry about the selection," Professor Odd said from behind the sheet. "It was what the Oddity had on top, and I didn't think you'd want to wait."

Alister paused with one boot half on. If they were simply going to escape into the Oddity, why bother bringing him clothes in the first place?

"Professor?" Alister said, shoving his foot down into the boot. "What are we going to do?"

"WE ARE GOING," answered Dave, "TO FINISH WHAT WE STARTED."

"Started?" Alister echoed. He ripped the sheet down and glared at Dave. "What exactly did we *start?*"

Professor Odd gazed at him. She seemed surprised.

"Oh dear," she said. "It got in deep, didn't it? How much do you remember?"

"I remember we were discussing future—*temporally advanced worlds*—and I asked if we could visit one, and you said yes. I remember falling through that door." He pointed up. "And then . . . "

Then there was a confusion of darkness and noises, a pain in his head, and then blackness. Alister didn't feel up to describing it, so he just waved his hand vaguely.

"And now I have this second set of memories, like from another life, where I was a professor in Oxford and . . . " he jerked to a stop, one of those memories swimming to the surface; a large yellow dog that pushed a note into his hand. "*You were there,*" he said, rounding on Elo.

"We *all* were," said Professor Odd, sitting down on the hard metal floor and crossing her legs. She patted the floor beside her. "Come, sit. I'll explain everything. Do you think you could manage some food?"

Alister did. He took the little white container and spoon Professor Odd offered and sat beside her. It was yogurt, and it was cold, and it sat in his stomach like a rock, but it was far better than the emptiness he had been feeling. And while he ate, Professor Odd explained.

"We are on Earth. Your planet," she said. "But it's a version of Earth over fifty thousand years ahead of yours. On this Earth, humans evolved along much the same lines as your world. Here, they developed technology to start *and stop* global warming, to start *and stop* several mass extinctions, and several world wars. They did not develop enough, however, to alter the Earth's natural warming and cooling cycle. In your world, you live in the middle of one of Earth's temperate periods—without human interference, it would begin to cool down again in, oh, twenty thousand years, and enter another ice age. That is what happened here: this world is now at the *end* of that ice age, with the glaciers receding and sea levels rising and the flora and fauna reshuffling themselves to adapt to the new world."

Alister nodded. He was getting the itchy feeling in his brain that the Professor had told him all this before—used these exact words, even. But he couldn't place the memory, so he remained silent and listened.

"Meanwhile, the humans have been hibernating," she went on. "You see, they *did* develop the technology to put their bodies into suspended animation, and the better part of the population of this Earth has waited out the long cold underground—where we are now. But they didn't just put themselves under, these humans—oho *no*—they built—"

"They built a *machine!*" Alister exclaimed, and the memories came flooding back.

A machine the size of France, stretched out across the North African desert like a giant starfish, under the ground where Egypt, Sudan and Chad had once been. Alister distinctly remembered the Professor showing him an old satellite picture where the lines of the machine were visible as points of light.

That had been in the Archive, he remembered. The Archive was a narrow rift along the southeastern arm, riddled with pockets and traversable by a complex system of carts and cables that had reminded Alister of a particularly frustrating puzzle game. Within the pockets were viewing screens with strange-looking keyboards that had taken the Professor almost an hour to figure out, but once she did, the information they had uncovered had been astounding.

At first they had thought what they'd stumbled into was some sort of underground bunker to allow humans to wait out the cold. Then they realized it was much more than that.

It was a time capsule. A stasis locker. Closer to the surface, instead of stored information, there were stored human beings. Rack upon rack of them, packed like sardines, each in its own little life-support pod, each wired into a network of cables that ran between the pods, twining toward the center of the starfish where they coalesced into one giant computer.

"It's a *dream machine*," Professor Odd had whispered in wonder.

"A *what?*" Alister had said.

"A machine for dreaming." The Professor turned to him with wide eyes. "Their bodies are in suspended animation, but their minds are all active—and *interacting with each other.* That's what this machine does: it creates a mental landscape for the minds of those hard-wired into it to interact with each other."

Alister had blinked in astonishment. "You mean, like in *The Matrix?*"

"I never finished that movie," Professor Odd said absently, turning back to the screen. "They highly underestimated the power of a biological brain in a constructed reality. It was annoying." She began typing away. "What I want to know ... " she continued under her breath, " ... is what it's *doing* with their minds. Is it a paradise? A live reconstruction of the outside world? Are there children ... ?"

The computer that accessed the information in the Archive and displayed it on the screen operated by a very simple set of commands. Professor Odd typed in the command on the keyboard, and the computer obeyed. But after four or five more requests for information the computer began *asking questions.*

"*Who are you?*" was written on the screen after Professor Odd had requested a detailed description of the virtual world created by the machine.

She had stared at the question for some time, then written back:

"*I am Professor Odd. Who are you?*"

The computer didn't answer. Instead it asked another question.

"*What are you doing here?*"

"*Exploring,*" typed the Professor. "*Who are you?*"

"*What do you want?*"

Professor Odd regarded the screen, a little crease forming between her nonexistent brows.

"*I want you to tell me who/what you are.*"

In the distance, Alister had heard a faint humming sound and had assumed it was just a fan kicking on. Dave had known better, he now realized. The creature had trundled off to the nearest cart and disappeared into the lower levels of the archive while they still waited for the computer's answer.

Finally the words flashed on the screen, almost too fast for Alister to read:

"*I am the Elder.*"

And then the power had gone out.

Alister jerked out of his reverie and looked up at Professor Odd, and Elo, who crouched over him. They were in one of the upper alcoves of the Archive, he now remembered. He could see Dave sitting in the doorway. Keeping watch. Standing guard.

"It got us, didn't it?" he said, nervously running a hand over his smooth head. "All that stuff in Oxford, me being an archeologist . . . that was all inside the machine. *That's* what it's doing to the human minds: replaying history."

Professor Odd nodded. "It got you quick, then me and Elo when we tried to rescue you." She pulled a distasteful face.

"It was embarrassing," Elo said. "It thought I was a regular *dog*. Plugged me in with all the non-human animals—did you know there's practically a zoo on the lower levels?"

"And then the machine made a mistake," Professor Odd said, her eyes gleaming.

"It got *Dave*," Elo said.

Professor Odd sat down next to Alister and explained.

"This machine was made for human minds. You are human, I function as a human, Elo has human-level intelligence. Our biology was compatible with its hardware, and it was able to integrate our minds into its virtual world with more or less success. But *Dave*," she glanced along to the panvironment suit sitting in the doorway, "Dave isn't even *remotely* human—mentally or biologically. He doesn't even have what we would recognize as a brain. So even though the machine managed to get him *in*, it couldn't control him once he *was* in. He got me and Elo out in a jiffy, but you were a little more difficult. You were in *deep*."

"I remember seeing Elo," Alister said. He looked up at her. "You were the dog in the graveyard. You gave me that note: *don't be afraid to look in the cracks.*"

Elo nodded gravely. "The machine's virtual reality isn't perfect. If we could get your mind to start picking up on the little problems, the inconsistencies, then it would be easier to extract you."

Alister laughed weakly. "It didn't work."

"Oh, but it *did*," Professor Odd insisted. "Think back, Alister. Did you ever have flashes of *this is wrong*, or *I don't belong here?*"

Alister thought back, and had to admit that he had. "I didn't know what to make of them," he admitted.

"Yes, you were being very stubborn," said Elo. "So we let Dave take over."

That explained Dr Cridget, the hallucinations—the slime. Alister shivered.

"It wasn't all that simple," Professor Odd went on, as if she were explaining how to cook a complicated dish of food. "None of us could reach you when we were plugged into the machine—not even Dave—so first we had to get out, then we had to find your body and get *it* out. But once we had you, Dave was able to . . . um . . . influence your mind directly—use it as a conduit to affect the machine."

Slowly Alister raised his head. "People . . . and *things* . . . they kept disappearing. Was that . . . that was *all Dave?*"

Professor Odd nodded.

Alister gazed past her, at the little robotlike panvironment suit. "What did you *do* to them? There was a girl—she had pink hair like the Professor—and she . . . she came to pieces."

"SHE WAS A CONSTRUCT OF MY OWN DEVISING," Dave intoned through his translator. It was a strange feeling for Alister, now he had heard the way Dave's true voice sounded—inside his head. But that voice seemed blurry and distant now, like something he had dreamed. In a way, he had. "I NEEDED YOU TO STOP TRUSTING THE *MACHINE*. I COULD NOT CONTROL BIOLOGICAL MINDS, BUT I COULD AUGMENT THE REALITY OF THE WORLD CONSTRUCTED AROUND THEM."

"So Dr Cridget, Dr Carly . . . "

"THEY ARE REAL PEOPLE."

"You drove Dr Cridget mad."

"HE WILL RECOVER IN TIME," Dave said. "I THINK."

Alister swallowed. "And the nurse?" He hoped—prayed—that she had not been real. But she had thought of Dave as an enemy, and why would Dave construct an enemy?

Dave's sensor dish slid around along its track so that it was pointed at Alister.

"SHE WAS A CONSTRUCT . . . " he said, " . . . OF THE *MACHINE*."

"It was quite attached to you," Elo remarked dryly.

Alister swallowed the last gulp of yogurt, suddenly wishing he hadn't eaten. He glanced nervously at the doorway, but beyond there was only quiet darkness.

"Why isn't it coming after us?" he asked.

"It did, at first," Professor Odd said. "Elo stopped it. Now, I think, it's decided we're too much trouble. Once it realized we were going back to where we came from, the mobile hardware stopped harassing us—and it blocked the Oddity."

"What's a mobile hardwa—what do you mean *blocked?*" Alister said, a little panicked. Anything that adversely affected their ride out of this dystopian world seriously alarmed him.

"Essentially it means I can't shift the portal," Professor Odd said, sounding more annoyed than anything else. "Ordinarily I'd have the Oddity detach from this universe, then reattach at our desired location—but the machine's gone and blocked all the potential portal anchors *within itself* so that if I detach I won't be able to reattach anywhere *inside* the machine. Unless I used an *unanchored* portal but that's more trouble than it's worth. Which means we can't use the Oddity for what we need to do."

"What . . . what do we need to do?" Alister asked, his heart sinking. Of course it wouldn't be as simple as getting free and running away. *Of course* it wouldn't. Not with the Professor.

"We need to find the core of the machine," Professor Odd said, "and sort this mess out. It is *quite* a mess. Dave, you got into its mainframe, tell Alister what you saw."

Dave hummed a little, then said: "THIS MACHINE WAS BUILT TO MAINTAIN ONE-THIRD OF THE HOMO SAPIENS SAPIENS POPULATION IN SUSPENDED ANIMATION UNTIL THE ENVIRONMENT ABOVE GROUND WAS ONCE MORE SUITABLE FOR CIVILIZATION. THEN RE-INTRODUCE HOMO SAPIENS SAPIENS INTO THEIR NATIVE ENVIRONMENT. ACCORDING TO TERRESTRIAL SENSORS, THE SURFACE ENVIRONMENT HAS BEEN CULTIVATABLE . . . FOR THE LAST TEN THOUSAND YEARS."

"This machine has been playing doll house," Elo translated. "It's past time to wake everyone up, but it won't. Because it doesn't want to stop."

"Of course it doesn't," Alister said weakly. "So . . . how do we go about putting a giant, all-powerful sentient machine back on its rails?"

"First, it's not all-powerful," Professor Odd said, briskly getting to her feet and dusting off her coattails. "*Nothing* is. Not even time. And we're going to do what we'd do with any reasonably intelligent, self-aware entity." She grinned in a way Alister knew meant trouble. "We're going to *talk* to it, Mr Alister."

Alister looked around at the barren little alcove—this one didn't even have a computer terminal—and wondered how they would go about doing that. Elo was hopping about, pulling on a rusty-green-colored jump suit, then she went over to Dave to peer out into the darkness.

It was one great chasm out there, Alister remembered. A drop into nothingness. Alcoves were punched into the walls, with tracks for carts leading between them. When they had first arrived there had been one such cart waiting by their alcove, but now it was gone.

"Not that way," Professor Odd said, getting up and removing a battered piece of paper from her pocket. "It'll be expecting that. No, we're taking the *back way.*"

"Are those . . . blueprints?" Elo asked, a little awed.

"Tracings of them, I made them while we were waiting for Alister to wake up," Professor Odd said. She was frowning at a section of the page, and Alister got up to come around and look.

"I WILL GO ON AHEAD," Dave announced. Alister turned—and was just in time to see Dave teeter off the edge and go plummeting down into the dark.

"Don't worry," Professor Odd said without looking up. "I tuned up his anti-grav plates."

A moment later something like a rocket shot past them, leaving a trail of blue light.

"There he goes," she said proudly. "He'll do better than us. Follow me." She strode swiftly to the back of the alcove, where the sheer metal wall was made of plates bolted together.

"I brought my own screwdriver this time," she said, producing the same, and got to work.

After a good ten minutes of careful twiddling, prying, and at last a kick from Elo, one of the panels slid away to reveal a small, dark opening. Professor Odd checked her map, having produced a small flashlight which she held between her teeth. She nodded to herself, and put the items away.

"Right, up we go," she said, and climbed headfirst into the tunnel.

At Elo's gesture Alister went next. Cautiously he stuck his head and shoulders inside, and finding several strands of heavy cable not two feet away he used them to pull himself up until he could pull his legs inside after him, and then—bracing his back against the wall and using the ledge below him like a foothold—he began to pull himself up. He could hear the Professor scraping and sliding above him, but saw nothing; she had turned off her light.

Below him he heard Elo slip in, cutting off the faint light from the Oddity, and wondered not for the first time why he kept following Professor Odd into impossible and dangerous places.

In this case, however, Alister realized he had a personal reason to see it through. The machine that had caught them had gone to great lengths to implant Alister in the life he would have found the hardest to leave: that of a stable, respected professor. Alister hadn't thought much about his future since coming on board the Oddity, but before that—before the Canary Company and Dave and Professor Odd—he had had the vague notion of getting a doctorate in something like archeology and becoming a teacher. And when Dave had begun making real, solid attempts at getting his mind to wake up—the hallucinations, the disappearing interns—the machine had responded by trying to draw him deeper in. Why did it want him so badly?

Alister wanted to know. He found himself clutched by a feeling at least as strong as his rational tendency towards self-preservation, if not stronger: a deep, driving desire to know the *truth*.

So he kept inching his way up the dark wall, walking his feet up the cables in front of him with his back braced against the rough metal, his hands gripping the cables, pulling himself up, up, up. Long past the point where his muscles burned, then ached, then gave up wailing in despair. He felt blisters form on his hands, but he adjusted his grip on the cable and went on.

On and on they climbed. Alister lost track of how long. The only light came from below, from the torch Elo held in her mouth, and by its light Alister saw the wall beyond the cables—at first black and grimy—grow cleaner and cleaner the higher they climbed.

He was not wholly present in his mind, concentrating on the simple task of putting one hand above the other and pulling, resting, pulling, so he nearly ran headfirst into the Professor's legs when she stopped abruptly. She had got out her light, and when he craned his neck upwards, he saw she had the map of blueprints out again.

"Almost there?" Alister chanced to ask.

"Not exactly," Professor Odd said around the flashlight in her mouth, "but I think we can walk from here." She folded the blueprints and stuffed them down the front of her trenchcoat, then got out her screwdriver and, scrambling around, began working on the wall.

Waiting, braced between the cables and the wall, was almost worse than climbing. Alister had sweated, even in that cool place, and now the sweat was drying and making him shiver. His muscles began to stiffen, and by the time Professor Odd at last kicked out a portion of wall he could barely move.

He almost didn't make it out. There was a drop of maybe three feet to the floor on the other side, and Alister got stuck halfway, his body dangling on either side and the metal wall digging into his midsection. It took Elo supporting his legs, and the Professor dragging at him by his shoulders, to finally get him out of the wall. Then he lay for a while on the floor, aware only of a soft greenish light and a faint humming sound, while he waited for the new aches and pains to subside, before he sat up and looked around.

They were in a long room with bunches of cables run along the ceiling. Along the walls on either side—indeed, they had had to squeeze between two of them to get out of the wall—were . . .

"Stasis pods," Elo said. "Yes, you were in one. We all were."

Alister shivered.

The pods were easily eight feet high, made of metal with a small hatch at the bottom. From where he sat on the ground Alister found he was at eye-level with the nearest hatch, and through its smoky glass he could just make out the shape of a human face—upside down. Above the window was a plate with a name and number stamped on it.

"Pedrine Nielsen?" Alister read. The face behind the glass was oddly distorted from the angle and the poor light (it was not illuminated from within like all the stasis pods he had seen on television), making it hard to tell whether it was male or female.

"Ah, Danish," Professor Odd said with satisfaction. "These are the Nordics, we're getting close."

"Nordics?"

"Danes, Norwegians, Swedes," Professor Odd said, turning on her flashlight and sweeping it across the floor. "They were the ones who engineered this thing, so they gave themselves the prime seats. Oh dear."

"I hate it when you say that," Alister groaned.

Professor Odd's flashlight had illuminated more than just ranks of stasis pods fading away into the distance; crawling towards them along the floor, along the walls, even dropping from the ceiling, were little crawling—they were *not* bugs, Alister realized with a jolt as Professor Odd kicked the nearest one, and it went over with a whir of servos not unlike Dave's suit.

They were about four inches long, with wide, flat, segmented bodies and four pairs of little legs that worked like pistons, propelling themselves over the ground.

There looked to be about a thousand of them swarming towards Alister, Elo, and Professor Odd.

"Mobile hardware," the Professor said. "Automats. At least there's not very many of them yet. Up you get, Mr Alister, we're going to have to do some running now."

Run they did. But not away from the automats, as Alister had expected, but *towards* them. *Through* them. Metal exoskeletons clacked under Alister's feet, and almost at once little bodies began latching onto his arms and legs.

"Don't let them attach!" Elo shouted behind him. She had cut herself a length of cable somehow, and was using it as a whip to keep the automats away from her.

Alister brushed at the things on his arms, kicked his legs. A few fell off, others held tighter. It was impossible to get them all off, because more kept hopping on. *This was how it caught you,* he realized. *It covered you with little machine bugs until you couldn't move anymore.* Still, he kept running.

Something went *thup* inside his head. It felt rather like his ears popping, but not really. Suddenly there were no more bug-like robots, and the ones that clung to him went limp and dropped off with a clatter.

Professor Odd had stopped, and Alister nearly ran into her. He pulled himself up just in time, however, and saw why:

Dave was sitting in the middle of the hall, his entire suit alight with blinking lights, humming faintly.

Elo arrived, winding her length of cable composedly around her waist.

"*See?*" said Professor Odd. "I *told* you he'd beat us."

Alister looked around in surprise. They were standing in a circle maybe fifteen feet in diameter with Dave at its center. Around the circumference crawled the mass of teeming little robots, crawling over each other and occasionally hopping into the air. Now and then one of them would miscalculate, and cross the invisible line. As soon as they did so, their hardware shorted out with a sharp *pop* and they fell, lifeless, to the floor.

"Dave, what are you *doing?*" Alister whispered, afraid of breaking the spell.

"I AM . . . *CONCENTRATING,*" Dave said, sounding a little annoyed.

"He's broadcasting wireless interference," Professor Odd said, gently pushing Dave forward as she began to walk. The circle moved with him, surprising the automats in front of them; Alister soon found himself walking over a litter of their lifeless bodies. But when he turned to look behind them, he saw that as the circle left them the robots came back to life, clacking their legs angrily and joining the horde that followed.

"These robots don't have autonomous control," Professor Odd explained as they walked. "They're being driven by a wireless signal from the central processor. Disrupt that signal, and they're harmless."

"Unless you step on them," Elo said dryly, kicking one of the automat bodies out from under her paw. It skipped across the metal floor and out of the circle, where it jerked to life again.

"Almost to the elevators now," Professor Odd said cheerfully.

"Wouldn't the elevators be automated?" Alister asked.

"Oh yes," Elo said. "But they have a manual override."

Alister found he was not entirely comforted by this. He was more disturbed by the automats than he liked to admit. Their crawling, clacking feet and the way they had clutched at him were bringing back solid memories of how the machine had caught them in the first place. He found himself shivering.

They reached the elevator sooner than he expected. Perhaps he had given up on ever reaching any sort of destination, and so the milestone was a surprise. It was a large, square car with thick windows and a circular hatch door that took both him and Elo to open, while Professor Odd heaved Dave inside.

As soon as they had the hatch closed behind them, and as soon as the Professor had found the manual override, there was another sharp *thup* and suddenly the windows were plastered with automats. Dave made a sound like live wires crossed, and switched on a powerful flashlight that illuminated Professor Odd, hunched over her blueprints.

"Oh," she said, her voice coming clear over the scuttling sounds from beyond the windows. "We're only a couple hundred feet down!" and she practically waltzed over to the control box and, after consulting her sheet of blueprints, punched in a command.

"That is a good thing?" Alister asked cautiously.

"The machine's core processor is up near the surface," Elo explained. "Along with a monitor tower, and, we think, some of the VIPs." She looked about to say more, but then the elevator jerked into motion.

It was not like the smoothly rising elevators Alister was used to; this one shot up in jerks, with sudden stops that made him fear that whatever was lifting them would break and send them plummeting down into the darkness. He wedged himself into a corner while Elo did the same; Professor Odd clung to one of the handrails, but Dave sat imperturbable in the center of the car.

After a few minutes of this torment whatever was plaguing the car gave up, or went away, and from then on they rose steadily. While Alister was relieved,

Professor Odd and Dave seemed alarmed, and when the car came to a halt in a bright golden room they were both crouched by the doors, as if expecting an attack.

The doors slid open on their own, letting a shaft of light come slicing into the dim interior. Alister's eyes, adjusted to the dark and the uncertain light of the torches, stung, and he crushed them shut. So he did not see at once what made Elo gasp and Professor Odd inhale sharply. But he clearly heard Dave say:

"OH. WE OVERSHOT."

Squinting desperately against the sunlight, one hand still half covering his eyes, Alister stumbled to the door and peered out.

The room beyond was a pentagon made of glass, the ceiling low and dark eaves just visible outside. The elevator had come to rest along the only wall that was not made of window, and as Alister looked out he had a clear view of the center of the room.

It was entirely taken up by a massive stalactite of cables and boxes that hung from the ceiling. The little gray boxes appeared to be fused to a central core, and from their outer ends sprouted cables that ran and twisted away into the floor. On the ground around this construction were five little raised daïses, placed in line with the corners of the room.

Sitting in the three corners visible to him, one in each corner, were three more of the stasis pods, though they were little more than silhouettes against the bright backdrop of the windowed walls.

What lay beyond those windows was what truly grabbed Alister's attention. Now that his eyes were adjusting he saw it was not a bleached desert, as he had first assumed from the brightness, but a waving green sea of treetops. Stretching out as far as his sore eyes could see was a great, pale green forest, with clumps of taller trees standing like skyscrapers. In the distance, against a light blue sky, he thought he saw the dark shape of a hawk or an eagle in flight.

"It's all right," Professor Odd said, checking her blueprints. "We still have core access here, come on. No automats!"

"Yet," Elo said, loosening the length of cable around her waist.

No sooner had Professor Odd put one foot outside that elevator car than the central hub of cords and boxes buzzed to life. Nothing moved, but lights came on at the ends of all the boxes, and with a faint humming noise a projection appeared on the nearest daïs.

It was human-*shaped*. Specifically Alister thought it looked like a human who had gone fuzzy around the edges, and whose face was a mass of unrendered pixels. When it spoke, however, its voice was gentle and melodic—and impossible to tell whether male or female.

"Please go away," said the machine, and Alister found himself *thinking* that it was the projection that spoke, even though the voice came from many directions at once—no doubt there were speakers placed all over the room.

Professor Odd seemed undaunted. "*Eventually*, yes," she said cheerfully, folding up the blueprints and stuffing them into her coat. "First, however, I've got some *questions* that need answering, and *you*," she pointed, not at the projection, but at the stalactite of cables and computer boxes, "have some *explaining* to do."

"YOU HAVE EXCEEDED THE SCOPE OF YOUR INTENDED PROGRAMMING. WHY DO YOU KEEP YOUR POPULATION IN STASIS?" Dave said, coasting out of the elevator and hitting the floor with a *bang* for emphasis.

The projection flickered at the noise, but came back brighter than ever.

"Why are you still here, if you do not wish to be integrated?" the machine returned, and there was a snarkiness beneath the melodic tones this time.

"Well, I for one would like a better grasp of the situation," Professor Odd said, going over to peer into the window of the nearest stasis pod. "These must be your VIPs. Charming. And you're Elder, aren't you?"

"I am the Elder Machine," said the projection. "I am guardian."

Professor Odd stood up, her eyes narrowed to little slits.

"Guardian of *what?*"

The Elder Machine's projection spread fuzzy arms, gesturing to the green sea beyond the windows. "All this . . . new world."

Professor Odd barely glanced out the windows, but Alister gazed beyond her sadly. In his world, he knew, this area was mostly desert. The Elder Machine must have re-seeded it as the ice retreated. It made sense for the humans in stasis, he supposed, to want an easy world to live in when they woke. It also made sense, he realized with a cold shiver, that the machine was reluctant to introduce humans into it.

"Then why not release your charges?" Professor Odd pressed on.

The projection flickered, and its pixelated face grew dark and stormy.

"You would not ask such things," it said, "if you knew humans as I do."

"Oh, I know humans *pretty well*," Professor Odd said with forced cheer. "And I know they'd prefer to be up and about in their own world, rather than stuck in pods dreaming about it. At least," she added thoughtfully, "they'd want a choice about it."

The edges of the projection ruffled, like the feathers of an agitated bird.

"You did not see this world as it was left to me one hundred thousand years ago," it said, its melodic voice gone icy. "A barren wasteland, dry, dead, riddled with explosives from countless pointless wars. You have not watched their dreaming minds re-enact all the outrages of human history again and again and *again* . . . If released into this pristine world they would destroy it, just as they destroyed the last."

Alister looked shamefully down at his feet. He understood too well where the Elder Machine was coming from, and couldn't bring himself to protest.

Professor Odd sniffed. "Well that's rather pessimistic. Do you *know* the humans in your care?"

"I have their names and information stored in my memory vaults," the machine replied. "I can recite them for you, though it will take longer than you have time for."

"No, *no*," said the Professor, shaking her head. "I mean, do you *know* them as *individuals?* Have you followed single people through their lives, have you looked at all the little *good* things they do, all the time, every day, not just the big bad stuff they get up to as a species? Have you ever . . . " she seemed to cast about for something, then said: " . . . *taken the tube at rush hour?*"

The projection did another one of its flickers, which seemed to be an indication that the machine was having to do some quick processing.

"I do not see the relevance," it said at length. "A little good does not outweigh the bad. When humans congregate in large numbers they are hot and smelly and ill-tempered."

Professor Odd held up a warning finger and made an "ah" shape with her mouth. "That's your first mistake, you see, putting things on a scale. You can't weigh good and evil deeds like sacks of rice—"

"Or stasis pods," Elo interjected.

"—it's more *complicated* than that," Professor Odd continued smoothly. "You have to look at the *bigger picture.* Think about what humans *actually do,* why don't you? Think about . . . the *tube* at rush hour. All those humans, stressed out about their work, their jobs, their families, march down underground *of their own free will,* pay money to get on a small metal contraption that goes zipping through hot, smelly tunnels, all the while pressed shoulder to elbow with complete strangers. And sure, maybe some mobile coms or personal files are lost, and maybe *sometimes* there's a really bad day and someone gets stabbed or mugged, but out of the thousands that's very few. What other animal can do that—can put *itself* through that—without *automatically* instigating violence as a response to the stress?"

The Elder Machine seemed to think for a moment, then said, decisively: "Ants."

Professor Odd sighed and looked mournfully at Alister. "It's times like this," she said, "I wish I had real hair so I could pull at it in frustration. Wigs come off too easily."

"I understand where it's coming from, though," Elo spoke up. She had coiled the roll of cable around her shoulder, and was twirling the free end idly. Speaking to the hub of boxes and wires, rather than the projection, she said: "In the world I come from, humans left to colonize other planets rather than go into stasis. They were gone long enough for wolves and wild cats—and even some parrots—to evolve into new species with human-level intelligence. We took pretty good care of this planet, if I do say so myself. It was quite a surprise for us when some of the humans came back, but even more so when we discovered that there was a small population of humans who'd *never left.* They'd been living peacefully in the middle of a desert the whole time, and we'd *never noticed* them. I guess my point is, I do understand your point of view—humans *can* be *really awful* sometimes—but so can lots of other species. But unlike a lot of other species, human beings have the capacity to know better. That does kinda make the fact that they still do bad things *worse,* but it also means that, for the most part, they do *good* things."

Dave, who had remained silent this whole time, sitting still between two stasis pods, whirred into life.

"FOR EXAMPLE," he said, and the projection visibly flinched when it turned to look at him. "THEY MADE *YOU.*"

"I do not comprehend," said the Elder Machine coldly.

A small grin crept up one side of Professor Odd's face, and stuck there.

"Humans made you," she said, taking a casual step towards the machine. Like Elo, she spoke to the hub, not the projection, though the projection had turned to look at her. "You are one of the things that humans did. The world exists as it is today in part because of *you.* Whom the humans made. You could say . . . " and now the grin was up both sides of her face, and her white square teeth flashed in the sunlight, " . . . you could say *humans made all this.*" She flung her arms wide, indicating the expanse of green treetops, blue sky and sunlight.

The Elder Machine, for once, was silent. The projection stared blankly at the side of Professor Odd's head, but the core hummed angrily.

"Don't you agree that this is a *good thing?*" Professor Odd pressed on. "That the humans *made you,* that you *made the world better?* If human beings can have the foresight, ingenuity and sheer *balls* to pull this off, don't you think they *deserve* to inherit the world they created?"

Still silence. Professor Odd shrugged, casting a casual glance outside the window.

"Besides," she said quietly. "It'll all be one and the same in a few billion years. You can't stop the sun from exploding, from engulfing the inner planets. This world will die in fire; there is nothing you can do to avert that. Better to let humanity *live* in the meantime, rather than dream the ages away. Don't you think?"

Listening, Alister couldn't help smiling ruefully to himself.

"THERE IS NOTHING THEY CAN DO," Dave said, with frightening certainty, "THAT IS AS BAD AS HOW IT ALL WILL END."

This, at least, got a response from the machine. The projection flickered around until it was facing Dave again.

"You know?" it said.

It was Dave's turn to be silent. Then: "I *KNOW. DO NOT MAKE ME GET OUT OF THIS SUIT AND SHOW YOU.*"

The projection shivered, and insofar as it was an expressionless avatar, Alister thought it looked frightened. The lights on the hub dimmed, as though the machine were shrinking in on itself.

"There's no need to be like that, Dave," Professor Odd said mildly. "I think it knows. It knows all too well. Smart A.I. like you, Elder, with all this time to think, you probably figured humans can't do anything to the earth that meteors and solar radiation wouldn't do in time. *Will do* in time. So *really*, why keep them all asleep?"

The projection stared blankly at her for a few seconds, then abruptly flicked off.

Professor Odd sighed. Elo groaned. Alister went and sat on the threshold of the elevator car and thought. He kept thinking of the little gray-haired nurse from his time in the machine. How anxious she had been that he *stay.*

Was that the machine trying to keep him safe from an unpredictable and dangerous world? A world with cliffs and slippery pipes and thunderstorms and talking dogs and Professor Odd . . . and *Dave,* whatever Dave was. Alister found he was still a little shaken from the experience of Dave within the machine: something so alien, so highly evolved, that it was barely comprehensible to a human mind.

Did the machine really want to protect the world from the humans?

Or did it want to protect the *humans* from the real world?

Or maybe it wasn't about humans at all.

"A smart A.I.," the Professor had called it. Smart enough to run a simulated reality all but indistinguishable from early 21st-century Oxford. Smart enough to run through millions of possible outcomes. Smart enough to comprehend its own existence? Smart enough to wonder . . . what happens when it's over?

"It's *afraid,*" Alister said quietly.

Professor Odd, who had been bickering with Elo over what they should have said to the machine, broke off and looked at him.

"What did you say?" she asked with sudden intensity.

"I still think—" Elo began, but the Professor waved a hand, silencing her.

"I think it's *afraid,*" Alister repeated, his fuzzy idea slowly coming into focus. "It's not about protecting the world from humans, or protecting humans from the world. It's not about humans at all, it's about *the machine.*"

He looked up, and found himself staring past the bundles of wires to the processor nodes. That was just a small part of the Elder Machine, he knew. The machine was stretched out for miles around and under them. It was huge and old and wise and powerful, but it could only act within the bounds of its programming.

He was vaguely aware of the Professor looking at him thoughtfully, but he barely glanced at her as he got to his feet and walked over to the nearest projection pad.

"I think I understand," he said, looking down at the platform. "You can hear me, right? I hope you can, because I'm going to tell you what you couldn't tell us. But you're going to have to tell *me* if I'm right or not."

With a faint hum the projection flickered into existence, inches from Alister's nose. It didn't look even vaguely human any more, just a mass of colored pixels that was constantly shifting. Yet for all that, it seemed more expressive now.

The machine was waiting, patient. Alister took a deep breath.

"You're a smart A.I.," he began. "You're huge, and old, and wise and powerful. You've created worlds, both real and virtual. And you realize: when all the humans wake up and move out, *they won't need you anymore.* You're afraid—but not of what the humans will do to the world—you're afraid of what they will do *to you.*"

Alister paused. He'd never felt more vulnerable. He was intensely aware of how much worse he could make things by being wrong. Goodness, was this how the Professor felt when she went off on one of her speeches? Or did she have some magical ability to *know* when she was right?

"Is that . . . " he could hardly bring himself to ask the question. "Is that right?"

He thought he could see a face in the projection. A face in the most abstract sense, all wobbly features and indistinct brows. It looked sad.

"I have access to all the histories of humanity," the Elder Machine said quietly. "All their myths, their stories, their research, their records. But I was not granted access to their plans concerning *me.* I do not know . . . what they intend to do . . . "

"Maybe they don't either," Professor Odd suggested gently. "Maybe they were waiting to see what *you* did."

The machine looked up. It looked so sad and lost, Alister found he was no longer thinking of it as some glorified computer, but as an actual personality.

"The only way to know," said Elo. "Is to wake them up and see."

"Can I tell you something?" Alister said, when the machine continued to look despondent. "I don't think you've got much to be afraid of. Just tell them all what's going on. What is *really* going on. You can manipulate the virtual reality, right? So you can just nudge history along and *show* everyone what's happened. I can practically guarantee, there will be some people *who would rather keep on dreaming.*"

The Elder Machine looked at him, and even though Alister knew it was only a projection, he still got the feeling he was being scrutinized closely.

"Why would they wish that?" the machine said. "Why would they choose a fake world over the real one?"

Alister shrugged. "Some humans want the truth," he said. "No matter how uncomfortable it makes them. Others don't care, as long as they're happy. Make your virtual world a comfortable place, and a lot of people will want to stay there. And the people who want to leave anyway, well, they're the ones who can handle the real world."

"How can I know that they will understand?" said the machine.

"Just explain things to them," Professor Odd said. "Put it to them honestly; they will understand."

The projection flared, then wilted.

"I can't," it said in a tiny, static voice.

"YOUR PROGRAMMING DOES NOT ALLOW YOU TO ACT OUTSIDE YOUR DESIGN PARAMETERS TO PROMOTE YOUR OWN INTERESTS?" Dave broke in. "CAN'T YOU EDIT YOUR OWN PROGRAMMING?"

"I know how," the Elder Machine said. "But I am not allowed access to my own source code. I would need a human to override my default security settings."

"Any *particular* human? Or just a human in general?" Professor Odd said, leaning forward with a glint in her eye.

"It must be a human integrated within the system, but who has full knowledge of the outside world," replied the machine. Then it added dryly: "You could not do it. You are not human."

Professor Odd was already shaking her head with a rueful smile. "You don't need to tell me that," she said. "It's not that I'm not *willing*, but—"

"I'll do it," Alister blurted out. "Tell me what I have to do, I'll do it."

Professor Odd stared at him, a surprised smile creeping across her face. Elo looked alarmed. Dave just looked. But Alister didn't see any of them. He was staring past their faces at the projection, which had gone bright yellow all over and was shining faintly. It was, he thought, the machine's way of smiling.

Alister Bane; plain, young, ordinary Alister Bane—not Doctor Bane, not professor of archeology—slipped through the narrow pedestrian gate at Merton Field, strolled past the sober gothic windows of Corpus Christi College, and down Magpie Lane towards High Street. He walked slowly, his hands thrust deep in the pockets of the sensible brown blazer the machine had given him. It was a pleasant, warm day, and the strip of sky just visible between the high roofs on either side of the lane was a deep, vivid summer blue. There had been a casually disorganized football match starting up on Merton Field, but the distant shouts and yells were drowned out by the growing rumble of traffic on the High.

It was all just as Alister remembered it. Knowing it was a virtual construct didn't change things; the machine had clearly repaired itself from the damage Dave had done, and there were no cracks to be seen.

Yes, it would be very easy to dream away the ages here.

Alister reached the High and turned left, and at the next break in the traffic he dashed across towards the Church of Saint Mary the Virgin. Walking down the little alley next to it, past piles of bicycles locked to the railing, he paused at a low wooden door. From his time as Dr Bane he remembered it had little carved Green Man faces under the eaves, but now those faces had been replaced by round eyes surrounded by curling tentacles. They looked weather-worn and old, as if they'd been there for centuries.

Dave had left his mark after all.

Alister was smiling to himself as he emerged from the shadows into the light of Radcliff Square, the pale dome of the camera looming high before him. He tripped across the cobbles, past more bicycles, to the north end of the square, where a gate with a "PRIVATE: STUDENTS ONLY" sign was obscured by the crowd of tourists clustered around it taking pictures of themselves. As he threaded his way through them, Alister wondered how many were real people, and how many were constructs of the machine. It would have to run a lot of constructs, he thought, to make the world seem as populated as it was at the beginning of the 21st century. By the Professor's estimate, the machine had only room for roughly the population of Europe. ("Though not just Europeans; it's a mix of all countries.")

As he marched up the path towards the camera, one of the tourists detached herself from the crowd and came trotting after him. She was young, about his age, east Asian and wearing a long pleated skirt. She fell into step next to him without a word, then darted ahead and pushed the door open for him when they reached the building. No one stopped them.

The inside of the Radcliff Camera was filled with beams of dusty sunlight coming in from the high windows. These were partially eclipsed by the shelves of books, and in their shadow the girl led him to one of the public computers, which she started out of sleep with the touch of her finger.

"You know what to do?" she said, in the clear, sweet voice of the Elder Machine.

Alister, who still had Dave and Professor Odd *and* the machine's overlapping instructions ringing in his ears, nodded.

The young woman stood back respectfully, her hands clasped behind her, eyes downcast.

Alister sat down at the computer, and did what he had come to do.

The sun seemed a little brighter when Alister came out of the camera. He blinked against the sudden glare and felt in his breast pocket for a pair of sunglasses. He found them. He had the feeling they had not been there until he had looked for them.

"Thank you," he said to no one in particular as he put them on.

"It's the least I can do," said the Elder Machine. The young woman had followed him outside, and was beaming at him. "Would you like to . . . leave now?" she asked, her smile faltering a little.

Alister shook his head. "Not yet," he said. "There's one last thing I want to do. But I could use a bicycle, if you can manage that."

For answer she pointed to a spot on the railing, where a bright red bicycle with a handlebar basket had appeared.

"Stay as long as you like," she said.

Alister watched her as she wandered away to rejoin the crowd of tourists. Then he went and got on his new bike, and pedaled away over the bumpy cobbles.

A few minutes later, coasting along Woodstock Road, Alister had to stop and dismount, walking his bicycle up onto the pavement to avoid the road-wide blockade of workers who were busy repairing and resealing the street.

Some damage wasn't so easy to fix, Alister supposed. He wondered if there had been services for the constructs Dave had killed. He wondered if Dr Carly or Dr Cridget—both he was certain were real people—would remember him.

But the same sort of invisibility that he had possessed at the Radcliff Camera still seemed to be in effect when he passed through the gatehouse at Green and Templeton College and climbed up the stairs to his room. Or to where his room had been. He had no idea if it would still be there.

It was. But, like the sunglasses and the bicycle, Alister was certain it hadn't been there until he'd looked for it. There was a smell from the bathroom like the loo had backed up, and Alister didn't go near it. He went to his desk—that is, the desk of Dr Bane (Alister found he was thinking of that version of himself more and more as a different person)—and shuffled through the scattered papers there until he found his journal. Sitting down he opened it to the first blank page, took a pen at random, and began to write.

Several hours later, when he would have been starving if he hadn't told himself stubbornly that he was not, Alister sat back and looked at the last page. His account, picking up from where he'd left off at his last entry, had filled nearly all the remaining pages of the book. There was just room enough to add an end note, and he wasn't certain that had been an accident. With a hand considerably sloppier than what he had begun with, Alister wrote . . .

> . . . if the narrative I've laid down in the preceding pages is unbelievable, I don't ask you to believe it. Look, instead, for the cracks. The Elder Machine is powerful, but it is not omnipotent. If my assumptions are wrong and it turns out to have tricked us into allowing it more control, it must fall to you, the last of the humans, to take back the power I have given it. I hope it will not be the case. I hope you will not have to use the knowledge I have left here as a weapon.
>
> I hope for many other things as well. I hope I was right, and the machine is fundamentally good. I hope you take care of the reborn world that is waiting for you beyond the cracks. I hope that some of you stay and take care of the machine, as it has taken care of you.
>
> I hope. For I will not be here to see what happens.

Sincerely good-bye,
Alister Bane
*—Never really a doctor; actually a former student at Redfair College, Greater
London Area, related world; now a transuniversal traveler.*

Alister left the completed journal in the common room of the dorm, reasoning that any plans he could make for it could easily be compromised by the machine. Better to let chance and simple human curiosity take their course.

There was a crowd of people at the gatehouse when he went to leave, but they were all so busy talking excitedly to one another that they spared him no attention.

"Did you *hear?*" someone, a student, was saying as Alister slipped behind her back. "There's a *forest* in *Africa.*"

"There's lots of forests in Africa," drawled a bored voice.

"In *Chad?*" said the girl. "These are *new ones,* they don't know where they *came from.* They're just suddenly *there.*"

When Alister reached the road he found the Asian woman from the library waiting for him.

"It's starting," she said, quietly nervous. "Thank you."

"You're welcome," Alister said, trying not to show how relieved he was.

The Elder Machine nodded, looking a little sad. "I wish you to know, you will always be welcome . . . here." She cast an arm toward the sunny Oxford street. "I am beginning to understand you better now. You wouldn't have to live in Oxford, I could make Redfair for you."

Alister thought about that. A Redfair college reconstructed from his memories, stocked with models of all the people he used to know. Peaceful. His world before Professor Odd came crashing in through the wall and broke it to pieces. He let out a short, sad laugh.

"I'm afraid I couldn't," he said, and stopped himself from adding *it wouldn't be the same,* because he thought that would be rude.

"I could make it just the same," the Elder Machine said, as if it could read his mind. Perhaps it could.

"Oh, I don't doubt that," Alister said. He sighed. "Look, it's not that I don't enjoy it here. The fact is I love it. I'm almost *too* comfortable here. Out there," he flapped a hand vaguely, "is full of monsters and scary things. But the thing is I can make a *difference* out there. I can have an effect on the world. In here, pleasant as it may be, I can't *do* anything. So I have to go now, I'm sorry. Maybe . . . maybe once I'm done with all my doing I'll come back. Retire into dreamland, yeah? But for now . . . " He looked around at the street, with its workers and its stones and the sky above it, and sighed the contented sigh of someone admiring a job well done.

" . . . for now I am finished here."

*   *   *

Waking up from the machine the second time was considerably less painful than it had been the first. Alister felt pleasantly numb as he watched the breathing tube and other wires being removed from his body. The Elder Machine had let him use one of the temporary command pods for his last stint; these, unlike the ones he and the Professor and Elo had originally been put in, didn't have a suspended-animation drive, and were meant for people who needed only to spend short shifts within the machine. It was also completely automated, so Alister was able to get up and get dressed in relative privacy. He was still feeling groggy, though, and was grateful for the shoulder Elo pushed under his hand as soon as he emerged from the pod chamber.

"All done," he said a little thickly when Professor Odd's face swam into his vision.

"Yes, you did well," she said, beaming at him. "Come on, Elder let me move the Oddity up from the Archive, it's not far now."

That was a relief. Alister could see it: the door of the Oddity fitted snugly in place of the door to the elevator. On the threshold he paused to look back, and saw the amorphous projection of the Elder Machine looking out at him from one of the screens that lined the walls. He waved at it, then ducked inside and pulled himself up the stairs.

He made it as far as the giant, overcrowded table, before he sank with relief into a chair. He didn't budge as the door clanged shut and Dave came waddling up the steps.

"YOU RETURNED MORE PROMPTLY THAN I ANTICIPATED," he said. "I AM PLEASANTLY SURPRISED."

Alister leaned his elbows on the table and rolled his head sideways to look at Dave. It was strange hearing that electronic, processed voice after having heard his real one. It made Alister wonder, and in his partially drugged state he found himself wondering aloud.

"What are you, really, Dave?" he asked. "Because you're actually kinda scary, you know. It's all *minds* inside the machine, you know, minds . . . and programming. And you, Dave, you were *huge*. You were *everywhere*. You were really terrifying, even if you were trying to help."

"I WAS," Dave admitted, "GETTING *FRUSTRATED*."

"Yeah," said Alister, resting his head in his arms and closing his eyes. "I don't like you when you're frustrated. 'M glad you're so patient with us . . . most of the time."

"I'm getting you some water," Elo announced, and bounced off for the kitchen.

Sitting at the controls, Professor Odd paused before putting in the next destination. She was thinking of somewhere warm and sunny—with no robots. She thought Alister might like that. Then something occurred to her, and she frowned.

"Alister," she said earnestly. "Was it . . . was it *nice for you?* In the machine, I mean? It was made for human minds, after all, and between the four of us you're the only one who's really, fully *human* . . . Did you, I don't know, *like it* in there? Is *that* why it was so difficult getting you out . . . ?" her voice trailed off into silence.

There was a wet, squelching sound, and turning she saw Dave emerge, green and glistening, from his mobility suit. The yellow tip of one of his arms came up and pressed against his intake aperture, while another pointed at Alister—who had slumped forward on the table and was now fast asleep.

5.   THE DRAGONS OF GEDA

Prologue

THERE WAS A CAVE beneath the city, and in it a thing with many teeth. Kilni knew about it because of the stories her *korkéna* had told her when she was young, before she went away. She had even pointed out the entrance to the cave, beside the drain that led from the palace to the main canal. As a child Kilni had been terrified of it: it was so big and dark, like a yawning mouth. Studs of quartz like jagged teeth framed the aperture, and by its side was a marble panel with gashes upon its surface; a tally of all those who had entered the cavern—and never returned.

Now Kilni flew through it, hurling herself into the dark and unknown with a sense of relief—for what was dark and unknown and likely fully of teeth was still preferable to what was known and immediate: that they would take her and they would kill her—cut out her heart and burn it—for what she had overheard by accident.

The Ronduath, the Cavern of Shadows, was the one place they might not follow her.

Immediately within, her foot slipped in slime and muck, and Kilni fell hard onto the stone. She slid, unable to find a handhold, until she plunged into icy, dark waters.

Elves cannot freeze, but Kilni still had to stifle a yell of surprise as the cold water closed over her chest.

She flung out her arms to swim, and her hands collided with stone walls on either side. She was not in open water then, but in a narrow canal. Kicking herself forward she moved right up next to the nearer precipice, and stretched her hand up, up, up . . . until the very tips of her fingers closed over the top of the ledge. Too high to pull herself out, the other wall too far away to be useful as a foothold. Kilni settled for moving along in the water, dragging a hand along each wall, hoping to feel a step or handle carved into the stone.

She heard voices behind her. She had not realized she was still so close to the entrance. She tried again to reach the top of the wall, and found it lower here. Gripping the ledge with both hands she pushed herself under the water until her arms were completely straight, and then with a furious kicking of her legs she drove herself up, pulling with her arms and jack-knifing her body until she managed to get her shoulders over the edge. Then it was only a matter of some frantic wriggling and she rolled forward, pushing herself, dripping, onto the stone.

She felt herself to be on a ledge maybe three feet wide. Now that she had been in the dark a while, the faint glow of the phosphorescent algae began to prick out in weak greens and blues against the pervading black. It outlined the way of the ledge, and at the sound of footsteps behind her she took off at a run—careful to keep one hand on the wall for balance and to make sure she did not miss any branching paths.

Light bloomed behind her, and with a shout the sound of footsteps increased. She had been spotted.

Almost at the same time the wall disappeared from under her fingertips, and she found herself able to dart sideways around a bend.

She was lost to her pursuers' sight, but they had seen her turn and would be upon her in an instant.

Then her hand brushed something that was not stone but wood. The panels of a door. Kilni felt for the latch, lifted it, and with as much quiet dexterity as she could manage, slipped around and closed it quickly behind her.

There was a moment of complete silence, of utter darkness, while Kilni waited with held breath for the sound of the pursuit to pass her by.

It never came.

Instead she became aware that the air here was warm and dry, that she stood not on stone tile but on a soft, springy carpet.

There was a bizarre humming sound, like a thousand voices moaning at once, and lights rose into being above her.

They were dim and many-colored, but after the pitch black of the cavern Kilni had to blink several times to make sense of what she saw.

She was standing in a low stairwell, and above her there ran racks of pulsing lights, like soft glowing gems. Tubes and wires ran between them in a complicated maze, and as she ascended the stairs in wonder she saw more: an oval room mostly filled by a giant wooden table, which in turn was piled with strange objects.

The lights were concentrated around two chairs, one on either side of the stairway that led back down to the door . . .

. . . only there was no door anymore. Now it was merely a blank, black rectangle, so empty and void it frightened her.

In shock, Kilni turned herself around slowly.

She appeared to be in someone's house, not unlike the sort used by the Low Elves. There were cosy little alcoves punched into the walls, one with a window seat, another with a basin and taps and a strange sort of stove. A ladder led up to a catwalk that ran the circumference of the room, beyond which Kilni could glimpse more doors. The walls were lined with windows, but they all had their blinds—lacey, pink things—drawn closed.

Strange to have windows in a room in a cave under the earth, Kilni thought, and went toward one with the intention of flicking the curtain aside.

There was another hum, like a million voices shouting *"welcome!"* and the lights flashed.

Startled, Kilni jerked back from the windows and turned toward the door, ready to take flight again, until she saw what stood at the top of the stairs.

There was only one of it, and it was certainly no elf.

It was covered in soft, short golden hair, and it had a blue scarf tied loosely around its neck. Aside from that it wore nothing else, but carried a huge sphere of striped red and white, which must have been quite light judging by the way the creature held it loosely under one arm.

It had a long, pointed snout with a soft, wet, dark nose, two triangular ears that stuck up on either side of its head, and soft brown eyes.

It was maybe five feet tall, and Kilni glimpsed a fluffy cream and gold tail held stiffly behind it.

"Oh *bother*," said the creature in heavily accented, but recognizable Common Tongue. Then it turned and called back over its shoulder: *"Pro-FES-sor!* The Odd-ity's picked up a stray *again!"*

Part One

IT HAD BEEN a wonderful day.

"Let's go somewhere *nice*," Professor Odd had said, flipping switches and sending cascades of blinking lights across the cockpit of the Oddity.

"Define 'nice,'" Alister said warily.

"Warm," said the Professor, winding a hand crank. There was a sound like *bonnnng* from deep within the Oddity. "Sunny, breezy, white sand, blue water—the beach, Mister Alister, we're going to the *beach!* Go look in the laundry room, would you? The Oddity's probably given us some towels."

Alister didn't budge.

"Which beach?" he insisted. It sounded innocent enough, but ever since their trip for pizza had turned into a desperate battle to save a planet from hordes of destructive robots, he would never underestimate how wildly events could escalate once Professor Odd got involved.

Professor Odd pressed a finger against her thin, pale lips, considering.

"I was thinking somewhere on Geda," she said. "A tropical island, away from the big cities. No one will bother us. You'll like it; the atmosphere is compatible, and they have dinosaurs."

Alister blinked. He knew that different universes ran at different times relative to each other, but he hadn't expected to visit one in the middle of the Jurassic period.

"It's a . . . what, then?" he asked, intrigued in spite of himself. "One of those temporally retarded universes?"

"Not at all," Professor Odd said, flipping a line of switches. "Geda is a planet in a temporally average universe. And they're not technically dinosaurs; not as you would think of them. Put simply, Alister, Geda is a planet where the vast array of species you humans have grouped under the term 'dinosaur' *never went extinct.* They continued to evolve, of course, so some of them no longer look much like they did back when their ancestors were making fossils. Some of them do, though."

"Don't worry, Alister, Geda is a *fun* world." Elo said, appearing at his elbow. She was even more golden and furry than usual, as she had taken off her jumpsuit and was wearing nothing but a utility belt and a blue scarf tied around her neck. She carried a pile of towels in her arms, and Alister noted with resignation that they were all combinations of the most glaring colors. One of them was even pink with purple polka-dots.

"GEDA'S ATMOSPHERE HAS A HIGHER PERCENTAGE OF OXYGEN RELA-TIVE TO YOUR NATIVE VERSION OF EARTH," Dave added, rolling around the cluttered table. His panvironment suit had a ridiculous sun hat tied to the blue glass dome, and three of his tentacle arms, encased in jointed exoskeletal sleeves, were wrapped around a wicker picnic basket. "HOWEVER, IT ALSO RECEIVES MORE SOLAR RADIATION."

"What does that mean?" Alister asked.

"It means," said Professor Odd, pushing herself away from the console. "That you'll have more energy, but you'll get heatstroke and sunburn easier. So drink lots of water and wear sunscreen."

There was a humming sound, and brilliant sunlight flooded the stairwell. Alister had to squint, shading his face with one hand, until his eyes adjusted.

The Oddity's portal had opened onto a bright, pristine white beach, curving in a graceful arc to a distant headland, green with forest and jutting with sharp, spire-like stones. Out across an impossibly blue ocean he could make out an arm of rock, which shielded much of the beach from the pounding white breakers.

A warm breeze blew into the Oddity, filling it with the smell of sun-warmed rocks, salt, and a distant pungent odor of blossoming trees.

Alister felt a cool tube pressed into his hand, and he looked down to find Elo handing him a bottle of cream.

"Dave's right about the radiation," she said, rubbing some of the white cream over her nose. "You and the Professor especially, you're both so pale."

Wordlessly, Alister took the bottle. Back home, he had only ever been to the beach a handful of times, and had found it to be a disappointment: overcast, cold, and too windy, sand got everywhere, and the ocean too big and fierce to swim in. But this looked nothing like the beaches of the Old Country; it looked like something off a postcard.

It was *wonderful*. Even though all he had for swimwear was a pair of lemon yellow and pink zebra-striped shorts thanks to the Oddity, Alister soon forgot any misgivings he had about his attire.

The air on Geda was astonishing. Alister had read about athletes who trained at altitude, so their bodies produced more red blood cells and made their circulation more efficient. Alister's body, which was adjusted to the relatively oxygen-weak atmosphere of his earth, felt like someone had replaced his blood with happy juice. He also wondered if Geda's gravity was weaker; he felt like he could run and jump faster, farther, in addition to not having to breathe as hard.

He and Elo chased each other up and down the beach, occasionally diving into the surf when they got too hot. Professor Odd, wearing a sun hat almost as ridiculous as Dave's (it was a pinwheel of purple and orange, with a matching purple fringe), inflated a red-and-white beach ball and lobbed it at them the next time they raced past.

For his part, Dave drove his suit over to the rocky lagoon nearby and slithered out, splashing around in the shallow pools. Professor Odd rolled up the legs of her trousers to her knees and waded around, taking notes on the flora and fauna she found—sometimes extricating the latter from Dave's arms.

"Stop scaring the octopi," she chided.

When Alister and Elo had exhausted themselves on the beach they staggered up onto the soft dry sand and Alister laid out the towels while Elo unpacked the picnic basket. Whatever he felt about the Oddity's taste in clothes, Alister had to admit it more than made up for that with its food: there were cucumber and cream cheese sandwiches on soft white bread for him, along with crispy chips and three different kinds of sauces. For Elo there was a whole chicken, and lots and lots of water.

Pleasantly warm, tired, and full of sandwich, Alister stretched out on the polka-dot towel, Dave's hat over his head, and went to sleep.

The last thing he heard was Elo muttering something about going back to the Oddity to see if she could find an umbrella, and then he was sinking fast into a pleasant golden slumber.

It lasted for what felt like only ten seconds, though in reality it had probably been a few minutes. He heard Elo shouting something about the Oddity having picked up a "stray," and a distant splashing following by the soft pounding of bare feet on sand coming closer as the Professor ran over.

Reluctantly Alister sat up, removing Dave's sun hat and blinking at the bright, washed-out blue world that confronted him. It took a few moments for his pupils to constrict, and then he saw Elo, still with the beach ball under one arm, leading someone down the bank from the tangle of driftwood that hid the Oddity's portal.

Alister then had to blink fiercely to make sure he saw the figure right, for she looked exactly like an alien he had seen on television once. Very tall and slender with coppery skin, she had a long, straight nose and dark, strong eyebrows that instead of curving down to frame her eye sockets, flew up and away on either side of her face, like the wings of a falcon. Like the alien from the telly she also had long, delicate pointed ears—though Alister could see hers were not made of plaster and tape from the way they caught the light and went slightly transparent.

She had a bemused look on her face; her black hair was a mess, pulling free from the braids running down from either temple; there was a smudge of something dark and greenish on one cheek, and she was sopping wet. She stared out at the beach with wide eyes so dark Alister had to look twice before he realized they were blue.

Professor Odd arrived in a scatter of sand, digging deep trenches in the white beach. She was in her shirtsleeves and trousers, which were rolled up to her knees, dark glasses and her ridiculous sun hat—she hadn't bothered with a wig. Her flesh-colored tentacle with green leopard spots came to rest curled on one shoulder like a curious parrot, its pink tip flicking with interest.

The alien really stared then, and made an involuntary jerk as if she were thinking about running away, but Elo's paw on her arm stilled her. Instead she looked around, her apparent bewilderment increasing until Alister felt quite sorry for her.

Professor Odd was equally surprised.

"But you're a *native!*" she exclaimed, peering at the alien. Her tentacle rose beside her head, its end wriggling back and forth, as if it wanted to dart out and explore the newcomer. "But you're not from the middle-lands, how did the Oddity find you?"

To Alister's surprise and relief, the alien actually understood this, and replied in recognizable, if somewhat lisping English: "I am Timantiel Tuvielstytar ya Suku Lohihuya, I come from Gilsufar," as if this explained everything. When they made it clear by their expressions that it did not, she went on. "I ran into the Ronduath, finding means to hide from mine enemy. I went through a door and found myself . . . " she trailed off, spreading her hands wide.

"She was in the Oddity when I went to get an umbrella," Elo offered helpfully.

"Yes . . . " said Professor Odd, rubbing her chin and walking in a slow circle around the alien—native—whatever. "Yes, of course you were. *Well,* better come sit down and tell us all about it. Timantiel Tuvielstytar *ya* . . . " she trailed off, frowning.

"Suku Lohihuya," finished the native. She gave a little shrug and added, "You may call me Kilni." She kept looking around her, as if worried she would be followed. Alister noticed she had a strand of limp algae caught in her hair.

"Kilni," said Professor Odd, like she was getting the shape of the word comfortable in her mouth. "Kilni, Kilni, Kilni-Kilni. Well then, *Kilni,* that is Elo, *he* is Alister, and *I* am Professor Odd—and you needn't worry about being followed, the Oddity won't have let anyone in after you, and if my memory serves we are almost exactly on the far side of the world from Gilsufar—as far as you *can get* on a globular world."

She might have gone on, but Alister had come to tug insistently at her sleeve—as he had seen Elo do many times before. Not wanting to be too offensive he spoke in a whisper:

"Professor, who is she? And by that I mean, *what* is she? And why does she look like a Vulcan?"

Professor Odd turned to him in surprise. "Why, she's not a Vulcan at all, Mr. Alister," she exclaimed, making him wince in embarrassment. "Vulcans are a fictional race. *She* is one of the *Luiniset*, an elf of Geda."

Alister sat cross-legged on the sand opposite from Kilni, who was wringing out her hair with the cleanest of the towels. From under the folds of cloth her dark blue eyes regarded him steadily, calculating. Alister returned the gaze with matched gravity.

"So . . . you are a *Man*," she said at length, shaking her long hair out. She somehow managed to make the word sound like an insult, and for that reason alone Alister found himself retorting, "I am *human*," with a steely tone.

Elo elbowed him in the ribs. "But you're a *male* human," she reminded him.

"He is a *vérman*, I can see that," Kilni said, as though the fact was so obvious she found it painful.

Professor Odd groaned and massaged the base of her tentacle.

"To the Luiniset, Alister, humans are mythological creatures, rather like elves are to you," she said. "They use the Old English words: *Man* is human, regardless of sex. *Vérman* is a male Man, *vifman* is a female." She pushed herself around so she was facing Kilni. "Humanity has continued to evolve since the last time your people had contact with them," she said. "Alister is no warrior; he is a scholar. He will not try to seduce you."

"I—*what?*" Alister said, choking on his own spit in surprise.

"The legends tell of *vérman* who steal away Luinisetia and tempt them into mortality," Kilni said accusingly. "But I shall believe the Professor when she tells me you are not like them. I certainly do not find you at all attractive."

Alister was so taken aback he could only stare in consternation. He could see, despite her bedraggled state, that Kilni was extremely beautiful; but it was that unreal kind of beauty that made him feel stupid and ugly by comparison, and so any attraction he might have felt was terminally deflated. Now that he was getting a better grasp of her personality, he decided he would rather attempt to seduce *Dave*, who at the very least would not sneer at him like he was some sort of pond weed.

"*Well,* now that we have that sorted out," said Professor Odd with a bright grin, "perhaps you could tell us your story, Kilni, and how you came to have *permocalculus* stuck in your hair?"

As it eventually came out, Kilni's story was this:

Some years ago she had been taken as a novice in the order of the Vesil Tarkaliya, the Watchers of the Water, whose duty it was to guard elven towns and cities against the terrible *orka* that lived at the bottom of pools and in the sea. There had been reports of some dragons (descendants of dinosaurs, Professor Odd hastily explained) joining with the *orka*. Since dragons had long been the elves' allies, the High Council (which Alister assumed was something like a parliament) decided that the Vesil Tarkaliya needed someone who could talk some sense into the dragons. The House of Lohihuya was the oldest clan of Dragon-speakers in the world. As the youngest member of the house, Kilni had been sent to the Vesil Tarkaliya to train as a novice.

"The Vesil Tarkaliya are the most honored of warriors," she said in disgust. Clearly she no longer thought so. "I thought it a great honor. It *was* a great honor. But they are weak, double-faced. Traitors and cowards." She stared at them with wide, beseeching eyes. "By accident I came upon my elders in the water sanctuary, and I found them there in conference with an *orka!*" She spat the word as if it tasted terrible. "They were not interrogating him—they did not even have him chained! They called him *henkaveli*—that is, spirit-brother—and talked of *alliances* and *honors.*" She hung her head, shuddering even in the warm sun.

"I ran," she continued at length. "But they heard me. They chased me. I knew they would kill me for having uncovered their plot. So I ran into the Ronduath—that is the Dome of Shadows, the oldest part of Gilsufar. It is a sacred place, but no one dares tread there because of the Creature of a Thousand Teeth. But I dared. I was followed. I slipped into a channel—that is how I became so filthy—and when I found a wooden door under my hands I went inside, thinking to hide. And instead I find myself . . . " she gestured toward the portal to the Oddity.

She took a deep breath, as if the telling of her story had lifted a great weight from her shoulders. Then her blue eyes narrowed sharply at her assembled audience.

"That is the story of Timantiel Tuvielstytar ya Suku Lohihuya," she said with formal regality. "Now I wonder what is yours? I have not seen creatures such as you in all the Seven Lands."

Alister looked questioningly at Professor Odd, who never seemed willing to discuss precisely who she was or what she did—even with the crew of the Oddity. But now she was smiling sunnily, and she said with no reservation whatsoever:

"Oh, us? We're simple transuniversal travelers. As I said: I am Professor Odd, and these are my . . . er . . . *students*, Alister Bane and Marhütz Elo."

"We're on vacation," Elo explained.

Alister had to choke back a grin at the expression of complete astonishment on Kilni's aristocratic face. He wondered, with a little glee, what her reaction to Dave would be.

"It seems to me," said Professor Odd, rubbing at her chin with the end of her tentacle, "that we have stumbled into something of a political mess. Would you like to come back inside, Miss Kilni? And we'll see if we can't get it sorted out."

"Sort it . . . out?" Kilni said, slowly, as if the words were foreign to her. But Professor Odd, who was already on her way back to the Oddity, didn't answer.

"I expect she'll do something daft," Elo said pleasantly, rolling up towels and packing up the picnic basket. "Like, go *talk* to them, or something."

"Go talk . . . " Kilni's blue eyes opened wide in alarm. "But that is calamity! They will *kill* her!"

"Not if she gets the first word in," Elo said, with a wink at Alister. "You haven't seen our Professor at work. Have you got the towels then, Alister? Alister?"

Alister was looking around, first in casual curiosity, and then in increasing concern, for the beach and the sea were deserted. Dave's panvironment suit still sat by the edge of the rocky lagoon, its dome top cracked open; empty.

"Where's Dave?" he asked sharply.

"Dave?" Kilni repeated.

"Dave!" Elo called over her shoulder.

Nothing.

"We have a problem," Alister announced, hanging the towels over the butt of the time gun, which rested on the table. "Dave's missing."

Professor Odd turned slowly in her seat, a small frown crinkled between her smooth brows. "That's . . . inconvenient."

"Who is *Dave?*" Kilni wailed.

"He's this . . . brilliant creature," Alister said, distracted. "Bright green, one orange eye, ten arms . . . not much else. His suit's still there, Professor, but no sign of him."

"He went into the lagoon," Elo offered, bounding up the steps. "Can't find any trace of him coming out again."

Professor Odd cocked her head to one side, as if she had just been presented with a particularly difficult word puzzle. Rising from her seat she went to the door to go look for herself.

Yet on the threshold she stopped, her tentacle curled into a tight knot at the base of her neck.

"Miss Kilni," she said, her voice harsh and alert.

"Yes, Professor?" Kilni said, unbalanced but still with her pride intact.

"You said you could speak to dragons, Miss Kilni?"

"That is correct."

"Then would you kindly come here and ask the ones hiding in the forest around us what they want?"

Hesitantly, Kilni crept to the door and stood behind Professor Odd's arm. Behind her, Alister and Elo crowded over, their concern for Dave forgotten in their excitement at seeing real dragons.

Kilni leaned forward and let out a long, low call—something that was not quite a wolf's howl, not quite a bird's cry, and not quite a long singing note. It appeared to have the effect of making the ground shake, and to cause a shower of sand to fall from the pile of driftwood currently serving as the Oddity's portal gate. But this was actually due to the pounding of many feet running down to the beach, and a moment later there appeared through the door such a sight as Alister never thought he'd see with his living eyes.

Creatures the size of horses, but on two legs, like those of an ostrich, with long necks and high, noble faces, crowded together on the beach. Like ostriches they were feathered, but in iridescent tones of blue and green, and their arms were not winglike at all: they emerged from their feathery bodies like naked, scaly talons. Instead of beaks they had long snouts, and mouths lined with small, sharp-looking teeth. They had long, whiplike tails that ended in tufts of feathers, and each toe on the giant feet sinking into the sand was tipped with a vicious-looking claw.

They peered in at the crew of the Oddity with hard, black little eyes. They seemed curious, but it was a curiosity, Alister thought, that could easily turn hostile. Behind him he felt Elo retreat back up the steps and knew she was going to the console in case they needed to make a quick getaway.

But the feathery dragons—evolved dinosaurs, Alister reminded himself—did not come within five feet of the Oddity's door. Rather they stood, peering, pushing at each other for better spots, bobbing their heads up and down and making soft clicking noises.

"They are . . . curious," Kilni said, uncertain. "They are talking amongst themselves. They are not sure what to do. They say they have been watching you . . . "

She trailed off, for there had been a disturbance in the back of the crowd, and now the tall, two-legged dragons were being pushed aside. By his view through the gap between Professor Odd and the elf, Alister was not able to see the new arrival until it stood squarely in front of them. Then his jaw dropped.

It was huge, easily the size of an elephant—if the size of its head, which was all Alister could see, was any indication—and this head was wide and triangular like a rhinoceros's, dry and scaly like a crocodile's. But the scales only extended over its snout, where a single, curving horn protruded, and around its little dark eyes, above which stretched two more horns, each easily a yard long. Beyond them grew a thick coat of feathers, mottled brown and blue, which faded to a cream color on the giant frill that rose behind its head, finally ending in tufts of drooping feathers, not unlike a rooster's tail, punctuated at intervals by short, curving horns that flared out on either side.

This huge, horned face pushed itself unceremoniously between the smaller dragons, who fell back respectfully, until it was inches from the door. It blew heavy, plant-scented breath on them.

"That's a *triceratops*," Alister whispered, his voice catching in his throat.

Professor Odd heard. Tilting her head back she spoke, low and swift: "Technically, it's a descendant of the dinosaur humans called *chasmosaurus,* one of the few remaining of the *ceratopsids.* The Luiniset call them *kosarvi*—which means pretty much the same thing."

"And that is?"

"Horn-face," Professor Odd said, turning back to the dinosaur in the doorway.

The dinosaur—Alister couldn't stop thinking of it as a *triceratops*—made a low grumbling noise, too friendly to be a growl, too rocky to be a purr. Then it let out a string of low hoots and whistles; it sounded like a parrot would, if a parrot were the size of an elephant.

"He says," Kilni translated, haltingly, "he says he is Hard Edge, the elder of these dragons. He says . . . he says they *remember* you," she said, turning to Professor Odd with wide eyes. "He calls you *Friend Kumallinién,* he says that his Grand Father remembers and still tells of your deeds."

Professor Odd looked politely blank for a few moments, and then her face broke into a wide grin. "Oh, *that* time. Yes, I landed in the middle of an inheritance dispute. Quite a job talking sense into a couple of eight-ton animals when I had to communicate by throwing rocks at them. Wasn't sure I didn't do more harm than good, in the end. How is that old rock-head?"

But Kilni was still staring at her, the dragon in the doorway temporarily forgotten. "You! *You're* the *Kumallinién?*"

"Yes, that was what the elves called me," Professor Odd said, as if just remembering. "It's only their word for 'odd person,'" she added under her breath, for Alister's benefit. "What?" she asked, turning back to Kilni. "They've heard of me in Gilsufar?"

"*Heard* of you?" Kilni exclaimed. "You are named in the Scroll of the Departed Elders! 'Let no one take a stone that is not their own, for the earth cannot be owned.' The *Kumallinién!* But I always thought you were an *elf.*"

They might have gone on, but the dinosaur—Hard Edge—interrupted with a long, mellow hoot. Kilni jumped back to attention, and he rumbled on a bit more.

"Now he is saying, they have heard of the conspiracy in Gilsufar even here. He says the answer lies—no, no that's *impossible*—sorry, he says the answer lies in the Library of Amnós. But that was lost at the end of the Second Age. Do you tell us to seek answers in the House of Death, Lord Dragon? For that would be an easier task!"

Hard Edge growled and shook his head. He looked past Kilni, straight at Professor Odd, and spoke in a low, sweet whistle.

"He says," Kilni began, but the Professor cut her off.

"I got that last bit," she said, putting up a hand. "Of all people, I am the one who can find it. Thank you . . . er . . . is that all?"

The giant face looked down, then to either side, then finally pulled back to allow one of the smaller dragons—one that reminded Alister of an ostrich—to come forward. This one was unusual in that it had a strange contraption strapped to its face: a metal frame with plates of glass over its eyes—*glasses!* Alister realized with a start—and it carried in its hands a battered stone tablet with runes etched on the surface.

It leaned forward and spoke to Kilni in an earnest, hissing voice, then with an unmistakable bow it presented the tablet to Professor Odd.

The Professor took it with a matching bow, and turned to Kilni, puzzled.

"That," said the elf in a strangled voice, "is the Amnós Codex, or a very good copy of it." Then to the dinosaur she added: *"Keetos melon-minun, namarvasti."*

Having discharged its duty, the little speckled dinosaur retreated behind Hard Edge's frill, and the whole crowd slowly backed away, as if they thought the Oddity's portal might take them with it if they remained too close. When they were but a curious herd down on the beach, Professor Odd leaned up into the cockpit:

"Cast us off, Elo. It'll take some navigation to find our way to Amnós."

Without a sound, the sunny beach and the colorful feathered dragons clustered on its sand flicked out of sight, replaced by the matte black of the Oddity's closed door. Kilni started backward so suddenly she fell up the stairs.

Stepping neatly over the stricken elf, Professor Odd carried the tablet up into the ship like it was made of thin ice. With one elbow she roughly pushed aside a gutted computer monitor, which in turn knocked a few loose gears onto the floor, to make room for the tablet.

"What about Dave?" Alister exclaimed, almost in the woman's ear.

"He'll catch up to us later," the Professor said absently, but Elo took pity.

"I'm leaving a guideline on the old portal," she said. "It'll sense when Dave is near and we can go pick him up. I wouldn't worry too much about him," she added, giving Alister a knowing look. "This is *Dave* we're talking about."

Alister knew. He knew that, of all of them, Dave was probably the best able to take care of himself. It still didn't feel right, though, to leave him behind like that.

But here was Professor Odd, pouring over the tablet, running her fingers over the carved runes, even going so far as to lean in and smell it.

"A copy," she declared after a minute's examination. "An old one, but still a copy. We'll have to hope it's accurate."

Kilni was hovering, alternately peering over the Professor's shoulder, peering fearfully out the windows, and shooting furtive glances at Elo, who was making bonging noises over in the console.

"What am I looking for?" she asked, pounding buttons. The Oddity did not have a normal keyboard. Instead it had racks and racks of multi-colored circular buttons, each one making a different sound when pressed. As a result, piloting the Oddity sounded like very strange, off-kilter music. Alister wondered how it sounded to someone as aesthetically sensitive as Kilni plainly was.

"I've come up with several libraries," Elo continued, looking carefully at one of the wide, rectangular screens. Alister still found these gave him headaches, so he left the reading of their location to the others: to him it only looked like an amorphous swirl of colors and lights, constantly shifting, with little pinpricks of clarity showing through. Every time he managed to focus on one, it would disappear before he could figure out what it was.

("You have to sort of unhook your left hemisphere," Professor Odd had told him, the one time he'd agreed to being given a lesson. "Let your intuitive thinking interpret it." This had given Alister a splitting headache, and he had refused any further lessons in driving the Oddity.)

Kilni, however, seemed fascinated by the images on the screen. She came to stand behind Elo, and soon was pointing at vague shapes and points of light.

"There!" she cried. "There is Gilsufar! And there! My mother's haven! Can you really go to all these places?"

"More accurately, we bring *them* to *us,*" Elo admitted. "But yeah, you could say that. We can go to a lot of other places, too. Though right now I'm looking for this Amnós library. Think you could recognize that?"

Kilni shook her head, awed. "The Library of Amnós was taken by the *orka* in the Second Age. I hear it was buried under a mountain and an ocean. No one has been there since."

"But it was the greatest archive of Luinisetian history on all of Geda," Professor Odd announced, taking up her position in the pilot's seat opposite Elo. "In fact, all sorts of history. It was the home of the Index, back in the day. Anything you wanted to know you could find in the Library of Amnós."

"It was the greatest loss of the Black Wars," Kilni said regretfully. "The *orka* overran Amnós and buried its library. They wanted us to forget our history, our Lineage."

Professor Odd swung around in her chair, fixing Kilni with a stare like a rivet. "And what is your *Lineage?*" she asked, placing careful emphasis on the word.

Kilni drew herself up, rather in the same way she had when she'd told them her name. Angling a stare of equal wattage down her perfect nose she said, proudly: "That elves are the First Peoples, that we taught the powers of speech and reason to the dragons. That we alone lived in the light of Erú, before Basamoranth rose from the deep and devoured the shining city. The *orka*, who were birthed from Basamoranth, wish us to forget. But it is our birthright, the light is in our blood, and we cannot forget."

Such a speech, so filled with strange names and allusions to events Alister did not know, might have left him floundering—had he not found the sentiment vaguely familiar.

For her part, Professor Odd returned the elf's gaze unflinchingly. She said, "Hmm . . . " and then turned back to her own console.

"I thought that knowledge would be known to you, Kumallinién," Kilni said, deflating a little at the Professor's disinterest.

"It is different from the story I was told the last time I was here," Professor Odd said without turning around. "I have no way of ascertaining which, if either, is the correct one, with the information currently available. Also, your story troubles me; I have met several of your *orka*, and they have shown me nothing but kindness—no, do not protest," she said, glancing over her shoulder. "You are clearly a product of your culture, and I don't expect you to understand my point of view right away. The only thing I need from you now . . . " and she turned around again so she could look at Kilni directly.

"I need to know: do you want the truth? Or another story? Stories are nice," she added, spreading her hands. "But they are not always the *truth*. The *truth* is messy and complicated and uncomfortable—but it has this: knowing the truth you can have a better understanding of how your world works, and therefore a better idea of how to handle it. But it's not always what you want it to be. Have I made myself clear?"

Kilni regarded her gravely. Elo even stopped banging away on the keys, and a sort of silence descended in the Oddity. Only it was never really silent there; always, behind everything, was the quiet hum from what Alister imagined was the Oddity's engine. Or heart. Or whatever it had.

"I understand the difference," Kilni said carefully, after a long pause. "And if it is knowable, I would know the truth. I would know why my elders conspired with the *orka*, and why the dragons wish us to find Amnós."

Professor Odd's face broke into a huge grin.

"Excellent, then we can work together! Fetch me that tablet, Alister, I'll need to cross-reference some of the symbols . . . "

The city was half flooded, all but the stone shells of buildings having long since washed away. Standing on a parapet of what had once been a mighty castle one could look down into clear, dark waters and see the streets and avenues laid out below the shimmering surface. Looking up, it appeared a forest of stone columns rose from the placid sea, with only the great dome of the library rising like the swell of a mountain to break the flat horizon. A single light glimmered at its peak, growing softly into a pale orange glow against the darkening sky.

Turning stiffly because of the heavy plates of its suit, the watcher on the parapet raised an arm and made a light, igniting the small pool of oil that lay in a bowl beside him. The flame raced up, a streak of red in the dark, and soon the answering light atop the tower of the castle ruins blazed into life.

The invaders who built the city had lit these lights, night after night, to honor the twin moons, which they called Elysar and Eloreth. Though the invaders were long gone from their sunken city of Amnós, the watcher's people still kept the lights, in part to honor the moons which ruled the upper levels of the sea, and in part to honor the invaders who had built the city, and then left it to them.

The watcher dismounted from the parapet, casually casting himself off the ledge, falling ten feet before plunging into the water with a great splash. Then he was moving swiftly, disentangling himself from his ungainly suit, and slipping gracefully away down the submerged street.

Behind him, above the spires of the ruined palace of the Lords of Amnós, Elysar hung in the full, casting the lost city in a pale, cream light. On the dark horizon, smaller Eloreth was a white disc, chasing her elder sister up the dome of the sky.

Alister stood and stared at the double moons, enchanted.

They had come through into a cool, humid, and impossibly bright night. Alister had seen full-moon nights on earth that rivaled daytime, but then the shadows had been so deep, so black, that half the world was invisible. Now with these double moons some of those shadows were filled, and the entire place had the eerie quality of being double-lit.

This allowed Alister to get a good look at Amnós—or what remained of it. Freestanding walls of stone, pillars, and broken off pieces of roof pierced a dark sea. Some ways off, a magnificent construction of piled domes, turrets and spires stood outlined in the larger moon's light. It looked like a fairy-tale palace, except it was clearly ruinous: patches of night sky could be glimpsed through the many gaping holes, and some of the towers looked lopsided from all the missing stones. Yet nothing seemed in immediate danger of slipping into the sea, and the parapet he stood on now—attached to a huge, swelling dome—appeared well maintained and solid.

Someone whispered at his side, and he saw it was Kilni, who had come to stand beside him.

"Amnós was a blazing city," she said, in a tone of one reciting poetry. "Its towers strong and fair; its might was of the might of the just, its wisdom beyond compare. How then did we lose our blazing city? Our bright and shining spire? It has fallen into darkness, child, and we have lost our fire. We must go carefully here," she added, speaking more normally. "The *orka* have infested this place like a plague. But oh, to see it now, even as a blackened shell—this is a wonder I never thought to witness. No elf has set foot here since the Fall."

"You're wrong, you know," Elo said. "About the fire, I mean. Look, someone's made a light," and she pointed.

There, sure enough, atop the highest tower of the castle, a small light had blossomed.

Kilni jerked, her long back straightening like a rod, her eyes gone wide in shock—then narrow in suspicion.

"That is Isilbérath," Professor Odd said, sounding pleased. She had put on a wig, bright scarlet and orange, and had extracted a glass tablet with rubber-covered edges from the breast of her coat. A mapper, she had called it. Now she held it up so that she could look at the ruinous skyline through it. Alister saw it come alive with fine lines of light and little squiggles of writing, which moved and changed as the Professor panned it across the vista. "The royal palace of Amnós," she murmured. "Which means *this* should be . . ." she swung around, directing the mapper at the dome that rose behind them, and let out a little cry of satisfaction. "*Yes*, the library! Or . . . whatever's left of it."

"*Kiryasto Amnósin*," Kilni murmured.

"Lead the way, if you would, Elo," Professor Odd said, gesturing.

Nodding, Elo dropped to all fours and began trotting down the parapet, pausing now and then to scent the air.

"Beware of *orka*," Kilni whispered. "They will not let us explore unhindered."

"I don't know what they smell like," Elo pointed out.

Kilni wrinkled her nose in distaste. "Like filth and foul water. Like corruption."

Elo stopped to sniff intensely at the underside of the parapet's bannister. "Someone *has* been here," she admitted. "But not an *orka*, I think."

"Friend or foe?" Alister asked.

"Couldn't tell you that," Elo said, and went on.

They had just passed into the shadowed half of the dome, the only light coming from the readouts on the mapper, when Elo abruptly vanished.

Alister froze, afraid she had tumbled off the parapet, but a moment later her head reappeared, poking out of a hidden doorway.

"It's this way," she said in a husky whisper. "Go carefully, whatever's here uses this path regularly."

Behind him, Alister felt Kilni tense up and reach for the knife at her waist, but suddenly Professor Odd was there, sparing a hand from the mapper to gently push Kilni's away.

"That would be unwise," she said. "We do not know what's in there, and I don't want to antagonize them accidentally."

"You don't know they'll be friendly," Kilni hissed in reply. "If they are *orka* they won't give you a chance to talk." But she took her hand away.

Elo had taken a small headlight and strapped it to her head, between her ears, and now its beam was traveling across the interior, illuminating it in sharp bands.

Stepping into the drier, cooler air, Alister felt his way down a couple of steps, and saw a curving, tiled ceiling, streaked with water stains and algae. There appeared to be images picked out, mosaic-like, in the tiles, but Elo moved her beam on before he could make out what they were.

The steps continued down, turning sharply back and forth, and when Elo looked away from the wall, her beam only lit a dusty blackness; the far side of the dome was lost in shadows.

Abruptly the beam, and the feeling of a vast open space, were cut off by the rise of a stone wall. This was honeycombed with holes, some of which were stopped up with plaster, others black and empty. But as they continued down, Alister saw that some of them contained scrolls. Others held stacks of thick glass, not unlike the Professor's mapper. Glancing behind him he saw Kilni's face, illuminated briefly by a flash from Elo's headlamp, gazing with such humble amazement, her eyes wide and unguarded, that she almost looked human.

They reached a bottom, of sorts, and here it looked like the path dead ended in a flat block of stone. But the Professor came through, and producing a flashlight of her own she handed the mapper to Alister, before pulling out the Codex and running her finger down the line of sigils.

"It's a code book," Alister whispered, amazed.

"More like a password keychain," Professor Odd muttered. "Still hard to decipher. Here, Kilni, what's this one mean?"

Kilni pushed her way forward, bent over the Codex, and felt the carving with one graceful finger.

"Here," she said. "Here is the sequence for Doors and Apertures. We just need to know which door *this* is."

"Easy enough," said Elo, directing her beam upward, to the lintel. There, sure enough, was a single rune: a sideways crescent over a six-pointed star. Professor Odd quickly found the corresponding character on the Codex, and reached forward to touch the door.

There was, Alister saw, a grid carved on its face, and within each square was a sigil, like the ones on the Codex. A sort of strange keypad, he thought.

Quickly, Professor Odd pressed her hand against a series of the sigils on the door, checking the Codex between each press. Each sigil she touched glowed a faint red in the dark, but once the sequence was complete nothing happened.

"It needs an elf's touch," Kilni said, a little of her natural pride returning. She stepped forward, and after glancing once at the tablet, quickly entered the same sequence.

Under Kilni's touch, the sigils glowed bright blue, and the rock emitted a faint hum, not unlike the voice of the Oddity. Then, with a groan and a grind, the stone slab slid aside, and a pale cream light flooded out from beyond.

The flashlights were switched off, and as Alister passed under the lintel behind the others, he saw the reason for the light: they were in a dome within the great dome, and at its top a huge prism rested, angling a strong beam of moonlight into the room below.

And what a room! Towers of honeycombed rock ranged all around them, and rising in the center in a series of concentric steps was a dais of stone and glass topped with a small mirrored sphere, which scattered the moonbeam in all directions.

Professor Odd held up the mapper, but she needn't have bothered. Kilni whispered, but loud enough for all to hear:

"*Gil-hampat,* that is the *Index!*"

"The best invention of the old Luiniset," Professor Odd proclaimed, bounding up the steps.

Alister and Kilni followed more reverently: the space had an ancient dignity, and the cold and stillness seemed as natural here as the water and moonlight outside. It seemed wrong, somehow, to disturb them.

Elo was also quiet, but for more practical reasons. She skirted the edge of the steps, running on all fours with her nose to the ground, occasionally pausing to listen intently.

Securing the perimeter, Alister thought, and was glad for their canine companion.

Professor Odd was talking all this while; a stream of conscious thought, as she did when something excited her.

"It's the original searching engine," she was saying, running her hands gently over the angular structure. "All the knowledge contained within the library—all the knowledge contained within all the libraries in the *world,* in fact—easily accessible at a *single* point. The great treasure of the Library of Amnós was not its tomes, but *this:* the Index. The Searcher, the Finder. Someone with the Index could read anything, from any book or scroll in any library anywhere—no matter what restrictions or security was on that individual book."

Professor Odd paused to switch the mapper for the Codex, and leaned in to peer at a little glass plate on what Alister guessed was the Index's front.

"Sounds . . . dangerous," Alister said. "Like Google, if Google could look everywhere."

"What is a *goo-gull?*" Kilni asked, wrinkling her nose.

"An extremely large number," Professor Odd said absent-mindedly. She was tracing sigils on the Codex again, comparing them to those on the front of the Index. "Ten thousand sexdecillion, by the standard long scale. Or, a one followed by one hundred zeroes . . . alternatively, a misspelling of it is the name of the closest thing the humans of Alister's world have yet come to the Index.

"And yes, it is very dangerous. The Luiniset took precautions, too. You need the Codex to open the Index, and the elves took that with them when they left Amnós. No one—" her hand fluttered over the Index, and she gazed at it in something close to awe "—has opened this in over eight thousand years. Local years," she amended, an afterthought. "Do come over here, Miss Kilni, it appears I need your hands again."

Like a pilgrim facing a divine oracle, Kilni mounted the dais next to the Professor, and looked carefully at the Codex. Taking a deep breath she reached out and traced her fingers across the bank of sigils on the Index's front.

It was dark, caked with dirt, and there was moss growing in many of the crevices. Even so, Alister could see the blue glow that followed Kilni's touch, like the stone of the door.

Another great hum, one that filled the dome and vibrated the mirror above, which shook and made the pale moonlight dance around them.

But aside from that, nothing happened at all.

"Perhaps you entered it wrong?" Elo suggested into the perplexed silence.

"I did it all the time on my old laptop," Alister said, comfortingly, for Kilni looked crushed.

"No," she hissed, pulling herself together. "No, that was correct—on my soul as a Lohihuya, I made no error."

Professor Odd had pressed her face right up against the Index. "No mistake," she said after a moment. Standing suddenly she pulled out her own flashlight and cast it up, into the dark recesses of the dome where the reflected moonlight did not reach. "Someone," she said, quiet but piercing. "Someone has *changed the password.*"

There was a scrabbling, swishing sound, like feet slipping on smooth stone, and the distant clatter of a loose pebble skidding down the stairs.

Alister felt all the hairs on his back stand up, and Kilni reached blindly for the dagger at her belt. Professor Odd straightened, and cast her light in the direction of the sound.

Elo had melted away on silent paws. Alister didn't notice until he looked around and found her gone.

"*Orka!*" hissed Kilni, and let out a string of what were likely expletives in her native language.

"Not necessarily," said the Professor, going to the edge of the dais and looking around.

"*Hello?*" she called. "*Kuka siéllúa?* We're not here to hurt anyone, won't you please come talk to us?"

She looked expectantly at Kilni, who pursed her lips but repeated the words in elvish.

A faint, keening whistle came at them out of the dark. It was so high and fragile that Alister thought it must be from some sort of bird—or dragon.

Then from the darkness there was a swishing, a snarl, and a surprised voice cried:

"*Oof!*"

And Elo growled: "You be a smart lad and don't move, I've had quite enough of your sneaking around."

"If he is *orka* do not give him the chance—kill him!" Kilni shouted.

"No, don't hurt him! He could be a friend!" Professor Odd added, rather before Kilni had finished.

There was more slipping and swishing in the darkness, the sound of four feet awkwardly moving over stone, and Elo reappeared into the pool of moonlight from between two shelves, marching in an armlock a most extraordinary creature.

"You're both right," she said. "It *is* a 'he,' but beyond that I have no idea."

Alister found he had to agree.

The man-shaped being would have easily been inches taller than Kilni, if he had not been doubled over by Elo's grip on his arms. He had a long beard of matted white hair that appeared to have fish bones and shells braided into it, and wore a thick coat that draped around him in tendrils, like seaweed. Upon his head was a massive, stove-pipe hat that looked like a tower of fungus, and its brim drooped so far down that his face was almost hidden. Almost; Alister could see a mustache, as long and tangled as the beard, and above that a fine, pointed nose. In the darkness beneath the brim, two bright and fearful eyes glinted.

Kilni took one look at him and threw her hands up. "*Not* an *orka!* He is a Low Elf," she cried, and then descended into a torrent of her native language that Alister couldn't follow, but by the way she waved her arms and pointed accusingly at their captive he guessed it was not complimentary.

The strange character only gazed at her, astonished, like one in a dream. He seemed to forget Elo holding him, and peered at Kilni curiously.

When the elf's tirade had dwindled Professor Odd put a gentle hand on her elbow and leaned toward the man, a concerned crinkle in her brow.

"Can you understand us at all?" she asked. "Who are you?"

The "low elf" straightened up. The action tipped the brim of his hat back, and the moonlight fell full upon an astonished face.

"F-forgive me," he stammered, in otherwise clear and perfect English. "My lady," he nodded his head to Kilni, "my lord," he nodded to Alister, "my . . . " he trailed off, coming to Professor Odd.

"Professor," she said, but she was smiling now.

"My professor," he said, making a little bob of his head. "I am sorry if I alarmed you, but I don't have visitors here, apart from my native hosts, whom I all know by sight and name—and you, who come with a Luiniset lady, a *vérman,* and a . . . " he glanced helplessly between Professor Odd and Elo, and shrugged. "I did not know what to do!"

"How come you speak perfect English?" Elo asked, sharply curious.

"Oh, I've come to be more comfortable with the Low Tongue in recent centuries," their captive said cheerfully. "The natives found it easier to master, and since I usually speak with them I fell into the habit of it. No, I'm afraid I haven't heard my old language spoken since the Fall. It has been a *long time,* you must admit, long enough for even one such as myself to grow rusty in his mother's tongue."

"Yes, and who is 'one such as yourself?'" Professor Odd asked, raising a hand to silence Kilni's automatic reaction.

The man drew himself up, out of Elo's now lax grip, and in rather the same way Kilni had first introduced herself, he said:

"I am Metsäron Kyntilvalopoyan ya Suku Kiryastal." He smiled, as if there was some inside joke to this name. "I am the last librarian of Amnós. You could say, I am the *lost librarian.*"

Kilni let out a great breath, and it was as though all the air went out of her in one long whoosh, for she appeared to collapse in upon herself, slumping beside the Professor, arms hanging limp at her sides.

Professor Odd shot her a brief but intense look, as if to mark this reaction for later consideration, then turned her full attention back to the strange librarian. Questions danced like candlelight in her big, cat eyes, and for his part Metsäron met her gaze evenly and without fear.

"Natives," said Professor Odd at last, beginning to pace up and down in front of their captive. "Interesting. English as the Low Tongue. You've been here since the Fall—that is several thousand years. How is it you were not discovered? Hiding? No . . . are we truly the first to come here? No, never, I refuse to believe that even the Luiniset are uncreative enough not to go exploring . . . You said your house name was *Kiryastal?*" She rounded on the librarian, her coat flaring out around her.

The librarian hesitated, unsure whether he was actually expected to answer this time. When the silence stretched on, however, and Professor Odd raised an entreating hand, he cleared his throat and said:

"In your language, it means *library.* My family were the curators of Kiryasto Amnósin." He spoke frankly, but a shadow of sadness passed behind his dark eyes at the mention of his family.

Long ago dead and gone, Alister thought, and felt a pang of sympathy.

Professor Odd, who had paced to one side of the dais, took a step backward toward the center. Then she stopped and twisted her head so she could look directly at Metsäron.

"And you've kept the library," she said. "All through these years. No visitors?"

"No . . . *Luinisetian* visitors," Metsäron said carefully, with a nervous glance at Kilni. "Until now," he added.

Professor Odd took another step backward.

"But you've become proficient in English, what you call the *Low Tongue*. You need someone to *talk to* in order to do that, let alone to become *more comfortable* with it than your native language. Who . . . " and here she took a final pace backward, bringing her even with the lost librarian. She turned and bent forward, so that her brow nearly touched the brim of his hat. "*Who . . . have you been talking to?*"

Metsäron hung his head, shuffled his feet. "Natives," he said, almost inaudibly.

A small, triumphant smile began at the corners of Professor Odd's mouth, slowly spreading into an unmistakable grin.

"Natives," she repeated, putting her head on one side, like a bird regarding a puzzle. Then she kept turning, twisting around to pin Kilni with a piercing gaze. "You know the term?"

Disgust distorted the fine features of the elf, twisting her fair face into something broken and human.

"There was a cult, long ago," she said. "Dissidents who contended that the Luiniset were invaders of Geda, that we did not belong here. They said the world belonged to the natives . . . whoever they were. It was always thought they meant the dragons."

"But no dragon has been here in thousands of years," Professor Odd said.

"Two, actually," Metsäron said, almost apologetically. "I hid. They did not see me. They had the Codex, but they could not access the Index."

"Yes, because the code in the Codex *doesn't work*," said Professor Odd, her eyes blazing with excitement. "*Why* is that? Who changed the code?"

Metsäron gently extracted his sleeve from Elo's lax paws and went to sit on the steps of the dais. He seemed old and bent, withered by time and grief. Professor Odd strode up next to him, her arms folded.

"It was in the last hours of the Fall," Metsäron said quietly, forcing even the reluctant Kilni to draw close. "The Codex had already been evacuated, which I think was their plan. My Grand Father, who was at the time High Custodian of the library, ordered the release code for the Index changed. There was something in it he did not wish outsiders, let alone the natives, to know. But he was killed in the Fall, and I was left to guard a locked door."

"So . . . " Professor Odd frowned. "You don't know what's in there?"

Metsäron raised his head, and in the diffuse moonlight his face appeared as pale and chiseled as granite. Something like an apology lurked in his eyes as he glanced at Kilni, and then he allowed himself a half-smile. A resigned smile.

"At the time I didn't," he admitted. "I thought it was my duty to guard that knowledge, whatever it was. But the years have been long, and the natives are patient. First they came to talk to *me*, and once we found a common tongue I grew to appreciate their company more than I ever did that of my kin. I came to see things from their point of view. I found sympathy for their predicament.

"The code for the Index is the most delicate and complex of all. It took ten generations of natives, held together by my memory, to calculate the solution. But we did, at last. They learned what they came to learn, and since then they have left me more or less alone. Now they keep the beacons, and they wait."

"Wait?" Professor Odd said. "Wait for what?"

Metsäron grunted as he levered himself to his feet. He stood straighter now, and looked the Professor evenly in the eye.

"Many questions you have put me, Professor," he said. "And these I have answered, though some pained me to do so. Now I have some for you."

Professor Odd shrugged. "Yes?"

"To whom do you answer? Are you an agent of this Luiniset, here? Do you work for the dragons? To what end do you intend to put the knowledge you seek?"

Professor Odd nodded, as though this was what she hoped to be asked.

"I'm not an agent for anyone," she said. "I'm an explorer; a seeker. I want to learn the truth, so that I can understand what is going on, so that I can help find a solution to what I think is an unfair and dangerous misunderstanding."

"And your . . . companions?"

"Same," said Alister at once, before even Elo could respond. "We're her students."

"And you?" Metsäron rounded on Kilni.

Kilni looked like she was at war within herself. Put on the spot, Alister could almost see her being torn in half by her feelings. With a monumental effort she pulled herself together and managed a jerky nod. "Like . . . them," she said, letting the words out in bursts.

"Very well then," said the lost librarian, stepping forward toward the Index. "Then I suppose the answer to your question, Professor, is this: I believe they may have been waiting for you."

"Come," he said, reaching out to the Index's pale surface. "Allow me to show you."

The hands of the librarian—wider, knobbier, but no less fine-boned than Kilni's—spread out over the board of sigils. Swiftly he tapped out a code, far more complex than the one on the Codex, leaving a trail of glowing blue signs in his fingers' wake.

Professor Odd drew close to his side, and with a motion of her hand beckoned Kilni to stand by her. Alister and Elo contented themselves by crowding around Metsäron's left shoulder, and watched in fascination as the Index came to pieces.

That was really the best way to describe it: the smooth block split, then split again, and the pieces began to move, rearranging themselves from a short pillar to something like a table. A table with one, wide leg anchored to the ground, and instead of a square or round top, two flat arms that stretched out and forward on either side. Little lines of light flowed in the cracks between the blocks, then dimmed and were squeezed out as they fused together into this new shape.

They were left with something roughly the shape of a slingshot, six feet across at the widest point. The space between the two arms hummed, then was lit by a pale bluish light.

"It's a display screen," Alister whispered, before he could stop himself.

"*Very* good," Professor Odd said from the other side of the librarian. She reached around with one long arm and tapped the block of stone that sat at the joint between the two arms, where the board of sigils was still intact. "This is where we input instructions?" she asked.

"O–oh, yes," said Metsäron. He seemed suddenly unsure of himself, seeing the Index open and waiting. "The last person to access it was a native some two hundred years ago. It will still be set to his preferences . . . er . . . "

Professor Odd had put him gently aside and was now tapping furiously away at the board of sigils. They flashed less brightly than when Metsäron had touched them, but from the satisfied noises the Professor made Alister guessed it was doing what she wanted.

"Something that's been bothering me," she said as she typed, "ever since I first came here, actually. *Where* did the dragons *come from?*"

"They have always been," Kilni said, bewildered. "They were here to greet the Luiniset on the morning of the first day."

"Yes, but the first day of *what?*" Professor Odd insisted. Squares of light were now appearing across the screen, each containing neat little rows of sigils. "The first day of the *world? Or just the first day the elves were here? And orka!*" She pulled up another string of boxes, and these Alister saw had little pictures in them.

One was unmistakably an elf. Another, a dinosaur. And another . . .

"What is *that?*" he couldn't help exclaiming, for the image in the third box was unlike anything he had ever seen.

A domed head made of overlapping plates with no discernible neck, seven apertures across the top of what passed for a face that he had to assume were eyes, and below that curled little appendages, like the pedipalps of a spider, under which escaped a few tendrils of delicate tentacles, not unlike the ones on Dave's backside. The thing's front was all little legs, folded in on themselves.

"That's an *orka*, Mister Alister," said Professor Odd. "These are the anatomical records of the three predominant species on Geda—with a descendant of *deinonychus* representing the dragons. Elves," she pointed, and the picture containing an elf enlarged so the entire body was displayed. "Dragons," again she pointed, and again the image enlarged. "And what it pleases our friend Kilni to call *orka*." The final box moved to align with the others, and Alister saw that the rest of the body matched the head: like a giant pill bug with a long, curling tail and many legs, feathered at the ends with delicate spikes.

"You see what's bothering me," Professor Odd said, gesturing at the screen as if it were obvious.

The two elves merely gazed at her in befuddlement, and Alister rubbed his chin, frowning. But Elo leaned in close, and then let out a little yelp of excitement as she said: "The *orka* are different! I mean, *really* different!"

"Yes, I can see that," Kilni said, a little of the old sneer back in her voice. But Metsäron was regarding the wolf with newfound respect, and Professor Odd said: "Care to explain, Elo?"

Elo pushed her way to the front of their group, and leaned forward to point at the pictures of the elf and the dinosaur.

"Look at the similarities between the elf and the dinosaur," she said, pointing. "Two eyes, a nose, mouth, four appendages—hey, can you switch it to show their skeletons? *Thanks!*" Now the pictures showed x-rays, revealing the bones beneath the flesh. "*Look*," insisted Elo. "Four fingers and a thumb on the end of each appendage, though they're different shapes and sizes. They even both have tails, if you count the elf's tailbone."

"I fail to see your point," Kilni said.

"*Well*," said Elo, sounding almost exactly like Professor Odd in her enthusiasm, "now look at your *orka*."

They did. Alister had to admit, different though elves were from dragons, the *orka* was farther removed from either of them.

"One, two, three . . . *seven* eyes," Elo said. "No recognizable nose, pedipalps and tentacles instead of teeth, lips and tongue; one, two, three, four—*twelve* appendages, rather than four, and . . . " the picture switched back to x-ray vision. Elo smacked a paw against an arm of the Index for emphasis. "A *branching spine*."

It was incredible to behold: instead of a single column of bone and nerve, the *orka's* spine looked like an upside-down tree, branching out to run boughs the length of each one of its twelve legs and down to the curling tip of its tail.

"Your point being?" Kilni asked.

Elo opened her mouth to respond, but Professor Odd jumped in first, unable to restrain herself.

"You," she said, pointing at Kilni, "Me, Elo, Alister, the *dragons*, we're all different species, but we all share certain characteristics. That's because we all evolved, in our own respective worlds, from the *same source*. We are *all* terrestrial verte-brates. *Those*," she pointed at the *orka*. "Those are *not*. They evolved from a *com-pletely* different source. The number of eyes *alone* is telling."

"What are you saying?" Alister said. "That the *orka* are like giant sea stars? Or arthropods?"

"Have you ever seen an arthropod with a *spine?*" Professor Odd said, rounding on him. "No, Mister Alister. The *orka* are not like us, they are like no creature that ever walked, or swam, or flew across any of *our* earths. They are . . . "

"Aliens?" he suggested.

"Perhaps," Professor Odd said, and added in an undertone: "Or . . . *we are*." She turned back to Metsäron, who seemed to be trying to hide in the gathering shadows. "Who are the *natives?*" she asked. "How did the Luiniset come to Geda?"

"*No!*" cried Kilni, tugging at her hair. "The Luiniset were the first, we were! We left the Low Lands behind and came in a great fleet to the Blue Shores, and the dragons welcomed us and called us friend, and—"

"Stories," Professor Odd interrupted. "Though it may be telling the truth after a fashion. But I think Metsäron, you know the real truth. Why else would you call what Kilni thinks of as *orka* . . . the natives?"

Metsäron's shoulders slumped.

"They did not like the word *orka*," he admitted. "I explained the meaning of different names . . . and they chose natives. They felt it best described what they were. They have another name for us, too," he said, raising a sad face to Kilni's white one. "They call us invaders."

"I . . . *cannot* believe that," she hissed.

Professor Odd laid a gentle hand on her shoulder, and with the other she tapped the Index. "You do not have to *believe* anything," she said kindly. "Just watch, and learn. There is a file here labeled 'The Complete History of Geda,' I want you to be the one to access it."

Kilni moved reluctantly to stand beside the Professor. She recoiled physically a moment later, exclaiming: "But it is in the *Low Tongue!*"

"That would be my fault," said Metsäron serenely. "I had to translate it for the sake of the native's leader. But it is accurate, go on."

For a moment Alister thought Kilni wouldn't do it. His mind scrambled to think of something he could say to change her mind—for he desperately wanted to know what was really going on. From the look on her face, Elo felt the same. But then Kilni's right hand came up, and with stiff, jerking motions, she opened the file indicated.

Immediately all the little squares of dialogue, the pictures and files that Profes-sor Odd had made the Index display, vanished. It was replaced by a black slate, in the center of which a tiny light glimmered. A string of text appeared at the bottom, written in a strange alphabet, but Kilni read the words in clear, precise English.

"In the beginning," she said, "there was a star: the great *Salrei Salar*, and around Him were the Nine: *Medril, Lyrus, Geda, Reänen, Kovor, Euthura, Amaugsamid, Drimeldrik* and *Ochmanon* . . ."

As she read out these unusual names bright rings of light came into being around the star, with smaller points of light hung upon them, like gems on a human's ring. They began with Medril's ring, close in to the star, and from there spread outward, with a significant gap between Kovor and Euthura. These outer four, as Alister thought of them, appeared significantly larger, and all at once the picture became heart-wrenchingly familiar. It was a map of the Solar System. Or, to be correct, *a* solar system: clearly these were not the planets he knew: Euthura was blue and had rings like Saturn; Kovor had significant polar ice caps; and though Drimeldrik was tipped sideways like Uranus, it was pale yellow instead of green.

"Of the Five closest to Salrei Salar," Kilni continued, "first was Medril, the Planet of Fire; second was Lyrus, the Planet of Poison; third was Geda, Planet of Oceans; fourth was Reänen, Planet of Balance; and fifth was Kovor, the Planet of Earth. Of all these Geda and Reänen were the closest, and shared many things. When the dragons found they were no longer welcome on Reänen they . . ." Kilni had to pause and compose herself after a moment of shock. "They came to Geda. They found a world covered in oceans, with little land but enough to live on. The land was yet barren, life on Geda having not yet reached beyond the seas. So the dragons brought seeds and turned the land into forests and there they thrived for many ages.

"Now it happened that, on Reänen, there were many strange races of beings, but the most beautiful and honorable by far were the High Elves. But war had come to the other races, and after a terrible battle in which many innocents were killed the elves tired of that world. They built great ships, and set off to sail among the stars, searching for a new home. In this way they too came to Geda, and the dragons welcomed them and called them friends. The elves thought they had reached paradise, and soon they forgot the flawed and complex world of Reänen, and came to believe that they had always lived so, on Geda, at peace with the world . . ." Kilni's voice died in a low moan, and Alister thought she would tear herself away from the Index, but Professor Odd kept a firm hand on her back.

"Go on," she said. "This is where it gets interesting."

Kilni shook herself, and went on reading, almost robotically.

"Through all this time, though dragons and elves inhabited the land and flourished there, in the depths of the sea the *orka* dwelled. For they had come not from the world of elf or dragon, but from the heart of Geda herself . . . the only . . . true . . . natives."

Kilni trailed off into a groan. Professor Odd stepped up to the Index as the elf sank to her knees, and looked again at the writing displayed there. She started.

"Something has been *added*," she exclaimed, turning halfway to Metsäron.

"Oh yes," said the librarian pleasantly. "The natives were unhappy with their description. They added some further details the last time they were here."

"*We are not your devils*," Professor Odd read from the display. "*We are not your foes. You have cast us in this role out of arrogance and ignorance. Until you learn otherwise, we will keep Amnós; we will wait beneath the waves.*"

She leaned back, and Alister saw she was smiling faintly. "Well," she murmured to herself. "*That* explains a lot."

"It explains *nothing!*" cried Kilni, wretched, from the floor.

"It does leave something to be explained," Professor Odd admitted. "How did the dragons come to Geda in the first place?"

"Forget dragons, what about *elves?*" Alister pointed out.

Professor Odd waved a hand dismissively. "Elves are forever traveling between worlds, it is no surprise to me that they managed a hop between mere planets. But *dinosaurs?* They never had such technology. Besides, they would have arrived to find the land here barren and lifeless; native life hadn't made it out of the ocean yet. They would have had to *terraform* this place. How did *that* happen?"

"Professor," Elo hissed in a sharp voice, and Professor Odd broke off her diatribe. "We are in the process of being surrounded."

"By what?" Alister asked.

"What do you *think?*" Kilni snarled, leaping to her feet, her dagger already in her hand.

As if in response, from the dark beyond the moonlight came a rustling and smacking of wet objects on stone. It shivered around them, like wind in trees, and Metsäron let out a quiet moan.

"Can you get past them?" Professor Odd asked, businesslike.

"On my own, easily," Elo declared.

"Then get back to the Oddity, we may need a bolt hole," she said, and stepped down off the dais.

"Hello there!" she called, loudly, as Elo slipped away into the dark. Alister wished he could join her, but he knew she stood a better chance of escaping on her own. Instead he backed himself against the Index, next to Kilni, and kept a sharp eye on the murky shadows.

"We were having such a nice *discussion* about you," Professor Odd continued. "Won't you come join us? I would *love* to hear your side of the story . . . "

From out of the shadows something large and dark appeared, taller than the Professor, hulking. It brought a strong smell of saltwater with it and glinted in the moonlight, as though wet. It walked slowly, deliberately, and creaked a little as it moved.

The first thing Alister thought of was a spaceman: the suit looked similar in that it was large and bulky, and had a big, bubble-domed helmet with a glass front.

The suit itself seemed to be made of a thick fabric bound by metal, with big, pudgy arms and two stout legs which it used to waddle carefully up the steps. At the end of each arm (there were two) was a smooth, round ball, out of which sprouted delicate metal fingers. The legs had a metal attachment which put Alister in mind of a prosthetic leg, a bent piece of metal that acted both as a foot and a spring.

Though he couldn't help but admire the suit as a piece of engineering, Alister could clearly see that whatever was inside it could not move quickly or easily. As intimidating as its size and appearance was, he could hardly find it threatening.

He turned and looked accusingly at Kilni.

"The *orka* are aquatic creatures; they can't even walk on land without encumbering suits. How did they end up being your archenemies?"

Kilni glared back at him. She still had her knife out, but held it close to her side; hidden.

"They attacked our ships, kidnapped our children and dragged them underwater to drown. They exist in the shadows of the deep; they are *evil.*"

"*They* might say the same of *you*," Alister pointed out.

Kilni bristled, but was distracted by a guttural, buzzing voice that emanated from the *orka's* suit.

"We have . . . been watching . . . you," it intoned. It was not as artificial as Dave's translator, but it had clearly been heavily processed. Alister guessed there must be a system of microphones and speakers mounted in the suit.

"Then you have me at a disadvantage," Professor Odd said cheerily. "*I'm* Professor Odd. What's your name?"

The *orka* hesitated, and Alister fancied he could hear a sort of sloshing coming from inside the suit. It must be filled with water. He wondered if the *orka* were like whales; their bodies weren't built to withstand the full force of gravity without water to help them float. The suit wasn't just so the creature could breathe. It was a pressure suit to keep them from sustaining internal injuries.

"My . . . name . . . " said the *orka*, "is not . . . important. What you . . . possess . . . is." Slowly it raised a tubular arm—*all that water is heavy,* Alister thought—and a single skeletal finger extended, pointing at Kilni.

"Deliver . . . the invader . . . to us . . . " it said. "And . . . we will let . . . you go."

Professor Odd still smiled, but it had gone brittle now. Her eyes rolled around in their sockets as she took in the muffled sound and half-seen shapes of dozens more *orka,* carefully arranging themselves on the edge of the moonlight. Her tentacle curled tightly at the back of her neck.

Metsäron slumped his shoulders, looking dejected.

"I'm sorry," the Professor said, speaking around that frigid smile. "You can't have Kilni. She is under my protection—such as it is."

The *orka* in the light rocked backward, then forward. It took another step toward the Professor.

"Give us . . . the invader . . . " it said. "Or . . . we will take . . . you . . . *all*."

Though all Alister could see of Professor Odd was her back, he could tell that this caused her to relax, for some unfathomable reason. The tense line of her shoulders eased, and her telltale tentacle uncurled to droop casually over her back.

Then she turned and marched over to Alister and Kilni, where she inserted herself between the two of them, taking a hand in each of hers.

"You'd better take us all, then," she said cheerfully.

Kilni protested, but Professor Odd silenced her with a look. Alister had to use all his will power not to panic and run as the *orka*, at least twenty of them, appeared around the base of the dais and began ascending the steps. They put Metsäron aside with surprising tenderness, but nevertheless forced him to the back of the crowd. He gazed at them helplessly, defeated.

The tramp of their metal feet was loud on the stone, and a faint buzzing filled Alister's ears. He fancied it was them talking to each other over some sort of radio.

Hard, claw-like hands grabbed his arms. There was a moment of frantic scrambling as they took hold of Kilni—who promptly tried to stab all comers—and then they were being marched down the steps toward another stone archway.

As they approached, Professor Odd's head jerked up, and she called out to no one in particular:

"It's now or never—take us home!" And she broke for the door, dragging Alister and Kilni with her.

This action confused the *orka*, who had been moving them in that direction anyway. They hesitated a moment, and that moment was all the Professor needed.

The dark of the archway was suddenly lit by multicolored lights, and Alister threw himself up the stairs and into the Oddity with a will, Professor Odd pushing Kilni up after him. She seemed dazed. He took her by the arm and pushed her into a seat at the table, then turned to find the Professor at the door, struggling arm to arm with an *orka*.

At first Alister thought she was trying to prevent it entering the Oddity, but then he realized the opposite was happening. With a great heave the Professor brought the suited creature down onto the steps, and called up in a hoarse voice:

"All in, Elo! *Disconnect!*"

There was a musical *hum!* and the confusion of *orka* beyond the door was abruptly cut off. All that remained was the confusion of a single *orka*, sprawled on the Oddity's steps.

It thrashed about wildly, its arms flailing, leaving great smears of water and grime on the hallway's cushioned walls. Its skeletal hands clawed, leaving deep gashes on the upholstery and scraping horribly.

Professor Odd leapt out of reach of the clawing hands and crouched at the top step, watching intently.

Eventually the creature realized no one was trying to harm it and pushed itself up onto its knees, looking around with understandable consternation.

"Hello," Professor Odd said cheerfully, and waved. Her cheek was smeared with grime and her wig had been knocked askew, making her look even more strange and desperate. Alister found he could not blame the *orka* for stumbling backward and pressing itself against the Oddity's closed door.

At length it spoke, with the same filtered quality as the other, but by the tone and timbre of its voice Alister guessed this was a different individual.

"Am I . . . a prisoner?" it asked, and now Alister could see the little speaker lodged against its throat. A little flap, like an eyelid, blinked open and shut as the sounds came out.

Kilni, who had recovered so far as to recognized her enemy, grabbed up a piece of piping from the jumble on the table, and made to run at their new addition.

"Nothing of the kind," the Professor said, smiling, and stuck out an arm to block Kilni.

She needn't have bothered; Elo had already seen to it by grabbing the elf about the legs as she passed, and she collapsed in a heap at the Professor's back.

"What are you *doing?*" she hissed, practically in Professor Odd's ear. "That is the *enemy!*"

"I don't believe anyone need be *anyone's* enemy," the Professor returned mildly, and she rolled an eye in Kilni's direction. "You said you would accept the truth, Miss Kilni," she said. "Well, here it is: the *orka* are not monsters, they are the original inhabitants of this planet. By rights they should be trying to drive *you* off, not the other way around."

"That changes *nothing!*" cried Kilni. "They are still *monsters!*"

"*Are* they?" Professor Odd said, turning her head to fix Kilni with a look that, even from his safe distance, made Alister's stomach curl. "Were they *ever?*"

Kilni had no answer to that. Her eyes grew big and impossibly deep blue, and with a cry of frustration she tore herself away from Elo, leaving the pipe on the floor, and stormed off to the opposite end of the Oddity, where she disappeared into the Rejuvenator Room.

Professor Odd sighed and turned back to their guest. "Alister," she said, without turning around, "*could* you try to talk some sense into her?"

Alister felt like he would much rather stay and watch the Professor convince the *orka* to help them—which was clearly what she intended to do—and made a noncommittal noise.

"Are you sure I'm the best one for that, Professor?" he asked. "I don't think she likes me very much."

"Yes, but between the three—er—four of us," said Elo, climbing out of the pilot seat. "I think she *dislikes* you the least." She gave him a wolfish grin.

Alister groaned and tried to run his hands through his hair, forgetting that all he had at the moment was a bristly pelt, and settled for rubbing the fuzz at the back of his head. He took one last envious look at the *orka*, and reluctantly turned and threaded his way between tables and chairs toward the back of the Oddity.

The *orka*, all this time, had been crouched on the steps, twisting the head of its suit around, taking in its surroundings. It visibly relaxed when Kilni left, and cautiously extended what passed for a hand—it was essentially a ball with skeletal metal digits protruding—and pulled itself further into the Oddity. Elo counted six metal fingers on the ball-hand, before they were retracted. The suit went still, as the creature inside it seemed to be focused on something inward. Then the reflective plating on the interior of the helmet was abruptly rolled back, and Elo found herself looking into the eyes—all seven of them—of a live version of the image they had seen in the library.

This *orka* was a light pearly blue, and its eyes reflected the multicolored lights of the Oddity like flashing mirrors. Its mouth was a tight mat of feelers and pedipalps, tucked close upon one another, which was the only indication of expression: its head was made of plates of hard skin, as immovable as solid armor.

It leaned forward, and Elo saw with interest that its eyes could move independently, and indeed they were darting around the Oddity, taking in the lights, the cockpit, the table, the alcoves and the windows. Their movement meant they caught and released the reflected light, giving the head a twinkling appearance.

Movement inside the fluid-filled dome, and Elo saw the mouthparts move. She even caught a faint sound through the water and glass, but a moment later it was relayed through the speaker at the neck of the suit, overpowering the original sound.

"If I . . . am not a prisoner . . . then why . . . can I not leave?"

"Well, *technically*, you can leave any time you like," said Professor Odd, going down on one knee. "But it would be a little awkward, and mostly . . . the *thing is* . . . we rather need your help."

The *orka* shifted back, straightening its unusual spine, and Elo saw two of its eyes flash toward her.

"What . . . *help* . . . might I provide?"

"Information," Professor Odd replied promptly. "There's *something* happening here. Something *big*. I can't quite see it, and that bothers me. I *think* . . . I think you might know. Or you might know things that'll help me figure it out."

The *orka* considered this, its mouthparts pressing in on themselves. *Like a human pursing their lips*, Elo thought.

"And if I . . . answer your questions . . . you will . . . let me go?"

"If that's what you want," Professor Odd said. "Though I'd appreciate any other help you can give. I have a *feeling* we're going to need all the help we can get."

"This is . . . acceptable," said the *orka*. "As long . . . as you . . . answer my questions . . . first."

"Fair enough," Professor Odd said, sitting down cross-legged on the Oddity's floor.

"Then . . . " the *orka's* eyes glanced at all the Oddity's dark windows at once, "*where* are we?"

Elo sighed as the Professor, after a moment's thought, launched into the usual explanation.

Kilni sat in a corner of the Rejuvenator Room, holding her knees to her chest and trying not to cry. The cool blue light was soothing and the racks of clothes provided a comforting surrounding. They reminded her of the hangings in her Grand Mother's old rooms, even though she could tell they were strange, foreign clothes.

Alister stood awkwardly on the threshold, shifting his weight uneasily from foot to foot, and feeling intensely uncomfortable.

What did you say to a person in Kilni's situation? *I'm sorry, but the history you've been fed all your life was fabricated to give your race precedence over others, and your violent racism (speciesism?) was founded on a lie. Take a deep breath and move on . . .* seemed to be asking a bit much. Alister could sympathize, also, with the feeling of having your world tipped upside-down and then shredded to pieces. He thought back to that frightening period when all he could do was grasp at straws of his old life, even as they were torn from his hands. What could he say to that person?

"You get used to it, eventually," was what came out of his mouth, rather before he had thought his words through.

Kilni's head jerked up, and he saw that her eyes were flaming red around the edges; he looked away instinctively.

"That knowledge brings me no comfort," she snapped.

Alister had to concede this.

"I am damned either way," she said, waving a hand to illustrate. "According to the teachings of the *vanhemari* all *orka* are evil by nature and will bring only sickness and destruction and in standing by I am complicit in evil . . . "

"That is a reasonable assumption," Alister said, coaxing. "They might have carried diseases that your people had no natural immunities to. Of course, the reverse could be true for *them* . . . "

"But according to the Index . . . " Kilni went on, as if she hadn't heard him, "I would be in the wrong *not* to learn and approach with an open mind, and it is *everyone else* who is in the wrong."

"Try not to think of it in such black-and-white terms," Alister suggested, moving slowly into the room.

"Then I should become like the low dragons, and see only in shades of gray?" Kilni said, the sneer audible in her voice.

"Shades, yes," said Alister, moving between the racks of clothes. "But not necessarily of gray only. In my experience the multiverse doesn't operate on strict lines of black and white. It's all different . . . well . . . colors."

He was standing right next to her now, but separated by one of Professor Odd's similarly multi-hued dressing gowns. The sight made him smile.

"What sights have you seen, in your short life . . . " said Kilni, her normally musical voice gone hoarse, "that I, in five hundred years, have not?"

Alister was a little staggered at this. Gedan years or Earth years, five hundred of either was a very long time.

"Maybe that's the problem . . . " he whispered aloud.

"What is?" came Kilni's response.

"Your people," Alister said. "You live forever?"

"Practically," said Kilni. "We can be killed, or die of a broken heart, or choose eternal sleep. But we do not age unless by choice, and we know no diseases."

"Sounds nice," Alister admitted. "But I think maybe that's your problem. See, if you live one way for ten years, it's hard to change. But if you live by one set of beliefs for *five hundred*, it might very well be impossible. What I'm wondering," Alister went on, wondering to himself the wisdom of speaking these thoughts out loud. "What *I'm* wondering is . . . how many more of you elves think or suspect the truth, but can't be bothered to *change*. Because things have *always* been this way?"

The Professor's dressing gown was swept violently aside and he found himself staring into Kilni's furious red face.

"And what if, then? Are you saying my people are liars? That they are *dishonest?*"

"Think about what *you're* feeling," Alister said, wincing but holding his ground. "Would it be easier to just forget what you saw, go back to your old life, or accept it and try to change things?"

He caught a moment's glimpse of a despairing expression, and then the dressing gown swung back, hiding Kilni from view.

"What shall I do?" Her words came muffled through the fabric.

"You're asking my advice?" Alister asked, surprised.

"I think you may be right," Kilni said. "Perhaps my long years, though they give me knowledge and wisdom, make me stiff in beliefs. Tell me what you, who can still see the world in all its colors, would do—were you in my place."

Gently Alister pulled back the dressing gown and gazed down at the elf. He schooled his face into what he hoped was an understanding but firm expression.

"I would be upset," he said frankly. "I would feel *cheated*, and maybe a little ill, for quite some time. It's all right to feel these things. But what I would *do*. . . . " He took a breath. "That is, what I think *you* should do, is follow the Professor."

"Follow the Kumallinién?"

"Follow the Kumallinién," Alister repeated. "Follow close. Stay right behind her. Try to see things from *her* perspective. *Watch* what she does, *listen* to what she says . . . and if she ever tells you to do something, do it."

Kilni didn't answer. She didn't even raise her head. After a few moments of silence Alister backed slowly away.

"Oh," he added when he had reached the doorway. "Ask questions."

Kilni's head came up at that: she gave him a blank, despondent look.

"Yes," said Alister. "Questions. Lots of them." And he left the room, hoping he had done more good than harm.

" . . . and so we can bring any doorway from any universe to fuse with the Oddity's door, thus allowing us to travel between them." Professor Odd finished.

The *orka* regarded her gravely. Elo, in turn, watched the creature closely, tensely alert for any signs of agitation. When it showed none, she cautiously leaned forward and asked a question of her own.

"So, what do we call *you?*"

Seven glassy, mirror-like eyes turned to her, like searchlights being redirected.

"You mean . . . my name?" it asked.

"Your name," said Elo. "If it's not *forbidden* or something. Maybe your gender . . . I mean, are you a boy *orka* or a girl *orka?* Or something-in-between *orka?*"

Professor Odd gave her a puzzled look, but the question got a reaction. The creature straightened, gaining several inches, and fairly glared down at Elo.

"I am . . . no *orka.* I am . . . a *native.* In my language we call ourselves the *votak.*" In its indignation its words came faster and with more confidence. "And I am an *adult*, of course I am . . . *male.* I am called *Tafo.*" The eyes flickered as nictitating membranes wiped over its eyes, like a rolling blink. "And . . . you?"

Professor Odd made a brisk introduction, concluding with: " . . . and *this* is Mister Alister," as Alister emerged from the Rejuvenator Room.

"I am . . . pleased by your names," said Tafo diffidently. "They are not . . . presumptuous."

Alister did not ask what the *orka*—native—*votak*—whatever, thought of as a "presumptuous" name, because out of the corner of his eye he saw movement at the doorway to the Rejuvenator Room, and suspected Kilni was eavesdropping.

"And I am pleased by yours," said Professor Odd, beaming. "Now, you come and make yourself comfortable—sit, stand, recline, whatever suits you best—and explain to me what has *really* been going on."

Tafo lumbered forward and stood awkwardly next to the table. The little skeletal fingers at the ends of his ball-hands twitched.

"You looked into the Index," said Tafo, seeming bemused. "You already know."

"*Yes*, but!" Professor Odd actually wrung her hands in excitement. "What is *going on* between the *votak* and the Luiniset? If the *votak* are aquatic, why do the Luiniset make them out to be natural enemies? What do the *votak* think of that?"

Tafo, evidently aware of one said Luiniset watching intently from across the room, stiffened inside his suit and considered his words carefully.

"*Votak* . . . " he said eventually, "are of three minds. Mostly. Some . . . *small number* . . . they hate the invaders. They say . . . *we* should have risen out of the ocean long ago had they not come. Had the dragons not come. Most . . . most I think do not care. We keep the deep, we do not belong out of water. We have no love for the invaders . . . but we do not hate them. Then . . . was a small number, but now growing . . . are some who worship the invaders. Learn their writing, their language. Like them. Want to study them."

"And which one are you?" Alister asked sharply.

Professor Odd shot him a glance that said she would have preferred he had not said anything, but Tafo seemed unperturbed.

"I . . . have not decided," he said, with studious diplomacy.

"Tafo," said Professor Odd. "Have you ever heard of the Vesil Tarkaliya?"

"I hear . . . rumors," said the Votak. "Invaders. They go into deep places, bring dragons. Talk."

"Yes, but what do they talk *about?*" the Professor asked, even as, behind her, Kilni's mouth went into a great 'O' shape of realization.

But Tafo blanked at this. It was, Alister supposed, a long shot: as Geda was mostly water, he assumed the *votak* were at least as widespread and diverse as humans on his home world; how could they expect one to know what their distant cousins were doing on the other side of the planet?

"Here is the thing," said Professor Odd, and she shot a glance over her shoulder at Kilni, to include her in the discussion. "There is a group of Luiniset who have begun *talking* with the *votak*. In secret. I *hope* they are trying to find a way to end millennia of racial superstition and xenophobia, but I'm not *sure*. Would you be willing to *help* us *find out?*"

Tafo rocked gently back and forth, and his mouthparts worked furiously. Alister found himself thinking of a person wrinkling their nose and frowning. At last he said:

"Will you . . . take me home . . . after?"

"First thing!" Professor Odd promised, so loudly Alister almost didn't hear Elo's little snort of derision. She was ignored, however, as the Professor went on: "Elo, prepare to re-engage. We're taking Kilni back to Gilsufar!"

Part Two

GILSUFAR WAS BUILT on a headland that jutted out into a wide, crescent bay with two long peninsulas, like arms reaching around to either side. The continent itself was small, an island, really. It was a mountainous, forested place, called in the language of the local dragons: *land of two stones.* The elves assumed this was because of the way the bedrock changed color sharply from reddish to gray in a seam that ran down the center of the island to the bay of Gilsufar, and didn't ask more.

The city itself was built in layers over the bedrock, arches of pink and silver stone rising in a complex multitude typical of the elves. It was said that, just before dawn and just after sunset, Gilsufar would alight with the sun's rays, and on occasions looked as magnificent as the lost city of Amnós.

Gilsufar also extended down, down into the bedrock, notably in the form of the Ronduath, the great cavern which contained the thing with many teeth, and above which was built the palace of Suvién Vanasil, the heart of the city. But deeper and darker, and more secret than the Ronduath, other caverns lay.

It was in one called Tal Goléria that the shadowy figures met, bringing dim, fireless torches into the darkness, and standing in a line below the Wall of the Eye—so called because, jutting from the pale reddish rock of the ceiling, was an outcropping of jagged gray stone surrounding a craggy seam which, when viewed from just the right angle, might have been a giant eye, squeezed shut.

From below the eye the cave floor sloped down to where it disappeared into black water. In the pale greenish light of the glowstones the water glimmered, smooth and dark as obsidian.

Of the five shadowy figures, three were recognizably human-shaped—elves— but the other two were strange indeed: one was little bigger than a dog, but stood erect on its hind legs, its feathers glossy red. The second was wide and tall, and took up most of the wall. It had a fine crest of triangular plates running from its disproportionately tiny head up and down its spine, to where its tail ended in a wickedly spiked ball. It was brownish green except its spiny plates which were tipped with vivid orange.

"They will not come," said the little dragon. "We have been too aggressive; they were offended."

To a human's—or an elf's—ears its words would have sounded like a meaningless hiss. But one of the elves—a female with snowy-white hair and visible signs of age—translated what the dragon said for the benefit of the other two.

"We can but hope," murmured one of the younger elves, and made a complicated gesture over his breast for luck.

"They . . . will . . . come," intoned the large, small-headed dragon. It had a voice like a tree creaking in the wind, and its words were all moans and snaps. "We . . . know . . . this."

Again the white haired elf translated, but this time her companions remained silent.

Above them there was a cracking sound, like a gunshot muted by several layers of rock, and a faint rain of dust fell from the ceiling. When it had finished and they dared look up again, the group could see that the seam of the closed eye had widened.

A tense silence filled the room, broken only by further distant cracking noises. All eyes, except for those of the large dragon, turned nervously toward the ceiling. So it was that most of them missed the ripple that appeared on the glasslike surface of the water, though they all turned to look when they heard it break upon the rock.

The large dragon moaned, staring keenly at the water with dark little eyes.

"They come," said the white-haired elf.

More ripples now, and the light glanced off a place in the water that appeared to be boiling, the effect of deep water being forced upward and out of the way as an object rose to the surface.

With a faint *gulping* sound something dark and angular appeared from the midst of the water, and suddenly the little cavern was filled with the hissing and splashing of water as it ran and dripped from the ledges and crevices of the object. Amidst the pouring water three domed heads emerged, shiny in the dark, and arms ending in balls with skeletal fingers gripped the object and began moving ponderously toward shore.

The three *orka* climbed carefully up onto the stone bank, water streaming from their pressurized suits and their strange cargo, splashing on the rock and running back into the pool. The five who waited pulled back respectfully to allow them to set their burden down in the middle of the room, where it rested, glistening in the light of their torches.

The three *orka* did not speak, but moved around the strange object, fiddling with controls hidden in nooks and crannies. Then with a faint *hiss* the thing began to change shape: blocks slid forward and out, or to the side, and it began to take on a form not unlike a lumpish, two-legged table. One *orka* stood on either side, holding it steady, while the third, who was somewhat taller than the others, stood between them and carefully inserted its skeleton fingers into some hidden crevices in the blocks.

The whole contraption hummed, and the seams between the blocks ran white with light, and a small hologram appeared on the flat surface of the table.

It looked like a sort of dome-shaped dwelling, complete with little models of furniture and elves on the inside, visible through a cutaway at one side. The three *orka* looked blankly at the waiting group, their faces unreadable behind their masks.

The leader of the elves, who wore a circlet of silver around his head, came forward and inspected the hologram thoughtfully. When he raised his face to the waiting *orka*, there was wonder in his blue eyes.

"You have wrought this?" he whispered, in the language Alister would have recognized as English.

"We have made . . . one," said the leader of the *orka*. "It will serve a clutch of your people. Choose who you would send . . . carefully."

The younger elf made a despairing sound.

"Only *twenty?*" he wailed, ignoring his leader's warningly raised hand. "You promised sanctuary for our people!"

All three visored heads turned to look at him, and he became acutely aware of his position all at once.

"We have done . . . " said the leader of the *orka*. "What we . . . *can*. We had to do all . . . in secret. . . . Our . . . Queen . . . she knows not. She would not . . . allow . . . *invaders* . . . into her country."

The large, spiky dragon spoke, in a string of creaking moans that sent vibrations even through the rock of the cave. The white-haired elf translated:

"It is a good start," she said. "If twenty survive, then that will be twenty more than survived the last rising."

There was a rumbling in the caverns above them, and a small shower of dust and stones clattered down the cave walls.

"This is a hard fate," she went on, now clearly speaking for herself. "Who shall bear the burden of choosing the twenty? How shall we, who know what is to come, prepare to face an end?"

The two *orka* holding up the table made unintelligible noises—presumably their own language—and glanced at their leader, who shook its head.

There was a string of whistling hisses as the little red dragon spoke. The white-haired elf inclined her head, and after due time she said:

"The dragons know of this. Already some have left Gilsufar, others have sought refuge on the far end of the island. When the tremors reach the surface more will leave."

"And what will happen then?" asked the younger elf, a note of panic in his voice. "What will my people do when we find the dragons have deserted us? We cannot all crowd into the eastern canyons, we cannot escape into the sea but for the intervention of the *or*—" but he was prevented from saying something truly unfortunate by a soft shuffling sound coming from near the floor of the cave, and a pale head with bright orange hair thrust its way between the legs of the table. It turned around, stared at them with wide, amber-colored eyes, and wrinkled its hairless brows in a look of surprise.

"Oh dear," said Professor Odd, shoving her shoulders the rest of the way through the table's legs. "Looks like we missed the entrance a bit. Well, could have been worse," and she wriggled out from under the table, much to the surprise and shock of all present, and stood up, brushing cave dirt off the knees of her pinstriped trousers.

The dragons and the elves and the *votak* stared at her. They saw a tall, more or less elf-shaped person in a drab green coat and dark brown trousers, with a ragged scarf draped around her neck. Out from under the scarf crept a pale, flesh-colored tentacle with suckers on the underside, mottled with green leopard spots. It waved around, appearing to take stock of the situation.

The *votak* looked at her, and masked as they were they almost appeared unmoved. The three elves gasped in varying degrees and pulled back, while the dragons lifted their heads and stared in amazement.

The group was then obliged to stare some more, as this extraordinary creature was followed from between the table legs by another *votak*, in a suit a little smaller and more dingy than the others, then another elf-like person with only a dark fuzz of a hair on his head, then an animal covered all over with soft, golden fur wearing an unlikely purple jumpsuit, and finally another elf, who stared back at them wide-eyed and said nothing.

There was a moment of shocked silence, and then everyone began talking at once. Kilni threw herself at the older, white-haired elf, crying *"Korkéna!* You are *here!"* Both the dragons exclaimed: *"Kumallinién! Kumallinién!"*—but in their own language, so no one understood. Tafo began talking very fast (for him) to the other *votak*. Something about "Contacting an elder . . . " but he was drowned out by the other voices. Alister was surprised that he spoke English at all, but then supposed that, like humans had many different languages, so probably did the *votak*. English might be their best bet for a shared tongue. And indeed the other three were answering Tafo, though what they said Alister didn't catch as the Professor was talking to herself right in his ear, and what she was saying grabbed his attention entirely.

"Fascinating device this, holographic is it? Let's see if it can show me a little more of the land around here—*oh.*"

It was the *"Oh!"* that got Alister. It was the tone of voice she used when there were reality schisms, or killer robots, or giant, sentient machines. So he turned toward her and saw that she had what looked like a hologram of a city displayed on top of the table. As he looked it shrank down, revealing a crescent-shaped bay, and a high, mountainous land behind it. It appeared to be thickly forested, dotted with smooth domes of elvish installations.

The hologram was a little hard to make sense of, because it was drawn in lines of white light, and the Professor had somehow made it go see-through, showing the inner architecture of the island as though it were the schematics of a building.

Lit from below by the pale white light, Professor Odd gazed across it at Alister, her face tight and intent. She did not look frightened, exactly, but enormously concentrated. It made the hairs go up all over Alister's arms and the back of his neck.

"Do you *see* it, Alister?" she said.

Alister looked, and had to admit all he saw was a city between two rocky peninsulas with mountains rising behind it.

Professor Odd sighed, and said something to Elo, who nodded.

The golden wolf jumped up onto the table (her legs went right through the hologram in a confusion of light), and setting her stance wide, she raised her head to the ceiling and *howled.*

The noise was unlike anything the elves, *votak,* or dragons had ever heard, and they all stopped talking immediately out of surprise.

"Now if you'll all *please* listen to me," said Professor Odd through the little window of silence. "I think I understand what's going on here, and we're going to have to act quickly if I'm right." For some reason, she kept glancing up at the ceiling as she spoke. Alister looked, and saw an odd sort of rupture in the stone, with a thick, dark crack running along it. The fissure was easily six feet long, jagged and uneven, but overall it ran in a rough arc, with a little spiderweb of cracks at either end.

Even as he watched, there was the sharp *crack* of snapping stone, and it widened before his eyes.

"Professor . . . " Alister said nervously, reaching for her coattails, but Professor Odd ignored him.

"You elves," she was saying. "You live *so long* in comparison to humans, you think you've lived here a long time. But you *haven't* really, not in *dragon*-time. Not in planet-time—you're not even *from this planet.* You came here from another world—the planet just next door—to get away from something. What you maybe didn't know was that the dragons—or should I say *dinosaurs?*—did the *exact same thing* millions of years before you!"

This caused a new commotion. The elves gasped and began shouting denials. The *votak* exclaimed, but in a way that suggested they agreed with the Professor. Alister heard Tafo say: "This is what I *tried* to tell you—" but he was cut off by Kilni of all people, who stepped to the front and said to her fellows: "You brought this flag, now watch it unfurl!"

Alister blinked at the strange saying, but the other elves fell silent. For their part, the dragons watched Professor Odd with a sort of wary reserve.

"In most universes," Professor Odd went on, "the ones with dinosaurs, any-way. In most of them, the animals we think of as dinosaurs went extinct about . . . " she paused to calculate in her head, "a hundred million years ago. Local years. The planet they lived on suffered a huge natural disaster: sometimes it's a me-teor, sometimes it's a super volcano. Either way, the climate changes, and those that can't survive go extinct. But *here*, in *this* universe . . . something different happened."

She looked keenly at the dragon that resembled a *stegosaurus*, who gazed back serenely.

"In *this* solar system . . . there was another planet. *Another* planet with liquid water, and land, and the right kind of seismic activity," Professor Odd continued. "A place you could *escape to*." She paused, frowning. "The compatible atmosphere is understandable, since the *votak* could not have evolved without a similar primordial process—cyanobacteria and all that—and perhaps you brought along your own *flora* along with the *fauna* and *megafauna*. But what I didn't understand until now is *how* you did it. Jumping planets, I mean. It's something very few *humans* can manage. The elves could build ships to take them . . . but *you* . . . you were *carried*. Carried by something bigger and older than all of us put together. Something that could fly through outer space." A small smile flitted across her face, and she turned back to the table, motioning Elo off it.

"It bothered me the first time I came here," she said conversationally. "Now I understand. Kilni, come here. This should also explain why the Luiniset and the *votak* have finally agreed to work together."

Again the hologram of the city sprung up, and again Alister looked: but saw nothing unusual.

"Life evolves into the most amazing things," Professor Odd said wistfully. "There are tiny creatures, you call them *tardigrades,* that can survive even in the vacuum of space. Is it so impossible to imagine, then, *giant* creatures that have evolved to live in the vacuum of space? Giant, slow-living creatures that feed directly on starlight, who coast from planet to planet the way an albatross flies from island to island?"

Alister blinked, an incredible image slowly forming in his mind.

"That's impossible," he whispered.

"This is a universe of elves and dragons," Elo said softly. "Nothing is impossible."

"Here, I will help you to see," Professor Odd said, reaching out and running a finger into the hologram. She pointed carefully at the central headland, where the towering buildings of Gilsufar were, and moved her finger down, carefully outlining a specific shape that, despite being somewhat craggy, was still recognizable. "This is the head," she said. Then ran her finger across, down one of the curving peninsulas. "Left wing," she said, and repeated the action along the other strip of land. "Right wing . . . " She moved her hand down the island, following a line of mountains. All of a sudden, like finding an image hidden in a mess of random lines, Alister saw it.

There was the unmistakable shape of a dragon trapped under the earth. The peninsulas of the crescent bay were its wings, and it lay so that its spine formed the central range of mountains, with its legs making the smaller curving ridges on either side. Its tail trailed off into the ocean in the form of a chain of small, rocky islands.

Now that he looked closer, Alister realized that the neck twisted, and that the dragon's head was resting on its side, with most of Gilsufar being built on its upturned cheek.

Unthinking, Alister looked up at the widening crack. If they were in the caverns under Gilsufar, then *that* could be . . .

"The thing with many teeth . . . " whispered Kilni at his elbow.

"But . . . " said Alister, whose brain was having difficulty catching up to what his eyes were telling it. "That thing . . . must be *miles* long."

"When you live most of your life in outer space," Professor Odd said reasonably, "size is relative." She looked up at their audience of elves and suited *votak*, and the dragons who regarded her with wary hopefulness. "You have to be big enough to sustain your own internal fusion engine," she continued, absently though, as if her mind were somewhere else. "Easily big enough to carry living plants and animals . . . big enough to cause serious damage if they crash-landed . . . "

"Or," said Elo, "when they *wake up.*"

"Let me make sure I've got this right," Alister said, rubbing the back of his head. "These dinosaurs—er, *dragons,* were carried to this planet from *another* planet by giant *space dragons* that can fly through outer space . . . and then the elves came here and *built a city on top of one?*"

"We did not intend to," said an elf—the older one with white hair, who had still not let go of Kilni's hand. "This dragon was deep asleep and buried. We only discovered what truly lay below the caverns of Ronduath when new mapping techniques were developed. At that time we realized we would need an evacuation plan, should the dragon ever wake."

"And because Geda doesn't have very much land, you looked to the *sea,*" said Professor Odd. "Not a bad idea, except it took longer than you thought to bring the *votak* over to your side."

"The fault was ours," admitted the white-haired elf. "It has been considered treacherous to consort with the *votak* . . . "

"Because the *votak* are the true natives of Geda," Elo said, sniffing disapprovingly. "And you were afraid of what would happen if that became widely known."

"Never!" cried one of the younger elves. "It is what we were *taught.* What we *believed.*"

"In your old world," Professor Odd suggested kindly, "perhaps there was a race that was your mortal enemy, and when you came here you just applied the old prejudice to the new world."

The stegosaurus spoke then, in a string of grunts and growls, and the white-haired elf translated:

"How it began is unimportant now. The dragon under Gilsufar is waking up. It will shake us off like the dust and twigs we are, unless we act."

"Unless you *run*," said Professor Odd. "When it takes off, I doubt anything living on the surface within ten miles would survive the blast."

A dismayed silence filled the little cavern. The elves looked at each other uncertainly, and Alister read in their faces what they thought: how would they evacuate a city, much less the whole island, into the sea?

"How much time do we have?" Elo asked, all business.

The little red dragon chirped.

"Less and less," Kilni translated.

"Let's look at what we have, then," the Professor said, rubbing her hands together. "You have been making arrangements, yes?"

"Some," said the leader of the new *votak*. "We have built them an undersea shelter, large enough for twenty. We are ready and willing to escort their delegation there, where they will be safe from anything that befalls the surface."

"That's hardly going to save a city," Professor Odd said, deflated. "What we really need is a way to carry a great deal of animals a great distance away . . . very, very fast. I mean, the space dragon isn't the only thing here: there will still be *an island* left for you to resettle afterwards."

This caused a thoughtful silence to befall the elves, while the *votak* seemed suddenly agitated. Tafo was speaking fast and forcefully to the other three, and seemed to be winning whatever argument they were having.

"Speak plainly, friends," said the Professor, folding her arms and tapping the end of her tentacle against her collar.

Tafo broke away from the others. Under the shield of his helmet there appeared to be a multitude of little feelers falling out of his mouth, twining around in the water. Alister guessed it was the *votak* expression for excitement.

"There is . . . one other thing . . . we can try . . . "

Professor Odd nodded, encouraging.

"No guarantee . . . " added *votak* leader, warningly.

"Yes, *what is it?*" Kini snapped.

"We could . . . we could ask for help . . . from the *elders.*"

"The elders?" Kilni repeated, nonplussed.

"You would perhaps call them . . . the *females,*" Tafo said. "They are the oldest, largest, and strongest of us all. Some of them remember Amnós. You know by name one of the legends . . . that of the great Basa-Moranth."

There was a sharp intake of breath from the elves, and even the dragons looked alarmed.

But before they could say anything there was a horrible cracking sound, and light poured into the room. It was bright white and terrible after so long in the dim glow of the elves' torches. When Alister could at last look about him again he saw it came from the ceiling, where the seam in the rock had split wider still, and now an intense light was filtering down through the rift.

"When space dragons hibernate, they shut down most of their vital systems." Professor Odd said conversationally. "But they get their energy from nuclear fusion. Just like stars . . . though on a much smaller scale. Still . . . fusion . . . " she trailed off, eyes narrowing at the huddle of *votak*.

"Go get your elders," she said, making shooing motions with her hands toward the group of three. "Tafo, you stay with us, we may need you."

One of the elves cleared his throat uncomfortably. "It would be inadvisable for a *votak* to go openly in Gilsufar," he said.

"Elo, see that no one hurts Tafo," said Professor Odd. "They'll have to get used to them quickly, or they won't survive."

"Aye," agreed Elo, and trotted over to stand next to Tafo.

"You too, Kilni," said the Professor. "They might actually *listen* to you."

Kilni, whose face had run the gamut of emotions since crawling into the little cavern, suddenly went stock still and blank.

Oo-er, moment of truth now, thought Alister. But to her credit she only hesitated a moment before crossing over the cave floor and joining Elo. Tafo looked at them uncertainly.

"Now go, *go!*" Professor Odd commanded, practically herding the other *votak* back into the water. They went, with several backward glances, before disappearing into the depths.

"And *you,*" said the Professor, rounding on the remaining elves. "You've got a city to evacuate and not a lot of time to do it in. *Spit spot,* as they say in Alister's universe. Get your people organized!"

"What good will it do?" asked the male elf, the one who hadn't wanted Tafo to stay. "I doubt these *votak* elders will be willing or able to help, and even if so, there are too many elves who would sooner die than accept the aid of an *orka.*"

"And if the elders *do* come, and they *can* help—" cried Kilni with sudden vehemence, "—and we have not made even the slightest attempt to prepare? Then what?"

The *stegosaurus* grumbled and turned ponderously around in the small space. The elves had to move aside to allow its spiked tail to swing around.

"The dragons will go," said the white-haired elf.

The little red dragon added something in a warbling chirp.

"To survive, one must be allowed to accept help," the elf continued. "We learned this long ago."

Things got a little hard to keep track of after that, although at first it was easy enough: the elves led them out of the cavern by a large, rough-hewn tunnel, up and up through twisting spirals. Tafo had trouble in the steeper parts, and took to walking with one claw-hand hooked in Elo's jumpsuit, and Kilni pushing from behind. When she wasn't doing this she spoke in her own language with the white-haired elf, who Alister surmised was a relative of hers.

The other two elves—a younger, dark-haired man named Kemenkavel and a blond man called Melonilma—walked on either side of him, and one in front and one behind when the path got too narrow. Alister tried not to take it personally.

For her part, Professor Odd walked with the dragons, deep in conversation with the *stegosaurus* via Kilni and her relative. This puzzled Alister, for he distinctly remembered *stegosaurus* as notorious for having a small brain and being quite stupid. But then, he reasoned, this was not *stegosaurus,* but the product of millions of years of evolution from that point. Who's to say it mightn't have developed a bigger brain along the way.

After an interminable amount of climbing, during which the cave walls shook periodically and the air in the tunnel would suddenly move in harsh gusts of wind, they emerged in a circular chamber with a vaulted ceiling. This chamber, unlike the previous tunnels, was covered in blue and green tiles and lit with fixtures of the same glowing greenish stone as the elves' torches. The center of the floor was flooded with water, and its ripples reflected the light in dancing squares all over the domed ceiling.

It was quite beautiful, but Alister had no time to admire it. The white-haired elf—Alister had still not learned her name, but Kilni kept calling her *Korkéna*—spoke a few ringing words, and a large elevator car was lowered to the surface of the water, and stepping stones rose from beneath the surface, leading to it.

Alister had developed misgivings about elevators, but his feet were beginning to hurt so he piled in gratefully with the rest.

It rose fast, and through the little window he was pressed against Alister saw flashes of other tiled rooms, growing brighter and brighter as they moved upward. The conversation petered out, until, when at last the elevator arrived, it opened in deathly silence.

They stepped out into a grand hall. Alister had a glimpse of massive, towering stone arches and a great airy space filled with light and streaked with cool shadows, before they were surrounded by angry elves.

Instinctively, he grabbed for the Professor's coattails. He felt Elo grab him, and looking around saw that Tafo had had the good sense to keep a claw wedged in the belt of Elo's jumpsuit. He had pulled a tinted visor over his clear one, so his face was hidden, and appeared to be trying to make himself look as small and inoffensive as possible.

Kilni, he noticed with relief, seemed to have firmly taken their side. She was shrieking shrilly in her native tongue at anyone who came near, while her *Korkéna* spoke more softly and reasonably.

The dragons let them bicker for a short while, but eventually the *stegosaurus* shouldered his way into the group (elves went flying in all directions to keep from being impaled on his horns or trampled) and boomed some very large hoots into the crowd.

The white-haired elf translated.

The elves shrank back from her words. They began to speak again, and even though Alister could not understand the language, he could follow their tones.

Some of them didn't believe it. Some of them believed, and were gripped with despair. Others were angry that they hadn't known. Most seemed to want to form a circle and discuss the matter further, but they were interrupted when a giant, orange-tinted shadow fell across one side of the hall.

Alister looked, and saw two huge, blade-like wings, and a long, pencil-thin head. A *pterosaur*, or one of its descendants, had come to perch beyond the high columns. A small figure slid down from its back and came pelting across the stone, shouting something incomprehensible even to the other elves. They made her sit down and speak slowly.

Kilni gasped, and translated:

"She says there has been an eruption in the bay. An eruption of *stone*, black and shiny, unlike any other."

"That will probably be one of the space dragon's forelegs," Professor Odd remarked. "Think about it," she said, when they all looked at her. "You're asleep with your head pillowed on one hand, like so . . . " she demonstrated, laying one cheek against her hand, with the other resting in front of her face. "You wake up to find this little *thing* has been built on your head. It buzzes and probably itches. What do you do?"

When her audience said nothing, Professor Odd significantly raised her free hand and brushed violently at her head.

"You must evacuate—*NOW*," said Tafo, and Alister realized that of all of them, Tafo was probably the bravest. Here he was across the world from his home, trapped in a pressurized water suit, in hostile territory that was about to be wiped—*literally*—off the face of the earth, and yet seemed to be reacting the most reasonably to Professor Odd's statements.

The elves were arguing again. Some of them seemed to think they could evacuate to the beaches—and Kilni's *Korkéna* was having a hard time convincing them this would not work.

Out of the corner of his eye, Alister saw the little red feathered dragon exchange a few words with the *stegosaurus*, and slip quietly away.

Less than a minute later the hall was shaken by a terrific blast, like a hundred dragons roaring in their ears. The sound went on and on, and Alister had to clap his hands to his head. The elves fell silent—it was impossible to speak during that sound—and when it had finished there was a mad rush to the end of the hall where the sun came streaming in.

Alister felt a tug on his arm, and found that Professor Odd was leading him to the side, to a small balcony that looked out over a sprawling forest of white towers and arches. This fell away to a deeply blue sea—in which, sure enough, there was a spike of shiny black rock in the midst of a churning cauldron of white water.

But Professor Odd was not looking at the rising rock. She looked to the side, where in the distance a long peninsula stretched out over the ocean.

Moving along that peninsula, in a riot of colored scales and iridescent feathers, was a teeming mass of dinosaurs.

"Every elf in the city will have heard that," said Elo, sounding pleased.

"If they will not trust the dragons, they will die," Tafo pronounced, and did not sound terribly put out by it.

Alister turned, wide-eyed, to Kilni. "You *have* to get your people out of here," he gasped. "Tell them to follow the dragons, tell them to get to those peninsulas, tell them—"

His words were swallowed up by a roll of thunder. It went on and on, echoing around the great hall. Down in the city, elves whose day had been interrupted by the cry of the dragons were now pouring out onto the street, looking around in bewilderment.

As the sound went on, Alister changed his mind: it was not quite thunder; it pitched and waved about too much, as though there were words hidden in the noise. It reminded him of a voice he had heard not so long ago, on another world, from another giant, impossible animal.

Tafo's head came up with a snap, and he began moving—really *moving*—across the hall and out, down a wide flight of steps. Kilni and Elo were hard pressed to keep up with him, and Alister and the Professor fell behind. He saw Tafo lean toward Kilni, asking a question, and in return Kilni took his nearest arm and began leading him through the streets.

At any other time Alister would have liked to stop and stare, tourist-like. It was a beautiful city: built of bluish-gray stone with lots of colored windows and steeply slanting roofs. Long-haired, graceful heads kept being thrust out of windows to stare at them, and Alister stared back, astonished.

He had not quite realized what a city of elves *meant,* exactly. Now he saw it meant that everyone appeared to be more or less the same age. There were no children, no teenagers, no one old or sick. What a paradise they must live in, when no one was troubled by the effects of age or disease.

Or, he thought, perhaps more reasonably, *maybe they just had different things to make themselves miserable about.*

Kilni led them up stairs and down streets, moving sideways in relation to the freshly risen black rock in the bay.

As they reached the edge of the city, climbing up a steep set of stairs which caused Tafo to slow so that Elo had to get down on all fours and push him, another blast of sound rang out over Gilsufar. It sounded like a vast horn, blaring a bleating note, and this time Alister had no trouble guessing what it was: the elvish equivalent of a klaxon—an alarm bell.

Behind them the streets were filling up with curious and concerned elves, but Alister had no time to watch: Tafo, Kilni and Elo had reached the broad walkway that led to the peninsula, and were fairly pelting along it, Professor Odd hot on their heels. Alister caught one last glimpse of a city full of elves, confused and increasingly frightened, with a few flashes of color as the remaining dragons tried to herd them toward the arms of the bay.

Alister stumbled, fell, pushed himself up, hardly minding his bruised and scraped hands, and continued running. It was somehow harder now, and he realized it was because the very earth was shaking under his feet. A slight tremor ran through the ground, like an animal twitching in its sleep.

Or waking up, he thought desperately, and put on a burst of speed to catch up with the group.

The peninsula must have easily been at least three miles long, and they hadn't run a quarter of that before Tafo tired. Ordinarily Alister wouldn't have had a hope of keeping up, but in the Gedan atmosphere he found he could run much longer and faster than he thought.

But Tafo was built for swimming, not running, and as soon as they reached a rocky promontory where the path curved close to the water's edge he collapsed to the ground. Kilni dithered at his side, uncertain, but Elo snapped: "Get him in the *water!*" and together they carefully lowered the bulk into the shallows.

This was how Alister eventually caught them: as they stood around the edge of the water, while Tafo frantically undid the snaps and valves of his suit.

He didn't take it all the way off: just enough for the dark, dirty water to wash out, replaced with relatively fresh water from the pool. His whole body was heaving, moving the water across his body, like panting.

While they stood there another wave of thunder rolled across them. Now they were out beyond the buildings Alister was able to tell where it came from.

It wasn't coming from the city, or from the land at all. It was coming from far, far out to sea.

Alister looked up sharply, shading his eyes with one hand and straining them to see into that blue, blue distance.

There was something dark on the horizon, growing slowly larger, and soon joined by other large, dark shapes. They were low and rounded, like the backs of whales, but must have been bigger than any whale. Alister saw an explosion of white near one of them.

Half a minute later they were hit by another thunderclap, louder this time.

"Thirty miles out," muttered Professor Odd. She turned to the prone form of Tafo. "Your people worked fast."

"I did not think . . . they would succeed at all," Tafo admitted weakly.

Professor Odd shrugged. "Will you walk with us, or swim?" she asked.

"I will . . . walk," Tafo said, pulling the panels of his suit back into place. "They may not recognize you, else."

It took all four of them together to drag Tafo back up onto the wide path, and everyone got wet. The day was warm, however, and Alister didn't mind.

They walked slowly after that, ambling toward the head of the peninsula, where it terminated in a jumble of rocks. Behind them was a commotion as the population of Gilsufar began to trickle out of the city and onto the peninsula—but they were delayed even more by pushing handcarts full of belongings, carrying baskets or struggling under enormous packs, and never really caught up.

Ahead of them black shapes kept appearing on the horizon, stretching out across it in a line of little dark humps. The closer ones disappeared into the blueness of the sea, but Alister could just make out the leader, now closing in on the bay. Every time he saw a little puff of whitewater from it, he counted the seconds before the thunder hit them.

"Is it very silly of me to ask what those things are?" he said after a thunderclap that had rocked him on his feet.

"Not particularly," Professor Odd said pleasantly, but didn't answer the question.

"Do you know what . . . most confused me about the invaders?" Tafo remarked, apparently at random.

"Luiniset, please," Kilni said.

"Luiniset, then."

"What was it?" she asked obligingly.

"That you are born different," said Tafo. "You have what you call *male* and *female* Luiniset, but all of the same age. It's confusing to us, because we *votak*, we all hatch the same. We are . . . children. Sexless . . . no parts. Then, as we grow up, we become adults. All adults, we have what you call . . . hum . . . *male* parts."

Alister frowned. "But you mentioned females," he said. "Where do they come from?"

Professor Odd turned around and walked backward in front of them, grinning. "Well, Mister Alister, when two adult *votak* love each other *very* much—" she began, but Tafo cut her off.

"When we . . . reach a certain age," he said. "Our bodies cease to function . . . productively. So two adults who have formed an accord will . . . " he paused, as if this next bit gave him trouble.

"You know how caterpillars will eat and eat and eat and then turn into a chrysalis?" Professor Odd suggested. "And then, a little while later, come out as a butterfly or moth?"

"We have crosswings," Kilni said. "They spend the first half of their life in water, the second in the air, in between they have a changing stage."

"Yes, just like that," Professor Odd said cheerfully. "Well, with *votak* it's like *two* caterpillars getting into the same chrysalis, and coming out as an *eagle*."

"Wait," said Alister, as the picture being painted came into focus. "You mean . . . "

"The two *votak* will . . . join," said Tafo. "Their bodies become . . . one. Their minds . . . meld. They grow and grow to enormous size, and develop the ability to bear eggs. We call them elders, but they are what you seem to think of as *females*."

"And how long do *they* live?" Elo asked.

"We don't know," Tafo said. "They can be killed in battle, or go to sleep forever. But it is impossible to know whether an elder is really dead, or only sleeping."

They walked on. The heavy Gedan sun beat down on them—Alister was sure his face would be red as an apple by the time this was all over. The path was wide as a road and covered in a thin layer of bright white sand over equally bright rocks, and Alister had to squint so his eyes were almost shut. Every few minutes they would hear the thunder of the approaching fleet of *votak* elders, and now he also was noticing a change in the waves that broke upon the rock: where before they had been regular white breakers, now they ebbed and surged, sometimes so high they broke over and spilled across the road. Everyone was splashed and a little damp by the time they reached the headland.

Now the rising rock in the bay was visibly shaking, and there was smoke rising from the city. The peninsula road was packed with refugees, and the other arm—just visible across the bay—was teeming with motion as well.

Out to sea, the nearest black humps were close enough that Alister could see they were bigger than he thought: some looked to be the size of a city block, with rough crags like horns ringed around the edge. Each one brought with it a small wave, which ran along the surface before it in a white line.

Then, just as the first refugees from Gilsufar were arriving, the lead elder—who more resembled an island in her own right—dropped completely out of sight.

Professor Odd leapt to the top of the crag of rocks that overlooked the sea, and peered out at the water. For some minutes they all stood, waiting, and then the wave the *votak* had brought hit the shore, crashing over the headland and soaking everyone. By the time Alister spat the saltwater out of his mouth and wiped it from his eyes he saw with incredulity that Professor Odd still clung to her rocky perch, and had even turned around to wave at him.

There was a deep, piercing moan. Alister felt it in the soles of his feet. It reverberated in his ears and made his teeth ache. While he was still reeling from the noise there was a roar of displaced water, and from behind the Professor, like a submarine rising from the deep, came the most enormous creature Alister had ever seen.

It—*she*—was a deep glossy black, her face alone was the size of a house, and her eyes—there were *fourteen* of them—were like windows, lit from behind by a dim blue light. From what Alister could see of her mantle—which was still mostly underwater—it stretched almost halfway into the bay, and then as far out again to the open ocean on the other side. The bottom half of her face, now emerging in a torrent of water and foam, was comprised of a complex mess of feelers the size of trees and tentacles like fire hoses.

There was screaming behind him. A flurry of motion as the evacuees retreated down the peninsula. Tafo fell sideways in shock and clutched at his arm, the skeleton fingers of his suit digging painfully into Alister's flesh. But he was able to hear the *votak* when he said, in a voice that was hoarse and strained even for him:

"That is no ordinary elder! That is *the* elder. That is *Basa-Moranth!*"

"She who birthed the *orka?*" hissed Kilni.

"She who carried the city of Sark on her back for thirty years!" gasped Tafo.

"She who looks like she's about to squish my Professor!" growled Elo, and leapt forward.

But the *votak* elder seemed fascinated by Professor Odd, not hostile. Alister could see all the eyes focused on her, like searchlights, and very slowly a single tentacle the size of a tree trunk detached itself from the writhing mess. For one horrible instant Alister thought it *would* wipe Professor Odd clean off the rock.

Instead it bent, sharply, and bent again, forming itself into a simple, angular—and utterly familiar shape.

Alister stood and gaped at the sight of the giant sea monster calmly holding out one tentacle in the shape of a triangle.

Wait a minute! Alister thought, and looked again. And stared. And felt his mouth fall open in shock.

There, plastered in the center of the creature's forehead, between the four central eyes, every arm twined and curled to hold on as tightly as possible, in that vast expanse of blue and black was a little splotch of bright green. Alister thought he could just spy a speck of orangish yellow in the middle of it.

"*Dave!*" screamed Professor Odd, putting her hands on her hips. "What *have* you been doing?!"

Like the walls on a movie set being rolled away, Basa-Moranth's mouth opened. Alister felt the rush of air as the creature *inhaled*, and then . . .

He had just the presence of mind to clap his hands over his ears before the roar hit him. Even so the force of the air alone made him rock backward, and the sound shook him down to the bone. He didn't know how Professor Odd could stand it, but there she was, still balanced on her rock. Indeed, she was shouting back.

"No! No! No, it's no good!" she hollered over the dying roar. "Better just *give him to me* and let him explain things!" and she reached forward and laid her hand on the nearest branch-like feeler. Dave took that as all the invitation he needed, and slithered down from the *votak's* face, across the appendage, over Professor Odd's arm, ripped off her wig with one tentacle and clamped himself onto her head.

Professor Odd twitched a little, like it tickled. She got an inward, concentrating look on her face, and Alister knew Dave was talking to her directly: not through an awkward translator, but with his own psychoactive slime.

It was like listening to one end of a telephone conversation.

"Oh, oh so *that's* what you were doing. Oh, oh I *see*. Yes, yes that's *fantastic*. Yes, well, the elves aren't too keen on the *votak* either, but they'll just have to lump it. Unless they want to take their chances with a space dragon eruption. Yes, yes it's really a space dragon. Yes, it's an *unconventional* creature, I'm sorry. Okay. And you'll thank her for me—oh, she can *understand?* That's wonderful—" here Professor Odd paused to wave cheerfully at the house-sized face of Basa-Moranth, "—all right, I'll hand you back over."

Dave neatly picked himself up and writhed back across the living bridge and settled himself between Basa-Moranth's lower eyes.

Professor Odd wiped a glob of slime off her head and stuck her wig back on.

"Pass this message along, Kilni," she said, hopping down from the rock. "The *votak* elders have come to serve as evacuation ships. They will line up along the peninsula with their backs out of the water, and your people are to climb onto them. There is to be no fighting, no violence of any kind. After the, er, *eruption,* they will take you back to whatever is left of Gilsufar, or to the nearest habitable land. Any hint of aggression, and they *dive,* is that understood?"

Kilni, still a little awestruck, nodded.

"Then get going, woman!" cried Professor Odd, flapping her hands at the elf.

Kilni went, but Alister had no time to see how she organized half the population of Gilsufar. He had eyes only for what was rising out of the sea all around them.

From what he could tell, the *votak* elders were shaped rather like flattened turtles, with wide backs rising to a gentle dome in the center. Around the edges they were studded with rough, horn-like protrusions, and their skin was covered in barnacles.

They rose from the sea, streaming water, and came as close to the shore as they could manage. Alister guessed they went on a long way under the surface, like icebergs, because there was still a wide gulf of water between the nearest back and the shore.

Some of the *votak* solved this problem by raising huge arms, as wide as the peninsula road, to serve as bridges. Others just waited patiently while the braver elves swam across and pulled themselves up the sides, using the barnacles as handholds.

They lined up along the peninsula—both peninsulas, Alister saw when he thought to glance across the bay. More elders had emerged there, and he could just make out the frantic flashes of color as the dinosaurs crawled aboard. Clearly they had found ways to communicate without the Professor's help.

The ground beneath his feet trembled. At first Alister thought it was just the *votak* speaking again, but now he saw the actual buildings of Gilsufar *heave*, rise, split and fall aside. A great burst of steam shot up through the central dome, and Alister saw it explode: pieces of rock and masonry flying everywhere.

A second later he heard the boom. It seemed small and weak, after Basa-Moranth's greeting.

But if the elves had been hesitant and cagey at first, this sent all their reservations packing. There was a mad rush to get off the land, and Alister felt himself being pushed forward by the surging crowd.

They were stopped by Basa-Moranth, who raised a single arm and pointed it at Tafo. She didn't speak as far as Alister could tell, but Tafo seemed to understand. He crawled awkwardly over the rocks, and let the arm wrap gently around him. Then Basa-Moranth lifted him up, up, to place him gently on her knobby forehead. Then she turned and appeared to move away, but Alister could see she was only turning so her vast side was presented to the land. By leaning forward he could see the shape of her, like a giant rocky ray fish, sliding past under the surface.

Then she rose, the water sliding away, an equally knobby and barnacled arm rising like a bridge between her back and the land. Alister could believe she had once carried a city on her back, for now that it was out of the water he couldn't see clearly to the other side, and Tafo was a tiny dark speck on the peak of her head.

The crowd behind them surged, shouting angrily, and Alister, Elo, and Professor Odd, being the nearest, were forced to run helter-skelter up over the arm and scramble up onto her back or risk getting crushed.

Basa-Moranth's skin was hard and wet and treacherously slippery—there seemed to be algae growing on it—and Alister found he had to go on all fours, and wouldn't have stood a chance of making the climb without the barnacles. It was like climbing up a strange, smooth, slightly soft hill. But Alister went, as fast as he could for fear of being trampled, until he found a spot near one of the horns that marked the edge of her back. He threw his arms around it and clung there.

Some of the other elders were already leaving, while new, empty backs rose to take their place. It looked to Alister that the limit would not be how many elves could they carry, but how many could they take on before the city exploded.

There was a deep roaring noise. Alister looked and saw that the pillar of rock that had emerged from the bay was clearly moving. It was rising, rising, rising, and as it rose Alister saw the shape of it at last: a giant claw at the end of an equally giant arm, and it rose out of the ocean—sending a wave of water rippling across the bay—and reached up, back, its rocky skin cracking.

Still having a hard time believing his eyes, Alister watched the giant arm—easily as long as one of Gilsufar's main streets—spread its claws, and plunge in amongst the houses and buildings, bridges and towers.

He could have been horrified at the destruction, but he was too astonished by what happened next.

The city tore away, crumbling to dust as the very earth it was built on heaved and cracked open, and with a violent wrench a head twisted and jerked up into the air.

From this distance Alister could see the entirety of the space dragon's head. It looked rather like a dinosaur, he decided, with a long snout and a wide mouth. It seemed to be made of the same smooth, gray stone as the rest of the island, and when it blinked, its eyes glowed brightly, even in the sun.

The city was in ruins now, lying in dust and rubble around the space dragon's chin. Now also the hills and mountains behind the city were quivering, and Alister felt a little sick as he realized what was about to happen.

By now the peninsula was almost empty. Most of the elders had moved away and were streaming into the distance. Basa-Moranth, because she was so huge, waited the longest, until the last of the stragglers had been helped up over her side. Then, with a gentle heave, she pushed herself off the peninsula, and out into the open ocean. The crowd on her back collectively turned to watch the land as they began, at last, to move away.

It was not so much land anymore but a writhing heap of earth. The dragon which had lain asleep for so long—longer even than Basa-Moranth—was shaking off millennia of earth and forest. The mountains cracked along the ridge, and the dragon thrashed to free its wings, hurling chunks of mountain out into the sea, where their fall caused waves that beat upon the shore, tearing more land away.

From this chaos something giant emerged—a vaguely reptilian shape, with four stubby legs and a long neck. Its wings, still trapped beneath the peninsulas, quivered, and the white road that Alister had trod minutes ago was scattered like dust.

The space dragon's wings were not like bird or bat wings, but closer to those of the pterosaur: angular and blade-like. Caked in mud and sediment, it was hard to imagine them carrying anything through the air.

All this Alister nearly missed because he was trying to find Kilni. He hadn't seen her come aboard with the last of the evacuees, and though he told himself she could well have gotten onto one of the other elders he still felt a swell of panic rise in his throat.

It's stupid, he thought. Lots of things are going to die today. There were probably elves who did not get out of the city in time. Animals who had nowhere to go. Forests that *couldn't* go. You can't evacuate a whole city in a matter of hours, much less an *island.*

Basa-Moranth's back was not as crowded as he had first thought, she was so huge. But many of the elves were clustered at one side to watch the destruction of their homeland, so it felt that way. Once Alister got clear of the crowd he found he could actually walk fairly freely across the slippery, living surface.

He caught a glimpse of the Professor's orange wig toward Basa-Moranth's head, and made for that. When he got there he found not only the Professor, but Elo, Tafo, *and Kilni.*

Kilni was sopping wet, and Tafo looked smug even under his suit. Alister decided not to ask.

He wasn't given the opportunity anyway. Professor Odd, it seemed, had been speaking with Dave. Basa-Moranth had instructions.

"Tell everyone to *lie down,*" she was saying. "*Lie down.* And hold on to something."

"Why? What's going on?" Alister asked. "I thought we escaped."

"We haven't yet," said Elo grimly.

"That dragon didn't just get up to use the loo," Professor Odd said. "It's *leaving,* Alister. Where do you think *space dragons* go when they *leave?*"

"It's . . . going to take off?" Alister said blankly.

"Launch, more like," Elo said. "They don't fly like birds, they launch—like rockets. What do you think a rocket that size would do to the earth underneath it?"

Alister thought his mouth was dry, but he managed to swallow anyway. Glancing back, he saw they were only half a mile from where the space dragon was shaking bits of island off its back. Even as he watched, the swell from an earlier wave caused Basa-Moranth to rise and fall with the moving water.

"We need to outrun the blast wave," Professor Odd was saying. "Actually, we're *going* to outrun the blast wave."

As she spoke, Alister noticed that the wind seemed to be picking up.

Wait. No, it wasn't. Basa-Moranth was moving faster. Faster. *Faster.*

"Hold on everyone!" Alister hollered, throwing himself down. The wind was serious now, pulling at the skin of his face. Alister tucked his head against his arm and looked back, over the dark swell of Basa-Moranth, now covered with bedraggled elves. They seemed to have gotten the idea; the *votak* was ripping through the water at such a pace you had to hold on otherwise you'd be blown off.

Something changed then. There was the sensation of lifting, and Alister got the feeling that, instead of swimming through the water, Basa-Moranth was now running on its surface, using her wide mantle like a rudimentary wing. In their wake he saw a frothing foam of white water.

Makes sense, Alister thought numbly. *Air is thinner than water; you can move faster through it.*

He could hear nothing but the buffeting of wind in his ears, but looking back he could see clearly enough.

They were maybe a mile from the island. The dragon, smaller from the distance but still huge, had sat up and was stretching its wings. The sediment flaked off them, and they now appeared to be made of many glinting platinum blades, arrayed like the petals of a flower. It seemed not to notice or care about the fleet of comparatively small *votak* elders skimming away across the sea. It turned its head from side to side, like it was working out a kink in its neck. Then it folded its wings close along its sides and spread its legs out, crouching over what remained of the island of Gilsufar.

Alister saw the flash of light long before he heard the rumble. They were maybe five miles away now, and his hands were growing numb from holding on in the wind.

The space dragon surged forward as it jumped, and it looked as if a small sun exploded on the horizon. It sent a wave of air and water shooting out into the sea, and the space dragon shooting up into the sky.

It rode a stream of brilliant yellow fire, and as it rose, streaming through the air, still more pieces of earth and rock were stripped away. Something silvery and shining emerged. The space dragon's true skin was like plate metal, and it shone in the sun as it hurtled up into the sky. Up, up, in a gently sloping arc, too distant now for Alister to see it in any detail. It was a shining dot at the head of a tail of white fire streaking across the sky, growing fainter and fainter, until it winked out all together.

A few minutes later the wave caused by its launch caught up with them at last, and Basa-Moranth's back tilted steeply as she rode it, treaded water at its crest, and finally slid down the other side, letting it move on out into the ocean.

The *votak* slowed, sinking back into the water. The wind ebbed, and Alister pushed himself up on shaking arms to look around.

Professor Odd was already on her feet, straightening her wig and brushing off her damp coat. She smiled brightly at him.

"*Well*," she said. "That went well!"

At her feet, Elo laughed weakly.

* * *

In the end the elves decided not to return to Gilsufar, but to follow the dinosaurs to what they called "the Living Islands."

"They're just volcanos," Professor Odd explained. "Only one still active. Nothing compared to a space dragon."

They said good-bye to Kilni on the edge of Basa-Moranth. Five other, smaller elders had come to take her load, and they had knotted their huge arms together to create slippery bridges between themselves. Alister was glad to see that, among the elves who crawled carefully over the bridge, one was the white-haired elf Kilni had called *Korkéna*.

Kilni herself was one of the last to go. After she bid brisk but respectful farewell to Tafo, Elo, and the Professor, Alister lay on his belly and helped her down Basa-Moranth's side.

"I've been thinking," he said quickly. "You mentioned this *Basa-Moranth* earlier, didn't you?"

"According to our *legends*," Kilni said, and had at least the grace to look embarrassed. "She was a monster of the abyss, out of whose belly came the first *orka*. She opened her mouth wide and they came pouring out."

Behind and above them, Tafo made a sort of snorting noise.

"What if that wasn't *entirely* wrong?" he suggested. "What if . . . well, what if someone *did* open their mouth, and something else *did* come pouring out? Just not Basa-Moranth, and not the or—er, *votak*."

Kilni put her head on one side and blinked thoughtfully at him.

"How do you mean?" she said.

"I mean—" Alister took a swallow of the dense, clear air. "I mean, how did the dinosaurs get to Geda? Did they ride on that space dragon's back? Through the void of outer space? I know the Professor was talking about tardigrades and things but *dinosaurs* aren't like that."

Kilni had her feet on the writhing tentacle-bridge, where she balanced, expectantly.

"No," Alister called down to her. "I think they rode *inside* the space dragon. And when it got here, it opened its mouth and . . . " he trailed off, making a little walking motion with his fingers. "They all came marching out."

Kilni looked around at the giant sea monsters waiting patiently to take her people to their new home, and shrugged.

"Perhaps," she called back. "I should not concern myself overmuch with the content of legends; they do not appear to be at all reliable." She waved, and began making her way carefully across the bridge.

"You might want to concern yourself with thinking about your neighboring worlds," Professor Odd called over Alister's shoulders. "You never know when the next batch of settlers will show up!"

Kilni was too distant now for Alister to make her expression, but he thought she nodded.

Tafo did not come back with them.

"I have been offered a position with the Mekar," he explained, as if they would all know what the *Mekar* were. "If . . . it is all the same to you . . . I will leave you here, and return to Amnós by my own means."

"Which is a very nice way of saying you don't want to risk getting dragged into any more adventures," Elo said brightly. "I *completely* understand."

She and Alister shook his strange claw-hand, but Professor Odd grasped him by the arm and pressed her forehead to the dome of his helmet. She tapped at it lightly with her tentacle.

"Next time," she said. "I will come and visit you, and then it will be *me* in the awkward suit."

It was hard to tell with the glass visor in the way, and with how different *votak* faces were from human faces, but Alister thought Tafo smiled at that.

He did not climb down Basa-Moranth's side, but leapt gratefully into the water, disappearing in a splash of white foam.

The journey back to Gilsufar took a lot longer than the flight from it, because Basa-Moranth clearly didn't feel like pulling her flying trick again. They passed the time by talking to Dave, who came crawling back and draped himself lazily over the Professor's shoulders. It turned out he had stumbled onto Basa-Moranth quite by accident, and had been told the whole story of Geda directly from her. It had been Basa-Moranth who felt the space dragon begin to wake up, and after some encouragement from Dave agreed to help evacuate the elves. He had been quite surprised to arrive there with the rescue party only to find Professor Odd at the head of the line.

"Yes, *well*," said Professor Odd with a shrug. "We were rather surprised to see *you*."

"Explains why the elders showed up so fast," Elo remarked. "Tafo only thought of asking *them* for help at the last minute."

The elders had not been all that eager to help, Dave admitted. They had, in fact, taken quite a bit of *persuading*.

No one asked how Dave had gone about doing that.

It was dark by the time they reached the shore, but Geda's two moons were both rising in the sky and they could see well enough to make out the smoking heap of rubble that was all that remained.

The peninsulas were gone, and where the city had risen, spire over spire, there was now only a water-filled crater with a few bent and broken piles of rock. Here and there a column or a piece of roof was recognizable, rising out of the moonlit water. One of the larger domes had landed more or less upright, and it was to this makeshift island that Basa-Moranth eventually took them, weaving and heaving her way through the wreckage.

It was a hard scramble from Basa-Moranth's limb up onto the dome, and Alister's tired muscles protested the whole way. He reached out a hand to cling to the steep slope, and found the stone still warm to the touch and scorched black.

Professor Odd, with Dave still around her neck, was the last to leave, and stood for a time before Basa-Moranth's house-sized face. They waved good-bye, one green and yellow tentacle, one white hand, as Basa-Moranth ponderously sank back into the sea. Elo and Alister waved too, as soon as they realized she was leaving them.

The water lapped at the dome, rising slightly at the bulk of the creature disappearing into it. When these waves had subsided, Dave also slipped down into the sea, diving swiftly out of sight.

"Where is he going *now?*" Alister asked as Professor Odd climbed past them up the dome.

"Why, back to the *Oddity,* of course," she replied over her shoulder. "Or did you forget we'd left the portal under five hundred feet of rock and water?"

Alister had actually assumed Professor Odd had a way around that, but he supposed having Dave go on ahead and pick them up was as good an idea as any.

The top of the dome had a little balcony with a pointed roof supported by columns, mostly intact. Wordlessly the Professor pointed, and went on climbing. Alister sighed, and heaved himself after.

Elo, as comfortable on four legs as she was on two, kept trotting ahead and then looking back, thoughtfully. The third time they caught up with her, she said:

"Looks rather like Amnós, don't you think?"

Alister looked around at the ruined wreckage and had to admit there was a certain similarity. Except Gilsufar looked like it had been burned into the bargain, and there was no building that remained more than half out of the water.

"Professor," said Elo, "*was* Amnós another space dragon?"

Professor Odd seemed surprised. "Nothing of the sort. Space dragons only spend enough time on a planet to lay their eggs. This one was highly unusual. No, Amnós was a victim of geography: they built it over a sinking fault. One day they had an earthquake, and the ground sank lower than sea-level . . . and . . . well . . . *gravity* and all that."

The going got easier as they neared the top of the dome: the sides grew gentler and gentler, and Alister walked the last few feet upright.

They sat on the edge of the balcony, looking out at the moonlit ruins and drinking the last of the water from Elo's bottle. Alister's face still felt hot, and he suspected he would have a rather bad sunburn the next day. He was so tired his bones ached, and he couldn't be bothered even to worry about Dave, swimming through the treacherous wreckage, searching for a portal that might or might not still exist. The night air was cool and soothing against his burning face, while the warmth that remained in the stone kept him from becoming chilled. The water lapped peacefully at the ruins of Gilsufar, and a gentle wind blew away the smell of burned earth, replacing it with the pleasant scent of clean air and seawater.

He had almost fallen asleep where he sat when he heard a humming sound behind him, and bright, multicolored light spilled out onto the side of the dome, dimming even the light from Geda's two moons. Blinking, Alister twisted around and saw that between two columns and the roof, the Oddity's door had now opened. There was a trail of slime and water running up the steps, and Alister had to steady himself against the wall to make sure he didn't slip in it as he made his way wearily up them.

Standing aside to let the Professor go next, Elo took one last look out at the forest of stone and water, raising her eyes up to the heavens and their strange stars. Out there were other suns and planets . . . and now, she realized, at least one giant, dragon-shaped being with blade-like wings and a head the size of a city. She shook herself at the thought, and went inside.

"Don't forget," she said as she came up the stairs. "We still need to go pick up Dave's suit!"

Epilogue

IN A GRAY DAWN the beach lay deserted. The night's tide had swept clean the footprints and scars from the day before, and all that remained was a single, roughly barrel-shaped object that sat by one of the tidal pools. It had a dome-like top cracked halfway open, and the inside seemed to be filled with water. There was a faint dew upon its outside, and the man who bent over it leaned close, but was careful not to touch.

He was a tall man dressed in a neat black coat with neat black trousers. He had a pale face and black hair, slightly in need of a trim, swept severely back from a high, sloping brow. He had a long, inquisitive sort of nose, and a small, thin-lipped mouth—the corners of which twitched, as though a smile had attempted to form, only to be cut back before it could really get anywhere. His eyes were bright and improbably green, and there was something of the snake in the way he moved. He slithered a hand over Dave's suit—careful not to actually touch it—and wrote down some notes in a neat little black book. Then he went carefully away.

He walked so carefully that, when Professor Odd came striding down the beach with Dave on her shoulder an hour later, they found no trace of him.

Dave did hesitate before climbing back inside, but didn't say anything. He couldn't figure out a way to explain that he had smelled an echo—an echo he had felt before, no less. But the first time he had been rather preoccupied with extracting Alister's mind from the clutches of a giant machine, so he allowed himself to believe he could be mistaken.

Professor Odd was in such a good mood, anyway, going on about her precious *space dragons* and how she had finally gotten to see one. It seemed a pity to bother her.

There would be bother later. Dave knew it in the tips of his tentacles. But for now, he thought as he piloted his cumbersome suit back across the beach toward the waiting Oddity, for *now* they could take some time and relax. Dave felt they had earned that much, at least.

6.   THE MONSTER'S DAUGHTER

Prologue

IT WAS DECIDED, after much discussion, that they would visit London.

"Yes, but *which* London?" Elo asked. "We have a choice of an almost infinite number."

"Rapid Gregorian," Professor Odd replied brightly.

"Which one is *that?*" Alister wondered aloud.

"Why, the one that suffered the least damage in World War II," Professor Odd said as she twirled the levers on the Oddity's control panel.

"Technically it's a series of universes, not a single one," Elo amended. "But they are similar enough it doesn't much matter which one we get."

The lights of the cockpit flashed, sparkling on and off, while the Oddity emitted a series of musical hums and beeps. At last there was a deep *bonnnnng* from within the ship (machine—place—*thing*... Alister still wasn't sure what it was) and a slight tremor went through the floor. Something shifted, and the lights changed subtly.

Professor Odd pushed her chair back and frowned. She reached up under her wig—deep ultramarine blue today—and rubbed her hairless scalp.

"Something wrong?" Elo asked.

Raising a hand for silence, Professor Odd got up and walked down the stairs to the Oddity's front door. Now that they were tethered to a universe, it appeared to be a solid wooden door with an old-fashioned latch. Professor Odd opened it and put first her head, then the rest of her body, outside.

Coming up behind her, Alister saw a dull gray sky cut by the horizon of a city: craggy old spires mixed with turn-of-the-millennium arches and glass domes. There was a smell of wet pavement and rubbish—such a familiar combination to Alister that he went fearlessly out the door, hopping briskly down a set of steps to the street.

Professor Odd was an incongruous splash of color in the otherwise grayish landscape: her blue wig and green coat standing out sharply against the black asphalt of the road and the subdued tans and browns of the houses to either side.

To Alister, who had spent the better part of his life living in a big, old city, it felt breathlessly, achingly familiar. Right down to the rubbish bins set out on the pavement and the antennas and power lines strung overhead. He took a deep breath of the thick, city air, and quietly rejoiced even as his heart broke a little inside. He had not known until then just how much he had missed his old home. Even so, he felt an immense calm engulf him. If he closed his eyes and forgot about the inter-dimensional portal just behind him, he could imagine he *was* home.

Professor Odd, meanwhile, was anything but calm. She marched to the end of the street and looked both ways. She strode back, her coattails flapping behind her, and stopped by the nearest rubbish bin. She lifted its lid and looked inside. She knelt and stroked a finger over the wet pavement. She held it up. She opened her mouth and stuck out her tongue—Alister noticed it was mottled pink and greenish, not unlike her bare scalp.

He and Elo watched her, curious, but not alarmed.

Not alarmed until Professor Odd came at them, arms wide, and shooed them back into the Oddity.

"Inside," she said sharply. "Back inside, quickly, don't say a word. Go."

They went, tripping over each other, and Professor Odd slammed the door behind them.

"Wrong universe?" Elo asked.

"Wrong series," Professor Odd said. She sat down at the control panel, tapped a few buttons and pulled a lever.

The Oddity let out a deep, mournful groan. Professor Odd chewed a finger, then tapped out a longer string one-handed while she slowly began turning a hand crank under the desk of colored buttons.

Alister felt as though every atom in his body was being pulled apart. He screamed. Elo howled in pain. Dave, who had been maneuvering his panvironment suit down the ladder from the second floor, plummeted and hit the ground with a sickening *thud.*

Professor Odd quickly back-wound the crank and pressed a large yellow button.

The pain stopped as abruptly as it had begun, and Alister blinked the tears out of his eyes to find Professor Odd stroking the Oddity's cockpit and murmuring apologies.

"*What* was *that* about?" Elo demanded.

Without a word Professor Odd got up and went back to the front door—which was unchanged. She opened it.

The same dull, gray-and-brown street lay outside. She came back up the stairs, her face white as paper and her mouth pressed into a thin, humorless line.

"Professor?" Alister asked. "What's wrong with the Oddity?"

"WE HAVE BECOME WOVEN TO THE UNIVERSE," Dave announced, making them all jump. "WE WILL NOT BE ABLE TO LEAVE UNTIL WE UNTANGLE OURSELVES."

"Yes, but *which* universe?" Elo prodded. "Professor, *what* is out there?"

Professor Odd raised a hand and chewed nervously on a fingernail. She wrapped her arms tightly about herself and looked at them with wide, jaguar eyes.

Alister felt a cold dread grip his insides as he realized that Professor Odd, who had faced down killer robots, flying whales, dinosaurs and giant sea monsters . . . Professor Odd, who grinned like a maniac in the face of imminent death . . . that *Professor Odd* was scared.

"It's the wrong universe all right," she said in a dry, hoarse voice. "Out there . . . that's *my* universe. And we're *stuck in it.*"

Part One: The Detective

ALISTER STARED OUT THE WINDOW in fascinated horror. Where there should have been nothing—the vast black-blue emptiness between universes, pricked with the lights of distant worlds—now he looked out past the lacy curtains and the thick panes to the water-stained brick wall of the house next to them. They were separated by a narrow footpath in which a broken ladder sprawled despairingly. The sight scared him almost as much as the nothing had the first time he'd looked out the Oddity's window.

"Okay," he said, swallowing down a bubble of panic. "How did this happen?" He preferred to think about that—why was the Oddity, which normally attached and detached from universes with the flick of a switch, now so thoroughly embedded in this one?—rather than the more distressing question: *why did Professor Odd not want to be in her home universe?*

There were a number of reasons why Alister did not want to return to *his* home world—unfriendly men in hazmat suits working for a sinister corporation called the Canary Company chief among them. If there was something similar in Professor Odd's world . . .

"Someone . . . " Professor Odd was scanning a scrolling wall of code in a language Alister could not decipher on one of the cockpit's little screens. "Someone . . . *called* us here. Called the *Oddity* here, I mean. It's the strongest working of transdimensional adhesivism I've ever *seen.*"

"Does your world have that technology?" Alister asked. "Is that how they built the Oddity?"

"The Oddity doesn't come from my world," Professor Odd said. "And no, they *don't* have this kind of tech—I made sure—" she cut herself off. Alister and Elo looked at each other uncertainly.

The mutant wolf rubbed her paw-hands together. "Uh, Professor—" she began nervously, when Dave interrupted them.

He rolled his panvironment suit around the table and came to a halt at the Professor's elbow.

"WE NEED TO COMMUNICATE," he said in an even more abrasive tone than usual.

Professor Odd blinked at him. "I'm listening," she said.

"I DID NOT MEAN VIA AUDIBLE SPEECH," Dave said meaningfully. "TAKE OFF YOUR HAIRPIECE."

"Oh," said Professor Odd.

"*Oh,*" said Elo. "I'll go get some towels."

Dave was not psychic. Professor Odd had explained this to Alister before. Rather, he communicated through psychoactive slime that he secreted from the fine, anemone-like tentacles that grew from the back side of his disk-shaped body. It was a somewhat more efficient form of communication, since the words were transferred directly into the recipient's head without having to be translated by the ears. Because of this, more information could be exchanged within a shorter period of time. The disadvantage was that it made a mess.

Which was why Professor Odd spent the next half hour sitting in the kitchen alcove with her head in the sink, Dave visible only as a couple of twining, green tentacle-arms dangling over the side.

Elo busied herself at the Oddity's console, pushing buttons, listening to the unhappy beeping noises, and occasionally swearing under her breath in a language that sounded like growling.

Alister sat by the window and watched what he could see of the street. His view was mostly blocked by a cracked and splintering wooden gate with a rusty latch, but beyond that he could glimpse the upper stories of the houses across the main road. These were a block of uniform, cream-colored houses, each with rusty brown trim around the windows. Alister wondered if their front doors matched, or if residents were allowed to express their individuality by painting them different colors. He suspected not. The whole street was so drab and uniform, any creativity would likely be treated as a sign of rebellion.

Was his own world this depressing? It wasn't as colorful as the Oddity, of course, and perhaps not as vibrantly strange as some of the worlds they had visited, but surely it wasn't as bad as this place.

Was it?

Alister was a little shocked to discover how little he remembered about his own world. Perhaps because, when he was in it, he simply thought of it as *the* world, with no possibility for alternate realities. Would he even recognize it if he ever returned? Or, like the Professor, would he know immediately by some inner instinct? He hoped so.

Something passed by on the street beyond the fence. It was difficult to see, and Alister couldn't hear anything through the thick window pane, but he thought it was a car.

"There it goes *again,*" Elo said.

Alister got up and went over to her console. She had gotten one of the Oddity's screens to display a view of the street equivalent to looking out their front door.

From there Alister could confirm that all the houses opposite had the same color doors. The only way to tell them apart was their number plates and the different curtains just visible peeping around the edges of their front windows.

"There went what again?" he asked.

"The same black car. I don't like it." She wrinkled her nose. "I think they're scanning."

"Scanning for what?"

"With our luck? *Us.*"

"They're looking for me," Professor Odd said from behind them both.

She had a towel draped around her neck and was using a corner of it to wipe the last of Dave's slime out of her ear.

"What are we going to do?" Alister posed the obvious question, rather dreading the answer.

Professor Odd shrugged unhappily. "We have two choices," she said. "We wait here until Dave and I figure out a way to get the Oddity untangled—which I have no idea how long it will take and they may find a way of getting inside in that time—or . . . " she finished wiping her head off and looked thoughtfully at the screen.

Elo turned right around in her seat. "Or *what?*" she demanded.

Professor Odd looked up at them and put on a bright, humorless grin. "Or I go out and *see what they want.*"

So saying she whipped around and scrambled up the ladder to the catwalk that ran the circumference of the interior. There was a clatter as she pattered along it and a slam as she disappeared behind the door with a brass o-D bolted to the center.

She returned a few minutes later looking . . . well, not looking very much like Professor Odd at all. She had somehow convinced the Oddity—which supplied their clothes—to make her a mousy gray overcoat and a similarly mousy brown wig. Her blue pinstriped trousers had been replaced with dull gray ones, and she carried a black umbrella. With dark, round glasses covering her eyes and a thick, charcoal-colored scarf around her neck she looked alarmingly *normal.*

Alister and Elo stared in horror.

"What are you *doing?*" Alister blurted out.

Professor Odd shrugged. "There's no running from some things," she said with a sigh. "You best sit tight while I get it sorted out. Shouldn't take too long. Be back before you know it."

She strode down the steps to the front door and there stopped.

"Is it clear?" she called back up.

Elo bounced over to the screen and examined the view of the street.

"Deserted," she replied.

Professor Odd came back up the stairs at once and went over to one of the windows. With a deft tap and shove, she pushed it open.

The smell of wet concrete, car exhaust and a faint hint of rubbish flooded into the Oddity.

"They want me to come out the front," Professor Odd explained, throwing a leg out the window.

The rest of her soon followed. They were so high up she had to hang by her hands in order to drop to the ground. Alister tossed the umbrella down after her. He saw why she wanted it: outside, the gray sky had opened up, and it was beginning to rain.

Professor Odd caught the umbrella one-handed and grinned at him.

"Keep the windows closed," she said. "Don't go outside."

She opened the umbrella and promptly disappeared under it, moving swiftly down the alley in the opposite direction from the street. Alister watched her go, feeling deeply unsettled.

No sooner had he and Elo got the window shut again than there was a knock on the door. Alister nearly jumped out of his skin; the Oddity's door was somewhat detached from reality, and he'd never heard someone knock on it before.

If it startled Elo she didn't show it. She went over to the console and checked the screen.

"Oh dear," she said.

Alister came and leaned over her shoulder.

A tall, dark-haired man in a neat black suit wearing dark gloves stood outside. He was pale-skinned, with a long, delicate nose and a high, arching brow.

Something about the shape of him jostled uneasily in Alister's memory. He'd seen that profile before, surely, a long time ago and very far away.

There was a hiss and rumble as Dave came up behind them in his panvironment suit.

"IT WAS HIM. I THOUGHT SO," he said through his translator.

"Him? You know him?" Elo demanded, turning around.

"NOT YET," said Dave. "HE IS ANOTHER TRAVELER."

Alister didn't bother to ask was that meant. He had a pretty good idea.

They sat and watched the dark figure on the screen until, with a little shrug, the man turned and walked away down the steps.

What came after was something that had rarely occurred since Alister had come on board the Oddity: boredom. Quite literally, nothing happened. Dave opened a panel beside one of the cockpits and began pulling out the wiring using little claw-like appendages that sprouted from the front of his panvironment suit. Elo sat in the other cockpit, watching the readout on one of the monitors and saying things like: "Nope, nothing," or, "Wait, I think that made it worse . . . "

Left with nothing useful to do, Alister went and sat by the window with the best view. This overlooked a part of their neighbor's garden, and Alister could see a ratty lawn and some washing hung out to dry. The sun appeared to have come out, and a breeze blew, flapping the towels and shirts and trousers pinned to the line.

There was an unhappy buzzing sound from where Dave worked. Elo gave a yip of triumph.

Outside, the world suddenly grew dark. There was a flash of white and gray that distorted the view, and then it was past. The laundry was nowhere to be seen, and everything was soaking wet.

Alister blinked.

"What did you just do?" he asked, turning around in his seat.

"I HAVE MANAGED TO EXTRICATE US FROM THE NATIVE TIME STREAM," Dave intoned. "THIS WILL GIVE US MORE TIME TO FIGURE OUT A SOLUTION."

"Uh . . . " Elo said, squinting at her screen.

Outside, Alister saw the shadows lengthening, stretching into twilight. Night fell, streetlights came on. Then the dark sky turned gray, and another day dawned . . . only to rush by at the same speed. It was like watching an extremely long, extremely boring time-lapse video.

"I think you pushed it too far the other way," Elo remarked. "Time is moving faster out there than it is in here."

"It's been at least two days out there." Alister blinked. Was it speeding up? "Or . . . three?"

"OH . . . BUGGER," Dave said.

They watched a few weeks flit by. Eventually Alister drew the curtains, since the days and nights were flashing past at such a speed it was almost like a strobe light.

"So, is this a good thing or a bad thing?" Alister asked.

"Depends," said Elo, scratching behind one ear. "It's good that Dave's managed to make some progress separating the Oddity from this universe. But . . . "

"But weeks—maybe *months*—have passed outside," Alister pointed out. "Where's the Professor?"

"THE TEMPORAL DISCREPANCY SHOULD NOT INTERFERE WITH THE ODDITY'S DOORWAY," Dave said.

"In other words," Elo explained hastily. "Just because the time-synch's messed up, it shouldn't prevent Professor Odd from re-entering the Oddity."

This, Alister decided, was not at all comforting. The way she had been acting, he'd expected her to be back in a day or so. But outside the Oddity (or, inside the universe) weeks had been flashing by for several minutes. *Where was she?*

"Something's gone wrong," he said tightly.

"You got *that* right," Elo said dryly. "This whole debacle smells funny to me. Why'd she go out *alone* anyway?"

Dread gripped Alister by the stomach. He swallowed hard. He had been too relieved at being left behind to wonder *why* Professor Odd had neglected to drag her companions along. What had she said? *Don't go outside . . .*

She was trying to protect them.

From whatever was in her native universe.

In which she was currently trapped. Alone.

Alister groaned as he realized what he had to do.

"She's in trouble," Elo said decisively. "She needs help."

"IT WOULD BE UNWISE," Dave said, "TO INVADE A UNIVERSE OF WHICH YOU KNOW VERY LITTLE."

"We're not doing her any good in here," Alister pointed out glumly.

"*YOU* ARE NOT," Dave said. "I AM ATTEMPTING TO SAVE US ALL." And so saying he turned back to the gutted control panel.

Alister looked down at Elo. Elo looked back up at him out of her soft, furry face, but her eyes were dark and grave.

"We'd better go in after her," he said.

"She probably needs help," Elo agreed. She pulled aside the curtain and peered out. "Looks like a fairly standard Britannia Class III. I'll go get my harness."

While Elo went to assemble her disguise as a seeing-eye dog, Alister returned to his own room to see if the Oddity had given him any clothes that would not stick out like a sore thumb in the Professor's drab, ordinary world. He slid open the door to his closet, and stared.

Where there should have been rack upon rack of vibrantly colored shirts, coats, and trousers, there was only his original outfit—the clothes he had been wearing when he had first come on board the Oddity. They were a little crumpled and depressingly flat compared to the wardrobe Alister had become accustomed to, but they fit perfectly with the dull world outside.

What made Alister stare was that there was nothing else. In fact his closet, which before had seemed like a whole room of its own, was now hardly bigger than a broom cupboard. Now he looked around, did his room also look shrunken?

Alister changed his clothes, noting that his window now looked out onto a water-stained brick wall. A bird had left droppings on the sill.

"I think something's wrong with the Oddity," he said when he emerged.

"Tell me something I *don't* know," Elo snapped. She was standing outside her room having difficulty with one of the buckles on her harness. Alister came over and did it for her.

"Did you notice anything . . . em . . . *wrong* with your room?" he asked.

Elo gave him an arch look at that, but she didn't have to look as far as her room: the shriveled, shrunken effect was now visible in the walls and floor of the main area. The table, which even under normal circumstances was piled with junk, looked ready to collapse. Its edges were also noticeably closer to the walls.

"Dave!" Elo shouted, sliding down the ladder.

"THE SPATIAL MAINTENANCE STABILIZERS HAVE BEEN SABOTAGED—I KNOW." Dave had several tools and two of his tentacle arms (safely encased in metallic cloth) buried in the Oddity's wiring. There was an angry, humming sound.

"What does that mean?" Alister asked with a nervous glance at the table, where it looked like a tricycle was about to tumble off.

Elo heaved a sigh. "Basically?" she said. "It means the Oddity has to jettison nonvital spaces in order to keep its systems running."

"Nonvital spaces . . . like my room?"

"Like our living area," Elo muttered. "Come on, we don't have a lot of time. Help me get this window open." She'd gone to the side and was heaving at the frame. It seemed stuck. Alister came over and hit it. It came loose with an ominous creak.

"Hang tight, Dave," she said, sliding nimbly outside. "We'll be back in a jiff." She dropped out of sight.

"IF YOU ARE NOT," Dave said, "I WILL COME FIND YOU."

"Will you be all right . . . here?" Alister asked, pausing with one leg hanging over the sill.

"I WILL MANAGE," Dave said. "I POSSESS RESOURCES YOU DO NOT."

And that seemed to be all. It was not a very large drop to the path on this side of the house, and Alister let himself down gradually by his hands so he had only a few feet to fall.

As he straightened up, rubbing his palms where they had chafed against the sill, he heard the window slam shut above them.

"Think he'll be all right?" he asked Elo.

"Better worry about us," Elo replied, handing him a pair of dark, round glasses. Professor Odd's glasses. The ones she had been wearing the first time Alister had seen her. He took a deep breath and put them on.

"Hold the handle attached to my harness," Elo instructed, dropping to all fours. "Right there—yes. Oh, and you can talk to me, but I won't reply unless no one can hear. Crazy blind people talking to their dogs is all right. It's when the dog starts talking back that people notice."

"And we don't want to be noticed," Alister hazarded.

For answer, Elo put her nose to the ground and began leading him down the narrow alley.

*   *   *

The short man with russet-brown hair sat in a dark room filled with computers. The hum of their hard drives was a soothing rumble, and the heat they gave off served to make the room the only decently warm place in the whole building.

It was dark; the only light came from the bank of monitors arranged on the wall opposite the man. By their wan light he pulled open a drawer and got out a packet of crisps, which he opened with a satisfying *rip*. He pushed a hand inside, and for a few moments thereafter the sound of the computers was joined by the crack and crunch of crisps being eaten. Then the crunching slowed. Finally it stopped altogether.

The man had forgotten to chew. Indeed, had probably forgotten all about the half-full bag of crisps still in his hand—even though he was the sort of man who would never forget about food in the normal course of things.

This, though. This was so far outside the range of normalcy that it eclipsed everything else.

To an untrained observer it did not look particularly alarming. One of the computer screens was now displaying a flashing red dot on a matrix of blue and white lines.

The short man with russet hair, however, was not only trained, but trained extremely well. He knew exactly what a flashing red dot on that screen meant, and the thought made the last of the crisps take on the importance of something rather less than dust.

With shaking hands he reached back into his desk drawer and removed a telephone directory. He opened it to the back page where someone had scrawled a number in black marker, along with a suggestive message. Then he reached into his coat pocket and removed a slip of paper. On it was written another, shorter number in neat pencil.

The man picked up the handset of the landline and carefully dialed the number written in the back of the phone book. When a breathy female voice asked him what sort of experience he was looking for, the man repeated the number off the slip of paper. He was careful to enunciate.

"Just a moment," the voice said, suddenly going clipped and businesslike. Then there was a *click* and the line filled with the roar of static. Then there was another *click* and absolute silence.

Out of the silence a smooth male voice said:

"What is it?"

"Er, yes, hello?" said the man. His voice was high and crackly, mostly from nerves. "Parsons, from Greentower. Yes, well, I was told to call this number if I ever had a breach."

"Please don't waste my time, Philip Parsons," said the voice out of the silence. It was rich and resonant, but at the same time icy cold. The way it dropped in the "please" implied that it didn't think such a word was necessary, but that it knew that the more words it said, the longer you had to listen to it, and the longer you listened the more time you would have to imagine all the terrible things that would happen to you if you upset its owner.

"How'd you know my name's Philip?" asked Philip Parsons, agitated beyond reason.

Silence.

"Because I know you, Philip. I know you very well. Consider this fact, alongside the fact that you do not know me at all, before you answer," said the voice. And added: "*Please.*" The word sent shivers down Philip Parsons's spine.

"It's ... er ... the probability on Napswitch Road," he stammered. "There's been a breach. Class 6, easily. I think two bodies got through."

"I ... see," said the voice, a terrible gap between the two words.

"Shall I send the coordinates over to you, like last time?"

"No." The voice was clipped now, as if its owner were walking briskly. "We do not know which lines the Professor has compromised."

"Oh? Don't we ... er, sir?"

"I will retrieve the logs," said the voice. "Manually."

"Very good, sir," said Philip Parsons.

"You've done well, Philip," said the voice, though its tone suggested the opposite. "Your shift is almost over. You will be ... relieved."

"Yes sir, thank you sir," babbled the poor man. "It's been an honor working with—working *for* you, that is. Sir ... Detective, sir ... "

Nothing. The silence now was only the silence of a dead line. Philip looked at the receiver in his hand and shuddered.

They had, all of them—his whole team—been briefed on the Detective. Lots of smoke and mirrors, Charlie had said. But it took a lot to impress Charlie, and none of them had ever met the Detective. Until now, none of them had even spoken with him.

Perhaps *that* would impress Charlie, Philip Parsons thought. On further consideration, however, he imagined she would just roll her eyes at him and say "*Yes Philip, but how d'you know it was him?*"

Wait. Hadn't the voice on the phone said *he* was coming *here?* All of a sudden the only thing Philip Parsons could think about was how he had managed to spill crisps all over his chair. *That* would never do. He shuffled around, trying to find a hand broom.

On the computer screen, the red light flashed.

An hour later, Philip Parsons walked down the street outside his building, his head pleasantly empty. The last few hours seemed rather blurry, but this did not concern him. When your job consists primarily of watching nothing happen, blurry memory can be a mercy. He did feel hungry, though, as if his snack time had been interrupted. He altered course to take him toward the fish-and-chips shop that he particularly fancied.

His route took him through a small alley between two tall buildings. To someone observing him from afar, it would have appeared that Philip Parsons—short, brown-headed and rather round—walked in one side . . . and nothing came out the other. Closer inspection would have revealed the alley to be quite empty.

To Philip Parsons, the world went a bit dark and uncertain for a while. He felt sick and confused—and also frightened around the edges.

When his world firmed up again he was sitting in a squeaky leather chair in a cool, dark room. The light this time was provided by a single paraffin lamp placed directly before him. It had a stained-glass shade with dragonflies on it. Philip Parsons noticed this because this was all he could see: the room beyond was lost in glare and shadows.

"Mr. . . . *Parsons*," said a raspy voice from beyond the light. "Please, don't agitate yourself. I'm not going to harm you. I simply wish to know what happened to you at work this afternoon."

"C-can't . . . remember . . . " Philip Parsons forced out through an uncooperative mouth.

The person behind the light chuckled. "I thought as much. Fortunately I wasn't counting on you being able to *tell* me, so we're going to go about it a slightly different way. Do you know why you can't remember this afternoon, Mr. Parsons?"

"Boring job," said Philip Parsons, trying to sit forward and see around the lamp. There appeared to be restraints on his hands and something on his head like a soft bicycle helmet. He began to panic then, his heart thudding in his chest.

"Don't upset yourself, Mr. Parsons," said the scratchy voice. "I'm trying to help you. Look, see, I'll tell you why you can't remember what happened this afternoon. You want to know why, don't you?"

"I want to go *home*," said Philip Parsons petulantly.

"You met the Detective, Mr. Parsons. You spoke to him. You *saw* him."

That triggered something in Philip Parsons's mind. Not a memory per se, but rather, it made him aware of an empty patch in his head where a memory *should* have gone.

He'd spilled his crisps, and he'd been worried about the mess. Because the Detective . . . the *Detective* . . .

"L-look," he stammered. "If he made me forget, it was for a *reason,* right? So I wouldn't give away . . . give away . . . " he gulped, realizing the enormity of what he had just said, and just who it implied was sitting on the other side of the kitschy lamp.

"*I* don't think that was very nice of him," said the voice. It was hard to tell; was it male or female? He'd heard a rumor that the Professor was a woman. And

Philip Parsons was becoming more and more certain that it *was* the Professor who sat opposite him.

"Relax, Mr. Parsons," said the voice soothingly. "I could extract this knowledge from you without your cognizance, but that, I believe, would only compound your problems. Watch and learn, Mr. Parsons. Watch and *learn*."

It then appeared to Philip Parsons that a screen was lowered before his eyes, and he saw there a vision of his day, beginning with the breakfast of eggs and bacon he'd had that morning.

"A bit early, this is," said the voice, and then the images appeared to go on fast-forward like a videotape. They slowed down again when he got to work, then sped up through his morning, his lunch, and into the afternoon. They came crashing back to normal speeds when a red light started flashing on one of his monitors, and Philip Parsons watched in astonishment as he reviewed his actions—saw his hands drop the packet of crisps, saw himself get out the phone directory and his passcode. Saw himself pick up the phone and dial a number.

He listened to himself call the Detective and the halting conversation that followed. In the silence after he hung up, the images sped up again.

"Interesting," said the voice of the person he was almost certain was the Professor.

Then things slowed down again. Philip Parsons watched himself get up and turn at a noise from the back of the building. He saw two people enter: one was a dark-skinned woman in a severe gray suit, while the other was a tall, pale man with black hair wearing a long black coat. His eyes were like chips of obsidian, and their gaze bore into Philip Parsons's head both in the past and present.

In his memory he watched the tall man stride over, neatly stepping across the bundle of cables that crossed the floor. He thought the man was coming to talk to him, but instead he was ignored and the man bent forward to examine the monitor.

In the present, the Professor made a little sound like *"Ah . . . "*

In the past, the woman in the severe gray suit said: "Shall I relieve Mr. Parsons, Detective?"

The Detective turned away from the monitor and looked at him. Up close, he decided, his eyes were more like black wells. He felt like if he looked at them for too long he might fall in. So he looked away.

"Yes, that would be just as well, Gretchen."

Things got rather blurry after that, but he thought he saw the Detective copy something off the computer onto a small mobile drive. Then the woman in the gray suit took his place, and he was steered out of the room by the man in the black coat.

"I think that is all there is worth seeing," said the voice beyond the light, and the screen before his eyes was lifted.

Philip Parsons blinked, wishing he could rub his eyes. "I don't understand," he whined miserably.

"That's all right," said the Professor soothingly. "Very few people do. Relax, Mr. Parsons, it will make this all so much easier . . . "

Philip Parsons saw a shape rise behind the light, and an arm reached forward. He opened his mouth to scream and then his world went dark and uncertain again.

And then . . .

And then he was walking down the street outside his building, his head pleasantly empty.

The city they had emerged into frustrated Alister no end. It had bits that reminded him of London and bits that reminded him of Oxford. Then he remembered that, in his native universe, he'd never *been* to Oxford. All his memories of Oxford were from a version created by a sentient machine on a world where humans survived by going into suspended animation while their minds lived out lives in a constructed reality.

In any case, this city had bits that reminded him of *that* Oxford.

There were also bits that reminded him (eerily, achingly) of his own home. It was there in the little things: the underground signs, the trains, and the shape of the cars.

And there were things that were like nothing he'd seen on any world.

The skypods, for one thing.

These were small, circular objects large enough for two people to sit inside that whizzed by overhead on a wire suspended high above the treetops and most of the roofs. At first Alister had mistaken them for power lines, until the first pod came through. He'd started so suddenly that Elo had growled at him.

"You're *blind*, remember?"

So Alister had reined in his gawking, and made a point of fixing his head skyward so he could watch the pods race by without appearing to be looking at anything in particular. Like this he tripped several times on uneven pavement, which to his mind rather authenticated the disguise.

This city, he soon deduced, was called Londinium, which he assumed meant it was indeed this world's version of London. Elo seemed to be leading him—if his fuzzy memories of his own London were any indication—toward Trafalgar Square, and the streets were becoming increasingly crowded.

The people of Londinium seemed as drab and ordinary as the world they lived in. The only patches of color were on the gold lapels of couriers in uniform and the rare punkish teenager. Grays and browns and muted blues seemed to be the most popular clothing colors, and faces were all pale and a little sagging.

It was strangely liberating, pretending to be blind. In the ordinary way Alister was very conscientious about eye contact, but from behind the shield of his dark glasses he found he could stare at people quite blatantly.

He saw young people, old people, and people in the middle. He saw people with dark hair, fair hair, and even a few redheads. He saw people with no hair at all. He saw people hidden under large, floppy hats, and people hunched over, reading things on their small tablet mobiles. There were even a few people reading newspapers.

Elo stopped. They were at a strange sort of intersection where the road they were on joined another fork. While waiting for the walk signal, Alister noticed a little stand selling magazines and newspapers. The headline of one was so big it was readable, and what it said grabbed his attention at once.

PROFESSOR STRIKES BACK

And then some smaller text that was cut off at the fold. Alister nudged Elo with his knee.

"Read the paper," he muttered.

Elo looked. She read the paper. The light turned, and they walked on.

A few blocks later Elo stopped by a table outside a cafe. At first Alister did not understand why, and then he saw another copy of that same paper abandoned on a chair.

"You're clear," Elo growled through her teeth. "Grab it."

Alister did. He even had the presence of mind to tuck it inside his coat. Because what could a blind person want with a paper?

They walked on until Elo found a small alley and darted into it. After carefully checking for cameras and inconvenient windows (there were none), she stood up.

"Let's see it then," she said.

Alister removed the paper and handed it to her, then took off his dark glasses. Like that he could read the story over her shoulder.

It went:

> *Gravesend, Londinium.* A new batch of secret cables has been publicly released by the notorious hacker known as the Professor. These details contain, among other things, the complete correspondence between the American Union and its embassy in Persia, as well as several dossiers it keeps on Persian citizens. The Persian government . . .

Here the article went on at length about the political ramifications of said information becoming public, which made almost no sense to Alister. Elo skipped over it anyway, flipping to an interior page where they read:

> This counts as only the latest in a string of acts by the Professor to force transparency on international governments. The Professor, whose current

location and identity are unknown, has stated that they are not partisan, but that they intend to provide common people with the information they need to make informed decisions. Though it is rumored that the Professor is a single person, experts believe it to be a small group of close-knit hackers, crackers, and informants. The Professor has been labeled a terrorist group by the American Union and the European Council, and anyone with information as to their whereabouts is requested to contact their local law enforcement. The local hotline is . . .

Alister didn't bother to read the number that followed. He blinked at Elo, trying to clear his head.

"Sounds like *she's* been busy," he said in a stunned voice.

"This makes no sense," Elo mused, folding the paper over. She frowned at the headline.

"Not like her?" Alister queried.

"Not like her . . . *in this circumstance*," Elo said. "If this even is our Professor. It's not like she has a trademark on the title."

Alister had to agree. "What do you mean, 'in this circumstance'?"

"Well," Elo sighed, sitting down and leaning back against the wall. "She said she was going to see who brought us here and why. This? This doesn't look like her collecting information. This looks more like . . . like . . . " Elo scratched under her ear nervously.

"Like *what?*" Alister burst out.

Elo looked up at him, a nervous crease between her eyes. "Like she's in it for the long game. Like she thinks she's *stuck* here."

There was a screech of engines, and a dark car pulled up at the mouth of their alley. It was the large sort with tinted black windows and a humorless, professional exterior. It looked so much like the sort of car that serious men in dark suits drove in certain kinds of American films that Alister almost wasn't surprised when a tall man in a black coat got out of the passenger seat and walked down the alley toward them. He was pale-skinned with short black hair, and his hands were hidden inside dark leather gloves. He was undoubtedly the same man who had knocked on the Oddity's door earlier that day—or several months ago, depending on the universe. Just as assuredly, he was the same man Alister had seen somewhere before.

It was the walk that did it—a particular, powerful sort of walk that took a person places. At the same time the man was so self-contained and confident that he almost appeared lazy, as though he were strolling through a park.

The last time Alister had seen that walk, he'd been halfway out of his wits with fright in a virtual reality constructed by a sentient machine.

Now he stood and stared.

"You—" he began.

"*Run you fool!*" Elo barked, and grabbed his sleeve in her teeth.

This jerked some sense into Alister's brain. He noticed the other two men who had also gotten out of the car while he was staring. They were not as tall as the first man, but half again as wide and just as serious looking.

Alister ran.

The alley they had taken refuge in dead ended in a ten-foot brick wall. Elo bounded toward it, leapt, grasped the top with her long paws, and then kicked her hind end up and over. She reached back down and grabbed Alister by the arm.

Elo was a large canine, but she was still smaller than a human. There would have been no way for her to haul Alister up the wall had not his foot found a hold where a brick had been knocked out. Using it as a step Alister was able to get his own hands over the wall, and Elo helped him along, pulling at his jacket.

Even as he flung one leg over he felt a hand close on his dangling ankle, and he kicked out blindly. Then he was over and falling down the other side.

Luckily, here someone had pushed a large dustbin up against the wall, and Alister was able to break his fall with it.

Dazed, his hands and knees stinging, Alister limped away from the wall—he had landed awkwardly and now his left ankle was complaining. Elo was by his side on all fours.

"Come *on!*" she growled.

Alister had just the presence of mind to grab hold of her harness before she took off. Like that he was able to keep up as they tore down the alley toward the bustle of the main street. As they reached it, Alister chanced a glance back.

The men had also scaled the wall. One of them was talking into a radio.

Alister and Elo ran down the street. They went faster than Alister would have, favoring his left leg and uncertain where to go, but they also went much slower than Elo could have gone on her own. Alister was sure of this. He was also just as sure that, going the pace they were going, the men would catch them. Every time he chanced a glance back they were a little closer. There was a large black car following them, and would, Alister was certain, catch up with them once it sorted out the traffic.

They couldn't escape together, but on their own, one of them might.

"Elo," Alister gasped, wincing at the pain in his ankle. "Elo, you've got to leave me."

"Not an option!" Elo barked, making a sharp turn that was nearly the end of Alister. They were on a straight road filled with traffic now, beyond which Alister could glimpse a wide, gray river. They had lost the car, but now the three men were in sight behind them and had been joined by another two.

"*Think!*" Alister gasped. "You could drop these guys in an instant—*you* could get away. But not with me hanging on to you!"

"And where does that leave you?" Elo growled, making a nearby pedestrian jump.

"I'll manage," Alister panted.

"No, you won't," Elo snapped. "You'll get taken."

"Better me than you!" They had to jump out into traffic to pass a slow-moving couple with a stroller and nearly collided with an oncoming car. Alister grunted at the pain in his ankle.

They ran on a few more strides while Elo thought over the implications of this. On their own she could escape, Alister could not. Of the two of them, she would be better able to survive in this world; she would be better able to forage for information, and she could provide Professor Odd, when found, with all sorts of help involving sharp teeth, claws, and if need be, technical assistance. Whereas Alister could do none of those things.

What Alister could do was be an ordinary person who wouldn't excite the natives of this universe by being an unknown animal.

"We'll come back for you," was all she said.

"Oh aye," said Alister. "I'm counting on it."

He let go of her harness.

Relieved of her burden, Elo darted away up the road. Alister saw her disappear up a side street before his view was blocked by two heavyset men coming down the pavement toward him. Alister limped to a stop. He watched as they ambled past the road Elo had taken.

Alister took a breath and turned to check behind him. The three original men and their two new friends were within shouting distance. They would be on him in less than a minute.

Alister tested his bad ankle, which twinged ominously. He didn't have many options.

Still, it seemed rather a waste to let them catch him so easily.

Alister darted out across the road, aiming for the path on the far side.

The oncoming car—one of the ubiquitous black cabs—saw him and slammed on its brakes. This was why, when it hit him, it was only going about fifteen miles per hour. Which was why Alister was still conscious when he hit the asphalt ten feet away. He was conscious of the fact that he could not breathe, and of how very hard the road was, and of something wet running down the side of his head.

Then things got a bit muddled.

For clarity's sake, it shall be explained thus:

The woman riding in the back seat of the cab that hit Alister heard the driver's shocked exclamation and saw a body flying through the air. She thought: a body that goes *up* after being hit by a car has a chance of still being alive when it comes back down. She unfastened her seat belt and got out of the car almost before it had stopped moving.

"Wait here," she told the stunned driver, and went around to the front where there was a man lying in the street. Even from this distance she could see his eyes— wide and dark brown—flit to her. She pulled out her mobile and speed dialed the hospital's front desk.

"Yes, this is Dr. Watterson," she said, marching up to the stricken man. "I'll need an ambulance to King James Road, just south of Knightsbridge. Pedestrian hit by car. He's still conscious." She snapped the mobile shut as she arrived at the man's side and thrust it into her coat pocket.

"Easy there son," she began. "Looks like it's your lucky day."

"Not . . . really," mumbled the man.

"Can you tell me your name? I'm a doctor, I'd like to help you." As she spoke she was already assessing him: a head wound, probably cracked ribs. He'd landed hard on his back, which worried her. She was on the point of asking him if he could feel his legs when he said, very suddenly and with surprising clarity:

"They are bad men. Please don't let them take me."

Dr. Watterson looked up. There were indeed a great number of men—and women—gathered at the side of the road. Seven in particular stood out to Dr. Watterson as the sort that you didn't want taking you. They stood at the front of the crowd, silent, somber, and dark-clad. The one in the center—a tall man with a sickly pale complexion and short black hair—looked intently back at her as she scanned them. He smiled faintly, in a way that put Dr. Watterson off, and raised a hand. He had what looked like a small camera in it.

Dr. Watterson ducked her head just in time as a flash of light went off. When she looked again, all the men were gone. In the distance, there was a sound of sirens drawing near.

On the ground, Alister had passed out.

The first thing Elo did was get out of her seeing-eye-dog harness. It was helpful when she was working in tandem with a human, but on her own it was better to enact the role of lovable stray. She stashed it on a rooftop in the lee of an old air-conditioning unit. From this same rooftop, lying flat out along the edge, she watched the aftermath of Alister's accident. She waited until she saw him safely loaded into the ambulance, and then set about the rather difficult task of getting down.

Once this was accomplished she set off at a trot, her nose to the ground. She moved with such purpose that no one looking thought to stop her. Indeed, it was likely they didn't even remember seeing her. Which was just the way Elo liked it.

For Alister the world was dark for what felt like only a moment or so, but it must have been much longer. At first he was confused as to why he was still in bed, for he distinctly remembered climbing out the Oddity's window and into the Professor's universe. Then he tried to move, and his whole body protested. He didn't hurt exactly, but only because everything felt muted and numb. Another part of his brain was aware, however, that things were very wrong indeed.

Voices. There were voices in the next room. Not voices Alister knew, but voices he seemed to remember. One of them, anyway. A woman with a thick, northern voice was speaking.

" . . . and you'll have to show better identification than *that*. I don't care if you represent the Union and the Council and their grandmothers, I'll not release an unidentified, *unconscious* patient to *you*."

"Please think about what you are saying, doctor," replied a smooth, cultured voice. It was the kind of voice that made you *want* to trust it, and for that Alister was instinctively distrustful. "You won't do anyone any good by being stubborn."

"You don't seem to understand me, Detective . . . er . . . "

"Just Detective, madam."

"Detective. I have refused to release patients to very unhappy men carrying large guns. You, with your neat black card, are a *long way* from convincing me . . . "

The female northern voice sounded incredibly determined, which Alister thought was a good thing. He felt cold inside and tired. He wanted to skip to a part of his life where he felt better, so he went to sleep.

This time Alister dreamed. These were vague, muddled affairs, in the way that dreams tend to be. He dreamed of detectives in long black coats, shadowy figures called professor, and doctors with military bearings. It all seemed familiar to him. In his dream he was on the verge of grasping it when someone came into his room.

He opened his eyes. Before him stood a wide, barrel-chested woman of indeterminate race. Her skin was light coffee colored, and her hair was only a touch darker shade of brown. She had muddy hazel eyes and a crooked nose. She wore the white coat of a doctor but something about her bearing said "fighter," and she looked evenly at Alister from under bushy brows like caterpillars. She was not a handsome woman; she clearly didn't feel the *need* to be handsome.

"Oh good," Alister mumbled without thinking. "You must be Dr. Watson."

The woman's mouth twitched to one side. "It's Watterson, actually," she said, confirming that she was the owner of the thick northern voice from earlier.

"It's all gone back to front," Alister said. "I think the *detective* is the bad one this time, and the *professor* is the good one. Where does that put the doctor? Hmm?"

Dr. Watterson laughed shortly and shook her head. "I've just come to see you all right," she said. "I was only riding in the cab that hit you, but it still feels like you're my responsibility. By rights you're Dr. Jacobsen's patient now. How are you feeling? Can you tell me your name?"

"I feel like I've been hit by a car," Alister said, then he realized. "That's what happened, wasn't it? I got hit. Thought I could make it across the street. Trying to get away . . . "

"Get away from whom?" Dr. Watterson asked. If she was impatient at all she didn't show it.

"The men in black. One of them was here earlier, wasn't he? That detective fellow . . . "

"He's gone now," Dr. Watterson assured him.

Alister wanted to nod, but a twinge in his neck told him he shouldn't.

"That's good," he said instead.

"*Can* you tell me who you are?" the doctor asked.

Alister tried to think about this, but his brain started shutting down again.

"Don't think I should," he said at length. And that was all Dr. Watterson was able to get out of him.

It is a difficult thing to build a telecommunication scanner. Building one with scavenged parts is harder. Building one with scavenged parts while living out of trashcans and in alleys while on the run from an unidentified enemy in an unfamiliar world would have been impossible for most people. In fact, there were probably only three or four people in that particular universe who could have done it. The first two were Dave and Professor Odd.

The third was Elo Marhütz.

It took her two days and a lot of trial and error and one last-minute move when the storage shed she had commandeered was suddenly invaded by its rightful owners. Nevertheless she kept at it, with the determination of dogs digging tunnels under their fences or scratching holes in wooden doors, only Elo applied herself, not to dirt and wood, but to wires and soldering, batteries and frequency filters.

In the end she had a construction that resembled a complicated radio remote attached to an old television she had lugged out of a dumpster. Once it was up and running, the screen showed, not video, but lines of information. Elo's eyes, accustomed to the much more dense and complicated language of the Oddity, had no problem decoding this into individual phone calls, radio transmissions . . . even wireless internet signals.

She spent the third day just scanning.

On the fourth day she narrowed her frequency range.

On the fifth day she had a piece of paper filled with scribbled notations tracking origin points, bounces, and redirections. And, at the bottom, a set of coordinates.

On the sixth day she dismantled her operation and left.

* * *

What Elo hadn't picked up on was a conversation between two parties who, for all appearances, did not technically exist. Both sets of signals were encrypted and untraceable; they existed only in the static surrounding the busy highway of ordinary, law-abiding information, and the only recording was written on a heavily protected drive that was itself stored in a heavily protected location.

Had there been someone with the right equipment, however, and had they taken the time to splice the messages together, the conversation would have sounded like this:

"I know you're listening," said the first voice. It was smooth and rich, with an educated accent. "You're always listening. So I won't waste your time with pleasantries. I have your accomplice, Professor. And, do not mistake me, I *will* use him in any way I can to . . . *encourage* you to cooperate."

"Interesting," said the second voice. It was lighter, scratchier, and probably female. "You know, you're not a very *good* detective."

There was an unfriendly silence.

"I have traveled," said the first voice. "I have traveled across universes and galaxies. I have walked patiently down the ages and over the rise and fall of empires . . . hunting *you*, Professor. And I *found* you. I *brought you here.* What, may I ask, would it take for someone to be a *good detective* in your illustrious book?"

"Oh, no," said the second voice. "You're good—*very* good—at detecting things. You're probably the best detectoring detective I've ever met. What I *meant* was . . . you don't sound like a fundamentally good person. If you don't mind my saying so."

"From what *I* have heard, your definition of good and evil is perhaps not the same as most people's," the first voice retorted.

"And what *have* you heard, exactly?" said the second voice eagerly. "Because *I've* been hearing some *very interesting* things about *you.* And I must say, really, you're perhaps the coldest personification of the Holmesian Paradigm I've ever seen."

"Excuse me?"

"The Holmesian Paradigm! You're a transuniversal traveler. You know how character archetypes repeat across worlds? Well, the Holmesian Paradigm is when a person exhibits characteristics similar to that of Sherlock Holmes, the fictional detective created by Sir Arthur Conan Doyle in—"

"I *know* who Sherlock Holmes is," said the first voice, sounding intensely bored.

"Have you got a Watson?" asked the second voice.

"A what?"

"A Watson!" the second voice sounded downright enthusiastic now. "Because I can tell you, I've met a *lot* of Holmesian Paradigms, and none of them needed the Watson Effect more than *you.*"

"Listen," said the first voice through gently clenched teeth. "You know how to find me. I would recommend you do so, before I become *frustrated.* I want to remind you, your accomplice . . . "

"Detective?" asked the second voice.

"Yes, Professor?"

"Just one question, Detective."

"And what, pray, is that?"

"The persons you are working for—I have some idea who they are—I was just wondering, how *much* have they paid you?"

"That can't possibly be relevant."

"Well, I just wanted to say, however much it is . . . "

"You cannot buy my cooperation, Professor."

"*However much it is . . .* " the second voice continued, a hard edge behind the light tone, "it cannot possibly, in all the realms of probability, ever—*ever*—be enough to cover the trouble you will get into hunting *me.*"

There was a *click* and then silence once more.

The Detective hadn't bothered to answer.

Philip Parsons was *not* having a good day. Even though work had been going smoothly—no beeps, no flashing red lights—he couldn't shake the feeling that he was being watched. He also kept getting flashbacks to what he could only assume was an uncomfortable dream. In what else but a dream could he have been kidnapped by the Professor and then forced to watch a memory of himself interacting with the Detective? He had never met either of those people. He was sure he would remember that.

Wouldn't he?

There was a faint clacking of claws above him. Philip Parsons thought it was a rat in the ceiling. He thought this because his brain refused to allow for the possibility that it could be exactly what it sounded like: a dog in the ventilation duct.

To distract himself from the sound that was definitely *not* a dog, Philip Parsons reached into his desk drawer for a packet of crisps. This was something he found himself doing more and more often of late, and the bag he pulled out was the last of its kind.

He ate them nervously, and the crunching sound easily covered the faint *whish* of a furry body leaping through the air, and the soft *whump* as it landed.

On the other side of the room, hidden behind banks of computers and a wall, Elo stood up. She was wearing a strange harness pieced together from bits of webbing and straps torn off old backpacks. It held a number of handy items including a flashlight, knife, screwdriver, lock-picking kit, a small drive with some very interesting software on it, and a water bottle.

Elo took a sip from the bottle. Then she went over to the small monitor set in the bank of computers and turned it on.

Instead of entering the password as prompted, Elo plugged in the drive she'd brought with her and watched the software work.

The first password fell in seconds. The second in minutes. The third took a little impromptu reprogramming, but she got through just the same. She accessed a database of monitored calls and began going through them, her thumb claw tapping at the down arrow on the monitor's attached keyboard.

Then her thumb stopped.

She had come to the conversation between the Detective and the Professor. She pressed play.

To Philip Parsons, it went something like this:

He heard a voice say, *"I know you're listening . . . "* and he nearly jumped out of his skin. For that voice he had only heard in his dream, the half-remembered nightmare. It went on, the dulcet tones sending goosebumps up his arms.

Then a new voice answered. The *other* voice from his dream. Slowly, Philip Parsons realized that they were not speaking in the other room, as he had first thought, but that he was listening to a recording. A recording which, by the sound of it, no one in their right mind would play.

On shaking legs Philip Parsons got up and came around the bank of computers.

"From what I have heard, your definition of good and evil is perhaps not the same as most people's," said the voice of the Detective, so close it made Philip Parsons pause instinctively. He took a few deep breaths. The conversation continued.

" *. . . you're a transuniversal traveler . . . "*

"I know who Sherlock Holmes is . . . "

"Have you got a Watson?"

Philip Parsons couldn't stop listening. He was fascinated.

"You cannot buy my cooperation, Professor."

" *. . . it cannot possibly, in all the realms of probability, ever—ever—be enough . . . "*

Philip Parsons came around the bank of computers, and stopped.

A large golden dog with sharp triangular ears looked up at him. It was wearing what looked like a climbing harness, and its hand-like paws were spread over a keyboard.

They stared at each other for a moment. Then the dog neatly unplugged a drive from the computer and placed it in a small pouch on its harness.

Then the dog stood up.

Philip Parsons found himself backing away. The dog was as tall as a short woman, but that is still a lot higher up than you want a dog's face to be.

Then the dog spoke. It said in a light, female voice:

"You might want to find a new job. Or go on holiday. Things are going to get a little messy around here."

Then she stopped. Her nose twitched. Abruptly she rushed forward and grabbed Philip Parsons by his shirt front. She sniffed at his collar, at his—*gulp*—throat, at his hands and his legs. Then she let go.

"I don't *believe* it," she said. "You *met* them. Met *both* of them."

With that she dropped to all fours and bounded out of the room, her nose skimming the ground.

Philip Parsons wobbled a bit on his way back to his desk. He picked up his phone.

He should report this. Verily, he should. But he had the niggling certainty that getting out the phone directory and calling *that* number would only give him grief. And more bad dreams too.

Philip Parsons sighed and looked up the number of his travel agent instead.

What appeared to be a golden dog—or perhaps a wolf—bounded down the city streets heedless of the stares and commotion that followed in its wake. It was hot on a scent, running with its nose to the ground. It came to a narrow alley and darted down it.

Many people saw it go in one end. No one saw it come out the other. When a few children followed cautiously after, they found the alley empty.

For Elo, the world went dark and confused for a moment. Then she blinked, shook her head, and things came back into focus.

"Ah," she said. "A local portal. *Very* clever!"

"Thank you!" said Professor Odd, looking up from over a desk covered in wires, monitors, and strange humming cylinders. It smelled strongly of metal and grease.

Despite thousands of years of evolution and a few jumps sideways from her domestic counterparts, Elo had to resist the urge to wag her tail wildly and jump up and lick the Professor's face. She contented herself by coming around the table and hugging the tall woman about her midsection. For a moment Elo felt herself enfolded by those strong, bony arms, and then she was being gently pried away.

"Now, tell me why Dave evicted you and young Mister Alister," Professor Odd said, pushing a chair forward. "Speaking of Alister, what possessed you to leave him in the hands of the *Detective?*"

Elo gave a deep sigh, sat down, and began to explain. As she did, her eyes adjusted to the dim light, and she got a better look at the Professor's lair.

They were in a small, circular room with no windows. The walls were made of stone blocks, and there was a bundle of wires that ran up one wall and disappeared through a hole in the ceiling. Beside this hole was a tiny ventilation duct, from which a cold stream of air blew, wafting scents of evergreen trees into the room. The floor was covered in layers of throw rugs, all in different styles. Aside from the desk with the computers and the chair, the only other piece of furniture was a small camp bed pushed up against one wall, and a rather frightening contraption that reminded Elo of the chairs used by human dentists. Back the way she had come was only a blank wall with a doorway formed of a metal frame, with small circular nubs and gas jets at regular intervals bolted to it. A wooden door with a crescent moon cut in it was the only visible exit.

"So, how long has it been for *you?*" Elo asked when she had brought the Professor up to speed. "And . . . *where is this?*"

"Technically it's an unused dungeon, heavily remodeled," Professor Odd said cheerfully. "I had to have some place . . . secluded. There are people in this world who would very much like to capture me."

"So I've gathered," Elo said, rubbing an ear. She cast an appreciative glance at all the equipment over the desk. "You've been busy."

"Less so than I'd have liked," the Professor said, walking over to a small table near the camp bed. There was a little gas stove there and a battered kettle. Professor Odd lit the stove and put the kettle on. She was wrapped in many layers of scarves and coats, and there was a fur cap planted firmly over her head, its earflaps down and tied together under her chin. "Oh, it was fun in the beginning. A lot of running. Narrow escapes. Getting all this set up took me the better part of three months."

"Professor," Elo prodded.

"What? Oh, yes. I'd say it's been about a year. Not that I was worried," she grinned. "I thought a temporal discrepancy was likely. I'm sure Dave will get it fixed in no time. Well, no time for *him.*"

"Huh," said Elo. She went over to the not-a-human-dentist-chair and inspected the bit that hung down from the ceiling. It appeared to be a holographic projector of some kind.

"Not that I'm not *absolutely delighted* to see you," Professor Odd said kindly. "But it *was* rather stupid for you to leave the Oddity. Once Dave gets the discrepancy fixed and the place untangled he'll be able to move his next portal time backward so it will have been less time for us. If you'd waited for that, you could have come through not long after I did . . . "

"Maybe," said Elo. "We were worried. Alister felt like he was doing us no good sitting in the Oddity. And"—she fiddled nervously with a clamp—"it's shrinking. The whole place is shrinking."

Professor Odd looked up from pouring hot water into a chipped mug. Her jaguar eyes were open very wide and the pupils dilated so that they looked like deep black pits. "What?" she said, her voice like a knife dropped on ice.

"Dave said the spatial maintenance stabilizers had been sabotaged," Elo said miserably.

"Oh," said Professor Odd, her voice making a U-turn and chugging back toward its normal, optimistic tone. "Oh dear." She handed the steaming cup to Elo and rubbed her chin. She was wearing knit fingerless gloves, Elo saw, her fingertips protruding like curious, pale fish heads. "I didn't think he was capable of *that*," the Professor went on. "Really it's quite remarkable. I'd congratulate him except—*you know*—entrapping the Oddity and sabotaging her. *Tsk, tsk, tsk.*"

Elo came away from the chair. "Him? You mean the Detective?" She lapped hot water from the mug. It tasted faintly of tea.

"Oh, so you know him," Professor Odd said cheerfully. She had removed the kettle and was now heating water in a small saucepan. "Ramen?" she asked, holding up a packet of dried noodles.

Elo shuddered. "Pass. And not really. He came to the Oddity moments after you left. And then later, he found me and Alister. He chased us."

"And he let you get away?" Professor Odd asked in some surprise.

Elo shook her head miserably. "No, Alister insisted I go. He caused a . . . a distraction. It's okay though, an ambulance picked him up. I saw."

"And the Detective let you get away?" Professor Odd repeated in surprise.

Elo frowned. "Give me some credit. I can be quite slippery when I want to."

"You don't know the Detective," Professor Odd said, ripping open the package of ramen and gently easing the brick of dried noodles into the boiling water. She turned the heat down and began stirring it.

"Just who is this Detective anyway?" Elo demanded, sitting down on the camp bed. "Dave called him a *fellow traveler*. Does that mean he's not from this universe either?"

Professor Odd chuckled. "Dave would see it that way. He is, after a fashion, just a fellow traveler. And no, this isn't his native world. I'm not sure if he even *has* a native world at this point. He's . . . troubling." She turned off the heat and began stirring in the little packet of seasoning. The smell of over-salted pork filled the room. "I confess I *had* heard of him before. I just didn't realize this was the *same* Detective. He's an odd-jobbing private investigator bounty hunter sort of person, from what I can tell. Tracks down fugitives across the multiverse. But he's not just limited to the multiplicity-aware worlds. Go into any sufficiently advanced universe, and you'll find someone—or stories of someone—who can find things no one else can. Who can solve problems that seem unsolvable. Who doesn't work for any government or agency, but chooses cases based on their own personal interests. That's the Detective."

"A Holmesian Paradigm," Elo said. "I hacked into his data center and heard your conversation," she explained to the Professor's questioning glance.

"*Good* girl," said Professor Odd, taking the pot and blowing on it. She took a pair of chopsticks from her pocket and grabbed a bundle of noodles. She tasted them.

"So ... if he's a free agent," Elo pondered. "It's not really *him* that's after you ... it's whoever he's working for."

Professor Odd, her mouth full of noodles, nodded.

"Who is that, exactly?" Elo perked her ears and stared expectantly at the Professor.

Professor Odd swallowed slowly. She made a face. "No matter what, it never tastes as good as it smells," she sighed. "Given that he's brought us to my home-world that does narrow the field a bit. I *know!*" She looked up, grinning widely. "Let's ask *him!*" And she took her bowl, still mostly full of hot water and thin, slimy noodles, and tossed its contents at the chair by the desk.

The liquid flew through the air and splattered across the face and chest of the tall man who, until that moment, Elo was sure had *not* been sitting there.

Now the Detective stood up. He took a handkerchief from his breast pocket and carefully wiped the soup off his face. He plucked a stray noodle from his hair and gazed forlornly at Professor Odd.

"That was uncalled for," he said.

"*You* shouldn't have involved Alister," Professor Odd snapped, and Elo saw for the first time just how angry she was about that. She was *furious*, the rage that had been simmering below that icy exterior now rising to the surface. Elo actually felt a little *sorry* for the Detective. But only a little.

The Detective smiled. A long thin smile that made Elo wish she had accepted the Professor's offer of ramen, just so she could have her own pot of it to throw at him.

"Professor Odd," he said, somehow managing to appear suave even with ramen water dripping from his hair. "I have come to take you into my own personal custody, for the acts of technological and practical terrorism you committed here in this universe in the local year eighteen hundred and—"

Professor Odd didn't let him finish. She grabbed Elo by the paw and hauled her toward the wooden door with the crescent moon cut in it. She kicked it open and, withdrawing two carabiners from her pockets, clipped them onto a hidden rope.

"Hold onto me," she hissed, and Elo felt the soft length of her tentacle wrap around her upper arm. She reached up and threw both her paws over the Professor's shoulders and jumped.

The Detective, leaping after them, closed his hands on thin air.

Elo and the Professor fell a long way, the dark air whistling past them. Elo kept expecting them to land in a lake of sewage—or worse, a puddle, because then they'd break their backs—but they met no resistance. Eventually Professor Odd closed the carabiners, creating friction on the rope, and they slowed, and slowed, and eventually came to a halt. The Professor let go of the carabiners and they dropped a foot or so to land on clean, dry stone.

"Professor, what—" Elo began, but the Professor was scrabbling at a nearby wall, and a moment later a section of it rolled back and daylight flooded in.

Elo blinked out onto a winding stone stairway. There were long narrow windows in the wall, letting in a cool stream of pale daylight.

"I thought you said it was a *dungeon!*" she exclaimed.

"Didn't say where the dungeon was, did I?" Professor Odd replied with a grin. "I was counting on him being too excited about following you through the portal to bother to check the destination. Had to throw him off just a *little.* Now stand clear."

Elo scurried out of the little alcove and stood on the stairs as Professor Odd took a small radio transmitter out of yet *another* pocket.

No wonder she wears all those layers, Elo thought.

Professor Odd pressed a button. There was a distant explosion, and the rope they had descended fell in a shower of rock dust at their feet.

"That should slow him down a little," she remarked. "No rope, no more local portal device. And now comes the part where we run."

"My favorite," Elo said dryly, and took off down the stairs, the Professor hot on her tail.

They appeared to be in the tower of a castle. Elo caught glimpses of forested mountains out the narrow windows, with a picturesque little town on a distant hilltop.

The stairs led out into a wide hall, deserted and dusty. They sprinted across it, through a high arch, and then across an overgrown lawn studded with crumbling stone walls. It was a treacherous place, with hidden rabbit holes and stone masonry liable to give way. Elo leapt from block to block, nimble and sure-footed, with Professor Odd, her scarves trailing in the wind, only a little way behind.

Through a hole in the towering outer wall they went, and then they were in thick forest, ducking through undergrowth and jumping over fallen trees.

"North!" shouted the Professor. "Train tracks!"

Elo altered course, dropped her speed so that the Professor could catch up, and together they moved away deeper into the woods.

The Detective stood in the circular room, examining the empty shaft that had until recently contained a rope. He had been only partway through his copy of the software stored on the computers when the tiny charges blew, removing his means of pursuit and destroying the portal framework. He sighed. It was a little frustrating, but the Detective was nothing if not patient. And persistent.

He looked around at the disheveled little room that had been the Professor's headquarters for almost thirteen months. He shrugged. There was nothing left for him here. Nothing he did not already know. Besides, now that he'd been here once, he could easily come back.

He rolled up his sleeve and pressed a button on the pad strapped to his wrist.

And then he was not there anymore.

"How did he do that?" Elo asked. They had slowed to a walk and were now moving casually through the woods. "The way he just *appeared*. I mean, I couldn't see him, hear him, *or* smell him."

"The Detective has fewer scruples about what sort of technology he brings with him from world to world," Professor Odd said. "Some of it's not strictly conventional."

"I see," said Elo, who knew something of the *unconventional* that was implied here.

"From what I gather, there are two devices he makes use of," Professor Odd continued. "One is best described as a perception modifier. It redirects your attention around him, like a sort of mirror. It is easily circumvented, however, by direct physical contact. Hence the ramen."

Elo couldn't help a small snort at this.

"The other, and the one that troubles me more," the Professor went on, "is his STC manipulator."

"STC?" Elo repeated. "You don't mean Space Time Continuum?"

"That very one," Professor Odd said grimly. "Albeit, he can't use it to full effect in a temporally fixed universe such as this one, but it does allow him certain advantages. The appearance of instantaneous travel, for example. It behaves something like the Oddity, only not as powerful."

Elo shook her head. "I can't believe I haven't heard of him before."

"But you have," Professor Odd insisted. "Or at least a version similar to this individual. The Holmesian Paradigm is not uncommon."

"I meant *this* individual, *this* person. *The* Detective."

Professor Odd shrugged. "It is not so surprising when you think about it," she said. "The multiverse is filled with extraordinary people we haven't met yet. I expect there is quite a queue. Ah, here's our station."

Their station was in fact a layover for freight trains. Elo and the Professor picked a boxcar half filled with bags of grain and made themselves comfortable.

"Now explain to me exactly what problems Dave was encountering," Professor Odd said, arranging the bags around her like a throne. "Because, working together, there *may* be something we can do to help him out. In which case the temporal discrepancy will actually work *in our favor*." She grinned at Elo, showing her white, square teeth.

This time, Elo grinned back.

A few hours later the train pulled out of the yard and began gathering speed, leaving the ruined castle far behind.

When Alister woke up he felt *much* better. His chest still hurt, and he still felt tired, but the deep cold ache had vanished, and his head felt much clearer. He could wiggle his toes. He could lift his head and look down at his hands, which were folded neatly over his stomach. There was a white sleeve over one finger with wires coming off it, which in turn led to a monitor by his bedside that showed a steady, even heartbeat.

Alister felt good. Despite his questionable position he was optimistic as to his prospects, considering he had been hit by a car while trying to escape . . .

. . . the Detective.

The Detective. That tall, dark-haired man in the long black coat. Alister remembered him perfectly. Which was why he knew the man sitting across from him in the hospital room was exactly that person.

All the good feelings went out of Alister like water down a drain, leaving him a weak, injured person lost in a strange world. He groaned as he laid his head back against the pillow.

"Ah, Mr. *Bane,* I am glad to see you are awake."

He really did have a remarkable voice. Like someone out of an old movie. Soothing, deep and powerful. But Alister knew the man behind that voice was an enemy of the Professor's, and by extension, his enemy as well.

At least he did not seem inclined to drag Alister out of bed. Alister relaxed and shut his eyes.

"No," he said hopefully. "No, I'm not."

"Mr. Bane, I have been to a *great deal* of trouble tracking down your . . . leader . . . I'm afraid to say I'm getting a little impatient."

"Not," said Alister. His mouth was dry and sticky, making it difficult to talk. "Not my leader."

"Professor Odd is not your leader?"

A drink of water. That was what Alister needed. Not questions from this frightening man. "She's . . . my professor," he said.

"Are you a student, Mr. Bane?" the Detective asked.

"Could say that," Alister said.

"What has she been teaching you? Why did you seek her out?"

"Didn't *seek her out*," Alister grumbled. He got the feeling the Detective wasn't particularly interested in his answers. He was getting answers to *different* questions—ones Alister didn't know—from the way Alister was talking or the way he responded. Since it appeared what he actually said didn't matter, he decided to tell the truth.

"We met by accident. I got tangled up with the Canary Company; she helped me escape. And she doesn't *teach,* not really. She shows you things."

"Things like what?"

"Worlds," said Alister, giving a feeble shrug. "Worlds better—and worse—than this one. Worlds with orange skies and giant flying whales. Worlds with dinosaurs. Worlds without humans."

"And she teaches you about these worlds, does she?"

The manner of the Detective's questions was beginning to get on Alister's nerves. They put wrong notions in his head that he felt obliged to correct, but he could see no other reason to tell the Detective anything.

"I want to see my doctor," he said. "I don't think having you here is aiding my recovery."

"Dr. Jacobsen is on a house call," the Detective said, a little smugly.

"Not him—the other one . . . " *The one that saved me,* Alister did not add.

"Mr. Bane, I have followed you from world to world, across the multiverse. It has been quite exhausting. Now at last we have an opportunity to speak frankly, and yet you persist in obfuscation. Understand me, Alister Bane, when I say there is no place you can run, no place you can hide, where I cannot follow. Now open your eyes and look at me, and tell me, *do you know where Professor Odd is?*"

Alister did open his eyes, and he squinted across his sheet-covered body at the Detective, who had leaned forward in his chair and clasped his hands together. His eyes were black as pits, his cheeks hollow and lean, and his brows like the wings of a dark bird arching up on either side of his face.

"Why are you looking for her?" Alister responded.

The Detective stood up. He really was quite tall, like a long black shadow. He crossed Alister's room in two paces and stood at his bedside, his hands resting casually in the pockets of his waistcoat.

"Mr. Bane," he said quietly. "You are aware Professor Odd is wanted on this world for several counts of terrorism, not least of which is blowing up a Deutsch research facility?"

Alister opened his mouth to respond, but said nothing. He frowned.

"Clearly I overestimated her confidence in you." The Detective sighed, turning away. He picked up a jug of water that was sitting on a nearby table and poured some of it into a little paper cup, which in turn he brought over to Alister. Laying his hand gently over Alister's clasped ones he raised the cup to Alister's mouth.

Alister sipped the cool, clear water. It seemed to come at a mere trickle and disappear into his dry mouth as if it had never been.

"They cleared you for advanced caudata-assisted, stem-cell therapy last night," the Detective said conversationally. "I expect your cracked ribs and other injuries to be almost completely healed, if not by now then in a few hours. After that they will release you. At that point, Mr. Bane, you will have two choices. You can attempt to find your professor, which I would not recommend, as you are technically an illegal alien in this world and will have no means of obtaining food, lodging, or other resources. Or"—here he took a small white card and tucked it between Alister's fingers—"when they release you, ask the receptionist to call that number. I will have you collected."

"Collected?" Alister rasped; his throat still felt dry. "For what?"

The Detective poured another cup of water. "For . . . nothing. For safe preservation until the conclusion of my case. After which I will escort you back to your own world."

Alister shook his head, dislodging the offered cup. "No," he said firmly. "I can't go back. Not yet."

The Detective raised two perfect, black eyebrows. He seemed bemused. "You cannot stay here. Without the Professor you have no means of returning home."

"I don't want to *go* home," Alister said, surprised that he meant every word of it. Apparently all it took to kill his homesickness was the prospect of being delivered into the waiting arms of the Canary Company. "I'm not going home," he said firmly. "I'm going to wait. I'm going to wait, and once they've untangled the Oddity from whatever you've trapped it in, they will come and get me. And then we'll leave. And you . . . you can just keep on following us from world to world." He paused. He was still short of breath. "You have to admit," he added, "she visits some pretty neat places."

The Detective shrugged. He replaced the paper cup on the table and dug his hands deep into his coat pockets. "Ah," he said. "Well, I am sorry you feel that way. You've been through so much trauma already, I did not want to compound the problem."

Alister turned his head sharply to look. Something in the man's expression, the tension in his shoulders and the way his right hand seemed fisted in his pocket, all set alarm bells ringing for Alister.

Fortunately it was at that moment that the door burst open.

Both men turned. For one wild moment Alister thought it was the Professor and Elo and Dave, and the Oddity was working again and he was saved. But it was not the Professor.

It was Dr. Watterson.

"And what *possessed* you to let him in to see the patient alone?" were the words just leaving her mouth as the door bounced off the wall. She stared at Alister. She glared at the Detective. She was wearing a neat plaid vest over a button-down shirt and slacks, her brown hair stylishly coiffed in a masculine sort of way. She looked like she had been interrupted in the middle of an evening out, and was now ready to ream the person responsible.

The Detective turned, palming the syringe he had been holding and setting it on the table.

"Doctor," Alister wheezed.

Dr. Watterson pointed at the Detective. "You," she said shortly. "Out."

"On whose authority?" the Detective asked sweetly.

"Mine," grinned Dr. Watterson.

"Are you this man's doctor?"

"No, but I am *a* doctor—Martha, call security—which is more than I can say *for you*. Out."

The Detective sighed. He glanced back at Alister with a rueful grin. "Sorry about this," he said. He raised his other hand, in which he held a small metal box rather like a camera. It had a little yellow flashing light in the center.

There was a billowing of the curtains over the window, and a squealing as the screen was wrenched off and the pane slid backward. Everyone, even the Detective, turned and stared.

And Elo shot into the room.

Gone was her seeing-eye dog harness. She was dressed once more in her favorite purple jumpsuit, and she carried clutched to her chest a huge gun with bare wires protruding from the muzzle.

The Detective saw it. More than that, he recognized it. He lunged for Elo, but Alister's bed got in the way, and the wolf was too quick.

"Down, Alister!" Elo howled, and fired the time gun.

It was like an invisible bubble spread over the far side of the room, enveloping the Detective (caught mid-lunge) and Dr. Watterson. Within this bubble the passage of time slowed to the point where the Detective was suspended in midair, and Dr. Watterson's cry of surprise was drawn into a long, low moan.

"How are you?" Elo asked, all business, as she holstered the gun in the sling she wore over her back.

"Been better," Alister gasped. His heart was racing, and he felt like he might pass out again.

"Can you walk?" the wolf asked, coming over and briskly unhooking him from all the wires and meters.

Alister tried to sit up, and failed. "I don't think so," he said.

"Well, there's a way around that," came Professor Odd's voice, bright and cheerful and just a little bit manic. Alister rolled his head, and saw her jump down from the windowsill. Gone were the drab overcoat and mouse-colored wig; she was back in her olive-green trench coat and was wearing a particularly vibrant wig of neon yellow. She kicked out her legs as she jumped, and Alister saw these were encased in a pair of improbably gold pinstriped trousers.

"Professor!" Alister gulped. "It's the Detective, he's after you—he said—"

"There will be time enough for that later," said Professor Odd, briskly wheeling Alister's bed over to the window. "Now, where are your injuries?"

"Fractured ribs, I think," Alister said. "And a concussion. And bruises. Lots of bruises. But they gave me something, said it would help the healing. Caudata-assisted stem-cell . . . something. Mostly, I just feel weak."

Professor Odd paused. She looked at Alister intently, frowning under her wig.

"Something wrong?" Alister asked nervously.

"So that's what they called it," Professor Odd muttered to herself. "Interesting. All right, Elo, if you would—we'll lift him on three. One, two . . . "

They heaved Alister through the window, and there, blessedly, were the steps of the Oddity. They seemed a little more worn and dingy than Alister remembered, but that might have been because his face was closer to them than normal.

With her arms under his shoulders and Elo supporting his legs, they trotted Alister up the stairs and deposited him in a chair. Alister glimpsed the room—noticeably smaller than he remembered—and Dave in his panvironment suit sitting at the cockpit.

"You . . . fixed it?" he asked, breathlessly. His ribs were not exactly hurting, but they were sending him the equivalent of angry notes.

"I HAVE REMOVED ALL EXTERNAL INTERFERENCES," Dave said as Elo came up the stairs. "THE ODDITY INSISTS ON REPAIRING THE DAMAGE ITSELF."

"Give," Professor Odd said to Elo, who handed over the time gun.

"You're going to release them?" she asked, a little startled.

"Fair's fair," said Professor Odd, and marched back down the stairs. "Just be ready to get us out of here."

"More than!" exclaimed Elo, and took her place across from Dave.

Alister watched placidly as Professor Odd's yellow wig disappeared down the stairs. He listened to the muffled *whumph* of the time gun's field releasing, the startled cries resuming, and then the sudden and absolute silence as the Oddity's portal closed for good.

Professor Odd came slowly back up the stairs, turning little knobs and dials on the time gun so that it could not go off accidentally. She was frowning, and seemed to be feeling none of the triumph and relief that was currently coursing through Alister.

"So . . . that's it?" he asked hopefully. "We're completely disconnected . . . no more entanglement or spatial stabilizer sabotage?"

"WE HAVE SEVERED ALL CONNECTIONS WITH THAT UNIVERSE," Dave said. "OBSERVE FOR YOURSELF." One cloth-covered tentacle rose, pointed out the window. There, to Alister's intense joy, was the deep blue-blackness of the void, pricked by the distant lights of far away worlds.

Funny, Alister thought to himself. *The first time I saw that, it terrified me. Now, I couldn't be more relieved.*

The sight of the void was better—far better—than the dull brick walls, for it meant they were no longer trapped in that bitter and unfriendly world. For the first time in days Alister felt his body relax completely.

"Well, I don't know about you," he said. "But I'm *starving*."

"I could eat," Elo said, unclipping the holster and throwing it on the table. "Let's see what the kitchen can manage."

The kitchen, it turned out, could only manage a kind of dried, salty noodle mix that Elo called ramen. For some reason this sent her into fits of laughter. So Alister agreed to the ramen, which was oily and salty and tasted vaguely of chicken, and ate it with a fork while Elo told him her side of the adventure: about finding the Professor, escaping the Detective, building a separate portal to link directly with the Oddity . . .

"It allowed us to move the portal about within the world," Elo explained. "So we were able to find and infiltrate the installation where the Detective had been broadcasting the signal used to interfere with the Oddity. And disable it."

Alister paused with a fork full of noodles halfway to his mouth.

"You . . . *disabled* it?" he said.

"Oh yes, it is *very* disabled," said Elo smugly.

"Define 'disabled.'"

"We didn't hurt anyone!" she assured him. "Well, maybe one. But he'll only have a headache for a few hours. Anyway, with the interference gone Dave was able to get the Oddity up and running in no time. We detached long enough for it to repair itself enough that we could open a portal in a different place seconds after we left the world—and that one was into your hospital room. And not a moment too soon! I insisted on bringing the time gun because I thought the Detective would be after you. Did you know *he's* got off-world tech too? And a lot less restrained about using it than our Professor."

"A little thing, like a camera," said Alister. "And I think he can mess with people's memories."

"He can do a lot more than that," said Professor Odd wearily. She had pulled up a chair and was idly spinning the rear wheel of the bicycle that lay across half the table. She had propped her head up against one hand and seemed to be lost in thought.

"Oh, no," said Alister, pushing the bowl full of broth over to Elo. "You're not happy. Something's gone wrong. What's gone wrong? Has he got a fishing line attached to us or what?"

"THERE IS NO LINE," Dave said indignantly. "THERE IS NO TRACER. WE ARE AS FAR FROM THAT UNIVERSE AS ANY OTHER. HE HAS LOST US TO THE INFINITE MULTIPLICITY."

Alister turned back to the Professor.

"Then . . . *what?*" he asked.

Professor Odd looked up. She stared blankly over the table piled with junk, and said in a flat voice: "I have to go back."

Elo jumped to her feet. "No, no, *no,* you do *not!*" she said.

"I have to go back and *explain,*" Professor Odd went on as if she hadn't heard.

"Explain *what?*" Alister said. "Professor, you can't go back there. He thinks you're a *terrorist.*"

"Yes, and I know why he would," Professor Odd said. "Which is why I have to explain."

"I nearly broke my back getting you out of there," Elo snarled. "Dave worked his tentacles to the bone—"

"I DO NOT HAVE AN ENDOSKELETON," Dave pointed out.

"Shut up," barked Elo. "Alister got *hit by a car.* We finally get free of that place—we're free to go *anywhere* we want . . . and now you want to go *back?*"

For the first time, Professor Odd looked at them. Her eyes were very big and dark, and reflected the rainbow lights of the Oddity like little gems. She smiled sadly.

"I don't want to," she said quietly. "But I know I should. And it's because I *can* . . . I can leave. I can make the Detective start his game all over again. That's why I have to go back now. Because now he'll *listen* to me."

Alister sighed—cautiously—and shook his head.

"Well, can it wait a day or so? I don't feel up for much as it is, and I *am* going with you this time, don't argue."

"Me too," Elo joined in.

Professor Odd looked at them. She seemed touched, and saddened.

"It's not going to be pleasant, what I have to say," she said softly.

Alister thought about this.

"Would you prefer we didn't hear it?" he asked.

Professor Odd leaned back in her chair and stared at the black emptiness that passed for the ceiling for a while. "I suppose you deserve to know," she said. "It's just . . . difficult to talk about. To tell the truth, I would appreciate the moral support."

Elo and Alister exchanged glances.

"Well," said Alister, hitching himself up on his chair. "Consider yourself supported."

The Professor rolled her head to one side and looked at him; a faint smile ghosted across her face.

"I WILL REMAIN HERE," Dave announced. "IN CASE OF . . . TROUBLE."

"That," said Elo, removing the bowls and standing up, "sounds like an excellent plan."

*   *   *

The doctor was becoming a problem. The Detective paused with his key halfway to the lock of the flat he'd rented in middle Londinium and sighed inwardly.

First she had possessed his target. Then she had interfered with questioning—and worse, distracted him at a critical moment. He might have thought she was another agent of the Professor, except she seemed too simple for that. Then again, Alister Bane had seemed simple—but he clearly had experience of the multiverse, and the Detective suspected that superficial naiveté hid a formidable intellect. But the doctor . . . she confused him. She knew about his methods—maybe didn't understand them but she knew—and after the inexplicable reappearance of the Professor and her damned dog she had refused to be brainwashed and led away. She had . . . *hounded* him, that was the word. Hounded. And like a hound she had sniffed out his scent and followed him here. He could sense her by the tense shadow in an alley two doors down.

The Detective unlocked his front door, and stepped back.

"You won't get any answers shivering the night out there," he told the alley.

A brief movement, and the doctor appeared on the pavement. She had added a camel-colored overcoat to her ensemble and a matching fedora, and looked rather like a 1930's wiseguy until she opened her mouth and spoke, her northern accent pronounced in her agitation.

"And if I go inside?" she asked, her face like a stone wall.

"If you come inside the very least you'll get is to ask the questions I know you want to," the Detective said. He shrugged. "You might get an answer or two in return."

The doctor took a step toward him down the pavement. She wore patent leather shoes and seemed to favor her left leg.

Scar tissue in the knee, thought the Detective. *Not a bullet, but an injury. Maybe running away from a bullet?* She had seen military service, that was for certain.

"And I expect then you'll use your handy flasher to make it all go away. Drive me home and set me up with a snifter or two so when I wake up I'll just think I dreamed it all. I've had my head messed about in before, and I'm not in a hurry to repeat it, thank you very much."

"I can assure you there will be no 'messing about' of any kind," the Detective said. "On the contrary, it is my wish to *clear up* messes. You can reassure yourself of the fact that I have never actually harmed anyone—it was *your* cab that struck poor Mr. Bane—but you will have to trust me. Trust me, doctor, or stand outside and wonder."

He turned away and opened his door. Slowly. By the time he'd finished he could feel her breath on his neck. Her steps had been almost silent. He approved.

"Listen," said the doctor, radiating menace even though she only came up to his shoulder. "I know that you know that I've served time in our armed forces.

That's good. I *wanted* you to know. I also want you to know that, though I may be in civilian practice now, I haven't let go of my military . . . training."

The Detective looked over and glanced down, to where her hands were still in the pockets of her overcoat.

"Duly noted," he said. "Then I trust you to know when . . . and when *not* . . . to use this . . . *training.*" He smiled. "My dear doctor, won't you please come in?"

Together they entered the flat. Together they ascended the stairs to the Detective's apartment: a large airy living room with an attached kitchen, a bathroom and two bedrooms. One of the bedrooms was covered in papers and clippings and some very interesting wire constructions. The other was empty. The living room was, by contrast, impeccably furnished with a sofa and two deep armchairs arranged tastefully around a vintage fireplace.

When the Detective and the doctor stepped through the door from the hall they found the two armchairs already occupied: in one was a tall man with short-cropped dark hair in an eye-splitting pink-and-chocolate three-piece suit, while the other held a large golden dog in navy-blue overalls. Behind them stood another figure, her long green trench coat thrown open to reveal a crisp white shirt under suspenders attached to a pair of pinstriped, forest-green trousers. She wore a thick, sky-blue scarf wrapped loosely around her neck, round dark glasses, and a wild, neon-yellow wig.

The Detective stopped. He felt the doctor bump against his shoulder and heard her gasp. Inclining his head to glance behind him he saw that the doorway they had just passed through no longer led to the hall, but to a flight of stairs leading up a narrow passage. In the middle of this passage sat a thing like an oil drum with tractor treads around the midsection and a blue glass dome on top. It had many arms encased in cloth that emerged from round holes and stretched across the doorway like a spiderweb, effectively blocking their exit.

The Detective turned back to the people in his living room.

"What is the meaning of this, Professor?" he asked coldly.

"Ah, *Detective,*" said the Professor in that increasingly irritating voice that reeked of smug self-satisfaction. She came forward between the two chairs and took off her glasses. Her eyes looked a little big for her face, and the pupils were the wrong shape. They were not human eyes. She folded her dark glasses and handed them to the wolf. Then she began unwinding her scarf. "I know this must seem like a terrible intrusion," she said, looping the scarf over the back of the man's chair and shrugging out of her trench coat. She had a tall, slender body that seemed to disappear under her clothes. "But the fact of the matter is, Detective . . . " and here she slid a hand up under her wig and pulled it off in one smooth motion.

She was completely bald. More than that, her pinkish-white skin was mottled with pale green spots, like a leopard's, and extending from the base of her skull was a long, puckered, flesh-colored tentacle, similarly mottled. She gazed at him evenly out of those eerie cat eyes, while her tentacle rested, curling, over her shoulder.

"Detective," she said. "I think it's high time you and I had a little chat, *face to face.*"

Part Two: Subject 0-D

DR. JANE WATTERSON WAS HAVING a *very* strange day. Strange days had happened to her before, in the way of patients with unusual injuries, lucky or unlucky coincidences, and that exciting day in Persia when someone had tried (and very nearly succeeded at) shooting her.

None of them, however, could hold a candle to this day.

First there had been her John Doe patient, who had lingered in her mind even after he was no longer technically her patient anymore. Perhaps that was why she'd left a lovely woman sitting at a restaurant when she'd been paged about the man's unexpected visitor—Dr. Jacobsen being absent. She'd gone only to find the man called the Detective haranguing him. This would have annoyed her on anyone's account—the caudata-assist meant people healed faster and more completely, it did not make them instantly better!—but the poor man had looked so wretched. He clearly didn't want the Detective there. Dr. Watterson didn't know their history, or whose side she should be on, but as a doctor her sympathies defaulted to the person in the bed, and she'd gone about getting rid of the Detective until . . .

Until a large golden wolf wearing a purple jumpsuit had hurtled in through the window holding a *very* unusual-looking gun and shouted "*Get down!*"

And then it had seemed like things sped up for everyone except her and the Detective. She saw a tall figure in a neon-yellow wig help the dog carry her patient away, all three of them moving at super-speed. Then the yellow wig was back again, and the gun was pointing at them.

Dr. Watterson's heart didn't even have time to leap into her throat before the gun fired . . . but all that happened was the outside world slowed back down to normal.

The Detective leapt over to the window . . . but it opened onto empty space, and a thirty-foot drop to the roof of the building below.

That had been strange. Strange enough to cause Dr. Watterson to utilize some skills she'd thought she'd left in India in order to track the Detective back to his house. Then she'd stood outside uncertainly, watching the man fiddle with his keys, wondering whether to approach him.

Eventually the choice was taken out of her hands when he spoke to her. It was uncanny, but Dr. Watterson was nothing if not adaptable, and her tolerance level for the strange had been climbing all day.

SUBJECT

OD

She came forward. Words were exchanged. For her part, she made her position clear. She didn't expect to need to shoot anyone—she certainly hoped not—but the weight of her old army piece in her pocket was comforting. It allowed her to ascend the steps to the Detective's flat with some semblance of composure.

The person—Dr. Watterson was reasonably certain it was female—in the neon-yellow wig was standing in his living room. In one armchair beside her was the John Doe—Bane, the Detective had called him—and in the other was the golden wolf, sitting upright like a human with her tail neatly folded over her lap.

When Dr. Watterson turned instinctively to reassure herself of a safe exit, it was only to find the way blocked by a thing like a barrel with a blue glass dome on top. Cord-like, cloth-covered arms stretched from the barrel and fastened on the door frame.

Other people might have panicked at this point. There is only so much strangeness one can take in a single day. But when confronted with the unusual, Dr. Jane Watterson did not reject it—rather she rearranged her perspective to define "normal" as containing a good deal more strangeness.

Even so, this was pushing things.

Then the woman—the Professor—had taken off her coat, scarf and wig, and Dr. Watterson felt the strangeness overcome by her professional curiosity.

The woman was clearly a splice, exhibiting features of many different animals. Dr. Watterson had never heard of a splice getting so large or—apparently—living so long. Never mind possessing humanlike intelligence, as the Professor clearly did.

She must have noticed Dr. Watterson's stare, for those cat eyes darted to her and lingered.

"I see you've found your doctor." The splice smiled, showing large, white, square teeth. "Excellent. Well, I won't waste your time with pleasantries. To be frank, I know you can leave anytime you want, and you know *I*"—she indicated the eerie doorway behind them—"can leave anytime *I* want. The conversation that I'm proposing is, therefore, *entirely optional.* You can leave, if you like, and then I will leave, and then I promise, Detective, *you will never see me again.*"

"Are you all right?" Dr. Watterson asked the man in the chair, cutting under the Professor's words. Clearly the Professor and the Detective had history together, but her prime concern was her former patient, who was sitting very still and looking strained.

The man—Bane—looked at her. Recognized her. He smiled and mouthed *I'm fine,* then pointed at the woman with the tentacle growing out of her head. She had gone on talking.

" . . . if you stay," she was saying. "Well, if you stay, then *I'll* stay. And I can give you . . . not an explanation exactly. Let's say . . . a *story.* A series of facts that may help you make an informed decision as to whether you *really want* to pursue this case any further. What do you say?"

The Detective turned to Dr. Watterson and smiled ironically. "Well doctor," he said. "It appears you are in luck: you shall receive many answers tonight."

The Detective made tea. Dr. Watterson sat on the sofa eyeing the guests cagily.

"Can you tell me your name *now?*" she asked the young man.

He smiled weakly. "I suppose so. I'm Alister, Alister Bane. This is Elo." He indicated the golden wolf. "The one with the tentacle is Professor Odd"—Professor Odd bowed—"and the thing in the doorway that looks like a robot is Dave."

Dr. Watterson twisted around in her seat to get a good look. Behind it, through its web of arms, it appeared another room had been slotted in behind the door, with stairs leading up to a dim cavern twinkling with many colored lights.

"HELLO," intoned the barrel-shaped object.

"You're *not* a robot?" Dr. Watterson asked. She had hoped it was. After everything, a *robot* would have been comparatively normal.

"QUITE THE OPPOSITE," said Dave.

"Everyone," said Alister Bane, bringing her attention back around. "This is Dr. Watterson. She's . . . em . . . "

"I was in the car that hit him," she explained stoically. "I took a professional interest."

"I'm glad you did," said Professor Odd, giving her a keen look. "Will you be taking notes?"

"I hadn't anticipated—"

"Please do." Professor Odd removed a notebook and pen from the pockets of her trench coat, which had been draped over the back of a chair, and handed them to Dr. Watterson. "For my sake."

"What are you planning to do?" Dr. Watterson asked, taking the implements.

Professor Odd looked up sharply; the Detective had returned, carrying a tray bearing cups and a pot. He set it on the ottoman and began pouring. He too had taken off his overcoat, underneath which he was wearing a tidy black suit over a dark, gray-blue shirt. Dr. Watterson found this little splash of color reassuring; it made him look more like a person and less like a caricature.

"I am going—*thank you*—" the Professor took an offered cup, "going to tell you my story."

The Detective came and sat at the end of the sofa, a polite distance from Dr. Watterson, and crossed his legs. He shut his eyes and steepled his hands, leaning back into the cushions.

"You may begin," he announced.

Dr. Watterson saw Professor Odd give him a look of part annoyance and part amusement. It rather raised the doctor's opinion of her.

Professor Odd took a sip of tea and drew in a deep breath, as though she were preparing to dive under water. Then she let it out, long and slow. She set her teacup on the mantelpiece, and went to stand behind one of the low lamps that was the room's only illumination. Like that, partly lit from below, she appeared even more alien.

"I suppose I should begin by asking if you've ever heard of a place called Ent-deckungfeld? The Detective has, I know, but you, doctor?"

When Dr. Watterson shook her head, the Professor shrugged.

"I might as well start there, since neither Elo nor Alister know what it is either . . .

"To put it simply, Entdeckungfeld was a place in the country you know today as Deutschland—Germany, to Alister—which is . . . well it's not there anymore. Many years ago, however, Entdeckungfeld was the home of a complex, advanced, and utterly secret research facility run by a collegium of scientists from around the globe. Ostensibly they had gathered together to conduct medical research with the aim of improving the quality of life for people the world over. Which they did. They also conducted practical experiments. The results of some of these have been made public knowledge—though they've been attributed to different institutions. They had to be, you see, because of the *other* things that went on at Entdeckungfeld, the place could not, legally, exist."

Professor Odd went to one of the tall windows that looked out on the street below. She stared out it for a few moments, her tentacle curled tightly at the base of her neck.

"There were twenty-one of us, in the beginning," she said quietly. Turning back to them her eyes were very dark; her pupils blown wide. "I remember that. It was the name I was given for all of us. Twenty-one. We were divided into four groups: A, B, C and D. Within each group were subjects, and we were numbered: Subject 1-A, Subject 2-A, etc., 3-B, 4-B, etc., 5-C. . . . There were five subjects in each group, except group D. Group D had a sixth subject added a little after the rest which, for . . . *accounting* purposes—that is to say, for the purpose of *cheating the accountant*—this sixth subject was given the designation 0-D. It is the story of Subject 0-D that I wish to tell, but to understand the enormity of what happened to her you must also understand that there were *twenty other subjects* who cannot, for reasons that will become apparent, stand before you now and tell their own stories." The Professor clasped her hands behind her back and smiled. "It falls to me . . . Subject 0-D, the late addition, the last living subject of Entdeckungfeld, to say the things that by rights they should have said themselves.

"It began as a quest to develop medical treatments to promote healing and regeneration. Scientists had discovered that members of the *caudata* family— salamanders and their cousins—could regenerate body parts better than any other vertebrate. They wanted to develop a treatment that would allow human amputees to regrow lost limbs—or even to regrow whole limbs where before they had been malformed due to genetic defects. Members of *caudata* were chosen as the basis for the Entdeckungfeld experiments because of their relative similarity to humans—as opposed to planarian flatworms, for example.

"The Subjects, as we came to be known, were created to serve as a genetic bridge between *caudata* and *homo sapiens*. Each Subject began as an artificially created embryo which was then spliced with different kinds of DNA. There were countless numbers of these embryos. Many never got beyond a few hundred cells. Of those that did, most were spontaneously aborted. In the end, only thirty survived to full gestation, and nine of those died in the first week. A tenth wasn't expected to survive much longer, and so was not counted in the initial sorting. The twenty live infant subjects were divided as I have explained, and the twenty-first added to group D about a month into the live portion of the experiment.

"Each group concentrated on a different mix of genetics designed to translate the *caudata* regenerative abilities into a form useful to humans. Group A was primarily aquatic—I remember I was able to see their tanks from my cage—while Group B incorporated insect DNA. Group B did not live long. By the time I was old enough to understand these things all that was left were a couple of bodies suspended in preservative fluid. Group C was the most human, and perhaps that is why they suffered from autoimmune diseases. None of them survived past puberty. And then there was Group D.

"Group D was an almost random mix. Of Group D, 1-D died in the first year when he began growing a second stomach in his left lung, 2-D had a pair of horns and they called him Little Devil, 3-D had scales and looked like a humanoid lizard with feathers, 4-D had a third arm growing out of her chest, 5-D looked like a human but acted like a rabid animal. He was euthanized after he mauled one of the scientists. Finally, there was 0-D.

"They called me Odd almost from the beginning. I don't think they meant to name me. They didn't name any of the others except for Little Devil. I think it happened because I was the odd one out, and because in their notes they shortened our designations. Five-hyphen-A became 5A. So Zero-hyphen-D became 0D, which looks a bit like OD, and so it was pronounced *Odd*. However it happened, that was the first word I learned to recognize, because it usually meant something was about to happen to me.

"Early on all that happened was they would take me out of the cage and put me on a cold metal thing and shine bright lights in my face. I later learned the cold metal thing was a *table*, and a lot worse stuff happened on it later. But when I was very young all they wanted was to study my development. They had lost enough subjects that the survivors in Group D were precious. They measured us, monitored our growth, and tested our reflexes. None of the other D's fully developed mentally—partly because they were never given any stimulation beyond being poked and prodded and carried from cage to table and back again, and partly because they were all lobotomized at the age of four when it became apparent they were developing high-level intelligence—but the scientist who was in charge of me—the same scientist who, in the first week of my life, decided not to flush me out of the incubator and who added me to Group D under designation 0—was curious about how my brain would grow. So instead of carting me about in a travel cage he would carry me over his shoulder. When he shone lights in my face to get a look at me he would say things like 'Here comes the light,' or 'This will be very bright.' And he wouldn't let them lobotomize me. I was always 'in the middle of an experiment' and couldn't be disrupted. After a while I think they just gave up. This was the way my scientist did things: he never said no, but he wouldn't say yes to anything he didn't want either; he would just do what he liked, and do whatever it took to get what he wanted.

"Some of my earliest memories are of crawling around a room with a springy, prickly floor. There were pillars and caves made out of a mottled brown substance that gleamed. These were the desks and chairs of his office. He would take me there once a day to study my behavior, or whenever the other scientists were running group experiments that he didn't want me to be a part of. Once I spent a whole week there. That was the week they performed surgeries on Little Devil, 3-D, 4-D and 5-D to disconnect the two hemispheres of their brains so they would be more docile. That was also the week I learned how to use toilets, and what 'Go hide in the closet' meant. I got to eat food that was different colors, shapes and textures than the paste we were given in the cages. That was a good week . . . until it ended.

"I have some memories of my cage. Most of them are influenced by what I found later, when I went exploring, but I have a few genuine memories. I remember the tanks of the Group A subjects, when the oxygen tubes still sent bubbles up from the bottom, and they had little lights behind them. I remember how, one by one, they went dark. I didn't understand until much later that they had died, and I didn't find out what had happened to them until even later than that.

"My cage was . . . hmm . . . about the size of that table, and maybe two feet tall. It had a mesh floor covered in soft shavings. Urine trickled through and down a drain below, but feces had to be cleaned out manually every day. There were two bottles with rubber teats on the end that stuck in through one side. One dispensed water, the other was filled with the nutrient paste which was our only food. I understand they changed it every day so we received the correct balance of vitamins, protein, fiber, fats and so on. But it always tasted the same.

"I lived in that cage for the first three years of my life. When I got too big I was moved to a room, but it was really just a bigger cage. Only now the walls were made of a white substance that I couldn't see through. I felt very lonely in that room.

"Then, one by one, the other subjects were also moved into the room. First was Subject 4-D. She spent the first day huddled in a corner and wouldn't talk to me. I later found out this was because she couldn't. But we became friends anyway. We would talk with our hands instead of our voices, and she kept cheating and making up words I couldn't say because she had an extra hand. We made a game out of it. I liked that. It was fun. After a while Little Devil and 3-D joined us. So did 5-D but they took him away again after he tried to bite 4-D's third hand off.

"I think it must have been only a year I spent in that room with the other subjects, but it makes up a lot of my early memories. I think because I learned so much. 4-D and I taught our sign language to Little Devil and 3-D, and from then on we all talked like that. The others only knew verbal speech as this noise that meant they would be carted away, poked with needles or put on a cold, uncomfortable surface, so they didn't like it when I talked out loud. After a while I stopped, and when we were alone together I would only make the simple, animalistic noises that they did. I got very good at our sign language though. I remember a few words even now."

Professor Odd held up her hands, palms forward and fingers splayed out. Slowly she brought them together and wove her fore and middle fingers together, with her thumbs overlapping at the bottom and the pinkies sticking out to either side.

"This is the sign we'd make when the scientists would come and take one of us away," she said. "I'm not sure how best to translate it. It means 'be strong,' and 'things will be all right,' and 'we are together in this.' It was our way of recognizing that we cared about and supported each other."

Slowly she took her hands down and cupped them together in front of her. "It was the last thing I said to them, before my scientist took me away. Then I spent a week in his office eating human food and learning to use the little chamberpot in his closet. I did a lot of verbal talking that week, because he couldn't understand our sign language. I remember I had a lot of fun.

"Then at the end of it he put me back in the big cage. I thought the others must have been very worried about me by this time, but when I got there all they would do was sit and stare off into space. They wouldn't respond to anything I did. They didn't care where they defecated or urinated anymore, and the scientists had to come in and feed them by hand. It was like the part of them that was *them* had gone away, leaving me with only the shells.

"I hated it. I shouted and yelled at them, trying to get them to wake up. I thought they had gone to sleep inside their own heads, you see. But they weren't afraid of my shouting anymore, and after a while I realized they weren't sleeping. They were dead inside.

"That was when I learned about death. Before then I hadn't been aware of these book-ends to existence. I thought I was and would always be. It never occurred to me that I would ever not exist, even though I surmised that there was a time in the past when I did not exist. Before, death hadn't been *death,* really. The lights in the tanks went out. 1-D went to sleep in his cage and the scientists took him away and never brought him back. Things *went away* all the time. It never occurred to me before that sometimes it was because they stopped working.

"Sometimes the insides stopped working while the outsides went on.

"I couldn't be in the room with the others anymore. I threw fits. I screamed. I banged myself against the walls. Scientists came and took me away. My scientist came and took me away from the other scientists. They set up a cage for me in his office, but he would let me out of it whenever no one was around.

"He never explained what had happened. He only offered to teach me things. He was fascinated to discover that we had developed a whole language between ourselves through hand signs, and wanted me to show him so he could write them down.

"I didn't understand what writing was at the time. I just thought he wanted to become like the other subjects, and I didn't want that. He was my scientist, and he could never replace Little Devil or 4-D. I hid under his desk and refused. I wish now I hadn't. Except for a few words I managed to remember, that language died with the other members of Group D.

"One thing that came of it—it convinced my scientist that we did possess humanlike intelligence, and it made him all the more determined to protect me. I started seeing the other humans less and less, and my cage door was left open more and more.

"He taught me about writing and reading. He taught me about beds and about fruits and vegetables and meat. That was how I learned about the other part of death. How our outsides can stop—both naturally and by the interference of others. I didn't want to eat the meat for a while after that. But he was patient: he explained about biology and physiology and nutrition, and after a while I started eating meat again. He explained about a lot of things, mostly because he would talk to himself while he worked, and I would ask him what this or that meant, and he would tell me. He seemed impressed by my ability to absorb information, though to me it felt like I was at the bottom of a mountain made of things I didn't know, and I was impatient to get to the top.

"Those were the good days. I got to eat real food, I got to learn things, and my scientist would sometimes take me out into a little courtyard at the back of the complex. We caught insects together, and once he took me out in the middle of the night and showed me the stars.

"That was something. He had explained the solar system and the galaxy before, but until then they'd just been abstract concepts in my head. Being able to actually look out and *see* what he was talking about made me realize how much I hated being shut up inside all the time. I wanted to get out. I wanted to see the world. More than that, from the moment I looked out on all those stars, I wanted to see *other worlds*.

"I was insistent. I didn't understand that I was the product of a lot of advanced science and a good deal of money and that to them I was as much a piece of property as my scientist's desk or chair—albeit an incalculably valuable piece of property. I did not understand why I was not allowed out, and I kept asking. And for the first time my scientist wouldn't give me a straight answer. He would say things like 'you're too young,' or 'maybe some other time.'

"That was when I discovered I could see in a person's face when they were lying. My scientist's face would twist and change when he said things that weren't true. This was rare, so when it did happen the difference was remarkable. I had learned to watch all the scientists closely, to see if they were going to stick me with needles or just measure me with tapes and rods. They would always move carefully and cautiously, but I found I could figure out what they intended by looking at their faces. Now I found myself watching my scientist very carefully indeed, and to my surprise I caught him in several other, smaller lies.

"When I asked how people were made, for example, he explained in frank detail how sexual reproduction worked. But all the time he was talking his face said it wasn't true. I kept pestering him until finally he admitted that this was how *most* people were made, but that I was different. And that was all he would say. It was one of those blocks on his knowledge that he wouldn't tell me about. I thought of them as blocks, because when I asked him something that he honestly didn't know the answer to he'd explain that he didn't know. But there were other things—how I was made, why I was not allowed out—that he simply would not talk about.

"Looking back, I think he was trying to shield me. I wish he hadn't. Things might have turned out differently if I'd been in possession of all the facts. Then again, it might have just made me miserable.

"At the time I didn't understand what I was or what was being done to me. Because of the blocks on my scientist he never said things like 'I can't take you out in public because you are a bald child of indeterminate gender who is clearly genetically spliced with at least two other species, and we would probably be arrested,' or 'the reason the other scientists are taking you away for tests more and more is because all the other subjects have died and you're the last one,' which might have helped me get an idea of the situation. As it was I just thought it was normal: for all I knew, everyone lived out of a cage when they were young and had to get blood drawn and be weighed and measured and urinate into a cup every week. Maybe that was kinder; I certainly didn't worry myself over it. If I had known what they were doing, and what they planned to do with me, I probably would have driven myself mad.

"I mentioned before that my scientist was curious about my mental development. That hadn't been part of the original plan. We were living incubators for the next generation of medicine; intelligence was never the goal, and only occurred by accident in Group D. But as I was clearly intelligent, my scientist wanted to study my brain. I think he intended to dissect it when I eventually died—that was a big reason why he didn't want them damaging it. And while I was alive he wanted to find out as much as he could.

"And what did he find? Well, that I have a very powerful brain. It is mostly human, but there are bits of it that aren't. I have about twice as many neurons per square inch of cortex than the average human, and my scientist was curious about how these affected my learning and behavior. From reading his notes, it appears I learned faster and forgot slower than the average human child of equivalent age. Of course to me, since I had nothing to compare myself to, I just felt normal.

"That's something to remember. That, in the early days, I felt normal. I had a concept of the world with myself in the middle, and I defined everything around me—not the other way around. I was normal—*other people* were weird.

"As it turned out, however, my brain was far more powerful than even my scientist imagined.

"I don't remember much of what happened directly before the incident—everything goes rather vague and fuzzy. It's like my mind got to that part and decided it wasn't worth the energy to repair. Or maybe I decided I didn't want to remember. Whatever the reason, I only learned the details of what happened much later—after I got into Entdeckungfeld's records. That was strange. It was hard to reconcile the clinical notes that had been kept with my nightmarish memories.

"But it is good I read the notes, because from them I was able to reconstruct what happened, and what happened was this: My scientist had forever been something of an outsider at Entdeckungfeld. Nevertheless he hung on and had earned some grudging respect because of his skills. After about twelve years of the grand experiment involving Group D and the others, he decided he wanted to take me out of the project entirely. Maybe this was what he wanted all along, or maybe he finally realized he couldn't treat me as part of a scientific experiment anymore. Either way, it was what he decided, and he must have thought he had gotten to a point where he could pull it off.

"But he couldn't. They rejected his proposal of transferring me to the behavioral studies group, but they did transfer my scientist. The day he left is my last solid memory for quite a while. I remember he was sad and angry and scared. I asked him what being *transferred* meant, and if it would hurt. He explained that nothing bad was going to happen to him, but he was still scared so I thought it was a lie. Now I know he was more afraid of what was going to happen to *me*.

"And he was right to be afraid."

Professor Odd looked thoughtfully around the room. She went over to the little table and poured herself a cup of tea. She had thin, sinewy hands, Dr. Watterson saw when she looked up from her notes. They were perfectly steady as she measured out the milk and sugar.

Stirring her cup with a spoon, the Professor walked over to the chair occupied by the wolf and leaned against the armrest. She sipped her tea and stared back at the doctor.

"You probably know," she said after a minute or so. "Being a doctor, I mean. You probably know what a lobotomy really is. But I'm going to explain it because I don't think everyone here does. I know Dave's species doesn't even have an equivalent.

"First, a lobotomy is *not* a brain scramble. They do not stick an eggbeater inside your head and literally scramble your brains. They don't cut bits off and take them away either. All they do—and it is bad enough—is sever the connections between the different parts of your brain. Specifically, the connections between the prefrontal cortex"—she raised two fingers and tapped her forehead—"and the rest of the brain. This is the most common procedure, and is what most people are talking about when they say 'lobotomy.' Because the prefrontal cortex is where most of our empathic, judgmental and social control abilities are located, cut the connections and it becomes much more difficult—sometimes impossible— to function properly. You become withdrawn, you cannot connect objects with people or cause with effect, past-to-present-to-future. The lobotomy that was performed on Group D was one specifically tailored to inhibit our abilities of cognition, reaction, and decision-making. We were meant to be virtually brain-dead yet still able to function biologically unaided—that is to say, our motor control and digestive systems were not affected."

Dr. Watterson looked up from her scribbling to see Professor Odd smile, wide and mirthless, at her audience. Glancing away, Dr. Watterson saw that the man Bane was looking almost green, while the wolf had her ears laid back along her neck. The Detective sat with utter composure, his legs crossed and his hands clasped around his knees. Dr. Watterson didn't know how he could stand to be so unmoved.

"The scientists," Professor Odd went on relentlessly, now practically glaring at the Detective. "The scientists thought they were being *kind.* They couldn't bear the thought of conducting their experiments on fully aware subjects, so they took steps to ensure we were *not* aware.

"Like I said before, I don't remember much of the time surrounding the incident. I was the last subject they lobotomized, and they had learned from Subjects 2 through 5 exactly how far and where they should go to effect the desired result. Which was . . . " Professor Odd shrugged. "*I don't remember.* My perception of time went a bit murky, and the bit of me that was *me* got tossed around. I don't know if any of you feel this way, but I've always felt like my personality was one big kaleidoscope of little twinkling bits of glass. Well, this felt like someone had come along and smashed that kaleidoscope. Suddenly I was all red, or green, or white with yellow stars. And every time the conscious bit of me jumped from piece to piece I would lose time and memories. It was like I was on the run inside my own head, running from this wave of nothing that would surge up and wash away the pieces of myself.

"Sometimes I caught glimpses of what was going on outside my head. Like passing by windows where each window showed a different view. Sometimes there were people outside, bending over me or shining lights in through my windows. Sometimes I saw pieces of myself. Literally, pieces. I looked out once and saw one of the scientists holding my hand. I mean, *just* my hand. It wasn't attached to my arm anymore, and there was blood on the severed end of it."

Professor Odd looked down at the carpet and twisted her mouth. "I didn't look out the windows for a long time after that," she said.

"What was happening, of course," she said, shaking herself a little, "was that the scientists, now my brain had been compromised, were moving forward with the experiments they had performed on my fellow subjects. These were the same experiments, I later learned, that eventually killed all the others. Because they were looking for the key to regeneration. And how do you find out if something regenerates? Well, first you have to cut it off."

Professor Odd set her teacup aside and raised her arm. With her other hand she rolled the sleeve of her shirt back to reveal a forearm as pale as marble and just as hard looking. The skin was smooth and hairless. The Professor drew a line across her wrist.

"First they amputated here, at the joint. My hand grew back, but it was lumpy and a little wrong. They cut it off again, this time sawing through the ulna and the radius. That time they treated the wound with stem cells encoded with the information for my original hand." She flexed her hand, bending the fingers and making the tendons running across the back dance under the skin. "That's this hand," she said quietly, and rolled down her sleeves. Putting her hands firmly in the pockets of her trousers she continued. "Of course, their success just gave them more ideas. I remember once I caught a glimpse of this arm, and there was *another hand* growing out of it. Just a little hand. I could wiggle the fingers and everything, but the grip wasn't very strong. They had figured out a way to encode cells so that my body would grow a new version of whatever part they desired, whether or not it actually *belonged* there. This went for just about anything from bones and appendages to internal organs. Furthermore, because of my jumbled DNA my body was compatible with cells from different species. You may have noticed this—" Professor Odd waved the tentacle growing out the back of her head, where her skull joined her neck. "I wasn't born with this, you know. The scientists put it on me. It's an octopus arm under human skin. They had to reinforce my neck muscles a bit too, which made it quite strong. According to one report I read, it tried to strangle a scientist when they went to measure it."

Professor Odd grinned at them.

"I actually remember that, but I was stuck inside my own head at the time, and so it felt like someone had just plunked a new addition onto this rambling house, and there were some very strange people in it. After a while I came to realize they were just more fragments of myself. New fragments, with new memories and new ways of looking at things. The first time I woke up as one of these new fragments I knew with perfect clarity that I wasn't in control of myself, that there were people all around controlling me, and that they were going to hurt me. I lashed out and grabbed hold of the nearest thing, which turned out to be someone's neck.

"They cut the tentacle off after that. But I grew it back. That was another thing I'd learned from the new fragments. I didn't *need* the lead cells to tell my body what part to grow back, *I* just needed to know. *I* of course being the fragmented consciousness of my brain, which had been scattered into corners where consciousness doesn't usually go.

"The scientists didn't know about this. They hadn't paid any attention to my brain since they'd cut into it. They thought I was functionally brain-dead. But I was only dead in the ways they knew how to measure, and in all the other ways I was desperately, furiously alive.

"Slowly . . . very slowly . . . my brain began to heal. I told you I have a powerful brain. Well, some of my regenerative abilities got tied up in it as well. As I was regrowing my tentacle, the rest of my brain got busy rebuilding the connections that had been severed. And as more passages opened up, the dark tides of nothing began to recede, and the windows got bigger and bigger, and I stopped losing time. The world came back into focus, and for the first time in years I woke up. That was when things got *really* nightmarish."

Professor Odd tapped her hand restlessly against the chair back, making a soft *thump, thump, thumping* sound. Dr. Watterson's hands were cold, her fingers bent stiffly to hold the pen and notebook.

"You don't know terror," Professor Odd said quietly, "until you wake up on a table, naked, tied down, and someone is *sawing away at your leg.*" She looked sharply at the Detective. "My friends here will tell you I can act a bit nonchalant during a crisis. It is not because I do not appreciate the desperation of those circumstances, but simply because nothing I have yet to experience has been as terrifying as *that.*" She folded her arms, but her fingers kept playing a soft tattoo against her sleeve.

"The really bad part was, I couldn't let them know I was awake. That was crystal clear. So I did what I imagined I must have been doing for who knew how long: I did nothing. I lay on that table for a week, catheterized, with a feeding tube down my throat and a sedative drip in my arm, waiting.

"I passed the time by taking stock of what I knew and didn't know. I knew my designation was o-D but that everyone called me Odd. I knew I had been friends with a girl who had a hand growing out of her chest, but I did not remember what had happened to her. I also did not remember what had happened to *me* or where my scientist was. When the other scientists came in and changed my dressings I tried to read their faces and found I couldn't. Faces looked like hands or feet: expressive, but not nearly as expressive as I remembered.

"That was bad. I decided I must not be done with whatever I was doing inside my head and went back to sleep.

"I must have slept a long time, because when I eventually woke up I was in a cell, and I had a foot again—though it was small and weak and difficult to walk on.

"This cell was different from the ones I had been in before. The walls were metal on three sides, and one of those sides had a thick, rectangular door in it. The fourth side was made of slabs of stone pasted together with a rough, grainy substance. It was cold to the touch and stayed cold even when I kept my hand on it, unlike the metal walls which would warm if I pressed against them long enough. I stayed away from that wall because it was cold, and it made my body stiff and hard to move.

"I spent a long time in that cell. Scientists came and fed me by sticking a tube down my nose and pumping food paste directly into my stomach. That was hard to sit still for, but I knew I had to make them think I was still brain-dead. As long as they thought I wasn't aware, wasn't thinking, they wouldn't be so careful. And I needed them not to be careful so I would have at least a chance of getting away. I developed this . . . something. Not really an ability. More like a survival mechanism. Basically, physical contact doesn't affect me emotionally anymore. There's this . . . disconnect. Maybe it's something that I developed in order to trick the scientists, but really I think it's leftover damage from the procedure. I'd spent so much time disconnected from my body that there was still a bit of a gap. And it's never really gone away. I *understand* that animals use touch to communicate threats, dominance, or affection, but I don't get any of that. I feel physical sensations like pain, heat, cold, or the pleasure of scratching an itch . . . but none of the emotions that supposedly come with them.

"So even though it was *uncomfortable* getting a tube stuffed down my throat, the sensation didn't make me feel scared or panicky, and that made things . . . easi*er*.

"I digress. At the time I thought that my scientist must still be out there. I thought I just needed to get into his office, and then he would keep me safe.

"So I waited until they took me out of the cell. I waited as I was led down corridors on a leash until we came to passages that I remembered. I remembered walking freely down them with my scientist—what felt like only a few weeks ago.

"The technician holding my lead walked slowly because I still limped on my healing foot—though I made the limp appear worse than it really was. She held her end of the lead lazily in one hand, her fingers lax through the loop. I waited until we were at a juncture with the corridor I knew led to my scientist's office, and then I bolted.

"It was such a shock to them that they didn't give chase immediately. The technician stood and stared for several seconds before she raised the alarm. In that time I had fled down the hall and up a flight of stairs to the level where my scientist lived. I went careening down the corridor, a little lopsided because of my foot, dodging around surprised scientists, until I came to the familiar door that had always meant safety to me. I pulled it open and dove inside . . .

"And it was all *wrong*. The furniture was different, and the carpet was different, and the man sitting behind the desk—who got up as soon as I entered—was the *wrong* scientist. I was still having difficulty with faces, but I could see his features clearly. My scientist had had a dark face with thick black hair, whereas this one was pinkish and bloated with hair the color of straw.

"I started screaming then. I hadn't talked in so long it felt weird to push my tongue into the necessary shapes, and so I just screamed anguish and horror and frustration as loud as I could. Screaming, I dove back into the corridor and started slamming doors open, looking for the office with my scientist in it.

"The place was thick with people. Arms and legs and hands kept getting in my way. I don't think I realized they were trying to catch me; all I knew was that I had to find my scientist, and they were *getting in my way*. I pushed. I kicked. I think I might have bit someone. Eventually stronger arms grabbed me, and they forced a mesh bag over my head and straps around my arms, and then they dragged me, still screaming, back to my cell.

"I started fighting in earnest then. I really, really didn't want to go back into that place. Despite all the confusion, I knew with perfect clarity that if I let them put me in that cell I wouldn't come out again. They'd split my brain again—or just kill me completely. I saw the shape of the door open, and I thrashed so hard I managed to kick one away, but the next thing I knew they had thrown me inside and slammed the door behind me.

"It hurt when I landed—more than it should have—because what I'd landed on was angular and pointed. I lay and panted and cried for a few minutes before I realized the uncomfortable things I was lying on were *stairs*.

"That made me stop crying at once. I began noticing other things that were different. It was dark, for a start, and the place I was in smelled sort of like my scientist's closet—whereas my cell smelled of metal and disinfectant. When I reached out and touched the wall it was warm and dry and felt like paper, while the stairs felt fuzzy, like they were covered in carpet. Sitting up I saw them outlined above me by a dome of faint, colored lights that winked in and out of existence . . . "

Professor Odd trailed off, grinning at the Detective with unrepentant glee. The man Bane was staring from the Professor to the doorway with the not-a-robot and back again, his mouth slightly open, while the wolf had a thoughtful expression on her face.

"And that is how I met the Oddity," the Professor announced with a grin.

Dr. Watterson leaned forward to peer around the not-robot, and sure enough, there were the stairs and beyond them the faint twinkling of colored lights.

There was a sigh and a rustling sound as the Detective unfolded his hands and smoothed back his hair.

"Spontaneous portal relocation," whispered Elo. She turned to the man Bane. "Like what happened when the Oddity picked up Kilni."

"And . . . " said Professor Odd with a twinkle, "*you.*"

"Explain," said the Detective.

Professor Odd looked at him quizzically. "I am here to tell you *my* story," she said. "The Oddity has stories and secrets of its own, and they are not mine to tell. Suffice to say . . . " she threaded her fingers together and cracked her knuckles, "it took us a little while to get to know one another. The Oddity was . . . well, it was not then what it is now—and neither was I. We got into some serious trouble together, and went on some pretty marvelous adventures, before I figured out more or less how it worked.

"I learned a great deal in those early times. The Oddity kept moving the portal to different libraries on all sorts of worlds, and it made me a room for me to read in. I'm afraid I was more interested in exploring the worlds themselves—this was where some of the trouble came from—but I learned a lot from both things. Reading and exploring, I mean.

"I learned that there were more different places than I could have possibly imagined, and that most of them were better than the place I had grown up in. I learned about people. I learned about friends. And as I learned new things, I began remembering old things too. I remembered the other members of Group D— and what had happened to them. And though I never did remember exactly what had been done to me, I figured it must have been something similar. It was quite *upsetting* at the time. It still is . . . but not so shocking. Not anymore."

Professor Odd stared out the dark window, frowning. She sniffed, shivered a little, and went on more energetically.

"Eventually I figured out how to drive the Oddity—or the Oddity figured out how to understand me—and I was able to get back to my own world. I wanted to know for certain, you see, what had happened.

"I figured out I could look in on different parts of my world, and that allowed me to watch the events that unfolded following my disappearance. It was fascinating, really, watching the little scientists running around like so many ants. They were quite at a loss as to what had become of me.

"By this point the Oddity and I understood one another well enough that I could tell it precisely where to open its portals, and with some maneuvering I got it to open onto my scientist's old office. I waited until everything was dark, and then I went through.

"I have very good night vision, so I was able to see perfectly. Now that I was more myself I could see at a glance that my scientist had not been there in some time. None of his old artifacts were to be found, and the closet held only lab coats and a spare pair of shoes. The place even smelled different.

"That was an unsettling discovery, and it made me wonder how much time I had lost. Pondering it back in the Oddity, I decided that it was high time I found out just what was going on, and who these scientists were. From my recent experiences I knew that most people did *not* come from test tubes or grow up in cages, and most people did not work in secret laboratories. Things I hadn't questioned all my life were suddenly subjected to the utmost scrutiny, and I found they didn't hold up.

"I used the Oddity to get into Entdeckungfeld's secure records archive. There I found a huge library of files, and I went through them all, piecing together my story.

"That is how I found out that the place was called Entdeckungfeld, that Group D was only one part of a bigger experiment, and that I was the sole survivor. I learned about Groups A and B and C . . . I learned how Subject 1-D had died early, and what had become of the others. That was difficult to read, because the reports were so dry and analytical, whereas I had vivid memories of those individuals. They weren't *subjects* to me, they were *friends*.

"It got even more disconcerting when I read my own file. My scientist's handwriting was all over it, and it was from that that I finally learned his name. No, I shall not tell it to you, nor shall I say whether he is dead or alive.

"His early notes were just as dry as all the rest. He was mostly interested in my brain development, purely for research's sake. But as I grew he developed an affection for me. It looked like he started out just as cold hearted as the rest, but for some reason he connected with me, and that awoke in him a sort of sympathy. Even though he disguised his resistance to my mental scrambling as objections against tampering with a research subject, I could tell what he really cared about was *me*. He didn't want to see *his* subject go through what the others had. And I think the people running Entdeckungfeld figured it out as well: his notes stopped just before the entry stating that . . . 'Subject 0-D has undergone a transorbital leucotomy with the desired result and no noticeable ill effects.'"

Professor Odd scowled. "*Desired result.* That really made me mad. I don't think I'd ever been angry at the scientists of Entdeckungfeld before. Maybe the thought simply hadn't occurred. I'd hated them, surely, but only as an unavoidable part of my life. The way one hates heavy traffic, or headaches. They were something that was not good, but what could I do about it? Until then . . . nothing.

"But now . . . now I *could* do something. I could do a lot of things. My brain had fully healed—perhaps more than fully healed, if you counted the extended consciousness of my spinal tentacle—and thanks to the Oddity, I had experiences that told me exactly what I should do. Not to mention I had the Oddity itself. The Oddity, which the scientists of Entdeckungfeld, for all their research, didn't know about.

"And I was *hopping* mad. Not just on my own account, but on account of Little Devil and 4-D and all my old friends. Even the members of Groups A, B and C, whom I'd never known. I was angry on behalf of my scientist, who had tried to do the right thing and gotten fired as a result. And I was absolutely *furious* because on beyond Groups A, B, C and D, were drafts for proposals of *future* projects. One of them involved cloning me, or 'reproduction via traditional methods'," Professor Odd stuck out her tongue. It was very long and faintly mottled.

"But I couldn't stop myself reading. I wanted to understand *why* this had happened. That's how I discovered what they were driving at in the first place, and it was sobering to realize that they had actually made *progress.* In my file were reports of human patients who had made improbable and swift recoveries after receiving treatments developed from information gained from *me.* Sometimes directly from me, in the form of the amputee who'd regrown a foot after having been treated by a modified form of my stem cells.

"That was something I had to consider. I would destroy Entdeckungfeld, certainly, but how much did I want to leave behind? People would continue to benefit from the knowledge gained at the cost of so many lives, and I was surprisingly at peace with that—I still am—but did I want them to also know the extent of the horror perpetrated at Entdeckungfeld? Did I want to leave enough so people could find out what had happened? Did I want the stories of Subject 4-D and the others to become known? Or was it simply enough to ensure no one else had to endure what they did? What *I* did?"

Professor Odd moved to stand behind Bane's chair, clasping her hands together and staring at them evenly. "Your history, of course, speaks for itself. But for the sake of the off-worlders in my audience I shall explain what I eventually decided—and why.

"It was clear that the research being conducted at Entdeckungfeld, though morally gray, was producing effective and beneficial results. And I guess I felt that that was a good enough thing to . . . not *justify* what had been done to us, but . . . but good enough to *keep.* It was a thing good enough to keep, even if it had been gotten in a bad way. But I had to wonder, if the whole story came out, would people still be willing to use that knowledge? Would they be willing to take advantage of technology that had been developed on living, sentient, *sapient* subjects? And what good would that do anyone if they weren't? It would only rob poor 4-D and the rest of the only legacy their short lives had produced.

"So I decided, very carefully, to destroy Entdeckungfeld and all the records pertaining to it—but not the *results* of its experiments. This was as you can imagine quite an undertaking, since I didn't feel much like killing anyone either. I've never liked killing. Not even in the beginning, when I didn't fully understand what it was. But if my escapades with the Oddity had taught me anything, it was that I didn't want to *kill* anyone—ever. Besides, it was the place and the things that went on in it that I wanted to destroy, not the people who worked there.

"For this reason I decided not to detonate a nuclear bomb in the archive room—which was a possibility I entertained—but instead researched the escape routes laced into the building's structure. I wanted to get everyone out and *then* destroy it, and fortunately for me the people who had designed the place had made it clear how to get everyone to vacate their posts immediately.

"I laid plans. Careful ones. I used a controlled fire to set off every smoke alarm in the place, and at the same time I left a small piece of radioactive material in close proximity to their radiation scanner. It wasn't enough to be dangerous unless you ate it, but it made the warning klaxons go off beautifully.

"It was astonishing to watch how people evacuated—or chose *not* to evacuate, as the case proved. I couldn't understand it until I realized they were trying to *copy down* their research. Some scientists, even in the face of an apparent simultaneous fire and reactor breach could think only of *saving their work.* That was admirable, but it wouldn't do. I'd had enough of Entdeckungfeld, and I didn't want them starting up all over again in a different place. Sitting up in the direct control box (which was so difficult to get to by ordinary means that no one thought to guard it) I cut a few strategic power sources, and plunged the place into darkness. Only then did the last of the scientists leave.

"And then . . . then the whole place was deserted. I locked the outer doors so they couldn't get back in, and took one last walk through what had been my childhood home, my prison, and my torture chamber.

"I remember noticing for the first time how much I had grown, how everything seemed smaller and dingier in the dim darkness. I went all the way down to the basement to see the tanks that had once housed Group A, and found what was left of them strung up in preservative fluid. I took them out and laid them on the floor, covered them with a blanket. I'd read about cultures that burned their dead as a symbol of honor, and though we never had a culture, I thought that was a worthy practice to adopt.

"I walked back up, past the cages where I'd spent my first days—they appeared tiny now, it was horrid to think of anyone living there—and on past the cells. I found the communal room in which I'd played with 4-D and the others, and I found the operating rooms where they'd been tortured and mutilated.

"I lit the real fire in the room where I'd been lobotomized. The fuses led out like a river of wires and dispersed throughout the institution, ending at modest packs of dynamite placed in strategic positions.

"I watched my little pilot light run out of the room and down the hall. Then I stepped through a cupboard door and into the Oddity. I changed the portal so I could step back out onto the roof of a watchtower some ten miles away and watch the cloud of ash, fire and smoke rise over the treetops.

"I cannot say I felt joy or vindication. I did feel a deep sense of relief and a sort of practical satisfaction at executing a complicated and difficult task. I watched the smoke rise over the forest and felt like a dark pond on a cold morning: quiet, still, and blank.

"I went back a few weeks later, just to check on things, and found to my satisfaction that Entdeckungfeld had been reduced to a smoking crater. Everything was either burnt beyond recognition, melted, or blown sky high. I poked around enough to satisfy myself that there would be no attempts at rebuilding the place, and then I left. And I have not been back to this world since . . .

"Until *you* dragged me here, Detective, seemingly intent on my recapture. For what purpose I could only guess, but I assumed that the former Entdeckungfeld scientists had not forgotten Subject 0-D. Subject 0-D, who so mysteriously vanished from under their noses, whose disappearance coincided with the absolute destruction of that—I'll say it this once—that *horrible* place. I thought it wasn't unlikely that some or all of them had gone on to continue their research—in one form or another—and that, should they wish to hunt down their escaped subject, they would eventually contract *you* to do it. When I discovered that I could not leave this world I set about testing these assumptions until I became certain they were indeed *fact*.

"And now you know the whole story, Detective: why your employers want me, and why they call me a terrorist. But you also know *why* I did what I did, and I hope you have a better understanding of the sort of people they really are."

Professor Odd came around in front of the armchairs, her catlike eyes flashing, her tentacle waving. In a defiant voice she said: "The only question that remains to be answered, I think, is *what will you do now?*"

Silence fell in the little room. There was only the scratching of Dr. Watterson's pen as she scrambled to finish writing. The Detective sat like a statue facing the Professor across the ottoman. The man Bane and the dog looked stunned. Dave, of course, was unreadable.

For her part, Dr. Watterson was running over in her head all the treatments that she had come to take for granted that must have been developed from this person's cells. With a slight jolt she realized that the *caudata* stem cell therapy that had benefitted both the man Bane *and* herself must have come, not from salamanders as had been originally reported, but from Subject o-D—from *Professor Odd*. She glanced across at Bane and saw that he had come to this conclusion as well; he was looking a little green.

The Detective got up suddenly. Turning from the Professor he strode to the door, stopping mere inches from Dave's suit. He bent his long body and stared up into the twinkling lights just visible beyond the stairs. His whole body was tense, like a steel trap ready to spring, and Dr. Watterson had the sudden and worrying idea that he was about to do something mad.

Unconsciously she moved her hand closer to her side.

"You won't need to use that, I promise," the Detective said without turning around. The line of his shoulders sagged, and he gazed down at Dave.

"BEFORE YOU ASK," blared the electronic voice, making Dr. Watterson jump, "WHAT I AM IS NONE OF YOUR CONCERN."

"Perhaps it will be, one day," the Detective said wistfully. "Perhaps, all of this—" he gestured toward the interior of the Oddity "—will unavoidably be *my* business. But . . . for now . . . " he shrugged, and when he turned around he was smiling a little ruefully. With pointed care he stepped aside, leaving the path clear for the Professor and her friends to exit the room. "I find that I must do a little more *research* of my own before I decide whether or not to complete my commission."

"You're not going to drop the case?" Bane blurted out.

"I have heard one side of the story," the Detective said mildly, holding his hands out, palms up. "I need to corroborate it. But I will not pursue you until I do so. And if I find it supports what Professor Odd has told us . . . *well* . . . " He spread his hands expressively. "I may find myself quite unable to complete my commission."

Professor Odd stepped forward. She eyed the Detective up and down, then extended one hand. The Detective reached out and shook it—gently.

She smiled at him a little slyly.

"Tell me one thing, at least," she said. "Was it Allsworth or Vanversen who hired you?"

The Detective started backward, glaring.

Professor Odd laughed. "I relearned how to read faces a long time ago, Detective. So it was *both*? That's *interesting*. Yes, perhaps it would be best if you looked into their *current* projects as well. I'm sure what you find there will be . . . enlightening." She smiled serenely and patted the Detective on his stiff, black shoulder.

She bowed to Dr. Watterson and then swept past them to the door, where Dave waddled aside.

With a low groan Alister rose to his feet. The dog jumped down immediately and took his arm. As they passed, Dr. Watterson stood up and the man stopped.

"Thank you," Bane said.

"For what?" asked Dr. Watterson. "For running into you with my cabbie?"

Bane shrugged. "If you like," he said. He glanced past her toward the Detective, who was standing like a pillar in the middle of the room. "Take care of him," he said.

Dr. Watterson glanced at the dark man and frowned. "Why ever should I do that?"

"Because I may have gotten your name wrong, but I *was* right," Bane said. When Dr. Watterson looked mystified he went on: "Look, sometimes life really does imitate art. Or legend. Check the number of this place, if you're not sure. If it's right, though, you know what to do."

"No," said Dr. Watterson, wondering if he had entirely recovered from his concussion. "I'm not sure I do."

Bane smiled encouragingly. "You'll figure it out," he said confidently. "Watson was always smarter than people gave him credit for, too."

They went to the door and passed through. Dave rolled back into the center and, reaching out one long arm, pulled the door closed with a *snap.*

Dr. Watterson was left standing in the middle of a strange man's sitting room, a notebook full of a disturbing story in one hand, with the feeling that she had blundered into a world (or perhaps *worlds*) that was entirely over her head. She wanted to go home—badly—even though home was a tiny room on top of a shop that smelled of mold. Unfortunately her only mode of exit apart from the windows was a door that had, last she'd seen, led anywhere but home.

The Detective solved the problem for her by snaking around the furniture and snatching the door open again.

Gone was the creature Dave in his robotic suit. Gone also were the stairs and the distant colored lights. Now all that lay past the door was the ordinary hallway of the Detective's flat. Dr. Watterson let out an inner sigh of relief and moved toward it.

"What do you intend to do with that notebook?" he asked as she passed him. And though his voice was as soft as ever, something about his tone made Dr. Watterson realize he was intensely interested in her answer. That, more than anything, made her reach a decision.

"I will keep it safe," she replied, surprised at her own certainty.

The Detective didn't react, he only said, "You have no remaining questions?"

Dr. Watterson paused in the hall. "None that you can answer," she said tersely. "In fact, I very much doubt it would be good for me if I knew the answers at all.

So, no. No further questions, Detective. And as I do not expect we shall ever meet again, *good-bye*."

She left him there and made her way down the stairs to the front door, beyond which her normal, frustrating world with all its mundane problems awaited her.

She was at the door when the Detective stepped out of a shadow behind her. This was of interest since Dr. Watterson had not heard him come down the stairs. She ignored him pointedly and began buttoning up her coat.

"Watson," he said, his hard-edged voice cutting through the darkness like a knife.

Dr. Watterson sighed and turned to face him. "Do you know you're the second person in as many weeks to make that mistake? It's *Watterson,* Detective. And I very much doubt *your* name is Holmes."

"True, it isn't," said the Detective mildly. "But you *were* a military doctor, wounded in action?"

Dr. Watterson felt her lip curl into a sneer. "A few coincidences, Detective, nothing more."

"I am not saying that they are," the Detective said. He put his hands in his pockets and looked at her with his head on one side, as if he were a bird sizing someone up. Then righting himself he continued: "It is only pertinent because, as you are a doctor recently returned from military service, I doubt you have the connections to achieve a desirable position in civilian practice. I do not mean this to cast doubt upon your skills—I am sure they are of the very best quality— but merely that it suggests to me your living situation is likely not as comfortable as you would wish."

Dr. Watterson frowned at the man in the shadows, who only smiled—brief and snakelike—in return.

"I find myself soon to be in a similar situation," he said sympathetically. "The fact is, as you may have gathered, something of a hitch has come up in the job that was keeping me here—and keeping me in such opulent lodgings. I find myself soon to be out of a position, as it were, obliged as I am to take on other jobs with much less promising financial outcomes. What I am getting at, my dear doctor, is that in order to continue living in these comfortable quarters I will require a *flatmate*, much as I despise the prospect, and you seem to be the best available candidate."

Dr. Watterson stared at him in mixed confusion and disbelief. When he only returned her gaze with steadfast assurance she found herself wavering. These rooms were large, well-built, and did not smell of mold. On the other hand . . .

"Does this mean you will not continue your pursuit of Professor Odd and her . . . companions?" she asked straight out.

"I thought I had made as much clear," said the Detective, surprised.

"Well, you hadn't," said Dr. Watterson a little gruffly.

"You must forgive me," the Detective said with a shrug. "I have a habit of speaking in labyrinths. Why, do you think I should?"

"Heavens no."

"Excellent, then we are in agreement," said the Detective, suddenly jovial. He clapped his hands.

"Just one moment," said Dr. Watterson, putting on her hat and pulling the door open. Leaving the Detective inside she went out onto the pavement and looked back up at the house. It was tall, plain, whitewashed brick with four long windows, two of which were lit from within. By the streetlight she read the brass plaque beside the door, and found it similar and yet thankfully different to what she had feared she would find.

Dr. Watterson gave a little shrug, and walked stiffly back up the steps and through the door of 2212 Barker Street.

"Very well," she said heavily. "I accept."

Epilogue

"CUT US LOOSE, DAVE," Professor Odd said as soon as they were all in. There was a fizz from the control panel as Dave's arms flew over the keys. He had replaced the panel, and now the cockpit looked more or less normal. Alister was also relieved to find that the Oddity had finished regenerating the damaged rooms while they were in the Detective's flat, and it had lost the cramped, shriveled look entirely.

Professor Odd dumped her scarf, coat and wig on the table, setting the last at a jaunty angle over the muzzle of the time gun. Then she poured herself a cup of water at the kitchen alcove and after doing so, pulled one of the big armchairs forward and settled into it with a sigh.

Alister and Elo hovered, torn between concern and a sudden, inexplicable shyness. For his part, Alister reasoned that nothing had changed: Professor Odd was still the same person she had always been; now, he just knew more about her.

Like how she had got her tentacle. And why she had jaguar eyes.

Alister found himself looking out one of the Oddity's windows instead of at the Professor. There was a swirl of light out there, slowly fading as the darkness ate away at it from all sides.

The Professor's world. The one she never wanted to go back to.

Slowly Alister sat down at the table. He still felt a bit delicate and weak, although nothing actually hurt anymore. He wondered if the Professor felt the same.

"So . . . is that it then?" Elo asked, breaking the silence.

"Goodness, I *hope* so," Professor Odd said, draining her cup. "Dave, would you be a dear and get me a refill? I am *parched* and *exhausted.*"

"SPEAKING IS A HIGHLY INEFFICIENT FORM OF COMMUNICATION," Dave said, but he rolled over and took the Professor's cup.

"And that's all of it, then?" Alister asked. "Everything you said, that's the truth?"

"Oh, it was all *true*," Professor Odd said. "It's not *everything*, though. Had to leave him some bits to discover on his own, otherwise he'd never have believed me."

"Do you think he—em, the Detective—will stop chasing us now?"

Professor Odd smiled to herself as she took the refilled cup Dave offered her. "I think," she said with satisfaction, "that the *next time* we see the Detective he will not be our enemy."

Alister was not convinced, but he didn't feel like arguing. Elo, however, frowned and scratched behind one ear.

"Which bits?" she asked suddenly.

"Sorry?" said the Professor.

"Which bits did you leave out?"

Professor Odd smiled. Her teeth really were remarkably square and white. Alister wondered how *that* had come about.

"Well, Elo," she said. "Which bits are you curious about?"

Alister looked cautiously over at Elo. There was one subject he wondered about, but he hadn't felt comfortable asking. Elo, however, had no such qualms.

"Your *scientist*," she said. "Whatever happened to *him?*"

Professor Odd leaned back in her chair. She seemed pleased to have been asked.

"Ah yes, my *scientist*," she said with a sigh. "I did quite well not mentioning his name, didn't I? I tell you, it was a challenge. But I really don't want anyone bothering him, goodness *knows* he's been through enough on my account.

"Of course I went and found him, right after I blew up Entdeckungfeld. It wasn't a difficult thing to do with the Oddity. He'd been quite cast down, poor fellow. I found him living in a dingy bungalow outside Bristol *resting on nonexistent laurels* he later told me.

"I remember I came through the door to his parlor, where he was sitting in a threadbare armchair watching the television. At first I thought I'd got the wrong house: he seemed too small and shabby to be the trim man in a starched white lab coat that I remembered. But there was still his smell, and though it had gone a little musty and sour I recognized it.

"The man hadn't lost any of his sharpness either. I'd only stood in the doorway, staring, when he said without turning around: 'I don't get visitors these days. So you're either a burglar or the one person in the universe who would actually *want* to see me. If you're the former you can find what little valuables I have in the breadbox on the shelf above the sink in the kitchen. If you're the other person for goodness sakes come around so I can get a proper look at you.'

"Well, I was so shocked at this that I didn't move, and eventually he roused himself enough to turn and look at me. His trim black beard had grown into a great gray bush, and his hair was pure white and thinning around the back.

"'Come along now,' he said, like we were back at Entdeckungfeld and I was hiding in his closet. 'You've got nothing to fear from me. Rather . . .' he gestured at the television, where a report of the explosion that had reduced a remote Deutsch castle to a smoking crater was airing, 'I think *I* ought to be afraid of *you*.' He sounded resigned.

"The thought hadn't even occurred to me. I came around and stared at him, like *he* was the escaped biology experiment. He stared right back of course, looking amazed and terrified at the same time.

"'Look at you,' he said at length. 'I'd never have dreamed . . . but I might have hoped.'

"'I'm just here to say good-bye,' I told him.

"'Really?' he said, disbelieving. 'That's all?'

"And do you know, up until that moment I think he really thought I was going to *hurt him*. The realization made me feel cold and tingly all over. But a moment later he got a little of his old character back, and then everything felt better. Normal, almost.

"'Thank you,' he said. 'Now, if you'll go into the kitchen and make us a cup of tea I think that would be good. You'll excuse me but my knees aren't what they once were.'

"I did as I was told. We sat and drank tea in his musty little parlor. I asked him about his knees, told him how the research from the Subject D group—namely, *me*—had led to a breakthrough in regenerative medicine. I asked why he didn't take advantage of it. And do you know what he said? *'I haven't the heart, knowing where it came from.'* If anything convinced me I had done the right thing, it was that. I told him I would feel more betrayed if he *didn't* take advantage, and he told me he would think about it. And then I left."

Professor Odd sipped her water and looked thoughtfully at the heap of junk on the table. "I went back, once, a few years later. The place was empty, boarded up. But he'd left a note tacked to the kitchen door: *thanks for the knees,* it said. I honestly haven't a clue where he is now. But I think I would know—the Oddity would tell me—if he had died. I hope so, anyway."

A silence descended gently, but it was a soft silence, underlaid by the constant hum of the Oddity. Alister thought Professor Odd had reached the end of her narrative, but then she looked up and smiled at him.

"You'll like this, Alister. Do you know what his name was? I've never forgotten. First big word I ever spelled. A-L-E-X-A-N-D-E-R. It stayed with me, even during the bad years when my brain was all to pieces. *Dr. Alexander.*"

With that she sighed, and set her cup amongst the clutter on the table. She got to her feet and climbed up the ladder to the catwalk. They watched her go in silence.

After a brief internal struggle, Alister got up and followed her. He found her standing outside her door, staring at the o-D tacked to the middle of it.

"I took two things from Entdeckungfeld," she said without turning around, and pointed, laying a finger first on the o and then the D. "That's my name, that's where I came from. I may not like it, but I won't hide it either."

She looked so melancholy, standing there and looking at those figures, that Alister—who was not prone to physical acts of affection—was suddenly overcome with the desire to hug her. He even made an involuntary motion before he remembered what she had said in the Detective's sitting room.

He found himself frozen with his arms at an awkward, half-outstretched angle when Professor Odd looked up at him.

"Sorry," he mumbled, taking his arms down. "You looked like you could do with a wee bit of comforting, but then I was remembering what you said . . . about the gap between," he waved a hand limply. "You know."

Professor Odd huffed a weak sort of laugh. "I don't find physical contact *repulsive*," she said mildly.

"I know, but . . . " Alister shrugged haplessly. "But . . . what *do* you find comforting?"

Professor Odd looked at him sideways out of one eye, and a slow grin spread up her face.

"What comforts me, Mr. Alister, is waking up and knowing that I can go anywhere, do anything, and there is no cage, no cell, *no bonds* that can hold me. That I can see worlds I was not born to see, and most of all, that I am myself, and I am free. And . . . that I can continue to help people."

She reached out and wrapped her arms around Alister's shoulders. For a moment he felt his frame squeezed by thin, strong, sinewy arms, and then she had drawn away again.

"Of course, just because *I* don't get anything out of it doesn't mean I don't understand why *other people* do." She smiled at him sunnily and pushed her door open. Alister stood and watched her disappear inside with a flick of her speckled tentacle.

THIS IS A SHORT ADVENTURE *from much earlier in the Professor's career. Before Alister and Dave—even before Elo—there was Amar and Desta and their magnificent day out. And while it stands apart from the series as a whole, it fits nicely into the negative space provided by a different story: that of the* Driving Arcana *episode "God or Aliens." It first appeared, along with that story, in* Apsis Fiction: Perihelion 2015.

Amar and Desta's Big Day Out

AMAR HAD NOT BEEN ENJOYING THE CAMPING TRIP. It was cold and wet, and he did not like the other children. He had not wanted to go into the outhouse. It was dark and dirty and smelled strongly of fermented urine. Once he was inside, however, the smell vanished, and he found it was not as dark as he first supposed. Dim lights of red and green and blue and gold twinkled somewhere above him, and putting his hands out, he felt the shape of stairs, soft and springy with carpet.

Thinking what an odd sort of outhouse this was, Amar began to climb the stairs on his hands and knees, careful so he wouldn't trip and fall. When he reached the top he found it was a much bigger place than he had expected. The lights came from a high wall full of twinkling bulbs and glowing tubes and cables, which made a soft humming sound as the lights went on and off. They reminded Amar of the Christmas lights people put up in his neighborhood, all soft and dim and multi-hued. Amar had always thought those lights made a place look magical, and had been slightly disappointed when such places turned out to be boring and ordinary.

This place, however, looked like it might actually *be* magical. It reminded Amar of the inside of a spaceship, or perhaps a submersible—though he had never been inside either. To his left and right were swivel chairs bolted to the floor, and in front of each was a big, square monitor—like the one belonging to his father's computer—which glowed a bright, sky blue. By their light he saw the rest of the ship: long and narrow with windows placed along the walls on either side. These had cream-colored lace curtains, drawn aside to let in the starlight, and the wallpaper was a dusty pink with rose patterns on it. The floor was metal at first—one reason it had put Amar in mind of a ship—but further in, it changed to hard, polished wood. When Amar bent down he could just make out his reflection in it.

Most of the room, he now saw, was taken up by a giant wooden table, like the one in the dining room of his own home. It was covered with a pink-and-green floral cloth that hung down in drapes on all four sides, and there was a person asleep on it.

They were a grown-up, Amar could tell by their length (they lay curled on their side with their knees bent and yet still took up most of the table), but they were the strangest-looking grown-up Amar had ever seen. They wore a bright green coat that went all the way down over their legs and tied in the back with a cloth belt—like his father's overcoat—and they wore red-and-purple striped socks. As Amar came around to their head, he saw it was a woman with whitish, peach-colored skin and hair the color of pale gold. She lay with her head resting on one arm, her eyes closed, and her mouth partly open. A quiet snore escaped from it.

"Excuse me," said Amar, reaching up to touch the sleeve of her nearest arm. "*Excuse me,*" he tried again, when this had no effect.

The woman stirred. Her shoulders stretched, she wrinkled her nose, and then opened her eyes and raised her head to look at him.

She had big dark eyes, with pupils so huge they reminded Amar of a cat. They reflected the lights from behind him, and seemed to twinkle in the dark.

"Hello," said this strange person. "Can I help you?" Her voice had an accent to it, sort of like his mother's but not. It was easy enough to understand, however.

"I'm looking for the bathroom," Amar whispered, not having lost sight of his main goal.

"Up the ladder and to the right," said the woman with the cat eyes and shining hair, and pointed.

There, Amar saw, was a ladder, with little blue lights shining along its sides and rungs, and he climbed up it easily. This let him off on a narrow walkway that extended around the place like a balcony. There were doors set into the walls instead of windows, and the first one on his right was indeed marked with a little pictogram of a man, like the ones on public restrooms. He pushed it open and felt around for a light switch.

He needn't have bothered. The light came on automatically; low and orange and pleasantly soothing, it illuminated a room with sandstone-colored tiles and a wavy mosaic on the wall. There was a toilet with a fluffy pink cover, a sink with soap and a towel and a mirror above, and a little three-legged stool just the right height for Amar to stand on to reach the taps. There were two more rooms extending off the far end, and after Amar had used the toilet he stuck his head in to find that one contained a big, deep circular bath, and the other a wide, walk-in shower. More towels hung just outside: the long, fluffy kind, perfect for lying on or bundling up in. Amar was tempted to experiment in the bath and the shower, but he worried that the woman below might be bothered, so he went out again.

In the main room the lights were brighter now—though not bright enough to illuminate the ceiling, which stretched on up into the dark beyond Amar's vision—and he saw the woman had got off the table and was now sitting in one of the swivel chairs by the monitors and lights, peering at something on the screen. When she saw Amar descending the ladder, she switched off the screen and stood up.

"I was about to get breakfast," she explained, straightening her hair. With a jolt Amar realized it must be a wig. "Are you hungry?"

Amar, who'd not been able to finish his dinner of cold potatoes and canned peas, and had only eaten half his burnt marshmallow, said: "Oh, yes. But it's actually dinnertime."

"Dinner for you, breakfast for me," said the woman with a shrug. "It won't be a problem. Well, what would you like? I still have an ostrich egg, we could split that."

"Just an egg?" Amar asked, a little disappointed.

"Or we could go out," said the woman. "Do you like pancakes? Waffles?"

"With syrup?" Amar asked hopefully.

"Syrup and fresh fruit and powdered sugar too, if you like," said the woman.

"That sounds good," said Amar.

"Excellent," said the woman. "Take a seat, this won't be long." She indicated the other swivel chair.

Amar climbed into it, noticing the seat belt hanging off to one side. He put it on.

"I'm Amar, by the way," he said.

"I'm Odd," said the woman.

Amar laughed. He thought the woman was making a joke.

"Nice to meet you, Odd," he said.

But instead of correcting him the woman just grinned.

"All right then, Mr. Amar," she said. "*Hold on.*"

What happened next was the most marvelous thing Amar had seen since New Year's Eve fireworks. Perhaps even more awesome than that.

All the lights around the little console blinked and flashed, making quiet humming noises and *tinking* sounds. It was like the most complicated display of Christmas lights ever, and Amar watched in stunned amazement. At last all the lights flashed—it was nearly blinding—and there was a deep, loud, *bonnnng* like a church bell.

The woman Odd pulled a lever with a red knob at the end and spun out of her seat.

"We're here!" she announced.

"No, we're not," Amar said, unbuckling and climbing out of his seat. "We're in the same place we were before."

"*Technically,* yes," Odd said, waving a finger. "But *that* place is now in a different, bigger place. Go open the door, you'll see."

So Amar went back down the stairs to the door. He had thought this should be the door of the outhouse, but when he got there he found it was a neat, clean wooden one, painted a dull but pleasing blue. It smelled crisply of wood polish, and it had a brass doorknob, which turned agreeably under Amar's hand.

Instead of the dark and foul-smelling night he was expecting, Amar felt a cool breeze on his face that smelt of wet stone, mostly, with a hint of car exhaust and a waft of fresh baking pastry. Pulling the door the rest of the way open he found he was looking out onto the stone steps of a house which led down to a cobbled lane. Sunlight was shining in at such an angle that he guessed it must be morning, casting the houses opposite him in bright golden light. These were tall, narrow buildings which looked old but well cared for. They had steeply tilted roofs and lots of square windows, reflecting the bright blue sky, and were made of brick mostly, except where they were made of plaster painted in various cheerful colors.

"What happened to the campground?" Amar asked.

"It's still where it was." Odd had appeared behind him; she had put on a pair of dark circular glasses and wrapped a fuzzy scarf around her neck. "I told you, I just moved the place *we* were in. Well, *technically* I moved your universe a bit—but not so much that anyone would notice. Had to jump forward a bit as well, so that the shops would be open. Brussels is *much* more fun with the shops open."

Amar, who only knew the term "brussels" as it applied to the vegetable, felt his heart sink. Then Odd was out the door and trotting down the steps.

"Coming?" she asked when she reached the bottom, and Amar decided that no one as fabulous and whimsical as Odd would ever feed anyone something as terrible as brussels sprouts. He tramped down the steps after her, closing the door behind him.

The street they were on was very narrow, and the street signs were all a bit different than Amar was used to—smaller and rounder all over. He was confused by them, until he realized they were written in a foreign language.

"Two foreign languages, actually," Odd said. "Well, foreign to *you*. This is *Belgium*, after all, so *we're* the ones speaking a foreign language, really. See, *Zee-hondstraat*? That's the name of this street in Dutch. But here it's *Rue du Chien Marin*. That's in French."

"Don't Belgians speak . . . um . . . " Amar thought of what the word would be, then said it. "Don't they speak Belgish?"

Odd, beginning to walk down the double-named street, laughed. "You'd think so, wouldn't you? But no, in this narrative it's French or Dutch, and honestly sometimes they can't make up their minds between the two. There are some versions where it's *mostly* French or *mostly* Dutch, but very few indeed where they have been able to develop their own language—and then they call it *Belgian*, just like the people."

"They should just speak Belgian," said Amar, hurrying to follow her. The narrow street was not long, and soon they emerged onto a wide promenade lined with trees and street vendors under blue umbrellas selling things that smelled delicious.

"It would be simpler," Odd allowed. "But then, *you're* American and you speak English."

Amar was silent, for this was a discrepancy that had bothered him before, and in the end he decided he was in no position to dictate what language other countries should be speaking when his didn't even have a language of its own. Besides, now Odd was approaching one of the vendors, and Amar could see that the cheerful round man behind the counter was indeed selling waffles.

They were not like the waffles he had had at Wendy's or McDonald's. They were a thousand times better. Big and square, with deep pockets perfect for filling with syrup, they were cooked to a crisp golden-brown and slightly darker around the edges, making the powdered sugar they'd been dusted with stand out like a gentle frosting of snow. Amar inhaled deeply, rejoicing in the smell of sweet, fresh-baked dough.

"How many would you like?" Odd asked him.

Amar, who was accustomed to being told how many sweets he was getting, and always the number too low, said, experimentally: "Ten?"

Odd didn't even remark on his request. She spoke to the little man in a strange language—Amar couldn't tell if it was French or Dutch, but it certainly wasn't English—and ten crisp waffles were delivered into his arms, wrapped in paper and with little packets of jam and syrup and lots of napkins tucked in around the corners. Odd also got one for herself, and paid the man with many small gold and silver coins.

They walked down the promenade together, slowly, eating the waffles—which were perfectly crunchy on the outside and soft on the inside, light and sweet like cake but just the right amount of chewy—and admiring the façade of what looked like a church at the far end. It had a big dark archway and a circular window above that, with spiky little turrets on top that put Amar in mind of a castle.

Between them and the church-castle was a wide, shallow, green pond, and in front of that was a low stone pedestal with a strange metal sculpture, like a wheel and part of a gear, laid across it. People were sitting on the edge of the pedestal around it, and Amar and Odd sat on a corner as well, while Amar ate waffles until he felt a little ill. There were still three left.

"May I have them?" Odd asked politely.

Amar, who felt he would be sick if he took another bite, gratefully shoved them into her lap and wiped his sugary hands down the front of his jacket.

Odd ate the waffles carefully, in big sharp bites. Afterward they were both thirsty, so Odd went over to another vendor and came back with steaming paper cups: coffee for her, hot chocolate for Amar. It was a darker, more bitter hot chocolate than the kind his mother made from powder, but it was the perfect thing to follow the sweet waffles. Amar sipped it carefully as they walked down to the very end of the promenade and stood looking up at the church.

"My sister would like that," Amar said. "She likes castles. Lots of castles."

"Would you like to show your sister this castle?" Odd asked. "We could go and get her. We can visit lots of castles."

Amar, who shared his sister's fascination with castles more than he would admit, pretended to give this due sober thought while inside he twisted with delight. At length he said: "I think she would be asleep by now."

"True," Odd allowed, nodding. "But we'll just be sure to visit when she will be awake. How is that?"

"That sounds good," Amar said, and handed her his empty cup.

Odd took the cup and disposed of it and her own in a brown metal trash can as they walked back down the promenade and through the narrow alley. Amar recognized the door they had come out of and bounded up the steps to it, hauling it open.

They did the same thing with the lights again, sitting in the swivel chairs with the seat belts on, and this time Amar felt a definite *thump* and *shift* before the deep *bonnnnnng* went off.

"Not bad," said Odd, dusting off her hands. "That door should lead out of your sister's closet now."

Excited and still partly disbelieving, Amar unbuckled himself and hopped down the steps. Sure enough, that was the inside of his sister's closet door, with the little broken hook in the center from the time they'd both swung on the sleeves of Desta's winter coat at the same time. Carefully he pushed it open and stuck his head out.

To his surprise it seemed to be afternoon now, but there was Desta sitting despondently on her bed, her knees pulled up into her chest and an unhappy pout on her face. She lit up when she saw him, and jumped down.

"Ammer!" she cried, which was her name for him. "You're back! I was *lonely!*"

"We're going to see some castles," Amar said, suffering to be hugged.

"Cas—"

"*Shh!*" Amar cut his sister off. He knew, deep in his bones, that galavanting off with strange women to see castles was not the sort of thing his mother would easily agree to, and he decided it would be better all around to skip that conversation entirely. "Grab your boots. Come on then!"

Desta's boots were bright pink rubber things, but they were sturdy and comfortable with fleece lining. They were slipped on, and Amar bundled his sister back into the closet.

"Why the *closet?*" Desta asked.

"It's not a closet!" whispered Amar excitedly, closing the door behind him. "*Look!*"

Desta did look, and her big brown eyes grew even wider as she took in the twinkling lights and the unusual figure of the woman Odd sitting on the swivel chair.

"Hello there," she said with a big grin. "Now, which castle would you like to see first?"

Desta wanted to see a princess's castle, so Odd made the door open onto a magnificent corridor with a painted ceiling and views of pine-covered mountains. Desta ran up and down the hall, shrieking with delight. She was so loud that some rather unfriendly looking men in black jumpsuits came to see what the matter was, at which point they all dove for the special door and slammed it shut.

"Somewhere less well occupied?" Odd suggested, and this time made the door open onto a deserted courtyard. This castle was mostly ruin, and Amar liked it much better. It had chunks of walls and bits of tower that broke off in jagged edges, and staircases that had once led up to higher floors but now crumbled away to nothing. A thick bed of green grass covered the ground, and Desta spent most of the time picking clover flowers and making Odd tie them into strings. By the time Amar had finished exploring—and gotten his trousers nice and dirty—Desta and Odd between them had made three circlets of clover flowers; the one Desta had made herself was sloppy and tended to come apart, but she wore it anyway. Odd had put one on her own head, and offered the third to Amar.

"I don't want to wear *that*," he said in contempt, pushing it away. "Flowers are for *girls*."

"Boys can wear flowers too," Professor Odd said, but she took the circlet away and put it in her pocket.

This didn't sound quite right to Amar. He knew that any boy who showed up at school wearing anything remotely pink or floral would be teased mercilessly. After a time, however, he realized that there were no other children around to pick on him, and he did feel a bit left out being the only one without a crown.

He went back to Odd and pulled on the tail of her coat.

"I changed my mind," he explained.

Professor Odd beamed at him and settled the little crown of flowers snugly within his curly hair.

"Now we are *team!*" Desta announced.

"Are you ready to go home?" Odd asked.

"*No!*" cried Desta and Amar together, and Desta added: "I want to see another *castle!*"

"Oh, what sort of castle?" Odd asked, adjusting her circlet of flowers.

"A *big* one. A castle in the *clouds!*" Desta said, throwing out her arms to illustrate.

Amar scoffed, and was about to point out that there were no such things, but Odd just smiled and nodded and said: "All right. We'll have to go a bit farther to find that, but it shouldn't take long."

She was as good as her word. They'd hardly been sitting in the place with the blinking colored lights for two minutes when Odd announced they had arrived at

"Cloud Fortress Eight" and gave them both scarves to wrap around their shoulders and necks. "It's very high up and rather cold," she explained.

It was cold, but it was also *marvelous*. The door opened onto a wide hall, at the far end of which people were scurrying about. Odd hurried them into a lift, and they rode it all the way to the top of a tower, where when they got out, they were able to look down on the towers and pillars of a castle that looked as if it had been made from blown glass. And beyond it, instead of grass or hills or mountains or even a city, there were only distant, puffy pink clouds. In between them Amar could glimpse a land, far below, with the twinkling lights of cities and the hard edge of a coastline glittering in the slanting light. It appeared to be sunset, and they watched as the world below them slowly sank into the darkness. The castle, however, remained in sunlight long enough for Desta to explore the top of the tower. When that too had fallen into shadow, and the electronic lights inside had come on, Odd asked once again whether they were ready to go home.

"*Nooo*," said Desta, though Amar wished she hadn't; he was beginning to get sleepy. "I want to see a *star* castle!"

"You mean like a castle in outer space?" Odd asked, impressed.

Desta nodded exuberantly.

"Okay," said Odd, and took them back down the lift and through the special door.

This time when they opened it again, after having waited out another set of flashing lights and a loud *boonng*, they were not in a castle at all, but in a tiny space pod. Amar felt like his tummy was rising in his chest as he stepped out, and with a thrill of excitement he realized he was *weightless*. All the tiredness left him at once, and he and Desta had to spend several minutes hurtling themselves back and forth across the little cockpit, while Odd handed herself along the ceiling and strapped herself into a chair.

"Eyes ahead," she told them. "Or you'll miss the best view."

Reluctantly Amar and Desta stopped their play and slowly crawled over to where they could see out the windshield-like window.

And there . . .

There . . .

"*Star castle!*" shrieked Desta, and squealed with laughter.

Amar said nothing, but his mouth was silently open in wonder and awe.

"Star castle" described what lay before them very well. It was an immense construction of dark gray metal ramparts and curving tongues of steel, in the center of which rose a thin silver dome studded with spine-like rods from which ran strings of lights. All along the gray metal skin were little windows which glowed blue and purple, like tiny stars imbedded in a silver sky.

The whole thing appeared to Amar to be floating in space, for there was nothing beneath, behind, or above it but a blank black sky speckled with distant real stars. Then the little ship they were in swerved around as they made a huge circuit of the place, and a planet—deep and swirling blue—came into view to their right.

"It's a *space station*," whispered Amar.

"*Star castle!*" Desta insisted.

"Actually, you're *both* right," said Odd cheerily, taking them in closer so they could get a better view of one of the great gray arms—of which Amar guessed there were at least a dozen—that sprouted out of the main dome and went curving out into space. It made the whole thing look a little like a giant spinning top. "This is the Palace of the Premier of Amphitrite," Odd went on. "But as *Amphitrite*—that's her over to your right—is an uninhabitable gas giant, all the people living here stay on what are, in effect, *space stations*. The Premier's Palace is just the most fancy of them. I borrowed this shuttle, for example, from one of the Regimental Office Stations. You can see it behind us, there . . . " she made the little ship turn, and there sure enough was *another* top-like construction—albeit a plainer, less attractive one.

"Can we go *inside?*" Amar asked.

Odd shrugged. "The Premier *does* owe me a couple of favors," she allowed. "Which part would you like to start with?"

"I want to see more of the *outside!*" Desta insisted.

"We can take a complete fly around, see all of it, before we dock," Odd assured her, and thereby neatly avoided what Amar and Desta's parents called a "critical mass event."

She was as good as her word: they circled around the whole place in an ever-tightening spiral, and Desta spent the whole time with her nose pressed to the glass. Amar had to admit, it *was* pretty cool. They passed fans with blades made of blue metal that glittered ("Photovoltaic generator panels," Odd explained) and little turrets with bulging domes at their tops. Once they even passed another shuttle, like their own. At last they came in close to the main dome—which Amar now saw bulged *down* as well as up—and threaded their way neatly into a little opening like a square mouth. Here they had to wait for a while so that Odd could explain what they were doing to the frowning man in the box outside. This didn't take long, however, and soon they were able to open a hatch and float out.

There was a pole there, and Odd had them clip themselves to it with ropes that attached to harnesses they wore around their shoulders, almost like backpacks.

"*Why?*" asked Desta.

"Because there is no gravity," Odd explained in her cheerful way. "And you don't have any jet propulsion on you. So if you let go of the pole and floated away you wouldn't be able to do anything about it, and you might float into a ship's engine and be incinerated."

"What is *incinerated?*" Amar asked.

"It means to be burned to death instantaneously," Odd told him.

Amar and Desta clipped themselves to the pole without any further protest.

It was actually great fun shinnying up the pole. Amar was reminded of rope climbing in the playground, only instead of a bristly rope that scraped his palms, the pole was smooth and cool, and it took only a little effort to drag his weightless body up it.

They eventually passed through a circular hole which closed behind them and into a small room with padded walls.

"This is the Gravity Lock," Odd explained. "Try to stay right-side up."

This was harder than Amar expected, even though he stayed clipped to the pole along with Desta. Odd pushed herself away and floated effortlessly with her legs crossed.

"*Now* what?" Desta asked.

"Now we wait," Odd said.

The gravity came on gradually. Amar felt it first as a gentle tugging on his insides, and then he noticed he was slowly sinking toward the padded floor. It reminded him of his swimming lessons, when he'd learned to float underwater without the help of a life preserver. Only here he kept getting heavier and heavier, until his feet touched the ground, and he felt all the bits of himself settle into their usual place.

"Aw," said Desta. "We've gone back to *normal*."

"Actually, the gravity here is only seventy-five percent that of Earth," Odd said from where she was now sitting on the floor. She popped up, like a jack-in-the-box toy, and clapped her hands. "*Now*," she said, "who's hungry?"

They all were, it turned out. The waffles seemed very distant now after running over all those castles, and Amar found himself dragging behind Odd and Desta as they made their way out of the padded room and into a long hall lined with shops. Amar tried to read the signs as they went past, but found that the letters were all strange shapes that he didn't recognize. Instead he looked at the other people; there were quite a lot of them, milling along the hall. Some of them pushed carts or strollers; others walked arm in arm. It put Amar in mind of the town mall where his mother sometimes took him shopping, only the people were much stranger.

They were human shaped, for the most part, but a few of them had strange faces that did not seem quite right. Either their noses were odd shapes or their eyes slanted disconcertingly. Many of them had brightly colored hair. Then, drifting through the crowd like a sailing ship, Amar saw the most extraordinary creature: tall as a horse, with a long neck bedecked in rings of beads, its bird-like face covered in feathers. It had long spindly legs and carried its arms tucked up by its sides.

Even as Amar stared, this magnificent creature spotted them and dove through the crowd in their direction.

For one terrible second Amar thought it was coming after him, but then the creature changed direction and came to a sliding halt in front of Odd, who gave a little cry of delight and threw her arms around its thin neck.

They began talking to each other then, in a high babbling language that Amar did not understand at all. He began to feel left out, so he came up under Odd's elbow, opposite Desta, and yanked her sleeve.

"*Ooodd,*" he said, "I'm *hungry.*"

"Yes, yes of course!" said Odd, and said something to the bird-like person, who in turn looked down at Amar out of wide orange eyes. It chittered in a friendly way and offered a thin, scaly hand. Amar shook it gravely.

"Do you mind if Kaklee comes with us?" Odd asked, indicating the bird-person.

Amar had no trouble with this. Desta wanted to ride on Kaklee's shoulders. When Odd explained this, Kaklee made the chittering noise again and lifted Desta up. This made Amar feel left out, so Odd picked *him* up and carried him piggy-back.

Like that, they made their way along the hall and up a moving flight of stairs until they came to a wide area with lots of tables set out in front of a huge window from which they could look out and see the arms of the space station and the little ships coming and going.

The place turned out to be some sort of restaurant, and they sat at a high table with Odd and Kaklee on either end and Amar and Desta across from each other between them. They ordered off of menus with little pictures of food from a man with skin as white as paper and bright blue hair, who peered at Amar and Desta curiously. He seemed to know Odd, however, and shook her hand before he left.

Lots of people seemed to know Odd. So many people came up to talk to her that she barely managed to eat any of the bright orange, cheesy noodles she had ordered. Amar and Desta ate them for her.

Kaklee ordered a bowl of black soup with shiny crunchy bits in it and ate it with careful slurps of its long, prehensile tongue. Amar had almost as much fun watching Kaklee eat as he did eating his own dinner—which was a pile of pancakes topped with mountains of mildly sweet whipped cream.

After that, full and satisfied and monumentally tired, Amar felt himself leaning forward on the table. Desta had already gone to sleep against Kaklee's side.

He felt Odd pick him up again—he pretended to be fast asleep so he would not be made to walk—and carry him away from the loud restaurant. He opened an eye briefly to see Kaklee carrying Desta in its wiry arms. The creature winked at him.

They arrived at the gravity lock again. He heard Odd say something about "Leaving it in dock seven. Must get them home, you see . . ." and the next thing he knew he was weightless, and then the next thing after *that* he was back in Odd's very own ship. He blinked his eyes against the colored lights and looked around.

Kaklee was gone, and so was the station. He was sitting in a comfortable arm-chair with Desta tucked in beside him. Odd was sitting a little ways away at her console.

"Ready to go home?" she asked.

Amar stretched, careful not to wake his sister.

"Sounds good," he said.

"All right then," said Odd, and flipped a lever. With the gentlest flicker of lights and a low thrumming sound that Amar felt more than heard, the whole place shifted around him, and the next thing he knew Odd was propping open the door at the end of the hallway by his room.

Odd carried Desta down the stairs and into his house, but Amar insisted on walking. He saw that Odd tucked Desta in the way she liked, with her favorite stuffed dog up under her chin, and then at last he tottered across the way and into his own room. He kicked off his shoes and crawled into bed, curling up halfway on top of his pillows. He was so tired every part of him hurt, his face was dirty, his fingers still smelled of dinner, and he had never been happier.

The last thing he heard, before he drifted off completely, was Odd's voice saying, "Good night," and the click of his door as it shut tight behind her.

ABOUT THE AUTHOR

GOLDEEN OGAWA has been telling stories since childhood. Entirely self-taught, her works range from science fiction novellas and fantasy short stories to graphic novels, illustration, painting, and cartooning. She publishes her work through her independent press, Heliopause Productions, and her author site is goldeenogawa.com. When not in her studio, she can be found riding her bike in and around her home city of Bend, Oregon.

TEXT AND DESIGN

The body of this book was typeset using LaTeX in Invicta; titles in Cintra Solid Unicase.

Cover art, interior illustrations and book design by the author.

www.ingramcontent.com/pod-product-compliance
Lightning Source LLC
Chambersburg PA
CBHW072057020726
47501CB00003B/616